Simon Shaw

Simon Shaw studied at Cambridge University
and the Bristol Old Vic Theatre School. He
worked as an actor until the publication of his
first novel, *Murder Out of Tune*, in 1998, since
when he has concentrated mostly on writing and
journalism. *Selling Grace* is his ninth novel. He is
an assistant editor of *The Week* and is a regular
freelance book reviewer.

By the same author

SIMON SHAW

Selling Grace

HarperCollins*Publishers*

A lot of people helped me to write this book.
Thank you to Julia and Anne for knocking it into shape.
I should also like to thank Andrew that is called Bill for
sharing his knowledge of the cards, and Daniel for his
linguistic experience. A big *spaseeba* to Shura.
And love and thanks, as ever, to Carolyn.

HarperCollins*Publishers*
77–85 Fulham Palace Road,
Hammersmith, London W6 8JB

www.harpercollins.co.uk

This paperback edition 2003

First published in Great Britain by
HarperCollins*Publishers* 2003

Copyright © Simon Shaw 2003

Simon Shaw asserts the moral right to
be identified as the author of this work

ISBN 978-0-00-710027-9

PART ONE

PART ONE

1

The case was over in half an hour. When Grace came out of the courtroom she was hoping to buttonhole Paul Murray, the solicitor, but she was too late. He was already talking into his mobile. She caught his eye to let him know she wanted a word, then went outside to enjoy the scenic view from the steps of Guildford County Court. It was a bright muggy day and it had been unbearably stuffy inside. She found a stretch of shaded wall and enjoyed the sensation of the cool stone against her back. It was a good five minutes before Paul made his appearance.

'Nice to be wanted,' she told him as he came down the steps.

'But never by the right people,' he answered, putting his phone back into his pocket. 'Exemplary testimony as ever, Grace. I always like to have at least one expert witness the beak is going to fancy. When she's an ex-policewoman too that really puts the icing on the cake.'

'Perhaps you'd like me to burst out of your cake wearing a bathing suit?'

'That might be too distracting. Thanks anyway, Grace.'

'No, no let me thank you.'

'For what?'

'For reminding me of why I'm an ex-policewoman.'

'Why's that?'

'Men like you.'

He laughed good-naturedly.

'Policemen have hormones too, Grace.'

'Don't I know it. As it happens, I'm having a bit of trouble with one now, though not in that way. I'm afraid I'm going to need some professional help.'

'Legal help?'

'Yup.'

'So it's true then?'

'What is?'

'That Jimmy Collins is hauling you over the coals.'

Now she laughed too, but there was nothing good humoured in the sound; it was a dry, ironical rasp.

'Word does get around, doesn't it?'

'Gossip travels faster than sound, Grace. You know that.'

'And what does the gossip say?'

'That you've been a very naughty girl and that nice Superintendent Collins caught you with your hand in the till. Is it true?'

'Not quite, but it was where it wasn't meant to be. My own fault, I was impatient. No, worse than that, I was emotional. Felt sorry for my client, you see.'

'I never had you down for the sentimental sort, Grace.'

'I try not to let it show. Anyway, she happens to be a very nice woman, and she's in the middle of a really, really shitty divorce. Husband a bastard, of the fat rich variety, of course, but he's run off with some bint and dumped her without a bean. You should see the pad they lived in, but that's part of her problem. She can't even get social security, they just won't believe that poverty and her address go together.'

'How'd she find you?'

'Through the phone book. Before they cut her off. She

4

actually admitted she couldn't pay me. That's when I started to feel sorry.'

'Who's her lawyer?'

'Someone I'd never heard of.'

'Someone who doesn't deserve to be heard of. Tell her to sell up and move somewhere smaller.'

'Property's in his name and it's now so derelict it's unsaleable. The husband's not only a fat bastard but a clever one. Lets his one indisputable asset go to seed, must prove he's skint. Claims his business is going bust and he's a cash-free zone.'

'And that's bullshit, I take it?'

'To put it mildly, yes. Maybe you've run across him – Jonah Wetherby.'

'The carpet chain?'

'The same. He sold the business last year. The wife knows he's got millions put away, but it's all offshore, impossible to find.'

'That didn't stop you looking?'

'No, and that's where I overstepped the mark. My client had a spare key to her husband's office. She also knew where he'd written down the alarm combination. Seemed like too good an opportunity to miss.'

'So what went wrong?'

'Surveillance camera. Hidden, unfortunately. I'd just made myself comfortable and was going through his stuff when the door bursts open and in come a bunch of security gorillas.'

'Ouch.'

'Yeah. Ouch. Bad luck it was on Jimmy Collins's patch, eh?'

'I think you'd have been in trouble whichever patch you were on. What did they charge you with?'

'What didn't they charge me with?'

'You know this isn't really my speciality.'

5

'Yes, but I need someone I can trust. Terry Hoffman's my usual man and I rang him straight off, but he's in Canada attending some lawyers' freebie. It was four o'clock in the morning when his wife told me that, she wasn't exactly pleased. I was feeling pretty frazzled by then, not quite all there, so I let them fob me off with the duty solicitor.'

'When did this happen?'

'Two nights ago.'

'You're in trouble, Grace.'

'Tell me something I don't know.'

'Well, I'd never have known from the way you conducted yourself in court. You are a class act, I have to hand you that. The original ice queen.'

'I'm not sure I want to take that as a compliment.'

'You ex-cops, Grace, I don't know. Throw away the warrant card and you get demob happy, running around sticking two fingers up at the law.'

'Are you going to help me or not?'

'I'll do what I can. Come and see me in my office as soon as possible. Give Jules a ring, make an appoint— I'm sorry.'

The apology was spoken hastily the instant he became aware of the cellphone ringing in his pocket. He snatched it out and put it to his face in one smooth practised motion. When he heard who was speaking on the other end his brow contracted into a frown.

'Sorry,' he muttered at Grace, holding his spare hand over the phone. 'Got to take this. Speak to Jules. Catch you later.'

'Yeah. Paul –'

But he'd already gone, his head hunched into his shoulders, the phone jammed into one ear and the flat of his palm against the other to shut out extraneous noise. She had wanted to ask him if he fancied a drink later, but after a moment's reflection she supposed that it was probably better to go through his secretary and do it all above board, as he had suggested. He was, after all, pretty damned good at his job, and if it was too much to hope for a knight in shining armour then a suit in pale charcoal pinstripes would have to do. She watched him walking away, talking animatedly. It occurred to her that she hadn't checked her messages since coming out of court. She stepped aside, found her shady spot again and rooted in her bag for her phone. She leant back against the pillar and rang her answering service. There were no messages.

Someone on the other side of the steps struck a match.

Grace glanced up at the sound, and wished she hadn't. Twenty-seven-year-old unemployed Dawn Kelly of 14 Inverness Mansions was taking her first drag of her cigarette and giving her the kind of look that merited a health warning. Name, address, age, occupation and that same look had already been aired inside. At least there were no tears now, although their effect could still be seen in the smudged black make-up all around her eyes.

'Enjoy that, did you?' said Ms Kelly, wreathing her bitter words in blue smoke. 'Another family chucked out on to the streets. Proud of yourself, are you?'

Proud of yourself . . . Grace replayed the venomous tone and felt herself wince. How come every aggrieved loser in the world watched the same bad movies?

'No,' she said tersely, determined to stay off the script, avoid any mention of job, as in *just doing it, ma'am*; or, worse, any glimmer of sympathy to suggest the heart of gold that surely must be beating beneath the rhinoceros hide she affected to show the world.

'I'll bet you are,' the woman repeated, undeterred by Grace's refusal to play the scene. 'Right proud. Chuck an innocent six-year-old kid out on the streets. All in a day's work for you, I suppose, taking the roofs from people who can't afford the smart-arsed lawyers to defend themselves,'

Grace remembered the innocent six-year-old: a grubby scowler who had given her a look of malevolence almost as pure as the one his mother was bestowing on her now. Easy to see where he got it from. If he didn't have a criminal record by the time he reached the age of joy-riding she'd come back to the steps of Guildford County Court and eat her hat. By the time he reached legal adulthood he might even have a record as long as his mother's.

'Perhaps you should have thought of that before you abused your tenancy,' said Grace, carefully putting her phone back into her bag. She knew the sensible thing would be to walk away and say nothing, but there was a limit to how much crap she was prepared to take in one morning.

'Stuck-up bitch!'

It was more of a snarl than a shout, but it was loud enough to attract the attention of passers-by. Two men coming down the steps, as likely a cheap-suited huckster with his legal aid brief as she had ever seen, kept their eyes fixed firmly in the middle distance as they pretended not to have heard. The woman stood on her tiptoes to maintain eyeball-to-eyeball contact as the men came between them.

'Fucking cow!'

The man in the cheap suit couldn't resist a little smirk. Grace followed the back of his head with her frostiest look in case he should have the nerve to turn round. He hadn't.

'Slag!'

Grace sighed to herself. Bitch, cow and slag in one volley. So much for feminism.

'Abuse isn't going to help you, Miss Kelly. You and I know perfectly well you'll be rehoused by the council, so forget the sob stories, please.'

'You get a kick out of this, do you?'

'It was nothing personal, I was just doing my job.'

Who said that? Grace thought to herself, even as the words

8

came out. If she couldn't come up with any better dialogue than that then it was time to leave. Time to leave anyway; she could hear her mobile phone ringing inside her handbag. Somebody more interesting than Dawn Kelly wanted to speak to her.

'Excuse me,' she said, and started walking towards where her car was parked, her eyes and her attention down in the recesses of her bag.

Which was a mistake, as she realized almost immediately. Always keep spitting distance between yourself and the human zoo, particularly if you've been rattling the cage; and never take your eye off the ball in the opponent's penalty area.

'This ain't nothing personal either,' said Ms Kelly as Grace drew level, jabbing her elbow into the side of her face.

The next few minutes were a blur. Afterwards Grace had a vague recollection of falling, and then of being shouted at and soothed in equal measure. Dawn Kelly had been doing all the shouting and Paul Murray most of the soothing. By the time she had regained her wits he had been joined by a couple of court officials and a policeman. Paul and the copper were on either side of her, each with a hand under her elbow, helping her back up the steps.

'Ambulance is coming,' said the policeman.

'Don't need an ambulance,' said Grace.

'Better get yourself checked out,' said Paul.

'Nothing to check, I'm fine!' she said.

'No you're not.'

They were at the top of the steps now. Paul released her elbow and came and stood in front of her. He had that look her father had once been so very good at, before he'd given it up in the face of her teenage recalcitrance, the I-know-what's-best-for-you look.

'Not what I'd call nothing,' he said, and showed her his white handkerchief before putting it back where she had failed to notice that he was holding it in the first place, against the back of her skull. The handkerchief was covered in blood. 'That was a nasty fall. You'll need stitches. So let's have no – Grace, are you all right?'

No, she wasn't. She felt suddenly nauseous, too weak at the knees to support herself. Fortunately the policeman had his arm out in time to stop her fall. She fell into his comforting bulk.

'I'll be all right,' she heard herself murmur as the young man took her weight. 'I need to clean myself up, please.'

They escorted her back inside, clustering round her all the way to the door of the ladies, like a rugby scrum shielding the ball. The nausea had receded; she had strength enough to stand unaided again now. She mumbled some embarrassed thank-you noises and stumbled through the door. One of the officials handed over her bag as she went in. The policeman took her mobile phone out of his pocket.

'Fell out,' he explained, in best minimalist copperspeak.

She grunted her thanks, a reply in kind, and went inside. Fortunately there was no one else around. She checked her answering service, but whoever had called hadn't left a message. She put the phone down next to the sink and turned to face herself in the mirror. Her right eye was closing up fast, puffy and red above the lid, the first smear of a black juicy bruise coming through. She wasn't going to win any beauty competitions tonight. Much less attract the attentions of a sex-starved judge. She touched the back of her head gingerly, feeling the sticky wetness in her hair. Must have twisted as she fell, cracked her nut against the pavement or the bottom step. Wonder she hadn't knocked herself out. Another great wave of nausea pounded through her. She clung to the sides of the sink to stop herself from falling, and to stop herself from throwing up. She laughed mirthlessly at her reflection in the mirror. What a way to earn a living. Nicked and assaulted in one week. She shouldn't even have been here in the first place.

It had been George Courtenay's job, not hers. A routine couple of hours' work, he'd told her, nothing he couldn't handle himself in the ordinary way of things, but he wasn't feeling too good at the moment and would she mind standing in for him as a favour? No problem, she'd told him, didn't she always? George and work didn't seem to combine too well these days. He'd once had a reputation for conscientiousness, but that appeared to have been folded away with his old police uniform.

Grace wiped the blood from her hair with some damp tissues. Perhaps George had had an inkling that the job might not prove as routine as advertised. Dawn Kelly had a history of violence. She had twice hospitalized women she thought were after her boyfriend and had once shoved a glass into a barman's face after he had refused to give her another drink. Grace hadn't discovered any of this till later. All George had told her was that there was a woman suspected of being in illegal occupation of a flat and the landlord wanted her out. Grace had duly obtained the evidence, which hadn't been difficult. The tenancy agreement was in the name of a man called James Carter, a local bruiser who had last been heard of working as a bouncer for a Guildford nightclub. Grace had knocked on the door and asked if Jim was about. Dawn Kelly had eyed her suspiciously and demanded who wanted to know. Grace had told her that she worked as a cashier at the nightclub and had some money that was owing to Jim. How much? Kelly had wanted to know, her eyes narrowing in instant calculation. I'll take it for him, she said, thrusting out a suddenly sweaty palm. Grace shook her head. Has to be in person, sorry. When's he coming back?

A simple enough question, but no answer was forthcoming. Kelly had tried to reason with her, she'd even offered to sign for the money. When reason didn't work she'd tried pleading and whining. With Grace still looking steely eyed she had played her trump card, throwing back the door to reveal her poor innocent defenceless son with no dad to take care of him and no money to buy him any toys. It was her least convincing ploy. The boy didn't look like a collector of Corgi cars or Lego, more a mutilator of stray cats. Nor did he look like Jim Carter's son. He wasn't. For one thing Jim was a bleached-blond Viking. The boy was black.

It was time for Grace to play her own trump card.

'Look, Miss Kelly, I'll level with you,' she said, in that tone she had perfected over the years to express the exact opposite of what she meant. 'There is a bit of money involved, but that's not the real reason I need to see Jim. He's been a bit naughty, you see, kept some keys he shouldn't have, and we need to know where they are for security purposes – you know, insurance and that. It's no big deal, we're not saying he's done anything criminal, but we need to put our minds at rest. If you could tell me where to find him, I'd be very grateful.'

It hadn't seemed to Grace like a particularly convincing story, but the way Dawn Kelly was staring at the twenty-pound note she waved casually under her nose suggested that plausibility was not a major concern. Her initial reluctance to talk was overcome the moment the money was safely in her grasp. So Jim had been a bad boy again, eh? Well, what did anyone expect from that useless two-timing bastard (one of the politer words she used). Her loathing had come tumbling out in a Niagara of self-pity and wounded pride. As for that bitch he was shacked up with in London, even a vocabulary as vividly scatological as her own struggled to do justice to the enormity of the outrage that had been inflicted on her. Grace had listened stoically and picked out the snippets of concrete information from the flood of abuse. There was no address but there was the name of a club in the Mile End Road where Jim had been last heard of practising his trade, and that was enough. Grace had gone up to London that

12

evening and easily tracked him down. Jim's initial reluctance to talk had faded as soon as he twigged that it was Dawn Kelly she was really after. To say that there was no love lost between them would have been a contender for understatement of the year. When he realized that the information might actually do his former lover mischief he confirmed with indecent eagerness that he was no longer residing at Inverness Mansions. It was all Grace needed. The court had weighed the evidence, most of it provided by her, and given Dawn Kelly notice to quit. And she had weighed in to Grace.

She finished cleaning herself up. There wasn't much she could do about her right eye, unless someone happened to have a spare ice pack handy. There was a pair of sunglasses in her handbag, but she'd always hated wearing shades indoors, they made her feel like a cheap gangster's moll. Moll she could live with; cheap she rebelled against. She started to leave, but stopped as her phone began ringing again. She didn't recognize the number on the display.

'Grace Cornish speaking,' she said in her best businesslike voice.

There was a pause at the other end. Then she heard a dry laugh.

'Is this a recorded message?' he asked.

She may not have recognized the number but she knew the voice all right. She was so taken aback she couldn't answer for a moment.

'Can you hear me, Grace?'

'Yes. Yes, I can hear you.'

'Where are you? You sound like you're in a tunnel.'

'Yeah. Something like that. Look, can I call you back?'

'I'll call you.'

'Give me a couple of minutes.'

She snatched up her things and went outside. The policeman was waiting for her.

'Mr Murray sends his apologies, he had to go.'

13

'Thanks.'

'Here, hang on a sec, miss.'

Grace stopped impatiently. The policeman looked aggrieved.

'We got Kelly downstairs,' he told her. 'You want to press charges?'

'Do you?'

'Well, there are no witnesses.'

'Then forget it.'

Grace shrugged and walked away. What was the point? If she could go into a courtroom now and display the blood and the swelling there might be a point, but by the time it came to a hearing there would be no physical evidence. She could always get her photograph taken, she supposed, but if no one had actually seen Kelly land the blow then no doubt her brief would come up with some cock-and-bull about Grace having slipped. If it came down to bare testimonies Grace would almost certainly win, but win what? Kelly would get a fine she couldn't pay and a meaningless slap on the wrist, unless there was a particularly draconian judge on the bench. Perhaps the same judge would be sitting when her own case came up. In which event the two of them might end up sharing a cell.

She found her shaded spot outside and sat down on the steps, nursing the phone in her hands. She cast a quick internal eye over her emotional state. Pretty composed, she concluded after a cursory examination. There was no time to probe deeper. The phone was ringing.

'Hear me now, Bob?' she said without preamble.

'Loud and clear,' he answered.

'Good. Tell me how you've been these last six months.'

'Busy,' he said curtly, his voice a defensive bristle.

She hadn't meant it to sound accusatory. There was no reason why it couldn't have been six years, not months. By long-standing mutual agreement neither had any obligations to the other on any account, notwithstanding the hours they'd once spent in bed together. But it had never taken much to get Bob Challoner's back up.

'I didn't mean anything, Bob. It's nice to hear from you.'

'You may not think that when I've finished. How's life in the glamorous world of private investigation?'

She hesitated. She felt no inclination to take on the sarcasm in his voice. It was meant to needle, and it usually did. The way he saw it the bulk of her life was spent with errant husbands and two-bit losers. Shaggers and wankers, to use his graphic shorthand.

'Making a living, Bob.'

'If you say so. You doing anything tomorrow?'

'Might be.'

'Cancel it. I'd like you to come up to London, meet a friend of mine.'

'You mean a blind date?'

'Ha ha.'

'I know what your friends are like. What's his rank?'

'Still sharp as a pin, eh, Grace? Good, that's why I need you. I told him you were bright.'

'Big of you. Why do you want me?'

'I can't tell you. Not over the phone. I need you to come up to town, and if it works out and you're willing, it'll be for a few days, till the weekend.'

'Now hang on –'

'You'll be well paid. What's your daily rate? A hundred?'

'What kind of cheapskate do you think I am? A hundred and forty.'

'I'll pay you two hundred a day, plus expenses.'

'But George –'

'I'll square it with George. Come up tomorrow and you'll get the full day's whack even if you turn straight round and head back to Guildford.'

'I'm suspicious already.'

15

'It's not easy money, I can tell you that much. If you throw it back in my face I won't be surprised, but I've got to ask you, because we need someone we can trust, someone with . . . well, a certain combination of qualities which turn out to be in pretty short supply. You happen to fit the bill, though I don't think you're going to thank me much for telling you that.'

'I'm intrigued.'

'Can you catch the 8.07 to Waterloo tomorrow? Wait under the main station clock, I'll send someone to meet you. I'll give him a description, but wear that long camel coat of yours.'

'He won't need a description. Tell him to watch out for a girl who looks like she's just had an argument with the back end of a bus.'

'What do you mean?'

'Got a hell of a shiner on my right eye.'

'How the bloody hell –'

'It's a long story.'

'When did it happen?'

'Five minutes ago.'

'Christ. I wish you'd take care of yourself, Grace. How long will it take to clear up?'

'Couple of days, I should imagine.'

'Well, it's Wednesday now. You should be presentable again by the weekend.'

'What's so significant about the weekend?'

'I'll tell you tomorrow. What's that noise? Is it you?'

The noise was the siren on the ambulance. She could see it slowing down on the other side of the main road, waiting for a gap in the traffic to make its turn.

'It's nothing,' she said.

'You'll be on the 8.07?'

'If I wake up in time.'

'Be there. And, Grace . . . ?'

16

'Yes?'

'Dress smart, no jeans, you know.'

'We going to the opera then?'

'No, no, just . . . you know, presentable. And bring an overnight bag.'

'A what?'

'In case you do decide to stay. Enough to last you till the weekend. Don't worry, we'll put you up somewhere decent.'

'It had better be the bloody Ritz, Bob.'

She didn't catch his answer over the piercing whoop of the siren. She put the phone away, shouldered her bag and walked down to meet the waiting ambulance. A paramedic in green overalls had jumped out of the back and was unfolding a wheelchair.

'It's OK, I can still walk!' she called out.

But only after a fashion. She stumbled down the steps. Her legs had gone horribly weak again.

Talking to Bob Challoner had always had that effect on her, she thought ruefully as she settled into the back of the ambulance.

2

Grace didn't have to wait at Waterloo for more than a few minutes. Just long enough to wonder what the hell she was doing playing the part of a walk-on in a spy movie.

It was too warm to wear the camel coat, as requested, so she draped it loosely over her shoulders. She was suitably dolled up in her best black skirt, white silk blouse and smart black velvet jacket. If it hadn't been for the shiny panda eye she'd have looked a knockout, even if she did think so herself. As it was, she just looked knocked out. Her fellow commuters hadn't seemed to notice. Perhaps they were used to seeing battered women on the 8.07.

She placed herself directly under the station clock and waited tamely. She scanned the faces of the commuters but saw no one looking notably furtive. She took out one of the magazines she'd bought to read on the train, but couldn't concentrate. She didn't notice the man who appeared from nowhere at her side. When he touched her lightly on the arm she jumped.

'Grace Cornish?' he said.

And that was all he said, then or later. When she had overcome her surprise enough to admit her identity he nodded, picked up her overnight bag and started walking,

18

clearly expecting her to follow. She did as she was expected. He was only a little taller than she was but he walked fast and she had to struggle to keep up. He led her to an unmarked blue Toyota saloon that was parked on the double yellow lines in front of the station steps, put her bag in the boot, then opened the rear door and waited for her to get in.

'Are we going far?' Grace asked, as the car pulled out of the station.

The only answer he gave was a slight shake of the head. As he drove he glanced in the rear mirror from time to time, but his eyes were on the traffic and never lighted on her for a moment. Any other time she would have been annoyed, but there was something oddly impressive about the man's silence. His appearance was equally intimidating. He may not have been that tall but he was big. He was very broad across the shoulders, and the bull thickness of his neck was down to muscle, not the usual fat-rolls she had noticed on some of the other fortyish men in her railway carriage. Though he wore a plain dark suit he didn't look at all like a businessman, and he didn't look like a policeman either. The suit wasn't flash, but it fitted him well, lending him a sartorial air quite out of keeping with what the average copper mistook for stylishness. Nor did he have a copper's hands. The skin on the back was dark and tanned, as weatherbeaten as the face she glimpsed in the mirror. When he lifted his palm to acknowledge a driver who had stopped to let him through she saw the calluses ridging his finger joints. They were labourer's hands, but this man was no civilian. She imagined him stripping down a gun or honing a combat knife. He had army as clearly written into his skin as the tattoo she noticed peeking over the edge of his crisp white cuff.

They were going east, along the south side of the river. They passed Blackfriars Bridge and she caught a fleeting glimpse of St Paul's. Signs for the Globe and the Tate Modern came up, prompting flashes of touristy inquisitiveness. Shortly after the turning for Southwark Bridge they headed right. It was an old-fashioned commercial district, full of warehouses and redbrick office buildings, most wearing a dilapidated air. The driver was slowing down; she sensed that they were nearing the end of their journey. Typical of Bob, she thought, to be nowhere near the smart end of town.

He'd been here more than six months now, doing whatever it was that he was so determined to keep mysterious. She remembered the one conversation they'd had on the subject, the autumn before in a Guildford wine bar. Her mind had been on other things at the time, she hadn't registered much, but she knew it was to do with drugs. A new unit, he'd told her, working directly with the intelligence services and answerable to the Home Office. He hadn't been meant to tell her even that much, it was all very hush-hush, but he'd been full of it and bursting to impress her. What did he want with her? Her knowledge of drugs was limited to the odd joint smoked in her student days, an experience which she recalled as not altogether unpleasant, possibly due to her unClintonesque willingness to inhale. But she'd had little to do with narcotics during her brief official career and nothing at all since. So what was it about? When did policemen ever employ private investigators, and pay over the odds too? Whatever Bob was up to it was certain that he didn't have the dead hand of police procedure guiding him. Which meant that he was pretty important. Which meant that he could be useful.

The thought had been in her head from the start of their telephone conversation yesterday, quietly nudging away at the back of her brain. Superintendent Bob, old friend of that nice foul-mouthed Superintendent Collins. Words had been dropped into ears before now, she knew how these things worked. He seemed to want her help, he could hardly complain if she wanted his. It was merely a question of finding out what it was he needed and suggesting the trade.

She'd know soon enough. The driver was parking the car down a narrow alley between two tall buildings. He turned off the engine.

He got out, retrieved her bag from the boot and opened the passenger door for her. It was an unlikely setting for an old-fashioned courtesy. The alley was filled with rubbish, the uneven ground pocked with muddy puddles. Grace picked her way carefully between them, anxious to preserve her one good pair of almost-designer heels. The driver led her round to the back, where an open loading bay led into the rear of one of the buildings. She followed him up concrete steps to a big square iron-grilled goods lift. They went up, very slowly, to the top floor in the building, the sixth.

Ahead of them was a dark landing, lit only by a frosted glass skylight. The driver went to a door and tapped out the code on a number lock. He beckoned Grace to go through, but didn't follow. Once she was across the threshold he handed over her bag and then shut the door in her face.

She turned around. Before her was a long corridor, its brown linoleum floor glassy under the glare of bright neon strip lights. Closed doors gave off to left and right. Had she been alone she would have bowed to her curiosity and peeked in, but there was a woman sitting behind a desk at the far end of the corridor staring at her. Grace advanced cautiously. As she drew near she attempted a smile, but the woman's mouth remained firmly shut. Grace wondered if everyone who worked in this place had taken a vow of silence.

'I'm '

'I know who you are,' the woman cut in, dispelling

Grace's theory. 'You're expected. Go through and wait, please.'

The woman stood up stiffly, and flicked down the handle of the door at the end of the corridor. She was stout in the body but pinched in the face, with naturally disapproving eyes and bloodless lips fixed in an expression somewhere between severity and primness. Nor had there been any warmth in her voice. She was probably only about forty but her plain dark suit and lank untended hair made her seem older.

Grace went into the room indicated and for the second time in a minute heard the oddly disquieting sound of a door being banged shut. She shivered, and not only on account of the cold bareness of the room. Whatever reason Bob had for putting her through this, she thought, it had better be good.

There were three plain plastic chairs in the room, which was as unadorned as the corridor outside. There was one other door, opposite the one she had come in by, but darker and heavier looking. She took the chair facing the second door. It also happened to be the one nearest the window, but there wasn't much of a view. She glanced out at the same alley where her car had come in. The windows in the building on the other side were all boarded up.

She took one of the magazines from her bag and scanned it uneasily. A couple of minutes passed. She took the mirror from her handbag and checked herself. The bruise had gone down and changed from black to yellow, but it wasn't a pretty sight. She touched up the make-up round her good eye. The other was beyond cosmetic salvage.

The dark heavy door opened suddenly. Grace shoved her mascara back into her bag and stood automatically. A young woman, a voluptuous and attractive brunette, dressed in a black skirt and top and a white blouse, stepped into the room. She seemed as surprised to see Grace as Grace was to see her. The two women stood silently staring at each other, and at their near-identical garb, for a good few seconds. Then the other door opened and pinched-face stuck her head through.

'Come along now,' said pinched-face impatiently, and the young woman did as she was bid. Grace saw her glance over her shoulder and caught her eye for an instant before the door closed. The look in her eye was an odd one: frank curiosity, mixed with something like sympathy.

It wasn't a look Grace enjoyed. She felt tempted to grab her bag and follow her out.

'Hello, Grace.'

She turned at the sound of Bob's voice, but she didn't answer him. She was too taken aback. He was smartly dressed in a blue tailored suit and a matching sober silk tie. He had lost weight, especially in the jowls, and his normally shapeless tangle of dark hair had been closely and stylishly cropped. His bald patch gleamed frankly, freed from the unconvincing camouflage of the traditional Bobby Charlton parting. He looked like he should have been fronting *Crimewatch* on TV. Was this the man once proud to be known as the slobbiest cop in the Home Counties?

'Come in, Grace. Let me take your coat.'

She handed him her camel coat and followed him through the door. The room on the other side was big and square and as characterless as the rest of the floor, but at least it looked lived in. There was a thick green carpet and a clutter of furniture, including a brown leather sofa on which two men were sitting. She couldn't see their faces clearly because the blinds in all the windows were drawn and there was no other light in that part of the room. When she glanced over at the other side, by contrast, she had to flinch from the bright white glare of a powerful desk lamp. The man behind the desk was reading some papers. He didn't look up as he spoke to her.

23

'My name is Dent, Miss Cornish. Please sit down.'

Grace looked around the room, her eyes adjusting to the light. On the wall behind the desk was a portrait of the Queen. She noticed that the other photos and prints on the wall were all of ships, some modern, some historical. Directly in front of her, facing the desk, was a plastic chair. She was obviously supposed to sit in it. There was also a brown leather armchair, matching the sofa, but set against the wall on the opposite side. She sat down in the armchair.

Dent looked up from his desk. Cool grey eyes stared at her through wire-rimmed lenses. She stared back. Dent was about fifty, neat and well groomed. He had a jutting jaw, high forehead, strong cheekbones. She could imagine him standing on the bridge of one of those ships on the wall, calmly issuing orders and looking as imperturbable as naval officers always looked in old films. It could have been quite a pleasant face, she decided, had it not been for the cold eyes. He was leaning back in his chair, examining her.

'A pleasant journey, Miss Cornish?' he said, his voice rising in ironical inflection. It was a smooth, cultured voice; the naturally superior tone of the hereditary officer class.

'Not really,' she answered. 'Can't say I'm into magical mystery tours.'

One of the men on the sofa chuckled. Grace looked across at him. He was whispering into the other man's ear.

'Suppose you stop enjoying your private joke and tell me what the fuck this is about,' she said.

The two heads on the sofa drew apart. Grace noticed Bob out of the corner of her eye softly shaking his head. He hung her coat on a peg on the back of the door, then came into the room and picked up the plastic chair that had been meant for her. He carried it behind the desk and placed it near Dent's. Dent waited for him to settle down before speaking.

'Miss Cornish appears to be an impatient young woman, Chief Superintendent. Still, you did warn me.'

'Yes, sir.'

Chief Superintendent. Grace stared at Bob. That was new. So was the quiet obsequiousness in his voice. She'd never heard him say *Yes, sir* in that tone of voice to anyone, the Chief Constable included. She looked back at Dent with new-found respect.

'And a very composed young woman too,' Dent went on, looking down again at the papers in front of him. He had the tone, if not the look, of an avuncular headmaster.

'Is that what all this stuff is about then?' said Grace.

'Stuff?' said Dent.

'The silent chauffeur. The Lubyanka décor. Miss Berlin Wall 1960 out there. You trying to spook me?'

'I suspect that would be a waste of time,' said Dent, his eyes on the desk. 'I see you have a degree in French and Russian from Bristol University. A very respectable 2:1.'

He let his words hang in the air, as if they were worthy of comment. Grace failed to oblige. He glanced up.

'Why did you join the police?'

'You do get graduates joining these days, you know.'

'Yes, I do know, thank you. Your police record is exemplary. A commendation for bravery, I see. Why did you leave?'

'Is there a law against leaving?'

'I understand you complained about sex discrimination.'

'It was a factor in my decision to leave, yes.'

'You didn't pursue the matter. Why not?'

'That's all ancient history.'

'It was only three years ago.'

'What is this place, Mr Dent? The Equal Opportunities Commission?'

'Very droll, Miss Cornish. Perhaps it's time we told you what this is all about.'

He opened a large manila folder and picked out a 10 x 8 colour photograph.

'Before we go any further, Miss Cornish, I must inform you formally that this conversation is bound by the terms of the Official Secrets Act, which I'm sure you will remember signing. You understand?'

Grace touched her temple with her fingertips.

'Scout's honour,' she murmured.

Dent handed Bob the photograph and he carried it over to Grace.

'His name is Mike Gallagher,' said Dent.

Grace stared blankly at the photograph. It had been taken at a poolside somewhere under a cloudless sky and a blazing sun. The man in the foreground was lying face down on a sunbed, dressed only in swimming trunks, his weight resting on his forearms and his chin tilted up, affording a view of a tanned and finely chiselled face. Thick dark hair spilled down over a face dominated by stylish aviator sunglasses and a huge grin. The grin may have had something to do with the bikini-clad blonde who was kneeling astride his back and kneading him with suncream-covered hands.

'Never seen him before in my life,' said Grace. 'Who is he? The new James Bond?'

'Not exactly, although he is something of a playboy. He's also a professional gambler. Thirty-eight years old, originally from Liverpool, Irish father, English mother, though you wouldn't know it. Speaks with an American accent, but still has a British passport. Left school at sixteen, worked on cruise liners, first as a steward then as a dealer in the casino. For the last twenty-odd years he's more or less split his time between Las Vegas, Florida and the Caribbean, with the occasional trip to Europe thrown in. Based in an apartment in Palm Beach, but a life spent on the move, going from hotel to hotel, casino to casino. Blackjack, poker, backgammon – he plays them all for high stakes, and wins regularly enough to sustain a pretty expensive lifestyle. Likes to relax by the poolside, as you can see here, when he's not making a living. This photograph was taken a few days ago in Bermuda. Nice life, if you can get it.'

'Where is all this leading, Mr Dent?'

'Please be patient, Miss Cornish. It's important you hear the whole story so that you understand precisely what we're dealing with here. This is not, as you may have surmised, strictly a local operation. Allow me to introduce to you Mr Tate.'

Dent indicated the sofa at the other end of the room. The man sitting on the left, thin and fiftyish with a high balding forehead and a long face, leant forward and rested his elbows on his knees. The man beside him, who was much younger, remained slumped in the well of the sofa.

'Mr Tate is with the American Drug Enforcement Administration. He and his colleagues have been keeping an eye on our friend Gallagher for a while now. He can tell you rather more about him than I can.'

Grace turned to face Tate, though it was so gloomy at the other end of the room that it took her a moment to lock on to his eyes. She wondered whether these people got a kick out of playing cloak-and-dagger. Or if the DEA was pursuing a policy of recruiting vampire agents.

'Pleased to meet you, Miss Cornish,' said the sepulchral agent in a solid and gravelly voice that was effectively more Bronx than Transylvanian.

'Very nice to meet you too, Mr Tate,' said Grace, in her most polite received English, sounding like the curate's wife at a parish tea party. *And what do you do, Mr Tate?* said a voice in her head that was far too prim and prissy to be her own. *You shoot and arrest bad-ass motherfuckers, do you? How delightful! One lump or two?*

Grace looked down again at the photograph on the arm of the chair to try to disguise the smile that was breaking

27

out from the corners of her mouth. She pulled herself together quickly. She had no idea what was going on, but she suspected that the best way to get it over with was to avoid riling them and to let them enjoy their feelings of self-importance. She resolved to be, if not meek, at least pliant.

'So what exactly has Gallagher done, Mr Tate?' she asked nicely.

'Nothing that we know of. He doesn't have a criminal record. But he was once arrested on suspicion of passing a stolen cheque in Las Vegas. This was sixteen years ago. There was no case to answer, he was released without charge, but not before spending a night in the cells. Sharing the cell with him was a man named Miguel Martinez, known as Mickey or Mikey, an Hispanic-American originally from Santa Fe. In those days Martinez was a small-time hustler and con man. He'd also been arrested for passing a stolen cheque, but in his case the charge stuck. Anyway, that night he seems to have struck up a friendship with Gallagher. Mickey and Mike, a couple of regular guys. Martinez was also a poker player, they really hit it off. What the two of them got up to together in that period, if anything, we don't know, because in those days Martinez was only a bit-part player. His big break came later, and that's when we started to take a look at his acquaintances.

'The big break came at the poker table. He took a lot of money off a guy named Poulson. Lot of money by Poulson's standards, anyway. Poulson was a customs officer, a guard on the US–Mexican border. He owed Martinez plenty, and Martinez kept giving him credit, suckering him in. At least, that's the way Poulson told it in his deposition. When it got to the point that Poulson owed twenty thousand dollars Martinez started to put the heat on. Said he was going to send round the debt collectors. Debt collectors he had in mind were a bunch of guys called the Juarez cartel. You may have heard of them. Martinez gave them Poulson on a plate and they were truly grateful. All Poulson had to do was look the other way when a certain few trucks came through at the border, and not only would his debt be taken care of but he'd have a whole big bunch of new chips to play with. Poulson didn't think too long about it. Got away with it for about two years, and probably would have carried on getting away with it if he hadn't gotten careless about the way he sprayed his money around. Kind of guy who turns up for work on a border guard's salary driving a new Mercedes isn't gonna win any prizes, I guess. Anyway, Poulson blew the lid on Martinez when we pulled him in – not that it did him much good. We put him on the witness protection programme, but he couldn't keep his big mouth shut even then. Cartel caught up with him a couple years ago, wiped him out with his entire family.

'As for Martinez, he's done a whole lot better, but then he's a much smarter guy. About a year after he met Gallagher, Martinez disappeared. I mean, really disappeared, like vanished into thin air. He hasn't been seen for fifteen years. A lot of warrants getting dusty in a drawer some place. We hear about him from time to time, though, seems like he's doing OK. He's a player on his own account these days. Not dealing, that's no game for a lone operator. He's a negotiator, and a real good one. Seems like he's a loss to the diplomatic service. Some heroin supplier in Colombia wants to talk to someone in Chicago he doesn't know, he calls Martinez. Martinez acts as middleman, and he offers a full confidential service, for a consideration. We don't have too many details about his operation because he covers his tracks pretty good. The money's all offshore and he's off the map. We're not even sure what he looks like these days. We have a photograph, but he's almost certainly had plastic surgery since. Whatever he looks like he keeps his face in the background. We know very little about him, but

29

we know that we want him. If our suspicions are correct then he could hold the key to an international criminal ring involving everyone, you name it, the Mexicans, the Colombians, the Russian Mafia. All we got to do is find him.

'He's got one weakness: he still likes to gamble. Secretive kind of guy like him doesn't like to be seen dropping cash. So he plays in private. Poker mostly, big stakes, though it can't be the money he plays for. Money's not a problem far as he's concerned. Maybe he plays for the thrill of it. And this is where his old friend Gallagher comes in. It's taken us a while to piece this together, but it seems like Gallagher sets up his poker games for him. As far as we can tell, he's legitimate, though how much he knows about what his friend Mickey really gets up to is anyone's guess. Anyway, this is the tape of a telephone conversation recorded by the Turkish police a week ago. A guy named Orhan the Turks have been trailing for a while is talking to our friend Gallagher. He's got a heavy accent, but his English is OK. You can follow it on this.'

He picked a single sheet from the top of the pile of papers on the table in front of him and handed it to the pale man. The pale man got up from the sofa and brought it over to Grace.

'The conversation goes on for about five minutes,' said Tate. 'This is the important part.'

He pressed the switch on a tape recorder that was sitting next to his pile of papers. After a few moments a crackly conversation started up. The voices were hard to make out. Grace followed it on the transcript, as he had suggested.

ORHAN: Saturday no good. I got to be here the eight-
eenth.
GALLAGHER: It's the only day he's available.
ORHAN: Week after better.

GALLAGHER: He's only in England for two nights.

ORHAN: Where is he after? In France?

GALLAGHER: He doesn't give me that kind of information. It's got to be the eighteenth.

ORHAN: You think I should be there?

GALLAGHER: I'm not going to tell you what to do, but you know he was pretty pissed off with you.

ORHAN: Yeah, I know. I owe you. We got a juicy babe shipment this month. You got yourself a woman yet?

GALLAGHER: I'll pretend I didn't hear that. You coming to London or not?

ORHAN: You gonna be playing poker?

GALLAGHER: They like playing poker.

ORHAN: The Albanians or the Russians?

GALLAGHER: All of them. It's a macho thing.

ORHAN: But not for you, huh?

GALLAGHER: I play with my brains, not my balls. Come to London. It'd be the polite thing to do. I'll make it worth your while.

ORHAN: Yeah? OK. It's always a pleasure to see the great Mickey Martinez in action.

GALLAGHER [ANNOYED]: I'm putting the phone down now. I'll e-mail you with details.

Tate clicked off the tape recorder, and looked at Dent, who had also been following a transcript, though he was presumably familiar with the contents. Both men were wearing the same solemn brooding expression. Grace had the feeling that she was watching a rehearsed double-act. She remembered the brunette who had come out as she had come in. How many others had heard this spiel already? And was there a queue even now forming up behind her?

'That conversation was recorded a week ago,' said Dent, picking up the baton. 'The Turks knew the DEA was interested in Martinez and sent them the tape. They informed us with the result you see today. Saturday is the day after tomorrow. Martinez will be in London for forty-eight hours, but where exactly we have no idea. Wherever he stays he won't be booking in under his own name. But Gallagher is the one who's arranging the poker game and we know which flight he's coming in on. We expect him to lead us to Martinez. You're looking perplexed, Miss Cornish. It's hardly surprising. I think it's time we explained where you fit into this. Chief Superintendent Challoner will put you in the picture.'

Bob Challoner opened another file. He kept his eyes on the papers as he spoke.

'These are copies of some of Gallagher's credit-card statements, supplied to us by our American colleagues. He's a globetrotter all right, there's payments in Atlantic City, Toronto, Monte Carlo, Nice, London – and that's only one sheet. Payments to hotels, restaurants, casinos. A lot of casinos, that's where he makes his living. He shifts around a lot but there are clear patterns here. One pattern in particular. Wherever he goes he likes to buy his women.

'He's made three trips to London this year. Two four-day visits, and one of a week. Different hotels every time, no pattern there. But on the last two occasions there's a payment to an escort agency called Amorous Liaisons. Before that he used other agencies, but the pattern seems to be that he sticks with the same one at least three times in a row. Hires a different girl each time, though, and always books her on the day he arrives. He's not interested in anyone he's seen before, though he does seem to have a preference for blondes. We know this because we've had a discreet chat with the man who runs the agency, a fellow by the name of Stan Economou. It would seem that Amorous Liaisons has been a bit lax in making declarations to the Inland Revenue. Our friend Stan is over a barrel. In return for keeping him out of prison he's agreed to help us. Next time Gallagher calls him he'll be sent a new girl all right. Only she'll be working with us.'

Bob's eyes were fixed on the papers in front of him. He was wearing an expression of iron concentration. Grace glanced around the room. Tate was looking at the floor, the pale man out of the window. Only Dent was prepared to meet her eyes.

'You still look perplexed, Miss Cornish,' he said calmly.

'You want to send me to Gallagher, right?'

'That is correct.'

'I don't fuck men for money, sir.'

Now the others did look at her, if only involuntarily, snapped to attention by her choice of words, or her tone, which was one thin notch below naked sarcasm. It was her turn not to look at them. She kept her eyes firmly on Dent. He didn't blink.

'We want someone to impersonate a prostitute, Miss Cornish. If we wanted the real thing we would not ask you.'

'Well, that's a relief. But even so, unless my impersonation's complete crap, I think we can safely assume that he's going to want me to do a bit more for him than hold his hand, right?'

'That cannot be denied.'

'So in effect you're offering to be my pimp. Do you want a cut, Mr Dent?'

'Miss Cornish, this is not a game.'

'You've seen too many movies. If you want to find where Gallagher is, why can't you just follow whichever girl he books, or wire her?'

'That has occurred to us.'

'It's a few years since I was a copper but it sounds like a basic surveillance job to me. The girl will lead you to Martinez via Gallagher. What's wrong with that?'

'Nothing, should it happen as you describe it. But this is

better. We've been through all the angles and the best option, for insurance purposes, is having someone on the inside. We want Martinez pretty badly, you see. We think it's worth going the extra mile.'

'And you'd expect me to lie back and think of England, is that it?'

'You can think of anything you like, Miss Cornish. That's your prerogative.'

'It's also my prerogative to tell you where you can stick it.'

'Of course. There's no way we could coerce you into this, even if we wanted to. We're looking strictly for volunteers, and if this isn't something you think you can do then that's fine, you can walk away from here and we'll forget this conversation ever took place. But we're hoping you won't exercise that option, at least not without hearing us out. The fact of the matter is that we've been having a fair amount of difficulty in finding suitable candidates for this business.'

'You surprise me.'

'Hear me out, please. A civilian won't do, we need someone who will understand the way we work. Now, with all due respect to the professionalism of the WPCs of the Metropolitan Police, glamour is not their strong point. To be blunt, only a couple of the ones we've seen would even turn any heads, let alone justify the Amorous Liaisons hourly rate. You, on the other hand, are a highly attractive young woman –'

'Mr Gallagher goes for the panda look then, does he?'

'I'm not flattering you, I'm making a statement of simple fact. You are an attractive, desirable young woman. I have had some experience of running honeytrap operations in the past, and not, I assure you, as the result of seeing too many films. You fit the bill, and not just physically. Chief Superintendent Challoner's report says you are intelligent, tough, resourceful and confident. That would appear to be the case. It is also the case that you are still here. I mean, you have not stormed out on us in high dudgeon, which would have been another of your prerogatives.'

'Maybe I'm too shocked.'

'No. You're not shocked at all. You have a fair amount of experience of undercover work; I've been reading your file. Six years ago you spent every night for two weeks walking through the streets of Horsham in the small hours to catch a rapist. And you did catch him too.'

'But I was never intending to get myself raped.'

'No, because Mr Challoner and his friends got to you fast enough. But if they'd been slower you might not have been so lucky. Tell me, why did you volunteer yourself as bait, Miss Cornish?'

'I was ambitious.'

'Was that all?'

'The bastard had raped six women. I wanted him put away.'

'Do you have any conception of how many lives Mickey Martinez has destroyed? A great many more than six. This is our chance to put him away and we're prepared to use anything or anybody it takes.'

'Well, thank you for letting me know where I stand.'

'You know that personal feelings aren't involved.'

'A good motto for a prostitute.'

'As it happens, sex does not appear to be Gallagher's sole concern. According to Economou, Gallagher claims that he wants intelligent company. He takes the girls to casinos with him and gets them to act as hostesses when he holds private gambling parties. The kind of party, we assume, that Martinez will be attending next week. He also specifies that his girls should have clean driving licences. The last one drove him around the South of France.'

'Sell your body and see the world.'

'The point, Miss Cornish, is that sex won't necessarily

enter into the equation. Yes, Gallagher does sleep with the women he hires, of course he does, but he doesn't appear to be in any hurry. We know he's arriving on Saturday because he's booked the flight with his credit card. He's playing poker on the same night. If all goes according to plan, we're expecting the entire operation to be wound up within a twelve-hour period.'

'So you're saying if I'm lucky I might get away with giving him a blowjob on account?'

'There's no point pretending, is there? We all know what we're talking about. You're not going to be much use to us if you tell him you've got a headache.'

'What if he doesn't fancy me?'

'Then he won't pick you. The procedure is that he phones Economou and asks for recommendations. Economou then faxes over photos of any girl he likes the sound of and Gallagher takes his pick. We're hoping to be able to offer him a choice of at least three girls. We have only two so far, and time is beginning to get rather short.'

'Was the girl who was in here earlier one of them?'

'You know I'm not going to answer that question.'

'All right, I'll ask another. What if Gallagher changes his routine and doesn't use his usual agency?'

'We fall back on ad hoc surveillance. We'll pick him up at the airport and go from there. But we'd rather not have to. These people Gallagher associates with are pros. If there's even so much as a hint that we're tailing him the whole thing could blow up in our faces. We simply want Martinez too badly to risk that. This is an exceptional opportunity, Miss Cornish, hence our recourse to exceptional measures. We would very much like you to help us. We are in a position to reward you handsomely for your time.'

'On top of what Gallagher pays me? Could do pretty well for myself then.'

'I wasn't thinking of money.'

'Good. That makes two of us. Thanks very kindly for the offer, Mr Dent, but I do have some self-respect. And I really don't think I'm cut out for this kind of undercover work.'

She stood up. She took a step towards the door. He said:

'I understand you're in trouble with the Surrey police.'

She stopped. She looked at Dent. And then she looked at her former lover.

'Nice one, Bob,' she said tonelessly.

Bob didn't flinch from her icy stare. If he was at all embarrassed he didn't show it.

'It seems you know rather more about me than I would like,' she said, turning back to Dent.

'We know that you're facing a potentially serious prosecution, Miss Cornish.'

'And you'll be prepared to make it more serious if I don't co-operate, is that it?'

'Please, we're not vindictive.'

'Pardon me if I split my sides.'

'I mean it. If you do walk out now there'll be no question of trying to make you suffer for it. I apologize if I gave you that impression.'

'What impression were you trying to give?'

'That if you help us we can help you. But it's a serious matter interfering with the course of justice. It's not something we could even admit the possibility of under normal circumstances. We need an incentive.'

'I see. And if I give you that incentive?'

'There will be no prosecution.'

'Who the hell are you, Mr Dent?'

'A humble civil servant, Miss Cornish. No prosecution. I give you my word.'

'The guy whose place I broke into won't like that. He might bring a prosecution of his own.'

'He won't. We have in our possession e-mails containing

details of his bank accounts in Austria and Liechtenstein. That information will be passed to Mrs Wetherby if he refuses to co-operate.'

Grace sat down again on the arm of the chair. She was feeling more or less how she had been feeling yesterday when Dawn Kelly thumped her.

'Is there anything you don't know?' she asked quietly.

'Yes. Your answer.'

'My answer?'

Her voice cracked, with tension, with surprise. She looked at all four of them, the two on the sofa first, then Bob, then Dent. She could see it written on all their faces, as clear as day.

They knew her answer.

3

At six o'clock, after an afternoon spent mostly waiting around to no purpose, the driver who had picked her up at Waterloo ferried her to a hotel by Tower Bridge. This time he spoke, but he wasn't interested in conversation. He gave her a set of instructions in a voice that sounded like a recorded message.

She would stay in her room, all night. She could use room service to order food, but she was not to speak to anyone else. He was obliged to warn her that her bill would be fully itemized and subject to scrutiny and that failure to heed this instruction would be treated as a serious matter. She had already been asked, at the end of her meeting with Dent, to surrender her mobile phone. Apart from the hotel staff she must talk to no one. She was at liberty to use the minibar and the video service. Her bill would be settled in full on her behalf. She would receive an alarm call at seven the next morning and breakfast would be brought to her room five minutes later. She should be down in the lobby by half-past seven, with her bag packed and ready, when he would collect her. She would be staying in another location for the rest of the week, he was not at liberty to say where. She would be provided with a telephone number to ring in the event of emergencies. He would be on the other end. Did she have any questions?

'I'd like to know what your name is if I have to ring you,' she said.

'Ryan,' he answered.

His voice had a slight lilt. She had thought at first that he might be Irish, but now she was sure that his long vowels had a West Country origin.

'That's it? No Christian name?'

'Ryan'll do.'

'Not even Private Ryan?'

They were sitting in the car outside the main entrance to the hotel. He had lectured her facing forward over the wheel, meeting her eye only in the driver's mirror. Now he swung round in his seat and fixed her with an appraising stare. His eyes were as grey as Dent's, but harder. Grace felt intimidated, as she knew she was meant to feel, but she stared him out boldly.

'Sergeant,' he said.

'Let me guess. Parachute Regiment?'

'Give over. Royal Marines. And that, young lady, is as much as you're going to get out of me.'

He took her bag from the boot and handed her a key.

'No need to register,' he told her. 'Go straight up. Fourth floor. See you tomorrow.'

'Seven-thirty and speak to no one. Aye, aye, sir.'

She gave him a snappy salute and walked away.

'Grace.'

She glanced back.

'You'll do,' he said, and became the first person all day to smile at her.

She felt a thousand times better for that smile and better still after a shower and a G&T from the minibar. The hotel room was basic but acceptable. She kicked off her shoes, sprawled on the bed and flicked through the TV channels.

She ate smoked salmon and scrambled eggs courtesy of room service and considered drinking her way through the rest of the minibar. It was too pathetic a fate to contemplate. She flicked off the telly, put her shoes back on and went downstairs to find the bar.

The bar was spacious, modern and as featureless as the rest of the building. A few obvious tourists were scattered about but the place was largely empty. A man and a woman were seated on stools, chatting at the bar. Grace moved to a stool further down and ordered a spritzer. She was about to give her room number when she realized that it would show up on her itemized bill. She reached for her purse.

'Please, allow me.'

The woman at the bar had got off her stool and was standing by her, pressing a five-pound note into the barman's hand. It was the brunette she had seen leaving Dent's office earlier. Grace laughed.

'You realize we could be shot for this.'

'In for a penny, in for a pound I say,' said the brunette in a Mancunian accent. 'I'm Jeanette, by the way.'

'Grace.'

'Shall we go sit somewhere quiet, Grace?'

They picked up their drinks and retreated to a table in one of the deserted corners. Jeanette gave a little wave to the man she had been talking to at the bar. He looked put out.

'German businessman,' Jeanette murmured for Grace's benefit. 'Says he's not married but I don't believe him. Maybe I'll give him my hourly rate.'

Grace smiled awkwardly. Jeanette sat down next to her, smoothing her – rather shorter – black skirt. The two women looked again at each other's matching outfits.

'Funny we both had the same idea,' said Jeanette. 'Doesn't look that tarty to me.'

'I should hope not. Anyway, we didn't know that was what they were after.'

41

'I had my suspicions.'

'Really?'

'Another girl in my department also applied, but she didn't get a look in. Figured it might have something to do with her having buck teeth and an arse like a truck. Hey, Dietmar's luck is in. Go for it, my son!'

Jeanette clenched her fist in a private gesture of encouragement. The German businessman was talking animatedly to a couple of women at the bar.

'What do you work in?' Grace asked.

'Traffic. Fixed-penalty administration mostly. Not exactly glamorous. When I heard they were looking for undercover volunteers I leapt at it.'

'You think this is glamorous? It's not the word I'd choose.'

'Everything's relative, isn't it?' Jeanette gave her cocktail an extravagant stir with the naff umbrella-stick provided. 'I know it won't seem that way if I'm the one gets picked and the guy's a perve, but I've been to bed with enough blokes I didn't really want to go to bed with not to worry too much about that. You know, a few too many drinks, go for a curry, oh what the hell. Then wake up the next morning and think: What the heck's that parked next to me? Easy come, easy go, me. Maybe it's different for you.'

Grace smiled ruefully.

'No, I've been there.'

'Reckon we all have,' said Jeanette. 'They show you that photo of Gallagher? Looked pretty tasty, I thought, for a Scouser. Wouldn't mind, I tell you. Wouldn't mind. I've had a lot worse – not that I'm proud of it. There was this bloke I got off with in Blackpool last year, Jerry Pratt was his name, would you believe it? Pratt by name, Pratt – No, on second thoughts, I don't want to go into that.'

'There have been a few Pratts in my life too.'

'Who was the worst?'

'Mm, that's a close call. But the one who still gives me the shivers when I think of him is from ages back. Guy I knew when I was a student. He was at Oxford, friend of my brother's, very full of himself. I hardly knew him, and what I did know I didn't like. But he invited me to go to his college May Ball. I knew he'd expect me to sleep with him, but I'd always really wanted to go to a May Ball.'

'So you went?'

'Yeah.'

'Dead posh. Were you at Oxford then?'

'No, no. My brother was. I was at Bristol.'

'Lot more than I managed. Did get an A-level, but I reckon they marked the wrong paper. What did you study?'

'French and Russian.'

'Bloody hell. What you doing here then?'

'That's a long story.'

'Well, we've only got all night. So what happened then?'

'When?'

'At the May Ball. Did you shag him?'

'Must have done. I was so pissed I can't remember.'

'Oh yeah, that reminds me.'

Jeanette took a long sip of her drink.

'You're only young and single once, Grace. Cheers.'

'Cheers.'

'Sound as if you mean it. Hey, you're not in a relationship, are you?'

Grace hesitated. She took a sip of her own drink.

'No,' she said.

'You don't sound so sure.'

'I was in a relationship till quite recently. I suppose I'm not completely used to the idea of being on my own again.'

'Does it help to talk about it?'

'No.'

'Can we talk about it anyway?'

'Why?'

"Cos I'm a nosy cow. What was his name?'

'Alan.'

'Alan? That's a neither here nor there sort of name, Grace, you don't want to waste your time hanging about with the Alans of this world. They're as bad as the Jerrys. He didn't give you your black eye, did he?'

Grace laughed. She shook her head.

'Why'd you split up then?' asked Jeanette.

'He went back to his wife.'

'His wife? This sounds juicy. So you were his mistress, like?'

'No, no, nothing like that. She was his ex-wife. They divorced a couple of years ago but I don't think he'd ever fallen out of love with her, though he wouldn't admit it. They had a kid, sweet little girl, he doted on her.'

'Was that a problem?'

'Not for me, but he was never really comfortable when we were there together. It became a problem. And then the wife decided she wanted him back. Funny that. He'd been single since they split up and she hadn't showed the slightest interest in him. Then as soon as I turn up she suddenly realizes he's the only man for her.'

'Yeah, women are bitches like that. I mean, don't get me wrong. All men are bastards, take that as read, but a lot of women are right cows with it. So much for the bloody sisterhood. Went back to wifey with his tail between his legs, eh?'

'Yup. A couple of months ago. We weren't even together that long, but . . . I thought it was quite serious.'

'Do you still love him?'

'Do I?'

Grace took another long drink. She contemplated her almost empty glass.

'I'll let you know when I've had a few more of these. What's that you're drinking?'

44

'God knows, but it's disgusting. I'll have what you're having.'

Grace went and ordered more drinks. Dietmar seemed to be getting along famously with the two women at the bar.

'I missed out there,' said Jeanette when Grace had returned. 'He offered to fly me to Hamburg and show me his plant. You don't get too many offers like that in a life-time. Cheers.'

'Cheers. What about you then? Single?'

'Yeah, you don't meet much talent in fixed penalties. There's Roger, but he's got flatulence and a gammy leg. And there's Dave, who's got all his limbs in order but thinks deodorant is for cissies. Mind you . . .'

She took a swig from her drink. She held up the glass.

'Few more of these and I'd be on for anything. Perhaps I should go back and lure Dietmar away from those two slappers. You know, get into practice.'

'You seem pretty relaxed about all this. You don't mind being the honey in the trap?'

'The what?'

'We're the honeytrap, that's what Dent said. I've heard the expression before, something I read about the Cold War. Sex is the only thing men like Dent think women are any use for.'

'I wouldn't go all militant on him, Grace, if I were you. I think you'd be wasting your time.'

'You might be right.'

'What do you work in, by the way?'

'I don't. I resigned a few years ago. I'm freelance.'

'That does sound glamorous. You done this sort of thing before?'

'Not exactly. And I'll tell you something else: I'm not planning to make a habit of it.'

'I'll tell you something else too, Grace. Don't look now but we're in the shit.'

Grace followed Jeanette's gaze. She turned round in her seat and found herself looking up into a familiar face.

'Come to buy us a drink, Sergeant?' she said sweetly.

Ryan didn't answer. He looked straight over their heads.

'I have to make my report in five minutes,' he said, barely moving his lips. 'I'm going to go out and come back in. If you know what's good for you, don't be here when I get back.'

He spun round and marched out, his head and back parade-ground straight. Jeanette whistled softly.

'Sends shivers down your spine . . . Thought we were in for a right bollocking there. I reckon he's got a soft spot for you, Grace.'

'Maybe it's you.'

'God, I hope not. Bloody great brute.'

'Ryan? Nah, he's a pussycat.'

'Oh yeah? You like a bit of rough then, do you?'

'Makes a change from a bit of smooth.'

'It's a pity he's buggered off, then. Dietmar's on the market again. We could have hit the town as a foursome.'

Jeanette waved gaily at the businessman as they walked out of the bar. The other women had deserted him. He was sitting on his own with a collection of empty glasses and a long face.

They returned to their rooms. It was too early to go to bed, and, in any case, Grace was far from sleepy. She watched some bad TV and drank more than she should have from the minibar. At midnight she went to bed and lay staring into the darkness. After a while she switched on the radio. When she heard the one o'clock pips she turned the light back on and fished the sleeping pills out of her bag.

She had been using pills for most of the last year, since narrowly escaping death on that ghastly frozen night in the Peak District. She hated taking them, but she had no choice.

46

The rapid turn of events since the morning had left her feeling even more of an insomniac than usual. The whole thing was so surreal. And she felt angry, too. Angry with Bob, obviously, and with Dent, and with the others in that room, all members of a smug male conspiracy. It wasn't hard imagining the way they thought. She'd lived with it for long enough, with the banter, the innuendo, the testosterone-charged primitivism of the canteen culture. It was changing, people said, old-fashioned sexism had no place in a modern police force, but irrespective of the progressive noises made for public consumption any changes would be surface deep. No matter how sophisticated the world became, coppers were always going to be an evolutionary throwback: a tribe of hunter-gatherers in a society that despised and needed them in equal measure. And the best of them – the ones like Bob with their gut instincts and predatory senses, and their unchallengeable sense of masculine superiority – were by definition going to be the most anachronistic. Venting her anger on Bob was especially pointless. How else did he know how to behave? Perhaps the anger would be better directed at herself. Why had she allowed herself to get into a position of such vulnerability? How was it Dent had described her? Tough, resourceful, intelligent. Try reckless, impulsive, boneheaded ... No wonder her life was such a fucking mess.

She was sitting bolt upright in bed, her upper body stiff with tension, her fists closed into tight balls. She opened her fingers, leant back against the pillows, tried to relax. It was no good; she was wide, wide awake. The sleeping pills hadn't yet had the slightest effect. The angry thoughts buzzed through her head.

She couldn't stop thinking about Alan. Alan was so different from Bob it was hard to believe they belonged to the same species. He had been kind, gentle, sensitive, and fatally weakened by a guilty conscience. She'd known it wasn't his fault even as she had felt him slipping away, but she was still angry with him, because he wasn't there. If he'd been waiting in her bed tonight there was no way she would have agreed to this squalid transaction. Let them threaten to throw it all at her, let her career go up in smoke and the cell door beckon, and she'd have taken her chance. If only he'd been there.

He wasn't there, and nor was anyone else. So much for being this highly attractive and desirable young woman. *Ha, ha, thank you very much, Mr Dent* ... She was on her own. Depressed, more lonely than she'd care to admit, and running low enough on self-esteem to agree to whore herself after only a token fight. At least she couldn't fall much lower, could she? Nothing to lose then, so what was she worrying about? Gallagher might not even pick her, and if he did, so what? She was tough, resourceful, intelligent, wasn't she? And loveless sex was nothing new. So no point getting precious about it. No point in anything at all.

'Now stop it.'

She spoke the words aloud. *Stop it*, she told herself again, mouthing the words the second time. *Stop the self-pity and cut that pathetic whine out of your voice. It's late, now go to sleep* ...

She repositioned the pillows and turned off the light. The bed was much too big, it was a waste being there on her own. She thought of Alan, and at once shrugged the image out of her head. No room for him any more, she told herself, as she felt the sleeping pills kick in at last. The tension was beginning to seep out of her, and if it was only a chemical courtesy, so what? Her eyelids were heavy, her busy brain was slowing down. She concentrated on breathing, slowly, deeply. Gradually the drug smothered her.

The next thing she knew the shrill bedside alarm was cutting through her head. She opened her eyes wide and saw the grey morning light filling the room. It was seven o'clock.

Ryan and Jeanette were waiting for her in the lobby when she came down half an hour later, looking moderately spruce but feeling immoderately sluggish. There was another woman with them, a small blonde with a slightly mousy expression. She too had a suitcase.

'Julie,' said Ryan, and then, deadpan: 'And this is Jeanette, in case you've forgotten. This is Grace, Julie. This way.'

The three women picked up their cases and followed him to the car. Grace took the front seat. No one spoke, but Grace caught Jeanette's eye in the angle of the driver's mirror. They exchanged a secret smile.

At Jeanette's request Ryan put on the radio and they listened to the usual mixture of pop music, traffic reports and inane banter. It helped pass the time. They drove slowly through the early-morning traffic, across the City and past St Paul's, down the Strand, Trafalgar Square, The Mall, Piccadilly. They rounded Hyde Park Corner and cut up through the park to the Bayswater Road. Past Queensway Ryan turned off into a small mews and parked.

'This'll be your home for the next few days, ladies.'

They collected their bags and followed him to the front door of one of the narrow houses. Ryan pressed the doorbell and showed his face to the camera beside it. They were buzzed in.

The pale young man who had sat on the sofa beside Tate the previous day was waiting for them, together with Miss Berlin Wall 1960.

'Thank you, Ryan,' said the pale man. 'That'll be all.'

'Yes, sir.'

The pale man consulted a clipboard.

'I'm Inspector Corliss,' he said when Ryan had gone. 'I'm Chief Superintendent Challoner's assistant and I'll be looking after you for the next few days. You've all met Sergeant Harrington.'

Miss Berlin Wall nodded. Corliss continued.

'Right, we've got a busy day ahead of us, so let's get on. First on the list is photographs. Two sets of photographs, actually. Some simple mugshots first. If you could all step next door with the sergeant, please, one at a time . . .'

When they had had their mugshots taken by Sergeant Harrington they reassembled in the living room. They were handed typewritten schedules.

'We want you all looking your best,' explained Corliss, 'so you're booked in separately with a manicurist, pedicurist, hairstylist, beautician, the lot. We'll do the other photographs then. That'll be mostly tomorrow, in the afternoon. In the morning, there'll be a little shopping expedition, to get you kitted out with essentials.'

'Essentials?' said Jeanette. 'You mean a jumbo pack of condoms and a tub of lubricant?'

The three young women smiled. Corliss and Harrington remained studiously monolithic.

'We'll get this briefing over quicker, Miss Dixon, if you don't interrupt,' said Corliss. He gave Jeanette a severe stare before continuing. 'Moving on, or rather moving backwards, we've set up a meeting for later this afternoon. Should prove useful to you. There's lunch before that, of course – if you've got any special dietary requirements, Sergeant Harrington is on hand to make a note – and also a briefing session. Also a special training session with Ryan. What else? We've got someone coming to streak Miss Dixon's hair. We'll get you looking as blonde as the others in no time. Oh yes, and since the manicurist is coming, you'd better go easy on the washing up, ladies.'

He essayed a tight-lipped grin at each of them in turn. When none of them responded he resumed his relationship with his clipboard.

'Dinner is at eight. All meals provided by us, of course. Nothing planned for this evening, you can all unwind, maybe even enjoy some alcoholic refreshment, in moderation of course. Now, what else . . .? Ah yes, sleeping arrangements.'

'I'm not having him,' muttered Jeanette.

Julie snickered. Grace put a hand over her mouth to disguise her laugh. Unfortunately they weren't the only ones to have heard. Two bright red splotches had appeared on either side of Corliss's pale face.

'There are two double bedrooms and a box room,' Corliss stammered. 'Sergeant Harrington will have the box room, and we'll leave it to you ladies to decide who has who. I mean, sleep together. I mean, shares. Twin beds. Electric blankets. Very comfortable. I'm told. One en suite shower. Bathroom on the first landing.'

His eyes scanned the clipboard desperately for more information. There appeared to be none. His eyes lit up suddenly as he had a bright idea.

'Coffee, anyone?'

They sorted the rooms out over coffee. Grace and Jeanette took one, Julie agreed to take the smaller one. Sergeant Harrington ran the day's menus past them. They agreed on chicken salad for lunch and poached salmon for dinner. She went out to shop in Marks & Spencer.

After lunch Ryan turned up with a black attaché case, which Corliss received from him with an air of religious solemnity. He invited the three women to follow him into the dining room, where he opened the case out on the table. He handed each of them a gold credit card, a driving licence and a passport, the documents featuring the photographs taken earlier that day.

'For security reasons it's essential during the operation that whoever is selected has nothing compromising about her person. We've kept your Christian names, but there's a false surname. We've given all three of you the same surname, because that way we figured you'll have a better chance to get used to it.'

Grace opened her passport. The given name was Grace Collins.

'Why Collins?' asked Jeanette, looking at her own passport.

Corliss shrugged.

'As good a name as any, isn't it? Only one of you'll be using it, of course. Chief Superintendent Challoner's choice, I think.'

We will have our little joke, Bob, thought Grace.

Corliss produced a mobile phone from the attaché case.

'Again, there's only one of these because only one of you will be required. But all three of you must be completely familiar with our communications protocol. You won't be bugged or tagged in any way – it's too risky – so the phone will be your only way of ensuring we know where you are.'

'Isn't that a bit risky too?' asked Jeanette.

'It shouldn't be. You'll be given numbers to memorize, but communication in clear should not be attempted except in case of emergency. Our encryption software is second to none, so if you get any significant information, e-mail us.'

'Won't there be a time lapse before you receive our messages?' asked Grace.

'Possibly. So if you need to get through quickly use text messaging. As you can see, the phone's quite bulky, and that's because there's a keyboard attached.'

He flipped open the panel on the bottom of the phone and showed them the tiny keyboard.

'I know some people can send rapid text messages cycling through the number keys, but this, as I'm sure you'll appreciate, will make things a lot quicker.'

'What if something goes wrong?' asked Jeanette. 'Like, we're in a basement, can't get a signal.'

'Obviously I can't predict exactly where you'll be, but I'm sure if you can't get a signal it'll only be temporary. But in the event of an emergency, don't worry: we'll be tailing you.'

'So why this palaver?'

'It's not a palaver, Miss Dixon, it's a series of safeguards. The crucial point is this: it's not just where you are, it's who you're with we want to know. We'll be giving you a list of codewords to memorize, but for now there's only one you need to know. Forget everything else if you have to but remember this one word, whatever happens. Ace. Got it? Ace. Simple enough, eh? We receive that word then we know you've identified Martinez, and we'll be straight in there, end of story. Right?'

'What if you have to stop off and get a warrant?' asked Jeanette.

'Don't worry,' Corliss insisted. 'Everything will be taken care of.'

'How are we meant to recognize Martinez when no one knows what he looks like?' asked Grace.

'Well, that's where you have to use your nous,' Corliss answered, beginning to sound impatient. 'It's going to be a private poker game, we don't know who else is going to be there, besides Gallagher and Orhan, but it's not going to be like Hyde Park Corner in the rush hour, is it? Hopefully it'll become obvious by a process of elimination. I mean, there are some things plastic surgery can't disguise. You're looking for a Caucasian man in his late thirties, five foot eleven, brown eyes, medium build, dark complexion and colouring. Narrows it down a bit, eh, even if he has acquired a pot belly and a blond wig. At the very least you should be able to make an informed guess, and if there's more than one person present who fits the bill then not to worry, we can make a positive identification later. We may not know where he is, but thanks to our American colleagues we have a DNA sample. But that's all by the by. Come on now, enough questions. We've a lot to do, so let's get cracking. First off I'm going to explain exactly how to access the net using this phone and then we'll start going through the rest of the codewords . . .'

The briefing dragged on for the next hour. After a short break they were ushered through a door in the kitchen into an adjoining garage. There was no car, only Ryan. He was standing on a large blue plastic exercise mat, his top buttons undone and shirtsleeves rolled up. His jacket and tie were hanging on a nail on the wall. He indicated for the women to line up in front of him.

'We've got time to go through a few basics,' Ryan told them. 'I've only been allocated an hour with you.'

'Yeah, that's what all the punters say,' said Jeanette.

Ryan turned his calm grey eyes on her and stared. After a few moments the snickering ceased.

'As I say, there's very little time, so I'd be grateful for your concentration.'

Jeanette coughed.

'What basics are you talking about?' she asked sheepishly.

'I think he means self-defence,' Grace answered for him.

Ryan gave her the benefit of his implacable stare. She met it coolly, although she was quite aware how intimidating it was intended to be. The man exuded physical power; the muscles pressed against the fabric of his shirt like exaggerated lines in the drawing of a comic-book hero.

'Should we take off our shoes?' asked Jeanette.

'No, let's try and keep it real. Those heels you've got on could be useful.'

'Useful for what?' demanded Grace. 'I thought this was going to be a one-night surveillance operation.'

'Useful for emergencies. But if you don't want to stay I'm not going to make you. This isn't part of your official training, and it's not my idea. If you want the honest truth there's not a lot I can teach you in one hour that's going to be much use in a real situation, but it's the only time I've been given and I'll do what I can, if you want me to. It's your call.'

'Sure, please go ahead,' mumbled Grace, feeling like a chastened schoolgirl.

'OK, nothing fancy, a few simple moves. No prizes for guessing the most sensitive part of the male anatomy, and that's what we'll work on first. Knee to the balls, followed by kick to the balls. Right, one at a time. Who's first?'

He demonstrated the first move and took them through it one at a time. None of them cracked any jokes or messed around, although the situation was ripe with possibilities. Grace did what was required of her efficiently and without fuss.

'Not bad,' commented Ryan, as she simulated kicking him between the legs and brought her knee up to his face as he doubled over. 'You done this before?'

'A bit.'

'Where'd you learn?'

'Guildford. How about you? Poole?'

He stood back and folded his arms. He stared at her.

'Smart,' he said.

'Don't know about that,' she said. 'But I do know that if I ever come up against anyone built like you it's going to take more than a kick in the balls to take him out.'

'You won't take him out. But you may buy yourself time.'

'For what?'

'Either to run away or find a weapon. Let's start with what you've got in your handbags. I've got permission to give you each one of these.'

He produced a hand-sized cylinder of red plastic. He held it in his palm for them to see.

'Mace. It's actually illegal for private citizens to carry it over here, but we figure it's exactly the kind of thing a working girl might keep in her handbag for protection. This is a pepper spray, fire it in the face and it'll blind any assailant, not to mention reduce him to screaming agony. You've got five one-second bursts. Flip up the top and press the trigger. I won't demonstrate, it's too confined a space, but it's pretty effective, believe me. I know, I've been on the receiving end.'

Ryan just had time to point out some of the hundred and one uses for nail scissors that had not featured in the manufacturers' original specifications and then his hour was up. He collared Grace as she was on her way out.

'One question,' he said brusquely. 'How'd you know I trained at Poole?'

She shrugged.

'Lucky guess.'

'Bullshit. Tell me, I want to know.'

'OK, it's no mystery.'

She tapped him lightly on the forearm.

'I used my eyes. A little trick they taught me at police college.'

He glanced down at the tattoo on his forearm, then back at her.

'I was right,' he said. 'You are smart.'

They both smiled.

'Thanks, Ryan. And thanks for the lesson.'

She walked back through the connecting door to the kitchen. Jeanette was waiting for her.

'What was that about?' Jeanette asked.

'Nothing. He wanted to know how I knew he was SBS.'

'He wanted to know how you knew he was what?'

'Special Boat Service. It's like the SAS, only they get wet.'

'Bloody hell! I knew I didn't want to meet him down a dark alley. So how did you know?'

'His tattoo.'

'What, that funny frog thing?'

'Yup, that's their symbol.'

'How the hell do you know that?'

'I've got brothers. One of them wanted to be a marine, his walls were plastered with posters and insignia and stuff like that. He used to tell me about the SBS, all the hair-raising stuff he was going to do when he joined.'

'And did he?'

'No, he became an accountant. The most hair-raising thing he does these days is commute on the Northern Line. But he makes a packet.'

'Oh. Is he single?'

The girls were given an hour's break. Grace asked for permission to take a walk. It was refused. The three of them sat around the kitchen table, getting to know each other and drinking too much coffee.

Late in the afternoon Ryan showed up again. He was accompanied by a woman in her early thirties, a strikingly pretty and leggy blonde. She was casually but expensively dressed in designer denim and cashmere.

'Ladies, I'd like you to meet Natalie,' said Corliss after Ryan had gone.

Natalie sat down at the kitchen table. Corliss remained standing.

'Natalie is on the books of Amorous Liaisons,' he explained. 'She spent four days with Mike Gallagher last time he was over here. We thought you might like to talk to her.'

The three women stared at her with more or less frank curiosity. Natalie recrossed her legs and lit a cigarette. She appeared nervous. Whenever she caught anyone's eye she looked away. A minute passed. Corliss cleared his throat.

'Come on now, one of you must have a question.'

'Yes,' said Grace. 'I've got a question.'

Corliss looked at her expectantly.

'Would you mind leaving the room, please? I think we'd all feel a lot more comfortable talking to Natalie on our own.'

Corliss was too surprised to speak. He looked at the others in turn. They made it clear that Grace had spoken for them all.

He tucked his clipboard under his arm and left.

'Thank Christ for that,' said Jeanette, when he had closed the door behind him. 'Give us one of those would you, Natalie. I left mine upstairs.'

Natalie offered round her cigarettes. Jeanette was the only other smoker. Natalie gave her a light.

'That's a smashing top you're wearing,' said Jeanette. 'Is it as expensive as it looks?'

Natalie offered the sleeve of her cashmere cardigan. Jeanette whistled.

'Feel that, Julie. Bet this didn't come from M&S.'

'Harrods,' said Natalie. 'Seven hundred quid.'

'Wow,' said Julie.

'Fuck,' said Jeanette.

'I did,' said Natalie.

They all laughed, Jeanette the loudest. Her shriek was so piercing that Corliss came banging on the door, demanding to know if they were all right.

'So how long you been at this lark?' Jeanette asked when they had got rid of their minder again.

'A couple of years. I wouldn't call it a lark.'

'What did you do before?'

'I was a cashier in a bank.'

'Kind of different.'

'You could say that.'

'How did you . . . you know, make the switch? I don't remember the careers officer at school mentioning this as an option.'

'I suppose it happened by chance. There was this one

customer at the bank, a girl about my age, well dressed, nice looking, always coming in and depositing large amounts of cash. One night I saw her in a wine bar, we got chatting. I must have been drunk. Anyway, I asked her how come she always had so much cash.'

'And the rest is history?'

'It wasn't quite as neat as that. It took me a while to pluck up the courage.'

'So what made you go for it?'

'Money. Simple as that. I had a mortgage and a one-year-old child to support and I couldn't manage on what I was making.'

'You've got a baby?' said Julie in a faint voice.

It was practically the first thing she had said since arriving at the house. The others all turned towards her and gave her their full attention. Julie wilted under their combined interest.

'Isn't that a bit, you know, awkward?' Julie went on, blushing furiously. 'I mean, what do you do with the kid when you're . . .'

Her voice trailed away to nothing.

'I don't do anything with her,' said Natalie, sounding a little put out. 'My mum looks after her when I'm working.'

'Your mum?' repeated Julie incredulously. 'Does she know what you do?'

'Yeah, what of it?' demanded Natalie, her voice rising. 'You got a problem with that?'

Julie shivered.

'I couldn't,' she whispered. 'I'd die.'

'You'd better not give it a go then, love,' said Natalie slowly, acidly. ''Cos talking about it is a hell of a lot easier than doing it.'

There was a sudden chill in the room. For a moment no one wanted to meet Natalie's eye. Even Jeanette found something of interest to stare at on the floor. Grace was the one who broke the silence.

'What have you been told, Natalie? About us?'

'I've been told bugger all, love. They're not exactly open and friendly, the people I spoke to. You're cops, aren't you?'

'As it happens, I'm not,' said Grace. 'But you're right, this is a police operation.'

'And they want you to pose as escorts?'

'That's right.'

'Good luck to you.'

'Thanks. It's very kind of you to help us.'

'Sod kindness. I'm here because they said they'd do me for tax evasion if I didn't co-operate. Same way they're putting the screws on the agency.'

'You're not the only ones they put the screws on, if that's any comfort. It would be helpful if you could give us some details about the way you operate.'

'What sort of details?'

'How much do you charge?' asked Jeanette.

'Depends. My basic's two hundred an hour. Never take less than that, plus the taxi fare there and back. I only do outcalls. If a client wants me for longer I'm open to negotiation. An all-nighter would be at least a grand.'

'Wow,' said Jeanette. 'That's a lot of dosh.'

'A lot of back tax,' said Grace.

Natalie laughed humourlessly.

'Yeah, exactly.'

'There's plenty of blokes'll pay that much, is there?' asked Jeanette.

'Plenty. If I was your age I'd charge more.'

'What sort of men?'

'All sorts. Only thing they've got in common is they can afford it.'

'What do you wear when you're working?' asked Grace.

'Depends. But if it's a hotel visit I like to wear a suit.'

'With a skirt?'

'Usually. But not too short. Nothing obvious.'

'Do hotel managements get bolshy?' asked Jeanette.

'Not if you don't make it obvious. You've got to be confident. I act like I'm on my way to a business meeting. Always wear my hair up. And glasses. Only time I ever do wear them. Over my contacts. Don't ever look tarty. I'm an escort, not a prostitute. There is a difference.'

'What about make-up?'

'Maybe a little eyeliner, lipstick, that's it. Look like a businesswoman, or a high-powered secretary. I always carry a computer case. There's no laptop in it, but there's room for everything I need.'

'Neat,' said Jeanette. 'And what do you need?'

'Not much. Condoms. Change of underwear.'

'You mean a lacy thong and a suspender belt?' Jeanette laughed. 'Simple souls, blokes. Eh, girls?'

'Isn't that stuff terribly uncomfortable?' asked Julie timidly.

'Lying face down chained to a four-poster is terribly uncomfortable,' said Natalie. 'But I don't suppose you'd know.'

The look on Julie's face implied that she didn't.

'The skimpier and lacier the better,' continued Natalie. 'As you say, men are simple souls. I usually wear hold-ups, or nothing at all if it's hot. Never wear tights. Remember, the quicker you get them excited the quicker it's over with.'

'Do you let them kiss you?' asked Grace.

'That depends. Some girls say never, but these guys are shelling out a lot of money, it's not like a quickie against the wall behind King's Cross. Yeah, if I like the guy and I'd be happy to take his money again, I'll let him kiss me.'

'As long as he lays off the garlic,' said Jeanette. 'What about the perves? You got a PVC bra, nurse's outfit, all that?'

'I sometimes get asked for white socks,' Natalie told her. 'You know, the schoolgirl look, very popular.'

'They want to spank you?'

'Usually the other way round. You'd be surprised how weird some guys are.'

'No, we wouldn't,' muttered Jeanette.

'It's not my scene anyway,' said Natalie. 'I try and steer well clear of that dominatrix stuff.'

'What about Mike Gallagher?' said Grace. 'What's his scene?'

There was another drop in the room temperature. Jeanette went very still. Julie was rigid already.

'What's the deal with Mike Gallagher?' asked Natalie casually, lighting another cigarette.

'We can't discuss that,' replied Grace quickly.

'Oh, don't worry, I'm not going to tell anyone. One squeak out of me about any of this and I'll be on my back paying off the taxman till I'm sixty. They made that very clear.'

'I bet they did. You spent four days with Gallagher, Natalie. Is there anything we should know about him?'

'Does this mean you're not pretending? You actually get to screw the guy?'

'Is that a big deal?'

'Let's just say you'll earn your money.'

'I was told that he's not especially interested in sex.'

'Oh yeah, and I'm Britney Spears.' Natalie chuckled hoarsely.

'They told us he took you to the South of France,' said Jeanette.

'Yeah. We flew to Nice, hired a car, then drove up to Deauville before coming back to London for a night.'

'And you did the driving?'

'Yeah, he likes to be driven. I actually drove back through the Chunnel on my own; he had a meeting, flew over and joined me later. He had a lot of meetings. I spent half the time by the swimming pool working on my tan.'

'Nice.'

'I've had worse jobs. He gave me a nice bonus at the end too. Generous guy. Though he's demanding. You've got to give him your full attention when he's around. You've got to be ready to pack up and go anywhere he says, any time of the day or night. You've got to look immaculate too, even at five minutes' notice. I think he's one of those guys who gets off on having a beautiful woman on his arm. He liked showing me off to his friends. He was very particular about my appearance, would tell me exactly what to wear.'

Natalie took a deep drag of her cigarette, then held it up in front of her face.

'He doesn't like these either. I had to pretend I didn't. He only asks for non-smokers.'

'They didn't tell us that,' said Jeanette.

'I'm guessing they didn't tell us a lot,' said Grace. 'How else is he demanding?'

'He wants it on tap. He's a sexual athlete. Even I was impressed, and I'm telling you, guys don't impress me much these days. He's not kinky, at least he wasn't with me, but he certainly doesn't hang around. I knocked on the door, I said hi, he gave me a drink, he discussed money and then he took off my clothes. He knows exactly what he likes and he's not shy about asking for it.'

'And what does he like?' asked Grace.

'Oh, that's easy.'

She jabbed out the butt of her cigarette in the saucer.

'I can tell you exactly what he likes, because he told me. He's a sucker for classy blondes. His own words. The longer and leggier the better.'

She looked Grace straight in the eye.

'He'll like you.'

4

Dent and Challoner both turned up at the mews for the final briefing on Saturday morning. It was the first time either had been seen since the interviews on Thursday.

'I should begin by apologizing for not having had the time to speak to you before now,' said Dent. 'Both Mr Challoner and I have been heavily occupied with other aspects of this operation. But I understand from Mr Corliss that matters have progressed more than satisfactorily in our absence.'

Corliss took time off from appreciating his clipboard to register his self-satisfaction. Dent consulted a clipboard of his own before continuing.

'I know that you've been well briefed and that most of what I have to say may appear superfluous, but the essential point of this operation cannot be stressed often enough. We want Mickey Martinez. Nothing else. It may be we are also able to arrest some of his associates. We may even recover a quantity of narcotics while making such arrests. But that is not important. We want Martinez, and you represent our best hope of finding him. Only one of you will be required, but I am grateful to all of you for volunteering. Whichever of you is selected will need to have her wits

64

about her, but essentially all we require is that she looks, listens and communicates. We need to know the venue of Gallagher's poker game. We need to know when all the players have arrived. Just two items of information. We will move immediately we have the information. The venue will be surrounded and entered, by force if necessary. Our squad will be equipped with battering rams and stun grenades, but they will only be used if strictly necessary. Once the raid begins, though, the safest place will be as far away from any doors or windows as possible. We don't know who will be present at this poker game. Some of the players may be ordinary citizens, high-stakes gamblers, we have no way of knowing. But we do know that Ralf Orhan will be there, and from his track record it's quite likely there could be an attempt to resist arrest. The same goes for Mr Martinez. There is one other thing I should tell you before I hand over to Mr Corliss. I've been informed that Mike Gallagher's flight has left Kennedy airport on time. He should be at Heathrow by half past two this afternoon. This operation is now officially underway. Mr Corliss.'

Corliss explained what would happen next, but they knew that already. He ran through a list of procedures, codewords, contingencies. They knew those things too.

They broke for coffee and sandwiches. No one was feeling very hungry. At two o'clock a car came to collect them.

The car was a black London cab. Ryan was at the wheel. The three women piled into the back. Dent, Challoner and Corliss went separately in a Jaguar. The journey was a brief one. The office of Amorous Liaisons was in Paddington, in a basement below a kebab shop. Grace rang the bell and they were buzzed in. Ryan stayed in the cab.

Corliss was waiting for them inside. He had a table set up with telephones and a radio transmitter. The table next to him had more telephones and a computer. Sitting at the keyboard was a small, moon-faced man with curly black hair and a thick moustache. He leant back in his chair and surveyed the three women in turn as they came in. It was the kind of look, thought Grace, that a butcher might bestow on a slab of meat.

'You done yourself proud, Mr Corliss,' said the man in a lazy, nasal voice. He flashed the women an ingratiating smile. 'It's an honour to have you on my books, ladies.'

'The feeling is not reciprocated, Mr Economou,' Grace answered.

Economou's smile expanded into a face-splitting grin. He sifted through some papers on his desk and pulled out a glossy photograph.

'Ah, you must be the lovely Grace. Your photo doesn't do you justice, love. But then, none of them do.'

Economou pointed at the pile of photographs on his desk.

'In fact, I'd go so far as to say whoever took these must be a complete tosser. Wouldn't you agree, Mr Corliss?'

The three women tried not to smile. Corliss's pale face tinged red spontaneously.

'Shut up, Stan,' he mumbled.

Corliss had taken the photographs the previous day. He had asked the women to pose fully clothed and in their new lacy underwear in one of the upstairs bedrooms. The results had been spectacularly varied. Jeanette had all the inhibitions of a Page 3 girl and her poses were entirely unambiguous. Julie looked like a nun surprised at an orgy. Fortunately their expressions didn't matter. Their faces had all been computer-distorted before being posted on the Amorous Liaisons website.

'I had a call asking for you last night, love,' Economou said to Grace. 'You ever need to make a few bob, let me know.'

'I think you ladies will probably be more comfortable waiting next door,' said Corliss. 'Come this way, please.'

He showed them through a door at the back into a tiny

utility room, equipped with a sink and a kettle and with barely enough space for three plastic chairs. The floor was uncarpeted and the walls were bare, apart from a nude calendar.

'I thought this was a high-class agency,' said Jeanette, carefully wiping the seat of her chair with a handkerchief.

'I don't suppose there's any point spending money on tax-deductible furnishings if you don't pay tax,' commented Grace.

'I hadn't thought of that. Coffee, anyone?'

Jeanette was the only one who was thirsty, which was fortunate as there was only one mug to be found in the sink. She helped herself.

Time passed. Jeanette drank her coffee. Conversation was stilted and conducted in hushed tones. The room was filled with stale air and tension.

Next door the phone rang. There was an almost audible collective intake of breath, followed by a moment of profound collective stillness. Then Jeanette, who was nearest to the door, slid off her chair and put her ear to the keyhole.

'He's talking to some bloke wants a bird with massive tits. Christ . . . he's telling him he's got a girl who's a 44DD.'

'Bloody hell,' said Grace.

'I don't believe it,' said Julie, her blue eyes almost popping out of their sockets. 'That's not natural.'

A sudden gust of laughter swept the room. Julie blushed, but only a little. She was used to being laughed at by now. Grace gave her arm a gentle squeeze.

They had only been together for a couple of days, but there was a bond between the three of them, even though they had nothing in common. Indeed, Julie and Jeanette might have been from different planets. Jeanette was loud, vulgar, brimming with confidence and explicit about sex. She was a pure modern ladette who drank lager, gorged on curry and brought every conversation round to pulling and shagging. Whereas Julie was shy, naive, self-consciously demure and sexually inexperienced. She had only ever slept with three men, she had confided to them, all long-term boyfriends. Jeanette claimed to have once slept with three men in the same night.

Grace tried to stop looking at her watch. It was agonizingly close to three. If the plane was on schedule then . . . she let the thought die out. She only wished she was as cool as the others thought she was. They both looked up to her in some way, they seemed to have decided – she wasn't sure when or how – that she was their leader, or at least their spokeswoman. It may have been because of her age. Jeanette and Julie were both twenty-five. They had affected not to believe her when she told them she was thirty. She looked nowhere near that, they had told her, sounding incredulous, at least for the first hour or so. After that they started joking about pensions and bus passes. But it was obvious that they respected her, and she was flattered. They thought that her being a private investigator was a very grown-up thing to be doing. She did try to explain that it wasn't like in the movies, but they didn't want to listen to that. Their own lives, they insisted, were humdrum. Jeanette thought life in traffic was bad, but Julie insisted that being the lowest-ranking PC in a suburban station with special responsibility for school liaison was worse.

Something else bound them together. Something that embarrassed them to different degrees, although they had not spoken about it openly. But it was there, and they were all aware of it. It was the knowledge that each of them was prepared to go to bed with a man for payment.

Payment in kind, but payment all the same. Jeanette and Julie had both been offered promotion. Grace had been promised salvation.

Only one would be chosen, but all would benefit. They

knew the deal. They knew too that there was a higher purpose, some might even call it a cause, or a principle, to justify the appearance of a squalid compromise. It was an act,
it wasn't real prostitution. And yet they couldn't help but
wonder where the difference lay, if difference there was,
between them and a woman like Natalie, who might be no
less compelled by necessity, but at least was honest enough
to ask for cash.

To the outward eye there was no difference. Natalie
would have approved of them. They were all wearing suits,
smartly cut jackets and skirts bought off the peg in
Kensington the day before. Grace and Jeanette were in navy
blue, Julie in bottle green. Their freshly styled hair shone,
their manicures gleamed as brightly as their new shoes.
They looked good. They looked expensive.

'It's gone three o'clock,' said Jeanette suddenly.

They glanced at their watches. Julie began looking nervously through her bag. It set off a chain reaction. They all
fiddled with the contents of their bags. It was something
to do.

'What have you got there?' demanded Grace, pointing
into Jeanette's bag.

Jeanette pulled out a garishly decorated packet of condoms. She offered it for general inspection.

'Banana, strawberry, licorice. That's my favourite.'

'Yuk,' said Grace. 'Let's see.'

Jeanette handed over the packet. Grace laughed.

'Tandoori flavour? Gross! Where'd you get these?'

'That chemist in Kensington.'

'They got flavours?' demanded Julie, her voice straining
with bafflement. 'What, like crisps? I don't understand.'

'No, you don't, do you?' said Jeanette sarcastically. 'Never
mind. Let's hope it never happens, eh?'

Jeanette leant across and patted Julie on the knee. Julie
looked offended.

'Anyone would think you wanted to get picked,' she snapped back, with a flash of spirit.

'Well, it's a good thing it's not going to be you, love. I reckon you'd pass out at the first sight of dick.'

'What do you mean, it's not going to be me? We don't know who it's going to be, do we?'

'I think we've got a pretty good idea,' Jeanette snapped back.

Grace glanced up. Jeanette met her stare with a hint of apology.

'You think it's going to be me, right?' said Grace.

Jeanette shrugged.

'We all heard what Natalie said, and I'm sure as hell no leggy blonde. Let's face it, Julie and me are here to make up the numbers.'

'You don't know that for certain,' said Julie hastily. 'He may fancy a change. You know, maybe he's bored of having cheeseburger all the time, might want to try a McNuggets.'

Grace smiled.

'It's OK. I think it's going to be me too.'

'You do?' said Julie.

'I do,' said Grace.

'And you're cool about that?' said Jeanette.

'I don't know if I'm cool, but I've had nearly two days to get used to the idea.'

'You figured out how you're going to handle it?'

'In theory, yes. In theory, you see, this is all happening to someone else who's also called Grace. Not me, Grace Cornish, but this woman Grace Collins. And this Grace Collins is just doing a job, starting any minute now and ending some time tonight. She isn't like me, so she isn't going to worry about the things I'd worry about, like whether I'll feel ashamed to look at myself in the mirror tomorrow morning. Thoughts like that are a luxury she can't afford. This Grace knows she's got to get through it somehow, and she's going to be professional, and dedicated and single-minded. No feelings involved, she's got that much in common with Natalie, but only that much. As soon as it's over, Grace Collins disappears in a puff of smoke, like that.'

'You'll get through it,' chimed in Jeanette. 'It'll be like that May Ball.'

'That what?' said Julie, wearing her familiar puzzled expression.

'Perhaps you'd better take these,' said Jeanette, offering Grace the packet of flavoured condoms.

Grace patted her handbag.

'It's OK. I've got some already.'

There was a knock on the door and Corliss poked his head round.

'Grace, can you step outside a sec, please?'

They all looked at their watches. Corliss guessed what they were thinking.

'Don't worry, he's not rung yet. He's clearing Customs now. Mr Challoner would like a word with you.'

Grace followed him out into the other room. Economou was still sitting at his desk, picking his teeth and leering at her, but there was no sign of Bob.

'He's outside,' explained Corliss.

Grace climbed the steps from the basement. She saw Ryan, leaning against the bonnet of the taxi and sipping coffee from a Styrofoam cup. He tipped his head to the side, indicating the rear of the cab. Bob was sitting there, hunched forward in the act of lighting a cigarette. She got in, and sat on the push-down seat opposite him.

'All right, Grace?'

'All right, Bob.'

'Good. You look fantastic, by the way. Haven't seen you looking this good in years.'

'You think I should go into prostitution full time?'

71

'Yeah, yeah. Same old Grace.'

'Same old Bob too. You didn't get me out here to tell me how nice I looked. What do you want?'

'I've got some news for you. I thought you might be interested. All charges against you have been dropped. It would appear that someone has mislaid a certain video in which you make a guest appearance.'

'That's very careless of someone. What about the security guards?'

'Oh, they've remembered that the door was already unlocked. As you were simply returning some papers that had been dropped in the corridor outside there's clearly no need for any further action. It was all a misunderstanding. Mr Wetherby is particularly anxious to draw a line under the affair.'

'A sentiment with which I'm sure Superintendent Collins is in full agreement.'

'Oh yes. There's nothing Superintendent Collins likes more than doing right by his old friends.'

'Not the only one, is he? How very considerate it was of you to put my name forward for this little job. Forgive me, but I haven't had time to thank you properly till now.'

Bob sighed.

'Grace, you may think I'm a hard ruthless bastard who'd sell his granny if the price was right, but the fact is I thought long and hard before involving you. I don't like you doing this, really I don't. If there was any other way round it, I'd take it, believe you me. And I sure as hell hope it's not you as gets picked.'

'But you know it will be me.'

'I don't know anything of the –'

'You've known all along, Bob. Don't lie, you know perfectly well the type of woman Gallagher goes for. The others are window dressing, aren't they?'

Grace had never seen Bob looking really rattled before.

72

It was an arresting sight to watch him fiddling nervously with the knot of his tie, then brushing imaginary ash off his lapel, and all the while twisting his head away from her and glancing at every passing car, as if the driver might suddenly slam on the brakes and throw open the passenger door and offer him a means of escape. Several times his lips parted, as if he were about to speak, but nothing came out. Eventually he took one long drag of his cigarette, wound down the window a couple of inches, and chucked it out, half-smoked.

'You may not believe this, Grace –'

'I said don't lie to me, Bob.'

'No, listen. This whole thing only blew up last week, remember? We knew we were up against the clock from the beginning, it's been a miracle we've got it together at all. We spent all last weekend looking for suitable girls. We found one, Julie, and God help us if Gallagher has a brainwave and picks her. Jeanette's an improvement, but she's no experience of undercover work. The point is, we were desperate. I thought of you straight away, of course. As soon as they said what they were really after was a classy blonde with brains I knew there'd be no one to touch you, but I didn't bring your name up. I didn't want you dragged into it, no way. OK, so we're not together any more, but I don't like the idea of other blokes sleeping with you, Grace. I can't help it, you know I'm the jealous sort and there's a part of me that still twists up inside when I think of you with anyone else. So don't think I'd serve you up on a plate to a jerk like Gallagher. I wouldn't, but on Tuesday Dent said he was thinking about cancelling the operation. And that was a hell of a blow, because we need Martinez, we need that fucker. Anyway, it was that night I heard about your scrape with Jimmy Collins, and I thought – well, excuse me for being naive, but I thought I could do you a favour. And in return you could save all our arses.'

'You didn't think you could do me a favour and leave it at that, for old times' sake?'

'Come off it, Grace. By what authority could I have got those charges dropped? I'm only a humble copper. But I knew that Dent might be able to do something. For the right consideration.'

'You're all whores really, aren't you?'

'Sure, if it makes you feel any better.'

'It's the twenty-first century, Bob. When are the police going to stop treating women as sex objects? Tell me this: if Gallagher was gay, would you be volunteering that nice young Inspector Corliss for my job? Or maybe you'd prefer to put your own arse on the line?'

'Keep your voice down, Grace.'

'Oh, I'm terribly sorry, Bob, am I embarrassing you?'

'No, but you are getting on my bloody nerves, so shut up, will you? You're right, OK? I see your point, OK? But there's fuck all I can do about it. OK?'

He wasn't rattled any more, he was just angry. His face was red and the veins in his forehead were tight and knotty. Grace folded her arms, and crossed her legs, and observed him coolly.

'OK,' she said. 'I think you'd better answer your phone.'

He was so steamed up he hadn't heard the muffled wailing of his mobile. He snatched it out of his pocket and pressed it to his ear. He grunted his name, then listened in silence for ten seconds. He grunted again and put down the phone.

'You'd better get back down there,' he said to Grace. 'Gallagher's gone to a hotel near Heathrow. He's checking in.'

She got out of the cab. They had been promised a warm autumnal day, but the sun had disappeared behind thick clouds and a wind was kicking up. Ryan smiled at her encouragingly. She hurried down the steps to the basement. She didn't want the men to see her shivering.

74

Bob came in after her. They stood silently by the door, watching Economou, who was sprawled lazily over his seat, and Corliss, who was sitting forward on the edge of his. Behind him the door to the utility room was open. Grace could see the others, huddled together facing out.

The phone started ringing. Economou took his time picking it up. He was the only one there enjoying himself.

'Amorous Liaisons . . . yes . . . ah yes. How very good to hear from you again, Mr Gallagher. Of course I remember, it was only, what, six weeks ago? Yes, sir.'

Economou's ingratiating nasal voice echoed emptily in the silent bare room. He laughed sycophantically into the receiver.

'Our motto, as you know, is total client satisfaction. Tonight you say, sir? And for the next four nights? Till Wednesday then, sir? Yes . . . yes . . . the same arrangement as last time, yes. Well, it's a bit on the early side, but I think that we can rustle you up something. Now if you could hold on one second, sir, while I consult the files . . .'

Corliss's clipboard was on the desk in front of him. He picked it up and scanned the paper attached to the top.

'I can offer you three lovely blondes, all very classy. Classy and sophist– What's that, sir? One moment, please . . .'

He lifted up the top sheet of paper and glanced at one beneath.

'The first lady is Julie. Petite, very delectable. Nineteen years old, five foot two, she's got . . . Yes . . . yes, I agree, she is a bit on the short side. But never mind, I think I've got just the ticket for you, sir, just the ticket . . .'

He lifted his head from the receiver and smirked at Grace. He mimed licking his lips.

'Let me tell you about Grace, sir. Yes . . . yes, it is a lovely name, isn't it, sir? A lovely name for a lovely lady. She's twenty-seven, medium-length blonde hair, blue eyes and cheekbones to die for. Five eight in her stockinged

feet, and very shapely with it. She's got a really fantastic –
What's that, sir? . . . If you let me have your fax number
. . . You prefer e-mail? Give me your address. Yes, I've got
a pen . . . yes, got it . . . Yes, she's on the website. You're
looking at the website now? Excellent, sir. Yes . . . yes. As
you know, sir, it is our policy to doctor the faces. The girls
prefer it, saves them possible embarrassment with family
and friends . . . Oh yes, sir, Grace has a full clean driving
licence . . .'

Economou swivelled round in his chair to face the computer screen. He carried on talking as he typed.

'The other girl? Yes, her name's Jeanette. Nineteen years
old, classic young English rose and very, very curvy . . . Yes,
yes, that's right, a mouth-watering 38D. Oh yes, of course
. . . I'm e-mailing you some other photos now, so you can
see their faces. Very pretty girls, you won't be disappointed.
Yes, that's right . . . A pleasure talking to you too, sir . . .
Indeed, I shall await your call.'

He put down the phone and clicked his mouse button a
couple of times, grinning charmlessly at Grace.

'He sounded very keen on you, darling. And who can
blame him after the build-up I gave you?'

'Fantastic what?' said Grace coldly.

'Sorry, love?'

'You told him I had a fantastic – dot, dot, dot. Fantastic
what, Mr Economou? Come on, the suspense is killing me.'

Economou grinned at her.

'Personality, dear. What else? You know, I'm serious: if
you should ever need a job –'

'Shut up, you Greek shithead,' snarled Bob Challoner.
'What the fuck's going on?'

'I've e-mailed him more pictures of Grace. Jeanette too.
He sounded quite keen on her and all, though I thought
he preferred –'

'Shut up. Now what?'

'Now nothing. We wait.'

Bob pulled up a chair and sat down heavily. He patted the seat of the chair next to him.

'Sit down, Grace, take the weight off your feet.'

'I'm fine standing, thanks.'

Bob shrugged. He lit a cigarette. Jeanette came out of the utility room and stood next to Grace. No one spoke.

'What's taking him so long?' Bob demanded when he had smoked his cigarette down to the butt and ground the filter thoroughly flat with his heel.

'It can take a while for the e-mail to arrive, sir,' explained Corliss.

'So much for modern bloody technology,' Bob growled. He lit another cigarette. He jabbed the match in Economou's direction.

'Business always this slow, is it?'

'Yeah, in the daytime. You should be here tonight. Phones don't stop ringing on a Saturday night. I'm run off my feet.'

'Bless,' said Bob.

The phone rang. Grace felt Jeanette reach for her hand and grip her fingers tightly. Economou picked up the handset in his customary lethargic style.

'Ah, hello again, sir, I trust that whetted your appetite . . . ah yes . . . Oh, really? You're sure? . . . Yes, right away, sir. What hotel are you at? . . . Oh yes, I know . . . It'll be half an hour, forty minutes max, depending on traffic. And how will you be paying? That's right, sir, same fee as last time. You'll e-mail me your credit-card details, as before? Excellent, sir. As you understand, this is solely for the introduction. Further arrangements are a private matter entirely at your discretion. Thank you very much indeed for calling us again. Any problems, please don't hesitate to ring.'

Economou put down the phone slowly. He looked mildly surprised.

'Well, well,' he drawled.

'Well what?' snapped Bob.
'Couldn't make up his mind, apparently.'
He jerked his thumb at Grace and Jeanette.
'He wants them both.'

5

The black cab sped through light Saturday afternoon traffic towards Heathrow, Ryan at the wheel, Grace and Jeanette side by side on the back seat.

'I don't believe this,' Jeanette was muttering under her breath. 'We're going to wake up any moment and none of this'll be happening.'

'Try and stay calm,' Grace whispered back, squeezing her arm.

'Easy for you to say that. You're the bloody ice maiden. But I'm in bloody shock.'

They were keeping their voices down so that Ryan wouldn't hear. The quietness in the cab made quite a contrast to the scene they had left behind.

Jeanette had been the first to break the silence.

'Oh, that's great, that is, bloody great,' she said after the long pause in which everyone had slowly digested the implications of Gallagher's choice. 'He doesn't just want sex with one of us, he wants a sodding orgy.'

Bob jabbed an accusing finger at Economou.

'Why the hell didn't you warn us this could happen?'

Economou held up both hands defensively.

'How was I supposed to know?'

'You said he only liked straight sex.'

'He does. He did. Ask Natalie.'

'Why didn't you tell him your girls don't do that sort of thing?'

'Because they do, actually.'

'What?'

'Well, most of them. I mean, if a punter asks for a double-up, most of my girls are willing. They reckon it's easy money. It's quite popular, specially with a white girl and a black girl. "Coffee and cream", we call it.'

'Shut up.'

'Phone for you, sir,' said Corliss. 'It's Mr Dent.'

Bob snatched up the receiver and marched into the corner. Corliss decided to take control.

'It'll be all right, girls,' he said confidently, addressing not just Grace and Jeanette but also Julie, who had emerged from the utility room to join the others.

'How the hell do you know, Corliss?' demanded Jeanette scornfully. 'You're not going to be there.'

'It's Inspector Corliss to you, WPC Dixon.'

'Oh, stick your clipboard up your arse.'

Bob finished talking to Dent. He threw the phone down on the table.

'All right, now listen to me,' he growled.

'Don't you love assertive men!' said Grace.

'And you can shut up for a start!' snapped back Bob. 'I've already had your twopennyworth out there, thank you, Miss Cornish. Right, listen, all of you.'

He looked around the room, at each of them in turn, to make sure he had their attention. He pointed at Julie.

'You, in there –'

He indicated the back room. Julie hesitated.

'Now!' he bawled, six inches from Julie's face.

She scurried off like a terrified small animal. Bob pointed at Economou.

'You – in there with her.'

Economou had experienced enough of Bob's tongue not to argue. He did as he was told. Bob helped him on his way with a shove and slammed the door shut behind him.

'OK,' he said, coming back and standing directly in front of Grace and Jeanette, the better, Grace imagined, to intimidate them. 'Dent and I are agreed. The operation goes ahead as planned. But if there's anything you can't handle, we abort.'

'And who decides that?' demanded Grace.

'You do. You knock it on the head, we go with your decision, no questions asked.'

'Oh great,' said Grace.

'Fucking great,' said Jeanette.

'And what's your problem, Dixon?' Bob shouted, standing as close as possible and breathing in her face.

'Pick on me, Bob, not her,' said Grace.

'All right then,' he said, transferring his attention to Grace. 'You tell me what the problem is?'

'Well, for a start we've only got one phone,' said Grace. 'So if we get separated –'

'Or something unexpected happens –' Jeanette chipped in.

'We're going to have trouble communicating. And then what if one of us gets into trouble –'

'And the other one doesn't –'

'And only one of us is there when Martinez turns up –'

'And there's no way of communicating –'

'What do you suggest we do then, Chief Superintendent, sir?'

Bob glared at them both in turn. They didn't flinch. He spun on his heels and glared at Corliss instead.

'Why the fuck have we only got one phone?'

Corliss flinched.

'Because there's only supposed to be one girl, sir.'

'Why haven't you got a spare, for emergencies?'

'We have, sir. It's in Southwark, sir.'

'You've got the planning skills of a fucking goldfish, Corliss.'

'Yes, sir.'

'He's not the only one,' said Grace acidly.

'And what do you mean by that?' Bob spat back at her.

'Very clever idea to give us the one surname, wasn't it, Bob? I'm Grace Collins and this is my friend Jeanette, er, Collins. Oh, what a coincidence.'

'And what a coincidence too that we're wearing almost exactly the same clothes,' added Jeanette. 'Again.'

Bob looked them both up and down.

'Tell him you're sisters. It'll make for one hell of a bloody orgy.'

Twenty minutes later the black cab swung on to the Westway, heading out of town along the M4. Ryan reported their location to the control room on his radio.

'I still don't believe it,' Jeanette was murmuring for the umpteenth time. 'Tell me it's not happening.'

'Listen, Jeanette, we've not got much time, we'd better sort this out.'

'I mean, what if he wants us to . . . you know?'

'What?'

'You know, like, it's such a bloke fantasy, isn't it? Watch two girls doing it, and then . . . I never done that before, you know, a threesome.'

'No, me neither.'

'Oh great. At least if one of us was bisexual you could give me a clue.'

'Look, we just tell him politely but firmly we don't do lesbian, right.'

'Oh, that'll go down a bomb, that will. Why'd we bother to come then? He'll probably kick us out, end of story. Then the whole operation's buggered and you know who they'll blame, whatever they say now.'

'We'll cross that bridge –'

'Probably kick us out anyway when we walk in. Nineteen-year-old English rose! Christ, I didn't look nineteen even when I was nineteen.'

'Listen a minute, Jeanette.'

'He'll probably sue us under the Trade Descriptions Act.'

'Listen, we've got to sort this out, it's important. I'll look after the phone, OK?'

'God, I need a cigarette.'

'Is that OK?'

'What if –?'

'Look, there's going to be a lot of bridges to cross, so let's take them one at a time, right? You get into trouble of any sort, you yell. Promise?'

'OK. I've been thinking.'

'What?'

'I think we should say we're sisters, like Challoner said. He can't make us do the lesbian stuff then, it wouldn't be decent.'

'Jeanette, love.'

'What?'

'Whatever we do with him it's not meant to be decent.'

The motorway was almost empty. The signs for Heathrow flashed past, the first junction, then the second, third, fourth. They passed the M25 turn-off. The cab pulled over into the slow lane. Grace saw Ryan talking into his radio. He caught her eye in the driver's mirror and signalled he wanted to talk. She slid across the floor and repositioned herself on the pull-down seat behind him.

'This junction,' he told her. 'They've given me the brief. It's a brand-new hotel. The lifts are on the right as you go in. You're to go up to the top floor, the seventh. Turn right when you come out of the lift, keep straight on, it's the end of the corridor. He's in the Concorde Suite. No room number.'

'Have we far to go?'

'No. I see it.'

Now she saw it too, to the right, a squat square building constructed in red and yellow brick, like a giant Lego house. They came off the motorway and negotiated a roundabout and traffic lights. A sign indicated that the hotel entrance was on the right.

They turned in and approached slowly over a series of sharp speed bumps. A vast, and mostly empty, car park stretched out on either side. Two huge continental coaches were disgorging their passengers in front of the main entrance. Ryan whipped the cab neatly in between them and stopped. Immediately a man standing on the pavement waved to attract his attention, but Ryan gestured him away brusquely.

'Sorry, mate, I'm on a job.'

Jeanette's was the door nearest the entrance. She got out first and Grace followed. She closed the door behind her, pulled down the window at the front and lowered her head to Ryan's level.

'How much do we owe you?' she said.

'No charge.'

'I'll report you to the taxi drivers' union.'

'Grace . . .'

She had started to go. She waited.

'Take care of yourself.'

She didn't like the concern she could see stamped into his granite-like face. Nor was she sure what good luck might mean in the present instance. She picked up her computer case and overnight bag and walked into the hotel.

Jeanette had a computer case and bag of her own. They saw their full reflections in the thick plate glass of the main doors, the Misses Collins in their near-identical navy suits, the Tweedledum and Tweedledee of the escort world. The doors swung open automatically. They stepped inside, brushing past the formless conga of tourists.

Grace walked fast. *Just get on with it,* she told herself. *Don't give the doubts time to creep in . . .* Jeanette, with her shorter legs, had to hurry to keep up. Grace saw the reception desk, the busy corridors, the thickly carpeted lobby with the white piano planted glaringly in the middle, but only out of the corner of her eye. Her attention was fixed on the lifts; one was waiting. She marched straight in and pressed the button for the seventh floor. The doors closed rapidly, leaving behind a couple of cross-looking guests who had assumed that Grace would wait. The lift rose swiftly, silently.

Out of the doors and turn right. The simple instructions were burnt into her mind. She strode purposefully down the corridor, Jeanette, her shadow, a step behind. She didn't take in the numbers and names on any of the doors. Until the last one. Concorde Suite. Black lettering on a silver plate. She raised her knuckles.

'Ready?' she said.

Jeanette nodded. She paused a second, took a deep breath. She rapped on the door.

There was silence. She turned her head to the door, pressing her ear up to the wood. She heard a faint sound, the murmur of speech, on the other side.

'Yeah?' came a muffled voice through the door.

'Mr Gallagher? It's Grace and Jeanette.'

A pause. Then the metallic click of a lock snapping open. The round handle turned and the door swung in a couple of inches.

'Come in,' said the voice, clearer now.

She took a deep breath. She counted slowly to three. She pushed open the door.

It was a big room, light and airy, the whole far wall a sheet of floor-length glass opening on to a balcony. There was a deep leather sofa in front of her, facing a glass and steel coffee table and a widescreen TV. The furniture was stylish and modern, the colour scheme pale blue and gold.

In the wall on the right was an open door through which Grace glimpsed a king-sized double bed. These things she took in instantaneously, but they barely registered. Her eyes were fixed on Mike Gallagher.

He had just sat down on the arm of the sofa, was leaning back idly with one foot on the coffee table, talking into a cellphone. But it wasn't his pose that caught her attention. A white towel covered him from midriff to mid-thigh. The rest of him was naked.

Stripped and ready for action.

Even as the thought struck her, his head turned towards her and their eyes locked. He smiled.

'That's OK by me,' he said into the phone. 'You take your time.'

Talking to someone else, but looking at her. Taking his own time too, and more than looking. Evaluating, appraising, appreciating. And imagining. His eyes flicked down briefly to take in her breasts, her legs, before returning to her face. She knew what he was imagining.

'Say eight o'clock then. But we shouldn't be any later than that.'

His tone was relaxed, unhurried, his inflection American. There was not even a residual trace of a British accent, let alone the distinctive vowels of a Liverpudlian. Nor did he look much like an Englishman. His hair was thick and black, his skin uniformly dark and glowing with the sun. His body was trim and muscular. His dark eyes, his strong jaw and long nose wouldn't have looked out of place in the pages of *Screen International*. He didn't look, somehow, as if he spent much time pining for the streets of Toxteth.

'Sure. I'll be there early. You come on when you're ready.'

His eyes were fixed on her again, bold and confident. If she had met those eyes and that smile across a crowded bar she might have thought their owner a little too sure of himself. She could have played hard to get, and meant it, but secretly she would have been flattered. She might even have smiled back. Even in her imaginary bar there wouldn't be many better-looking men than this one. And if, having encouraged him, at the end of the evening he should suggest ... Well, she had done that before, only in this case the preliminaries had been dispensed with and she was at the bedroom door already. No point in playing hard to get now, when she had been sold under contract and delivered on a plate.

So she smiled back.

'Hey, one more thing – don't forget your wallet.'

He clicked off the phone, chuckling to himself, and pushed it along the glass top of the coffee table, at the same instant rising and using his other hand to hold up his slipping towel. He was taller than he had looked sitting down, close to six foot. He gestured at the towel.

'My apologies, ladies, I was in the shower.'

He ran a hand through his wet glistening hair, like a model in a shampoo advertisement. The thick black hairs on his chest and legs were also matted with damp. He looked like he belonged on Copacabana beach, not in an anodyne English hotel room with a backdrop of dull grey sky.

'Can I get you anything? A drink, coffee?'

Grace shook her head. He turned his attention to Jeanette, for the first time.

'We're sisters,' she blurted out suddenly.

He looked surprised. Almost as surprised as Grace.

'Really?'

He looked from one to the other.

'Apart from the fact you share the same taste in clothes I can't see any physical similarity,' he said after a brief perusal.

'You're not the first to remark on that,' murmured Grace.

'That's cool,' said Gallagher.

He indicated the sofa.

'Grace, why don't you make yourself comfortable. Jeanette, come with me please.'

He walked to the open bedroom door. Jeanette hesitated. She flashed Grace a look of sheer panic.

'You coming?' Gallagher asked from the door.

Jeanette took a moment to compose herself, then walked slowly towards him across the pale blue carpet, a reluctant automaton. Gallagher followed her into the bedroom and closed the door firmly behind him.

Grace sank, almost fell into the sofa. A flurry of nerves, delayed-action shock, had overwhelmed her. The room was merely warm, but it felt hot and stifling. She undid the top button of her blouse. Her palms were clammy and she sensed perspiration breaking out on her forehead. She tore open the packet of tissues in her bag and dabbed away the sweat. She could feel her pulse racing, almost as fast as her thoughts.

What were they doing in there? Dumb question . . . But it wasn't Jeanette he'd been mentally undressing a minute ago. Why her then? She didn't know. Perhaps he was teasing them. Perhaps springing surprises turned him on. Would Jeanette be able to cope?

Grace willed herself calm. Jeanette had made lighter of it than anyone over the past few days, she had moaned constantly about how desperate she was for a good shag, pretended she wanted to be picked. *Wouldn't mind*, she had said – had kept saying, a monotonous joke – every time they had been shown Gallagher's photograph at the briefings. *I've had worse. Wouldn't mind a bit of that . . .* But her self-confidence had been blown out of the water half an hour ago in Economou's office and she'd had no time to recover herself. Would she give herself away?

A noise from the bedroom made Grace jump. A tiny noise, metallic. A bedspring creaking? Her imagination raced away. She wanted to go to the door and listen. No, what if he came out? Should she let Bob and the others know what was going on? Her fingers toyed with the keypad on the phone. But who could she say she was calling if Gallagher suddenly appeared? Anyway, what was the point in sending a message to say that he was in the bedroom with Jeanette? It was what she was there for, wasn't it? What they were both there for. Grace put back the phone.

Her turn would come soon enough.

She stood up. The fluttering in her limbs had subsided, but her mouth was dry. There was a tray with glasses and a bottle of mineral water on the coffee table. She poured herself a glass and drank it down. She noticed a laptop computer standing on a desk in the corner. She walked over. The laptop was switched off, but her eye was drawn to the printer and the pile of paper sitting next to it. On top of the pile was a sheet with the Amorous Liaisons logo. She saw one of the photographs Corliss had taken of her, sitting across a chair Christine Keeler style in her new black lingerie. Her age and measurements, some figures more accurate than others, were tabled beneath. She noticed that he had drawn a neat blue tick next to the line about her having a full clean international driving licence.

Gallagher's voice came to her through the bedroom door. It sounded very near. Jeanette's answering murmur was almost as distinct. Grace stepped away smartly from the table and plunged back on to the sofa.

The bedroom door opened and Gallagher came out, followed by Jeanette. He was now wearing a knee-length white bathrobe. She looked exactly as she had looked before going into the bedroom a few minutes ago, not in the least dishevelled, not so much as a hair out of place. She was trying to fit a large brown envelope into her small handbag.

'The taxi will be along in a few minutes,' Gallagher was

telling her. 'It's booked in my name. Wait by the reception desk.'

Gallagher opened the door to the suite. Jeanette shot Grace what she took to be a reassuring glance. She picked up her computer bag and suitcase from the spot from where she had left them. Gallagher saw her out and closed the door.

He came over to the sofa. He was carrying a black attaché case. He placed it on the coffee table and sat down, next to Grace.

'Your sister seems nervous,' he said.

He spoke the word, sister, as if it were in parenthesis. His expression signalled faint amusement, but there was an edge of suspicion in the tone.

'I've a confession to make,' Grace said quickly. 'We're not sisters.'

He didn't say anything. He merely raised an enquiring eyebrow.

'She is, as you say, a bit nervous,' Grace went on. 'She was afraid you wanted us to put on a lesbian show for you.'

He thought about it for a moment, and then he laughed. He relaxed and leant into the cushions, running his arm along the back of the sofa. His finger brushed Grace's collar.

'I prefer my women one at a time,' he said.

'You have to admit, it didn't look that way to us.'

'Yeah, I can see that. And would it have bothered you, if I had wanted the two of you together?'

Nonchalantly she brushed a stray lock of hair back from her face.

'Worse things happen at sea,' she said.

He angled his head away, as if to take a long-distance view of her. He gave a nod, suggesting he was satisfied with what he saw.

'OK. Let's discuss business.'

He reached for the black attaché case.

'Where's Jeanette gone, by the way?' asked Grace casually.

'To see a friend of mine. A little welcoming present. I think he'll appreciate her.'

Oh my God, Grace thought, and momentarily closed her eyes. *He's sent her to Martinez, and I've got the phone . . .*

Gallagher snapped open the case's twin locks and lifted the lid.

'You know the deal?' he asked.

'Of course,' she said. Feigning confidence suddenly didn't seem so hard.

He handed her a bulging brown envelope. She glanced inside. It was full of money. He didn't say anything, but he continued to stare at her. Maybe she was expected to count it. She lifted back the flap of the envelope. There were five slim bundles of fifty-pound notes inside, all the same size. She took one bundle out and flicked through it. Twenty notes, one thousand pounds.

'That's very generous,' she said.

'I am very generous to deserving causes,' he said. 'Besides, it's what you're worth.'

He stroked her neck again. With his other hand he touched her knee.

'I like only the best, Grace. Of everything.'

His index finger traced a small circle on the inside of her thigh.

'I want you to stay with me till Wednesday. Already I'm wishing it could be longer, but I've got to get back to the States. We'll be travelling to France tomorrow. OK with you?'

Her mouth had gone very dry. The tips of his fingers were travelling up her leg.

'I'll need your passport details. And your driving licence details. I booked a hire car for tonight. I'd like you to be my chauffeur, I'm not so relaxed about driving on the left. I'll want you to do some driving in France too. That OK?'

'Stan told me your requirements.'

'Uh huh. Well, he's pretty good at supplying my requirements.'

His hand was under her skirt, an inch above the hem.

'Pretty damned good.'

He was leaning in to her. She could see the concentrated look in his dark eyes, the purposeful set of his mouth and jaw. She knew he wanted to kiss her. What had Natalie said? Would she be happy to take his money again? The answer flashed into her head.

Wouldn't mind.

The thought ran through her like a shock. Her body stiffened, but if he noticed he didn't say anything. He had already pulled his hand away. His watch was making a bleeping sound.

'Damn, it's four o'clock already,' he said, turning off the alarm on his watch. 'You'll have to excuse me, I've got to make some calls. We've a busy night ahead, Grace, and I'm feeling tired. Still carrying some jetlag from last week, I think. I'm going to get my head down for a couple of hours. You be OK on your own for a while?'

She nodded, surprised. He reached into the attaché case and pulled out a wallet.

'Maybe you'd like to go shopping for a new dress. Don't get me wrong, you look great, but your friend'll be there tonight and you might be more comfortable in a different outfit. Take a cab, go into town. Be back by six-thirty, OK?'

He casually produced another bundle of fifty-pound notes and handed them over, like so many sweets.

'If you get back early charge anything you like downstairs to me. But don't drink too much, remember you're driving.'

'Where are we going?'

'I'll tell you tonight. You know your way round London?'

'Some of the time.'

'Well then, now's your chance to practise. You got a cell-phone? Give me the number in case I need to contact you.'

He walked over to the laptop and turned it on. He had to wait a minute while it booted up. She gave him the mobile number Corliss had made them all memorize and he typed it in directly. He put a hand up suddenly to his face to mask a yawn.

'Sorry about this,' he said, coming back to the sofa, and offering her a hand. 'Guess I should try a more regular lifestyle.'

They walked together to the door, his hand still holding hers. He indicated her suitcase.

'Leave that.'

'Of course. Where will I be sleeping?'

'With me.'

He pulled her towards him. He was standing very close, his hands resting lightly on her hips. She looked up into his eyes and saw a flicker of indecision. For a moment she was certain he was going to change his mind and order her to come next door with him. The moment passed. He gave a wistful smile. He brushed her hair with his lips. He murmured:

'I'm looking forward to it.'

6

The car was a two-door red Mercedes convertible. The afternoon clouds had long since blown by and the evening was dry and warm, so they wound down the roof and raced into London with the tangerine-red setting sun behind them, the wind in their hair and old pop songs blaring out on the radio. Between Slough and Brentford they had their own private karaoke session, belting out accompaniments to the Bee Gees, Elton John and Abba. He feigned shock that she knew the words to 'Dancing Queen', but she was at least as horrified by his high-pitch rendition of 'Staying Alive'. Grace begged him to keep it down as she dutifully braked back within the speed limit on the Westway, out of deference to the police car cruising ahead.

'You'll get us arrested,' she told him. 'Disturbing the peace.'

'Would they let us share the same cell?' he wanted to know.

The police car turned off at Chiswick and Grace stepped on the accelerator. She hadn't driven a car this powerful since her police training, and she'd never sat behind the wheel of anything half as smooth. She ignored the speed limits and the camera warnings and shot through Hammersmith.

'You always drive this fast?' he asked.

'Only when I can.'

Which wasn't for much longer. The traffic thickened and a tailback appeared from nowhere in the Cromwell Road. By the time they reached Kensington they were crawling. It was hardly necessary for him to tell her to slow down as they approached their destination, a tall white Georgian building with an imposing set of broad front steps flanked by Corinthian pillars. Grace pulled into the next side street and parked. She had driven barefoot. By the time she had strapped on her new Jimmy Choo's Gallagher had come round and opened the door for her. She kept him waiting while she checked her wind-blown hair in the driver's mirror.

'Best-looking chauffeuse in town,' he said approvingly.

She paused on the pavement to smooth down her new Karen Millen dress, a figure-hugging confection in cream silk. The dress, the matching handbag and the shoes had exhausted all of the money he had given her earlier, and a little more. His intention, she had decided, was not that she should go shopping in Marks & Spencer.

'Looking pretty good yourself,' she said.

He gave a mock bow. He was wearing a dark green Armani suit, a white silk shirt and shiny black brogues. He didn't hang around much in Marks's either.

He offered her his arm.

'These aren't my usual work clothes,' he said. 'Tonight's exceptional. Usually I dress down, it never pays to attract too much attention to yourself. You want to try and look like those guys.'

Up ahead a taxi was disgorging a full complement of passengers between the Corinthian pillars. The men were in baggy trousers and sleeveless shirts, the women in floral-print dresses. One of the men was wearing a baseball cap.

'You mean, like tourists?' said Grace.

'Like losers,' he said. 'London isn't Vegas, but casino staff everywhere are trained to sniff out winners. You dress like a high roller, you better be ready to lose like one. But this part of the evening's for fun, OK?'

'Sounds fine by me.'

They climbed the steps. A doorman in a double-breasted long coat doffed his top hat to them. A sign over the entrance welcomed them to the Blenheim Casino.

The losers from the taxi were signing in at the desk. They were in boisterous spirits, fuelled by drink. Gallagher stood patiently in the queue behind them. When his turn came he flashed a membership card. Grace was given a card to fill in.

'One of the quaint features of the British system,' Gallagher murmured. 'Like Beefeaters and warm beer. In the States they let in any bum off the street, as long as he's got sucker written all over his face.'

She filled in her name, Grace Collins, in block capitals. Her address she gave as the mews house. She paused over the line headed Occupation. She wrote down Model.

It didn't seem an outrageous fiction, she acknowledged to herself as she walked on Gallagher's arm along the mirror-lined corridor to the gaming room. The dress was the final element in a transformation so complete that she scarcely recognized the svelte elegant creature she saw reflected back at her. The careful grooming, the expensive clothes, scent, jewellery, had fuelled her confidence and given her poise. Beauty wasn't in the eye of the beholder; it was in the hands of the makeover artist. She had never in her life felt anywhere near this good about her own appearance.

She supposed if she were honest she had always thought she probably qualified as – in Dent's barbed phrase – an attractive young woman, but she'd never considered herself anything special. She knew she had nice eyes, a better than average figure, good legs. She wasn't afflicted with false modesty, but she wasn't especially vain either. She was too aware of her own faults. Her face was too round; if she didn't keep her head up it looked as though she had a double chin. Her hair was too dry, her skin too oily. Yes, her legs were her best feature, but there was always too much fat around the tops of her thighs for comfort. It didn't help that her diet was hopeless, the quasi-official regime of salads and fruit constantly compromised by junk food and iron-ration chocolate wolfed down at irregular and inhospitable hours. When things got too out of control she starved herself, dreaming of Ally McBeal. She didn't take care of herself properly in any way really, so why should she have made an exception about the way she looked? She tried to remember what had she had been wearing this time a week ago, last Saturday night. Her russet, wrap-around dress, £29.99 in a sale; her linen jacket, a nice cut but getting slightly frayed now in both sleeves; no tights; her comfortable sandals. Fair enough for a Guildford wine bar, and just sufficiently appealing should the man her friend Nikki was bringing along for her to meet turn out to be adequate (he didn't), but not enough to seriously turn heads in a place where any number of attractive young women had taken the opportunity to flaunt their charms as brazenly as possible. She had never been brazen, and nor was she now, but she was turning heads.

A man glanced up from the nearest roulette table as she came in. He whispered in the ear of his friend who looked up too and drank her in. It was odd, but she didn't feel self-conscious. Nor did she feel irritated, as she had had cause to feel so often walking past building sites. Somehow it was appropriate; no less than her due. At the next table a lanky young man with unfashionably long hair was frankly gawping at her through his black-rimmed spectacles. The woman beside him had clocked it and wasn't happy. She sailed serenely past them, a majestic liner disdaining to notice a field of icebergs.

The roulette tables, all full, were nearest the door. Next came the first half-dozen blackjack tables and a couple of poker games, also well attended. Numbers thinned out as they advanced through the room. They stopped by a table in the corner where only two of the places were occupied. Gallagher pulled out a chair. He indicated for Grace to sit down next to him.

'I'm going to powder my nose,' she said, a phrase she didn't remember ever using before, suitable for an experience she had never had.

'Sure. You want a drink?'

She asked for a mineral water. She promised not to be long.

She hugged the wall on her way to the cloakrooms, fascinated by the spectacle on view. There were between thirty and forty tables, a croupier or dealer at each one, other important-looking figures in the Blenheim's plum livery presiding over each cluster of gamblers. There were at least two hundred people crammed into the long rectangular room, their forms multiplied kaleidoscopically in the mirrors on the ceiling and the glinting glass of the chandeliers. The speed of the dealing and betting was astonishing to her untutored eye. Towers of plastic chips swept across the green baize tabletops in an endless procession of loss and, occasionally, gain. Some at the roulette tables whooped and hollered as certain numbers came up, but for the most part conversation rose little above a low hum. An air of concentration, like that in an exam room, hung over the tables. She wondered how much money would have changed hands by the time she got back. She decided that the five thousand pounds sitting in her handbag, more cash than she had ever seen in her life, would probably last a matter of minutes.

The washrooms were as sumptuous as the other interiors, all marble and glass and gilt. A Filipina maid in a plum apron was on hand to pass out individual fluffy towels to each lady as she finished. There was a small queue for the cubicles. Grace had time to examine the weight of jewellery on the neck, wrists and ear lobes of the woman in front of her, and to feel naked.

Once inside the cubicle she pulled down the lid of the toilet seat, sat down and took a moment to compose herself. She had got through the last few hours on such an adrenaline high it felt as if she'd been on some monumental bender. Whatever happened, she mustn't lose sight of her purpose in being there. She took the bulky mobile phone out of her bag.

The message she typed was brief. She gave the name and address of the casino, the colour and registration of the car and the name of the side street where it was parked. At the end she added the word VOID, one of the codes Corliss had made them all learn. It meant that she and Gallagher were still alone. She sent the message and waited. In less than a minute the acknowledgement flashed across the LCD: RING UNCLE BOB.

It was the second time she'd seen those words today. The first time had been back in the hotel, when she had warned them that Jeanette might be meeting Martinez. That was all she'd been able to do. If they wanted to keep tabs on Jeanette it would have to be the old-fashioned way.

She put the phone back into the bottom of her bag, amongst the packets of unopened condoms. An image flashed unbidden through her brain, of Gallagher disappearing with Jeanette through the door to the bedroom. She had been so certain that Gallagher would want her first she had felt almost put out. If she didn't know better she might almost have been willing to admit to a pang of jealousy.

She snapped shut her handbag and unlocked the cubicle door. The jewel-encrusted women had all gone, there was only the maid, hovering with her pile of towels. Grace accepted one with a smile when she had finished at the sink. She puckered her mouth at the mirror and touched up her lipstick.

I'm looking forward to it.

They might be staying over, he had told her, so he had packed her suitcase along with his in the boot of the car. Staying over where, he didn't say, and like a good call girl she was too discreet to ask. He was completely at his ease with her, he must have done this so many times before. Gambling and sex on tap, his perfect night. Only there wasn't going to be any sex. The second the poker game started she'd be on the mobile again and breaking up the party. When Dent and his coppers arrived they would take her into custody too, to make it look right, and afterwards she would quietly disappear. The raid was supposed to look like a drugs bust. Dent hadn't gone into details, but Grace had got the impression that they were prepared to plant something on Martinez to justify themselves. For a humble civil servant Dent certainly knew his way around the shady side of the block. Gallagher and any innocent parties would be held overnight, then released without charge. If Gallagher rang the agency again Economou would tell him that she had been so shaken by the night's events that she had disappeared without leaving a forwarding address. That was the plan anyway. Supposing something went wrong?

Then she didn't imagine she'd be getting a lot of sleep tonight, either way.

She dropped her fluffy towel into the bin provided and marched back into the gaming room. She watched Gallagher in profile as she approached the table, his manner relaxed, but his eyes fixed in concentration on the cards in front of him. He didn't look up as she slipped quietly into the stool next to him. He emitted a low groan as the dealer turned over an ace and raked in his chips.

'Not been doing so well without you, Grace,' he said. 'But it's a new deal, so maybe that's all about to change. You'd better stay and be my lucky mascot.'

He patted her hand, then reached into his inside pocket for his wallet. He peeled off a dozen fifties from the wad of notes.

'Hope this all goes towards your Christmas bonus, Charlie,' he said to the dealer.

The dealer, whose name was spelt out on a tag pinned to his chest, snaffled up the money expertly, slipped it into a clip and made it disappear into what must have been a hidden cash box under the table as if by sleight of hand. He pushed over a pile of rectangular chips. Then he began to shuffle the cards. There were so many he had to do it in relays.

'Four decks,' Gallagher explained to Grace. 'To keep them bad-ass professional gamblers away.'

Charlie presented a plastic cutting card to Gallagher. He handed it to Grace.

'My good-luck mascot will cut for me. Anywhere you like, honey. Split it wide open for us.'

He mimed what she had to do. She slipped the plastic into the pack and Charlie cut where she indicated. Gallagher banged the flat of his palm on the table.

'Deal 'em, Charlie.'

The cards flew out of the shoe. Gallagher bet and lost, doubled his bet and lost again. Again he doubled and this time he won. The cards came without pause, Charlie flicking them over at speed and with unerring accuracy, barely giving the players time to register the pips. Gallagher's manner never altered. Leaning forward in his stool, left elbow on the table, chin propped up on one hand while with the other he pushed out and collected chips in varying quantities, he kept up a more or less fluent stream of conversation, an upbeat bar-room banter that was unaffected by the swings of profit and loss. Grace reacted though, even if he didn't. She couldn't keep up with the speed of the play, but she could keep a rough track of his winnings. Gallagher meanwhile was egging on the other players and teasing Charlie and flirting with Grace all at the same time, never once taking his eye off the game. He played unhesitatingly, making his decisions to stand or hit or split without missing a beat. He played the whole shoe and then another. Midway through the third he suddenly announced that he was through. He exchanged his playing chips for cash chips and began transferring them to his pockets.

'Why are you stopping now?' Grace asked. 'You're on a winning streak.'

She reckoned that he had won about a thousand pounds.

'The first rule is like they say in the movies, always quit while you're ahead. And the second rule is, always obey rule number one. Come on, let's get you a real drink.'

He took her out of the room the way they had come in and into a long spacious bar. He ordered a bottle of champagne and an orange juice. They were shown to a quiet corner where all of the tables had reserved stickers.

He handed her a glass of champagne and kept the orange juice for himself. He hadn't actually asked her what she wanted but she wasn't about to object. The champagne was delicious.

'What about you then?' she asked. 'Don't you want anything stronger?'

He shook his head.

'The margins are close enough already. I'll catch up later.'

'Keeping a clear head so you can count the cards?'

He put on an innocent expression.

'Me? I never could do math.'

'Oh, really?'

'Yes, really.'

He laughed.

'I thought you didn't know anything about blackjack, Grace?'

'I don't. But I saw it in a film once.'

'Yeah? Well, I saw a lot of things in pictures that don't mean too much.'

'Are you saying you're lucky?'

'Luck is for losers.'

'But you're not wearing your baseball cap.'

'Damn. I knew I'd forgotten something.'

They both laughed.

'I was pretty impressed,' she said.

'I don't always win,' he said.

'I'm talking about your style. You didn't look like you were paying any attention at all.'

'Sometimes it's a bad idea to look like you're interested.'

'And not only at cards?'

He leant towards her over the table and rested his chin on his hands. He stared at her intently.

'Anything the matter?' she asked, suddenly feeling uncomfortable under his gaze.

'Nope. Just trying to figure you out.'

'How do you mean?'

'Something about you. Something different.'

'Oh. Is that a good thing or a bad thing?'

'Oh, it's good. All good. But you're different.'

'From what?'

'From the usual. You've got a quality of – what shall I call it? Freshness. Yeah, that describes it close enough. Though it's not all. Your friend now – your sister – she's fresh too, but in a kind of innocent way. She comes across as naive. The exact opposite of you. I look at you, I see sophistication, a lot of experience. But at the same time it's like you've never been with a guy like me in your life.'

He re-laid his chin on one palm, and with the other reached for her hand, his eyes on her the whole time.

'But I guess you have,' he added softly, stroking her wrist.

'I've been around,' she answered, her voice at the same level.

'Yeah, I'm sure. But as I say, you're unusual. No guy ever say that to you before?'

'They say all sorts.'

'I bet they do. You been doing this long?'

'Long enough.'

'Closed subject, huh?'

'I'd say I'm pretty open about myself. You're quite unusual too.'

'How's that?'

'Well, for one thing you don't look as though paying for it is the only way you're going to get laid.'

'You trying to flatter me?'

'No. Don't get me wrong, I'm delighted to take your money. But half the women in this bar would leave with you if you bought them a drink. That's quite a lot cheaper than phoning Stan.'

'Cheap doesn't interest me. Besides, I couldn't take the risk.'

'What risk?'

'You said half the women in the bar would walk out with me. What if you were in the other half?'

She shrugged. She took a sip of her drink. He said:

'So?'

'So what?'

'Which category do you come into?'

'That's for you to find out, not for me to say.'

'You don't give much away, do you?'

'I don't give anything away. I'm strictly a businesswoman. But don't worry. Your credit is good.'

He contemplated her in silence. Then he nodded to himself.

'I made a mistake,' he said.

'A mistake?'

'Yeah. I shouldn't have let you go this afternoon. I should have taken you straight to bed.'

Gallagher lifted his arm casually and snapped his fingers. A waiter appeared at his shoulder.

'Two more champagne glasses, please,' he said, not taking his eyes off Grace. He climbed slowly to his feet. 'We got company.'

Grace swivelled round in her chair. Jeanette, in her smart blue suit, was coming towards them. She looked pale and strained. Beside her was a bull-necked, stocky man with tight curly hair and a thick black moustache. The man broke into a broad grin when he saw Gallagher. The two of them embraced, slapping each other heartily across the back like locker-room jocks.

Grace had recognized the man at once. It wasn't Martinez. It was Orhan, the Turk.

Gallagher whispered into his ear. Orhan looked at his watch. Grace caught a few words. They seemed to be speaking Italian.

'Grace, say hello to my good friend Ralf.'

'Nice to meet you,' said Grace.

Orhan didn't reply. He gave her a quick, dismissive glance, then turned back to Gallagher. Another discussion ensued.

'OK, ladies,' said Gallagher when they had finished talking. 'Why don't you relax here a while? Ralf wants to concentrate on losing some money. Excuse us, will you?'

The two men went next door to the gaming room. Jeanette collapsed into the chair Gallagher had vacated. She reached into her handbag for her cigarettes.

'It's all right,' she said in response to Grace's warning look. 'He smokes all the time. They all do.'

'All?'

'Yeah, there's a bunch of them, six or seven. All Turks, I think. It wasn't a hotel I was sent to, it was this mansion block in Gloucester Road. Big top-floor flat, and when I got there these guys were all lounging around, smoking and drinking and arguing. They all stopped dead when I came in, all started staring at me, it was really scary. I recognized Orhan from the photos Corliss showed us. I gave him this letter Gallagher had given me. Whatever it said it made Orhan laugh, and then he read it out and they all started laughing, and pointing at me and . . .'

She closed her eyes and took a deep drag of her cigarette.

'And then some of them started poking and prodding me, you know, touching me up, but worse than that, like there was something really nasty about it. I really thought I was going to get gang-banged, but then Orhan got cross and shouted at them and they all went next door. So he calls me over, and he makes me sit on his knee, and then he starts touching me up, and I'm like, going along with it, and trying to act the part, pretending I'm enjoying it while all I can think is how much his breath stinks and how greasy his hair is. And then he, he like tries to kiss me, and I remember what Natalie said, and I push away and I'm trying to tell him, no, sorry, I don't do kissing, and then he . . . Then he slaps me really hard across the face.'

She patted her cheek with her palm to emphasize the point. It made her wince.

'Really hard. Like he was angry, like a punch. He's a pig of a guy, it almost knocked me out. I fell on the floor and then he stood up and grabbed my hair and started shaking me and shouting and calling me names. Bitch, he called me. "You fucking bitch, you do what I tell you. Do what I tell you, you fucking whore. You cunt."'

She jabbed out her cigarette in the ashtray. Her voice was thin and strained.

'That's what he called me. He treated me like a piece of shit.'

The waiter appeared with two clean glasses. Grace waited impatiently for him to finish pouring and go. Jeanette drained her champagne like lager. Grace took her hand.

'Look, it's not worth getting beaten up for, that's not the deal. I'll send Dent the abort message and then we quietly disappear.'

'Are you mad?' Jeanette hissed back. 'They'll kill us. Dent and all of them, this is their chance to get their rocks off and become big-time heroes. We jack it in now our lives won't be worth living.'

'I'm not –'

'It's cool, Grace. Really. It's cool. Look, nothing happened. He didn't even screw me; all he did was knock me around a bit, and then the phone rang, and he jabbered away in Turkish and then he and the other guys all left. He told me to stay in the flat and that's where I've been till about twenty minutes ago, when he picked me up in a taxi. I could have been a lot worse off, I'll tell you. There were a couple of other girls in the flat, they came out of one of the bedrooms after the men had gone. Really young girls. They didn't speak a word of English, but it was obvious they were scared out of their wits. One of them showed me these scars on her legs and bottom. She'd been whipped, it was really savage. At least Orhan didn't treat me like that. Look, he gave me these.'

She turned her head to the side to show off a gold earring.

'He wasn't nice about it, he just shoved the box into my hand. Like he was feeling guilty or something. But he wasn't nasty any more. He told me I was going to see some big-time gambling tonight, the kind of dough that would make my eyes pop out. That's how he said it, "the kind of dough, baby," like he was acting the tough guy and thought he was Robert De Niro or something. Christ, these gangsters are jerks. If they didn't have the movies to show them I bet they wouldn't know what the fuck to do.'

'Gallagher's coming back.'

'Yeah, OK. Look, the point is, the hard bit's over, we've got to stick with them till they start this bloody poker game and then we're out of there. It's better now you're around, I feel safe, so chin-chin.'

'Chin-chin.'

They clinked their glasses and drank. Gallagher came and laid a hand on Grace's shoulder.

'We'll be heading off in a moment, ladies,' he explained. 'We've got an urgent appointment. Grace, could you bring the car round to the front? I'm going to encourage Ralf to finish emptying his wallet.'

'Sure,' said Grace. 'Where are we going?'

'I'll give you directions. See you in a few minutes.'

'He doesn't give much away, does he?' Jeanette murmured as Gallagher went out. Grace gave her wrist a gentle squeeze.

'Nor do we, baby.'

Grace left the club and hurried round the corner to the Mercedes. She dashed out a quick short message on the keyboard: LEAVING BLENHEIM CLUB. WITH JEANETTE/ ORHAN. DESTINATION UNKNOWN.

It was the best she could do. She presumed that she was under surveillance. If she wasn't, she would want to know what the hell they thought they were playing at.

She started the engine and nosed the car round to the front of the club. There was no sign of the others. Idly she scanned the faces of the people leaving and entering. One of them stared back. She recognized the lanky man in glasses who had been gawping at her inside. He was coming down the steps, slowly, apparently unable to take his eyes off her, the same disgruntled girlfriend clinging to his arm. A blast of cold wind ruffled Grace's hair. She shivered. It was getting too late for open-air driving. She reached for the button to close the roof.

'Excuse me,' said a voice next to her ear.

She jumped. The lanky man was standing right by the car, his eyes still boring through her, a gormless, open-mouthed expression dominating the rest of his face. 'Excuse me, but I think I know you.'

It was Grace's turn to look gormless. She managed a nervous laugh.

'I don't think so.'

'Oh but I do, I do,' he repeated excitedly. 'It's Grace, isn't it? Grace Cornish.'

'I'm sorry . . .'

She gaped at him, entirely at a loss for words. It was not a condition which afflicted him.

'I knew it, I knew it, didn't I tell you, love?' he was burbling away to his studiously thin-lipped companion. 'Minute you walked through the door I said, I know that woman, I swear I know her, even though you're looking a damn sight sprucer than you ever did in your Lincoln days, lass, by heck you are.'

He threw back his head and laughed heartily, and something about that sound, or perhaps the tone of the once-familiar accent jolted her. The dimmest of dim memories began tugging at her brain. A café in the tourist season. A waiting job the summer after she left university. And a lanky charmless boy who kept pestering her to go for a drink, a boy called . . .

'Barry Statham. Remember me now, Grace?'

By heck she did, and he could see it in her eyes. He would have seen something else too, if he hadn't turned his attention at that moment back to his girlfriend – pure panic. Behind him the frock-coated doorman was doffing his cap to Gallagher and Orhan. They were walking down the steps, Jeanette trailing behind.

'Nice to run into you, Barry,' she said quickly. 'Sorry, I've got to go now.'

'Grace was thinking of going into the police like her dad,' said Barry Statham to his disinterested partner, in a voice that would have pierced lead. 'Doesn't look much like a copper to me, eh, love? So what you up to these days then? You a policewoman?'

'No.'

Grace pressed the roof and window buttons at the same time.

'I'm a prostitute. Goodnight.'

The hood swung up with a low mechanical whirr. The scrappy white face of Barry Statham gleamed at her softly through the window, fixed in a toothy Cheshire Cat's grin. The expression on the face of his silent companion was no less remarkable.

The passenger door snapped open and Gallagher thrust in his head.

'Those people hassling you?' he demanded, an edge of menace in his voice, as if to imply that hassle of any sort would receive short physical shrift.

'No, he was asking me nerdy questions about the car,' Grace replied smoothly.

Gallagher nodded, satisfied. He pushed forward the passenger seat.

'Jeanette, you'd better get in first, go behind Grace. You sit behind me, Ralf.'

Jeanette got in and slithered along the back seat. Orhan stuck his head in after her. He curled his lip at Grace.

'You let the hooker drive? Man, you're crazy.'

'Get in, Ralf,' said Gallagher impatiently.

The Turk muttered something under his breath and climbed in laboriously.

'Shit, man, you think I'm some kind of midget or what?' he complained.

Gallagher jumped into the front seat and pressed the lever to shift it forwards.

'Should have enough leg room now,' he said. 'Holland Park roundabout, Grace, then up on to the M40.'

'West or East?' she asked.

'West.'

She depressed the clutch and put the car into gear. Her foot brushed the accelerator.

'Put your seat belt on, Jeanette,' she said quietly.

Gallagher, she had noticed, had already put on his belt. She watched Jeanette follow suit in the rear mirror. She was also watching Orhan. He was shifting his weight around ostentatiously in the narrow bucket seat, trying to find a comfortable position. She waited until he was leaning forward, and then she jammed her foot to the floor.

The Mercedes shot out from a standing start like a bullet. Orhan yelped as his head was whipped back. Grace stood on the brakes and he was flung forward, like a rag doll. He swore loudly in Turkish.

'You ought to strap yourself in, Mr Orhan,' she said as she spun the car on the tightest of curves into Kensington High Street. 'With a hooker like me at the wheel anything could happen.'

Out of the corner of her eye she saw Gallagher's faint smile. She relaxed the pressure on the pedal.

'We going far?' she asked.

'Turn off the motorway at the second junction,' he said. 'It's a private house, a place called Burnham Beeches. You know it?'

'I've heard the name.'

'I'll direct you. Hey, quit that will you, Ralf? Feels like I got a baby elephant trying to kick me in the back.'

Orhan's squirming gradually abated. Gallagher turned on the radio and fiddled till he found music to his taste.

The traffic going out of London was a great deal lighter

than it had been going in. Once they got beyond Hangar Lane Grace was able to keep her foot down and cruise along effortlessly at a steady ninety. She had decided that this was a car she could become attached to, and she felt a pang of regret when she saw signs for Junction 2. She pulled into the slow lane. The evening light had faded appreciably since leaving London and she switched on the headlamps. Orhan leant forward and tapped Gallagher on the shoulder as they hit the exit ramp. He spoke in Italian. Gallagher twisted round in his seat and looked out of the back window.

'Slow down,' he told Grace.

She put her foot to the brake.

'Anything the matter?'

'He thinks we're being followed.'

Grace glanced into her mirror. All she could see was a diminishing trail of headlamps, but she was sure that Orhan was right. It was pretty smart of him, she had to admit. She hadn't noticed him looking out of the back during the journey.

'First left at the roundabout, then get into the right-hand lane,' said Gallagher.

She came off the roundabout and stayed in second gear as she pulled to the right.

'First turning, keep it slow,' Gallagher instructed.

She kept the speedometer down to twenty. The road behind was empty of traffic. She put her indicators on as she came up to the turning.

A pair of headlamps appeared in her mirror, coming off the roundabout.

'That him?' said Gallagher.

'Blue car, yeah.'

Grace turned into a narrow country lane, still idling in second. It was very dark between the high flanking hedges and trees. She put the headlamps on full beam.

'Do I carry on down here?' she asked.

'Yeah,' answered Gallagher. 'For a couple of miles. Road winds all over but just keep going. When you see a pub on the left you take the next turning on the right.'

Orhan said something in Italian.

'Yeah, I know,' murmured back Gallagher in English. 'Still with us.'

'Want me to lose him?' said Grace.

'You think you can?'

'Let's see.'

The road wound sharply to the right. Grace accelerated into the curve, went up into third and then straight back down to second as the road dipped sharply into a tight left-hand bend. The back wheels skidded and squealed but she was in full control. She raced smoothly through the gears as the road straightened and flattened and braked at the last moment before it wound up to the right. Up the hill in second and third, foot to the floor like a rally driver, and then one sharp turn as the reflection of another car's head-lamps appeared momentarily up ahead flashing across the hedge. She straightened out at the top of the hill and saw the other car coming towards her. The road had narrowed to single lane, there was a sign and a traffic island ahead. The big red arrow indicated that it was her right of way, but the other car was much nearer and wasn't slowing down. She didn't hesitate. Into second, foot hard down and the red Mercedes shot through the gap straight as an arrow. The other car braked suddenly and Grace aimed into the narrow space between it and the hedge. The car shuddered as its wheels skipped the road and shot over dirt and grass. The thin angry wail of the other car's horn disappeared as rapidly as its tail-lights in the rear mirror.

Orhan swore in Turkish. Gallagher laughed.

Another tight turn to the right and the rear of the car clipped foliage. The road was straightening out again, but it was rising and dipping sharply. All four wheels seemed to leave the ground as the car heaved up over the crests. Grace slipped into fourth for the first time since coming off the motorway.

Lights appeared up ahead. A car flashed at her and Grace dipped her lamps. The car shot past her as she slowed. She saw another car, in profile, waiting for her to pass before turning into the road. It was coming out of the pub car park.

She slammed on the brakes and cut in front of the other car without indicating. Her headlamps captured the startled white face of the driver for an instant and then he was gone. Grace crawled between the rows of parked cars. The pub was popular, the car park was almost full. She saw a space between a van and a Jaguar and swung into it. She turned off the engine and the lights.

It wasn't quite fully dark, but it was dark enough. Very little light came from the pub and even the vehicles at the other end of the car park had become colourless shadowy lumps. They would be quite invisible from the road.

'Nice work,' said Gallagher approvingly.

'I was that thirsty,' said Grace.

She was breathing fast, the blood was pounding through her head. A drink was the last thing she needed. She had quite enough natural stimulants coursing through her already.

The noise of a car engine sounded in the distance. It was coming closer, moving fast. All eyes turned to the road. A vehicle flashed past. It was going flat out, in the direction they had been headed.

'Was it blue?' asked Gallagher.

Orhan thought so, but no one knew for sure.

'How much further to our turn-off?' Grace asked.

'A few hundred yards,' said Gallagher.

'Then I suggest we get going before he realizes he's been done.'

114

She turned on the engine again and headed back to the road. Nothing was coming in either direction. She rounded a bend and saw the turn-off immediately. If the car that had flashed past hadn't turned around by now then it would be too late.

'There's another turning coming up on the left,' Gallagher warned. 'Careful, it's easy to miss it.'

She slowed and took the sharp corner comfortably when it came. She could see the lights of houses through the trees. They were few and far between.

'There's a driveway coming up on your right, black cast-iron gates. Pull into it.'

The car lights shone on the glossy black paint of the gates. Grace stopped in front of them. A camera attached to a pillar swivelled and pointed at them. Gallagher lowered the electric window and leant across Grace to speak into an intercom.

'Hey, Misha, *skolka lyet, skolka ziem.*'

Grace had to think twice before she realized she'd understood him. Not bad, she thought, as the gates swung open. Not only a smattering of Turkish and Italian, but Russian too, and pretty good if his accent was anything to go by. He seemed to have no end of aces up his sleeve.

Grace drove down a long straight tree-lined drive. A big, solid thirties house loomed out of the grey-black evening. The upper levels were in darkness but the lights were on downstairs. There was a circular area of gravel in front of the porch, surrounding a big ornamental pond, where half a dozen cars were parked. As Grace brought the Mercedes to a halt between a Porsche and a 4x4 Suzuki the front door opened and a burly figure in jeans and a black leather jacket stepped out. He had a muzzled Doberman on a leash.

'Mikhail Rostov, Misha to his friends,' Gallagher said to Orhan. 'Dmitri's brother and chief security guy. Let's go in and meet him. Grace, stay with the car a minute, will you?'

Gallagher, Orhan and Jeanette all got out of the car. Gallagher and Rostov engaged in a brief exchange of back-slapping and handshaking and then the four of them went inside. A couple of minutes passed, then the front door opened and Gallagher came out alone. He got into the car.

'I'm probably being over-cautious but there's a chance we could be seen from the road. Misha says if we park up round the tennis court we'll be guaranteed invisible.'

The drive extended down one side of the house for another hundred yards. The red clay tennis court was right at the end, with a chalet-style pavilion attached. Grace parked beside it and turned off the engine. The night became suddenly very quiet and still. She waited for Gallagher to say something. He seemed to be thinking.

'Where did you learn to drive like that?' he said eventually.

It was one of the questions she'd been rehearsing with herself over the last couple of minutes. She answered without pausing.

'Brands Hatch and Silverstone.'

'The motor-racing circuits?'

'A lot goes on there besides. I've always liked fast cars, I do courses there. Formula Ford and standard. The advanced courses are taught by ex-police instructors. You want to see my handbrake turn?'

It was almost true. She had driven a Formula Ford and she'd certainly been taught by coppers. Only they hadn't been ex when they had examined her.

'Who do you think those people following us were?' she asked, innocently.

'Who knows? Who knows if they were even following us. Ralf's got a vivid imagination, but then again, a lot of people don't like him.'

'I'm not surprised.'

'You don't like him much yourself, do you?'

116

'You kidding?'

'Yeah, I understand. When they were handing out the politeness genes they missed him out.'

'It's not only that. He's violent. He hit Jeanette in the face. Back at the club I told her to walk away.'

'He's got no call to be hitting her. I'll speak to him. Something I've been wondering about. Just a little thing. But how did you know his name?'

'Sorry?'

'Outside the club. You called him Mr Orhan. I introduced him to you as Ralf. I was wondering how you knew his other name, that's all.'

'Ah. That's what Jeanette called him in the bar. He must have introduced himself and she wasn't feeling like she wanted to be on first-name terms with him by then.'

'OK.'

She was glad it was so dark. There was a bit of light left in the evening sky, but not enough to penetrate the interior of the car. Had he been able to see her face she felt certain that her nervousness would have betrayed her. Maybe he could hear it anyway, in her tight voice and shallow breathing. She willed her pulse slower and concentrated on keeping the tension out of her words.

'Would you speak to him?' she said calmly, lightly. 'Jeanette's a sweet kid, but she can't handle him. As you guessed, she's inexperienced, a bit naive.'

'Yeah. Seems like I picked the right sister. You're pretty amazing, Grace.'

'Very kind of you to say so, Mr Gallagher.'

'I think you'd better call me Mike, in the circumstances.'

'OK, Mike. What circumstances exactly?'

'Oh, you know . . .'

She sensed his head turning towards her. She heard him moving in the leather seat. And then she felt him touch her arm.

'. . . when a man meets a woman kind of circumstances.'

His fingers trailed gently up her bare arm. His other hand was behind her neck, stroking her hair. His breath was on her cheek.

'Oh, that old thing,' she said.

She felt the warmth of his fingers through the thin material of her dress. They glided lightly over her breasts, her belly, her breasts again. She could smell him now, not just his aftershave but something stronger, earthier. It was a powerful smell, though far from unpleasant. His lips touched her neck. He kissed her there, and she lifted her head to expose her throat. He kissed her there too, a butterfly kiss, and a ripple of pleasure ran through her. His hand was beneath her dress now, stroking the outside of her thigh. She felt his fingers brush the bare flesh above her stocking tops and glide between them. She heard herself give a sigh as his fingertips brushed her groin. He was kissing her cheek, moving down towards her mouth. She remembered what Natalie had said about kissing. What was the point of holding back now?

She grabbed hold of his head with both her hands and plunged her tongue between his lips. He responded fiercely, crushing her even further into the seat and forcing his mouth against her so tightly that she could hardly breathe. Her head swam with giddiness. His hands were all over her.

He broke away suddenly. They were both gasping for air, but that wasn't why he had stopped. He was holding himself very still; she felt the tension in his neck muscles.

'What's the matter?' she whispered.

'Search party's arrived,' he said. He pecked her lightly on the forehead. 'Later.'

She glanced up and saw in the driver's mirror the flicker of an approaching torch. Gallagher disengaged himself and straightened his jacket. She sat up quickly, pulling her hem back down to where it should have been, somewhere rather nearer to her knees than her hips. Gallagher lowered his window as the heavy gravelled steps drew near.

'Hey, Misha, you getting some air?'

'Thought you got lost,' replied Misha in heavily accented English. He stopped at the window and rested his hands on his knees. Grace caught a flash of his white teeth.

'Sorry, my friend,' he said amiably in Russian. 'Did I turn up at the wrong moment?'

'No problem,' answered Gallagher smoothly. 'I expect Dmitri's anxious to get down to business.'

His accent, Grace noted, was refined Muscovite. Misha sounded much coarser.

Misha helped them empty the boot. He insisted on carrying both their suitcases, and on walking ahead, by himself. It didn't matter that he had the only torch, the path was broad and they had the lights of the house to guide them.

'Who are these people?' Grace whispered in Gallagher's ear.

'No need to keep your voice down. He doesn't speak much English. They're the kind of people your poppa told you to avoid.'

'And we're spending the night here? Poppa's going to want a word with you.'

'Hey, sometimes you can't choose your friends. It's like the guy said when the judge asked him why he kept robbing banks: "Because that's where the money is, Your Honour." This is where the money is, believe me. I don't ask how they make it. And they don't ask what I'm going to do with it when I take it away.'

'That's what you're going to do, is it? Win their money from them?'

'I sure hope so. I've got an expensive lifestyle to maintain. Maybe the cars and the hotels I could give up. But I wouldn't like to give up on you.'

'Let's hope you win then. I'd hate to have to waive my fee.'

He put his arm round her. He stopped walking.

'Hey, you're cold.'

She hadn't noticed, but he slipped off his jacket and wrapped it carefully round her shoulders. He put his arm round her again.

'Come on, and let me introduce you to some real live bad-asses.'

7

The short message she typed out was convoluted and imprecise. She was able to give the name of the pub, but thereafter it was a case of approximate distances. BIG HOUSE was how she described their final destination, an inadequate enough description on all counts. BLACK IRON GATES, SECURITY CAMERA was more helpful, but there had been neither a name nor a number, and if there had been a name on the lane where the house stood she hadn't seen that either. She was able to be a little more helpful with people: HOST DMITRI ROSTOV, 50–55, 5'10", STOCKY, GREY, BALDING – BROTHER MISHA, SAME HEIGHT/BUILD, YOUNGER, BLACK HAIR, BALDING, GOATEE BEARD – SHORT LONG-HAIRED BLOND GERMAN (?) CALLED SAMMY (?) + GALLAGHER + ORHAN + FIVE STAFF MIN (MALE). At the end she typed SPADE, Corliss's codeword for no sign of anyone who might conceivably have been Martinez.

She put the phone back into her handbag and examined herself in the bathroom mirror. She was definitely in need of some refurbishment. There was a slight smear of lipstick in the corner of her mouth and barely any on her lips. She knew where it had got to: she had just spent a minute on the doorstep wiping it from Gallagher's face with a tissue. She touched up her lips and eyes. She had no need of blusher, not with that flush in her cheeks.

She stood back and gave herself a full-length check in the mirror. It was a good thing she did; the zip at the back was half undone. She refastened it, and checked carefully for further signs of dishevelment. Eventually she was satisfied that she no longer looked like a well-groped teenager.

Cool, calm, collected, she mouthed to herself in the mirror.

All the things she didn't feel at the moment. She wouldn't let herself get carried away like that again, no way. No, she'd been too pumped with adrenaline after the chase. Speed had always excited her. She'd never understood the cliché of women supposedly falling for men with fast cars. Why be a passenger when you can drive? The first driving course she'd done she had been the only woman and most of the men had patronized her, including the instructor. She'd overheard him in the bar joking with some of the lads about her choosing her car because of its colour. None of the other jokes had been any less lame. It would have been enough to make her go out and show them, only she hadn't needed any incentives. She took to it naturally, even the instructor had been forced to acknowledge it, and when they did the final test hers was the fastest time. She didn't get top marks because she'd clipped some cones on a turn, but they'd all known she was the best, and she had known that they'd known. If they had made any more jokes after that they'd at least had the decency to keep their voices down.

That was all it had been then, she'd been turned on by the thrill of the chase. She nodded to herself in the mirror, as if settling a private debate. Sure, Gallagher was charming, devastatingly good-looking, undeniably sexy. But she'd only been playing a part. And now she had another, much more important part to play.

122

She came out of the bathroom and walked back downstairs and along the long, oak-panelled hall. A big shaven-headed man in an incongruously smart blue suit was sitting slumped in a chair by the door. He eyed her insolently as she drew level. She was on the point of telling him that his flies were undone, in Russian, but remembered in time that that probably wasn't such a good idea. She carried on walking, past the door to the reception room into which she and Gallagher had first been shown a few minutes ago, and on to the dining room, which they had all been about to enter when she had discreetly chosen her moment to excuse herself.

The dining room was also filled with well-polished oak: panels, sideboards, high-backed chairs and a huge rectangular table. Dmitri Rostov was at one end of the table, facing the door, his brother at the other. Gallagher was in the middle on one side, the fair man she'd been introduced to as Sammy on his left. Facing them were Orhan, Jeanette, and a woman she hadn't seen before, a striking platinum blonde who sat on Dmitri's right. The host, the first to see Grace, waved to her as she came in.

'Sit beside me, here please,' said Dmitri in his near-fluent but thickly accented English. 'I like always to have beautiful women close. It is rule of house.'

Gallagher and Sammy laughed politely. Misha looked quizzically at his brother. He hadn't got the joke.

'*Tak polojeno,*' explained the platinum blonde in Russian.

As she spoke, in a slow, bored voice, she turned her long neck just enough to be able to take in Grace comfortably. Her big emerald eyes glided rapidly up and down Grace's face and body, giving her the kind of once-over she had experienced from countless saloon-bar Lotharios, though usually with more subtlety. Although it was a frank sexual evaluation it was probably disinterested, Grace surmised. It was the kind of look a sleek, exquisitely pampered cat – a

Siamese, naturally – might bestow on a trespassing lesser breed.

She was beautifully groomed, expensively dressed and decked out with enough gold and diamonds to furnish a window display in Hatton Garden. Every inch of her seemed to sparkle. Only the gleam in her eye struck a discordant note; more alley cat than pedigree.

Grace sat down opposite her, between Gallagher and Dmitri. Dmitri indicated the bottles laid out on the table.

'Vodka, champagne? Vodka is Russian, champagne French. Lucky for you is not other way round.'

Not any old champagne, of course, but a magnum of vintage Cristal. She consented to his giving her a glass. He had to stand in order to get a balanced grip on the great bottle and pour it properly.

'Drink. Eat. Is good.'

It was a modest enough boast. In front of her sat a plate piled so carelessly with shiny black caviar that it might have been a child's portion of baked beans. A stack of blinis was beside it. Dishes with more blinis, red caviar, sour cream, cucumber, gherkins, black bread, ham, herring and a whole side of smoked salmon filled the centre of the table. A Russian feast, of a kind which most Russians could scarcely dream about. With the best will in the world the eight people seated at the table would have been hard put to do it justice. Perhaps the addition of the ninth would have made a difference.

The ninth place setting was between Gallagher and Sammy. No one had alluded to the missing guest and Grace had no intention of being the first to broach the subject. She wondered what name Martinez would be travelling under, and in what guise. When she had first been introduced to them it had occurred to her that Sammy might be Martinez, but then he had stood up and revealed himself to be shorter than Jeanette. As Corliss had said, there were some alterations beyond the capacity of even the most dextrous plastic surgeon.

'Dmitri's hospitality is legendary,' said Gallagher, passing Grace one of the bowls of cream. 'If we don't eat it all he'll be offended.'

The other guests, as if anxious to avoid the slightest implication of offence, had already driven deep trenches into their mounds of caviar. Only the platinum blonde's plate remained untouched. Her attention was fixed on Grace, and the stare she was bestowing on her was ripe with contempt.

I know who you are, her eyes said, *and I know what you do. Only I do it a great deal better.*

'*Chudesnie sergi. Nastoyaschie?*' asked Grace innocently. *Nice earrings. Are they real?*

The words were out before she could stop herself. Not that she wouldn't have done it again had she had access to the rewind button. The look of frozen astonishment on the blonde's exquisitely chiselled face was simply too good to miss. For a moment her poise and natural hauteur seemed to desert her. She looked more like a landed fish than a cat. It was Gallagher who filled the ensuing pause.

'Where did you learn your Russian?' he asked, switching effortlessly to the language. There was no surprise in his habitually cool tone, but there was perhaps a touch of suspicion, as there had been earlier out in the car.

Grace thought quickly. Was there any harm in blurring the details of her own past and her alter ego's? Was there any choice?

'Moscow. I spent six months there during my gap year at university.'

She spoke in Russian too. It had been a long time since she had used it in conversation, though she had kept up her reading, intermittently at least.

'Speak anything else?' he asked.

'OK French. A few words of German and Italian.'

'Ah. *Vsieznaika.*'

Vsieznaika, literally know-all – there was a good Slavic rolling word she hadn't heard in a long while. Her conversational Russian wasn't exactly flooding back; but she could manage.

'You're pretty good yourself,' she said, returning his smile. 'Where did you learn?'

'Not at a university,' he answered, a remark that prompted a small guffaw from the head of the table. 'But Dmitri was my professor.'

'I taught you too well, my friend,' said the professor. 'And how do you repay me? By taking all my money. Where's the justice in that?'

'Unlucky in cards, lucky in love,' said Gallagher mildly.

'Ah, then my number has come up. Thanks for that.'

Dmitri beamed. He reached across and pinched the cheek of the platinum blonde.

'But Tatyana costs me even more than you, my friend. So where's the luck in that?'

His brother Misha laughed sardonically. He murmured something to Orhan and the Turk gave a wolfish grin. The other man, Sammy, seemed to be in on the joke too. Only Tatyana was unamused. Grace was reluctantly impressed by how quickly she had recovered her icy poise.

'What's the matter, Dmitri? Can't you afford me?'

Her voice, naturally husky, had been marinaded in tobacco and spirits. It was a voice an actress would have killed for.

And for a moment it looked as if Dmitri could have killed her too. Only a hint of irritation flashed across his face, but the big coarse hand lying flat beside his plate had closed instinctively into a fist. His smile was strained.

'You're not eating,' he said.

Tatyana pushed aside her plate of untouched food and lit a cigarette. She enclosed the filter between two beautifully

126

polished rose-pink nails, inhaled deeply and blew a cloud of thick blue smoke over the table. Gallagher waved his hand over his plate.

'You're forgetting your manners,' said Dmitri crossly.

'At least I had them to forget,' she replied.

Dmitri hit her across the face. It was so fast and so sudden that Grace wasn't even sure that she had seen it, but the sound of flesh striking flesh was sharp and clear. Dmitri's hand was open, but he didn't pull the blow. The force of it almost knocked Tatyana out of her chair. She kept her seat only by grabbing hold of Orhan's sleeve. The Turk didn't react.

The conversation round the table, not unnaturally, had ceased. Grace couldn't help but reflect that it was all rather different from the last dinner party she had attended, a fortnight before in Cobham.

Tatyana got up and walked towards the door. She looked unsteady for a moment, but that could have been on account of her towering heels. She reached for the door handle.

'I didn't say you could leave the table.'

Dmitri didn't raise his voice. He didn't have to. Tatyana hesitated, but whatever inner struggle ensued didn't take long to resolve.

'I would like to leave the table,' she said tonelessly.

'Permission granted,' he said. 'Go to your room and do something useful. Like wax your legs.'

Misha laughed. Tatyana half inclined her head towards him, not looking at his face, simply noting the source of the sound. Then she went out.

Misha and Orhan resumed their conversation, talking over and ignoring Jeanette, who sat now, as she had sat since her arrival, like a statue. They were speaking in Russian, a language in which Orhan appeared to be confident but inaccurate. On the other side of the table Gallagher and Sammy were talking quietly in English.

'So then,' said Dmitri, turning to Grace with an affable smile refixed to his face. 'Have you been back to Russia since your student days?'

Grace shook her head. He carried on speaking Russian.

'It is all changed, you probably wouldn't recognize it. Even I don't recognize it, but then I don't go back much. I spend most of my time here and in the South of France. The weather is better there, but I like the climate here. The business climate.'

'I see. And what business are you in exactly?'

Grace felt Gallagher's hand pinch her knee under the table. It was done very smoothly; he didn't miss a beat in his conversation with Sammy.

'Buying and selling,' Dmitri answered. 'Very boring, you don't want to know about that.'

Grace smiled sweetly. Playing the dumb blonde didn't come naturally, but she could still feel the warm impress of Gallagher's fingers on her knee, and she could take a hint. Besides, she'd seen what could happen to blondes who acted smart.

'What delicious champagne!' she exclaimed, even as she reminded herself that she shouldn't drink any more of it.

'That is another of my house rules,' he answered. 'Only the best of everything.'

As if to emphasize the point he lifted his wrist towards her and rolled back his sleeve to allow her unrestricted view of the diamonds encrusted round the face of his watch. There was something childlike about his ostentatiousness; an eager ingenuousness quite out of keeping with the rest of him.

'It's half past,' he announced to the table, in English, tapping the precious watch with his finger. 'Is he lost?'

'He knows the way,' said Gallagher quietly.

'He knows the telephone number also,' said Dmitri.

Gallagher shrugged.

'Maybe his flight was delayed.'

'Maybe he tried to bring extra whisky through Customs,' said Dmitri.

The others laughed. Orhan translated the witticism for Misha's benefit.

'At least we have time to stack the decks in our favour,' Misha said to his brother, in Russian.

'The decks are always stacked in our favour,' replied his brother. He gestured towards Gallagher. 'How else do we get an edge over our friend here?'

Gallagher acknowledged the compliment with a nod. He looked at his own watch.

'We could start without him,' he suggested.

'Are you so eager to take my money? Enjoy the food.'

'I was thinking of Ralf. He's not got much time. And he's not a patient man.'

'I had already guessed that.'

The Turk heard them talking about him and swung round in his seat to face the head of the table.

'Why should I be patient when I see what I want and I know how to get it?' he said, remembering as an afterthought to pull up the corners of his mouth into the approximation of a grin. 'You are the same as me, I think. I tell your brother, men in our position must not be rivals. There is too much at stake to argue about crumbs.'

To illustrate his point he indicated the huge piles of food on the table. Most of it was untouched, although the heap of caviar on his own plate had been significantly more levelled than anyone else's. Everything about him suggested unfettered appetite.

'I have another rule of house,' said Dmitri. 'I do not discuss business at table.'

He spoke tonelessly, with a matching lack of expression in the face. Orhan sat back in his chair and watched him warily. After a moment he gave a shrug, as if to accept the rebuke. Dmitri seemed satisfied. He pushed back his chair and stood up.

'But you're right. Why should we wait? Let us go next door. Ladies, excuse us, please.'

Dmitri dropped his napkin on to the table with a flourish. One by one the others stood up and did the same. Gallagher was the last to rise.

'You'll be OK?' he said to Grace.

'Sure.'

'We could be some time.'

'Go wait in front room,' said Dmitri, waving vaguely in the direction of the hall. 'Ask Yuri, he will show you. Watch TV. You want anything else, ask Yuri.'

'Thank you,' said Grace.

'Or if you want to go upstairs, ask him to take you to my room,' said Gallagher. 'Your suitcase is already there.'

'It is best room,' chipped in Dmitri. 'Tudor oak, four-poster bed, Italian marble bathroom. Also big TV. Big bed too, you will be lonely on your own, but I will not keep him late. It does not take long to give him my money.'

Dmitri led the way to an oak door that fitted so smoothly into the wall panelling that Grace hadn't even realized it was there. He stood back and let the others go in ahead of him. Grace caught a glimpse of the room as the men filtered through. An overhead light, of a kind she had only seen hanging above pool tables, illumined the central feature, a large round baize-covered table. Dmitri pointed to the table as they went in and said something to Gallagher that made him laugh. The others took their places around it in silence.

The heavy oak door closed shut, restoring to the long oak wall the impression of unbreached solidity. Grace heard the sound of a key turning in a lock.

'Jeanette?'

Although there was no one to hear she kept her voice low. It took Jeanette a few moments to react.

130

'Jeanette, are you all right?'

She seemed sluggish. She stared at Grace quizzically for a second, and then gave her a big goofy smile. She lifted her glass, as if in a toast, and knocked back most of the inch or so of liquid in the bottom with a flick of her wrist and flip of her head.

'Never felt better, love,' she said with a laugh.

Grace pushed back her chair and walked round to the other side of the table. Jeanette was looking for something in her bag. Grace discreetly picked up the glass and sniffed the residue of alcohol. It was a champagne glass, but she had been drinking vodka.

Jeanette produced her cigarettes from her bag. She lit one clumsily, taking three attempts to spark the lighter. Grace watched her slow, deliberate movements, and felt her heart sink. She had hardly paid any attention at all to Jeanette during the meal, and nor had anyone else. Left to her own devices she had simply worked her way quietly through the nearest bottle and it was half empty.

'Go easy now,' said Grace gently, trying not to sound like a reproving older sister.

'Oh, I'm not drunk,' Jeanette replied hastily. 'Don't worry about me not being able to take care of myself or anything. This is for inner fortification, you know. In case, like.'

Grace didn't need to ask in case of what. She had seen for herself the way Orhan operated. In such a case alcoholic oblivion had its attractions.

'I got a message through earlier,' Grace whispered. 'They'll have found us by now, the place is probably already surrounded. The moment he shows up I'll send the code and they'll be here in minutes.'

'Yeah, I bet.' Jeanette gave a sour laugh. 'What if he doesn't show?'

'He'll show. He's the main man, remember? The reason they're all here.'

'Yeah? So why have they started without him?'

'I don't know. I wouldn't worry about it.'

But she was worried about it, and had been all the time that they'd been at the table, the empty place setting glaring at her like a fat hole in a jigsaw puzzle. The possibility of him not showing hadn't even been mentioned at the briefings, but then nor had the possibility of Gallagher picking more than one of them. What if any number of unforeseeable – or at least unforeseen – contingencies had derailed Martinez's plans? As Gallagher had said, his plane could have been delayed. Clearly things could still go ahead in his absence, so where did that leave the fate of an operation which – or so they had been promised – would all be done and dusted within a matter of hours? If Martinez didn't show then the consequences were pretty clear.

She would be spending the night with Gallagher.

And not just one night either. If Martinez called the whole thing off was that any reason for Gallagher to send her packing? He had booked her till Wednesday, and paid in advance. Well, she would deal with that when the time came. But could Jeanette deal with Orhan, even with half a bottle of forty per cent proof to give her fortitude?

'Jeanette, listen to me, this is important. When Gallagher paid you back at the hotel, did he tell you how long you had to stay with Orhan?'

'Yeah, all night. He gave me a grand. Can you believe it?'

Jeanette laughed hoarsely.

'I was counting the money in the back of the cab. Incredible, never seen that much cash. All them crisp new fifties. I thought, this is the life, eh, even wondered about popping back to have a quiet word with our friend Stan, get the low-down on my prospects. Can't afford to be too picky about your clients, I suppose. Pity. Makes a change from fixed penalties, though.'

'Hey, keep your voice down.'

'Oh yeah, we're meant to be undercover, aren't we? Ssh! The walls have ears!'

Jeanette dropped her voice to a hoarse stage whisper. She leant her head conspiratorially towards Grace.

'I didn't tell you the worst. You know, when we were talking at the casino.'

'How do you mean?'

'When he was hitting me. That phone call came in the nick of time, you know. When he got me on the floor he wouldn't let me get up. Told me to stay there, then came and stood in front of me, pointed at his crotch and gave me a big leery grin. In case I didn't get the message he started unzipping his flies. Hang on a sec, I says, I'll get a condom. He shakes his head, grabs a handful of my hair and yanks me towards him. I try and pull away and then he flips, starts screaming all that stuff again, slapping me about. No fucking condoms, he says. Suck it, bitch. Not exactly a gentleman, eh? And that was when the phone rung. Don't think I'd get away with it twice.'

Jeanette reached for the vodka bottle. Grace instinctively pushed out a hand.

'I think –'

'I've had enough? Oh no, love, I haven't had nearly enough. Tell you what, though. He tries to put his dick in my mouth again I might bite it off. *Skol*, or whatever it is they say round here.'

Jeanette took another long slug of vodka.

'At least if we ever have that conversation again, I'll be able to tell you the answer,' she said quietly.

'What conversation?' asked Grace.

'About the worst bloke I ever shagged. Our conversation in the hotel, you remember? Before Sergeant bloody Ryan came and gave us the third degree.'

'Hey, keep it down.'

Jeanette nodded.

'Oh yeah,' she whispered, trying to look and sound sober. 'It's all right, you can rely on me.'

'I know I can,' Grace answered, with a great deal more confidence than she felt. 'I know what I could do with, and I bet you could too – a pot of strong black coffee. I'll go and find us some. Why don't you go next door, put your feet up, watch the TV? We could be here for some time.'

Grace helped Jeanette to her feet without giving her a chance to object. She wanted to get her out of the room, and away from the alcohol, as quickly as possible. She steered her towards the door.

The shaven-headed man – Yuri she presumed – was sitting in the hall exactly as before, slumped into his chair. He sat up sharply when Grace spoke to him briskly in Russian.

'We would like coffee, please. Bring it to us next door, immediately.'

Dmitri had told her to ask for anything. He hadn't advised her on what tone to adopt when asking for it, but her peremptoriness did the trick. Yuri rose to his feet with more alacrity than his bulk would have suggested was possible and scuttled off, presumably in the direction of the kitchen.

'Wait in there,' Grace said to Jeanette, indicating the half-open door through which she could see a substantial acreage of leather-upholstered sofa and a proportionate widescreen TV. 'I won't be a minute.'

Grace bounded up the antique wooden staircase as rapidly as her spiky heels would allow. She turned right at the top, as before, and marched past three closed doors before opening the familiar fourth. She locked the bathroom door shut and took the phone from her bag.

She switched it on, typed in her password and accessed the internet mail icon, exactly as Corliss had shown them. There was no acknowledgement of her earlier message. She typed out another:

VOID – POKER STARTED WITHOUT MARTINEZ – WISH TO INFORM YOU THAT TARGET MAY HAVE CHANGED PLANS – PLS ADVISE ON PROCEDURE IF NO SHOW – PLS ACKNOWLEDGE URGENTLY.

It wasn't much of a message, but sending it at least gave her the illusion of action. She put the phone away.

She came out of the bathroom and started to walk back the way she'd come. As she passed the second of the three doors she noticed that it was slightly open. She gave an involuntary jump as she saw something move in the gap.

The door swung open all the way. Grace found herself staring into a pair of limpid green eyes.

'Oh, it's you,' said Tatyana, not attempting to disguise her lack of interest. She leant against the doorframe and stared the other way. She lifted an unlit cigarette to her lips.

Grace slipped her bag over her shoulder and folded her arms.

'Who were you expecting?' she replied, in Russian. 'President Putin?'

The big green eyes slowly swivelled round and locked on her. Grace didn't blink.

'Your Russian is very good,' Tatyana said after a pause. 'But my English is better. I suggest we speak English.'

'As you wish,' said Grace.

Tatyana lit her cigarette. As she exhaled she lightly brushed an earring with her thumbnail.

'Fifteen thousand francs,' she said.

'I'm sorry?'

'You asked if they were real. At that price I think we can assume they are. Do you not agree?'

The ironical inflection in her voice seemed permanent. Her accent was quite strong, but her English was faultless.

'French francs or Swiss?' asked Grace.

Tatyana's eyebrows rose by a millimetre. She took another drag of her cigarette. She rubbed her cheek.

'That is a good question,' she said, with her customary dryness. 'I think you are cleverer than the others.'

'What others?'

'The ones who come with Gallagher. A different one every time, although in essence the same. Same build, same height, same colouring. The last one had perfect breasts, but your legs I think are better. If I were to write a story about him I would call it "The Man Who Liked Only Blondes". But as there are so many men like him it would perhaps not be exclusive enough. Mr Gallagher has a reputation as a very discerning gentleman, and he is jealous of his reputation, do you not think?'

Grace tried to look indifferent.

'If you say so. It sounds like you know him better than I do.'

'I know the type. Which is useful. It saves me the bother of having to know the man. French, by the way.'

'Sorry?'

'The francs. Dmitri bought them in Cannes, but only after I drew his attention to them. In fact it was another pair that caught my eye, similar but three times the price. He bought me these instead, no doubt assuming that I wouldn't notice. Like most men who have no taste, Dmitri thinks no one else has any either.'

'But you took them nonetheless.'

'I take what I am given. The life I lead – you lead – doesn't come with a pension policy. Come here, I will show you something.'

Tatyana stepped back from the door and beckoned for Grace to come in.

'See where I am confined when I have been a bad girl.'

Grace paused on the threshold to take in the room. She had been in less comfortable prisons. The room was light and airy, finished in blue and cream, with none of the solidly oaken feel of the rest of the house. The large four-poster bed notwithstanding there was plenty of room for an armchair and a chaise longue and a whole wall of well-crammed bookshelves. A half-open door afforded a glimpse of an equally spacious, decidedly opulent bathroom. Another door, also open, led into a small room containing cupboards and a dressing table. A third door was closed.

'The door to Dmitri's bedroom,' Tatyana explained, watching minutely every stage of Grace's brisk examination. 'It's locked and I don't have the key. Which is a pity. Because then I could show you exactly what I mean by bad taste. Downstairs you cannot tell, because the house and furnishings are as the previous owner left them. Safe, but uninspiring, do you not think? When he is here Dmitri likes to think he is the English country squire. He sends his son to Eton, you know. The daughter is in a school for rich stupid virgins in Switzerland. She qualifies on all counts. Fortunately he doesn't like his children because they remind him of his wife. If you ever saw his wife you would understand. She looks like the captain of the Russian women's shot-put team. Little wonder he prefers me.'

She pulled on the locked door handle to Dmitri's bedroom, as if to demonstrate its solidity, and shrugged.

'No matter. Perhaps he will open it tonight. Perhaps not. Depends how much he drinks. The worst time is when he is drunk enough to be horny but not quite so bad he will pass out. Usually it takes him only a few minutes to fuck me, but when he is that drunk it takes long to get him hard. You will not have that problem, I think. What does Gallagher like in bed?'

'I don't know. Ask me tomorrow morning. Not that it's any of your business.'

'Ah, the ingenue. You will not sleep much, I warn you. Your room is the other side, that wall, the head of the bed. The last girl he brought here was screaming her head off all night. I needed earplugs.'

'I'll try to keep the noise down.'

'Perhaps you will have no choice. He is very virile, very good looking. It is not always necessary to fake pleasure with a man like that. He has an excellent body, no fat. Not too hairy, which I like.'

'Sounds like you know him pretty well.'

'I have not slept with him, if that is what you are suggesting. I have seen him sunbathing on Dmitri's boat, that is all. Though he would like to sleep with me, I see it in his eyes. Most men want to sleep with me, of course, but I am blonde, so it is natural for Gallagher to want me. But he knows that Dmitri would kill him, so I am in his fantasies only. Perhaps he will be thinking of me when he is with you tonight.'

'I doubt it.'

'You think you are good?'

'I don't get any complaints. Do you?'

'How much do you charge?'

'Enough. And I don't let anyone slap me around.'

'Ah ha.'

Tatyana let out a final long stream of blue smoke and walked over to the window. She threw the butt of her cigarette outside.

'Much cleverer than the others.'

Tatyana touched the left side of her face, where Dmitri had hit her.

'Let me tell you about Dmitri. He is the kind of man who needs to be in charge. Everyone around him must know he is the big shot, everyone must be scared of him. And they are scared, me included. But I do not show it. Instead I stand up to him, and now he must impose himself on me, and bend me to his will. Only then can he enjoy me, and this I understand, and that is why I am still here, after three years, and why I have many things worth much more than fifteen thousand francs. You see that wardrobe? I have ten fur coats. He has other women, all the time, but they show their fear and then he becomes bored quickly. Or else they are too stupid to be afraid, and that he finds boring too. It excites him that I am an educated woman with a sharp tongue. That is why I provoke him. Sometimes I go too far, and then I suffer, but it is better to anger a man like Dmitri than it is to bore him. It is simple really. As simple as he is.'

'I think I'd better be getting back downstairs.'

'What's the hurry? The men are playing at being boys, they may be there for hours. I invited you in here to show you something. Please stay at least until you have seen it.'

'What do you want to show me?'

'This –'

Tatyana headed for the bathroom, which was linked to the bedroom by a mini-corridor lined on one side by small cupboards. On the other side, resting on the floor and with its face to the wall, was a large oil painting. The frame was heavy, and Tatyana had difficulty lifting it. She moved it into the bedroom and propped it against the chaise longue.

'*Voilà.*'

It was a portrait of a woman in Victorian costume. She was wearing a richly embroidered white gown and a mass of expensive jewellery, but it wasn't her dress or accessories that caught the eye. Her features, framed by a mass of soft dark curls, were hauntingly exquisite.

'She's beautiful,' said Grace, conscious of the inadequacy of the response.

'She is, though I do not like the hand. He did not do good hands.'

Grace looked at the woman's hand, which was holding a closed fan across her breast. It didn't look so bad to her.

'It's a Winterhalter,' said Tatyana.

The tone implied that Grace ought to feel impressed.

'I'm sorry, I know nothing about art.'

Tatyana gave a smile, but there was no warmth in it. It was merely an expression of superiority.

'He was the most fashionable portrait painter of his time. Every crowned head of Europe sat for him. I had only seen his work in museums until this. It's one of several studies he made of the Empress Eugenie. Painted 1860 or thereabouts, I should think. She lived to a very great age, long after she had buried her husband and her son, whom she adored. She died here in England, very alone, a sad exile. She cannot have known her fate when she sat for this portrait – or could she? Do you not think there is much sadness in her eyes? It is what I like best about this picture. It is wasted lying on the floor beside the bathroom, but what can I do? I have asked that big fool Yuri to bring me a hammer and nail a hundred times, but he has a brain like a goldfish, always forgetting. I think he was shot in the head in Afghanistan, he is unusually stupid even for a professional thug. Usually I would ask Dmitri to give him a kick up his backside, but Dmitri is very sensitive on the subject of this painting, so it is not tactful for me to mention it. I would like him to forget about it, you see, so then he will not be tempted to sell it. He gave it to me, but he could easily take it back.'

'Isn't it a bad idea to hang it on the wall then?'

'I will hang it next door, in my dressing room, where he never sets foot. Though it does not matter. When Dmitri comes here he has only one thing on his mind and it is not art. If Mona Lisa was on the wall he would not notice. He is much more likely to fall over it on the floor on the way to the bathroom.'

'Why should he want to sell it if he has given it to you?'

'Because he does not wish to be reminded of his ignorance. You see, someone told Dmitri he was like Napoleon: the boldest, the baddest, the best. This Dmitri liked, very much. The only difference, he said, was that

Napoleon left Moscow in flames while Dmitri left it in shit. This is a joke, by the way, it is not always easy to tell with Dmitri. Anyway, now that Dmitri is Napoleon it is necessary to have things around to remind everyone of how important he is. So one day he brings me this painting, and he is very proud, like a peacock. I wish to give you the woman Napoleon adored, he says, so when I make love to you she will inspire me. This too might be joke, but I did not laugh. What do you mean? I say. Napoleon loved Josephine. Of course, said Dmitri, as if he talks to an idiot, and this is Josephine. It is not, it is Eugenie, I tell him. Dmitri explodes. It's the fucking Empress of France, he screams at me, do I think Napoleon had two fucking empresses? As a matter of fact he did, I tell Dmitri, but the second one wasn't Eugenie either. I tell him he has got the wrong Napoleon. You think I am an idiot? he screams at me, even louder. How can I have the wrong Napoleon? There is only Napoleon, any fool knows that. Not this fool apparently, I tell him. As a matter of fact there were three Napoleons, and the one who married Eugenie was no good. Now he starts to hit me, and call me names. This always happens when we argue, but this time I can tell his heart really isn't in it. Ah ha, I think, the great Dmitri has doubts about his own genius. This is rare and I enjoy it, even though he still hits me. He has to know the truth, but he will not believe me. So he sends me to my room, as usual, while he makes enquiries. And then I hear him screaming at people downstairs. Now I am glad I am in my room, for it is not good to be near an elephant when it is mad. He screams, he stamps, he breaks things against the wall. He is demented. I would not like to be the man who sold him that painting. This is a true story. It is much better than any of Dmitri's jokes, don't you think?'

'Yes,' said Grace uncertainly. 'I'm surprised he didn't try to get rid of it immediately.'

'Ah, but then he would have to fetch it from me, and

so he would have to admit it exists. But we pretend that it does not exist, and we pretend that he has never bought it.'

'He might send somebody to take it while you're not here.'

'No man is allowed in my bedroom, that is another of his house rules. No, if he wants the painting he will have to get it himself. And that is humiliating. I do not mention it, then it is mine. So. Now you understand. Dmitri is a pig. Yes. He slaps me round, as you say. Yes. But I have ten fur coats and a Winterhalter, all genuine. This is a pretty good deal, I think, though maybe you think you do better renting by the hour. How much did you say you charge?'

'I didn't. And if you'll excuse me, I really must be going.'

Tatyana opened her mouth to reply, but before she could say anything became distracted by a loud mechanical whirring noise outside. A helicopter was approaching the house. Grace had been vaguely aware of the noise for the last minute or so, but it had not occurred to her that the helicopter would be heading straight for them. From the way the window frame was rattling it had to be overhead right now. Both women instinctively took a step towards the window to get a better look.

Beams of light swept across the expansive gardens as the helicopter passed the house. They saw it hovering above them, brightly lit, already low and rapidly dropping lower. Out by the tennis courts, on the other side of the car park, a circle of landing lights had been switched on and shadowy figures could be seen moving on the lawn.

'Visitors do drop by at the most inconvenient times,' remarked Tatyana, above the rhythmic whooping of the helicopter blades.

Grace felt her pulse quicken. Her first thought had been that the helicopter must belong to the surveillance team and was straying dangerously close to the house, but now that it was clearly coming in to land it dawned on her that she should have expected it. Why wouldn't a man like Martinez opt for the grand entrance? She slipped her hand casually into her bag and made contact with the comforting contours of the phone.

'Who do you think it is?' she asked, with what she hoped would pass for casualness.

Tatyana shrugged. Her own casualness was unfeigned; it was clear that she couldn't have cared less.

'Thanks for the guided tour,' said Grace, heading for the door. 'Take care of yourself.'

Tatyana raised an eyebrow.

'I always do.'

Grace walked rapidly along the landing to the head of the stairs. She was in such a hurry that she had already taken the first couple of steps down before she noticed that someone else was coming up. It was Gallagher.

'I was wondering where you'd got to,' he said.

'I was with Tatyana. How's it going? You winning?'

'I already won.'

He stopped, a couple of steps below her, and laughed. He was looking very relaxed. His top buttons were undone and his sleeves rolled up. He carried his jacket over his shoulder. In his other hand he held his black attaché case. He raised it by the handle, and gave it a shake, as if to indicate that it was full.

'Not a bad night's work,' he said, coming up towards her. 'Now we can party.'

'We can?'

'Yup.'

He stopped on the step below her. He put down the attaché case and placed his free hand against the small of her back. His head was level with hers. He leant towards her and brushed her cheek with his lips. He said:

'I mean, a small, private party.'

'Sounds good to me,' she answered softly.

His hand slipped down to her bottom and pulled her gently into him. He whispered into her ear.

'We could go back to the car and pick up where we left off, but I figured it might be more comfortable up here.'

He pulled away and glanced down as footsteps sounded on the staircase below. A small, moustachioed man Grace hadn't seen before was coming up, holding a silver tray on which were balanced a bottle of champagne and two glasses.

'Thank you, Yakov,' said Gallagher in his smooth, barely accented Russian. 'I'll take it from here. Hold my coat, would you, Grace?'

She took the jacket, as requested. Yakov handed over the tray and returned to wherever it was he had come from. Gallagher gave his wrist a flamboyant twist and lifted the tray to shoulder height before setting off down the corridor.

'You coming?' he called over his shoulder.

Grace hesitated.

'I don't understand. You've finished the game already?'

'The game? Oh yeah. Didn't take long, I know, but these are busy guys.'

'But I thought you were waiting for your friend?'

'What? Oh, him. Nah, he didn't show. Come on, the champagne's getting warm.'

'I . . . I want to check on Jeanette.'

'Jeanette?'

He stopped walking, and gave the tray a little twirl. He looked amused, and faintly puzzled.

'She wasn't looking so good earlier,' Grace explained quickly. 'I think she may have drunk a bit too much, I want to see she's all right.'

'Oh, she'll be OK. Ralf'll take good care of her. I think he likes her a lot. He said he was thinking of keeping her for a few days.'

'I'm sure he'll look after her, but –'

'It's too late anyway, you won't catch her now. They've gone.'

'Gone? When?'

'Now, I guess. You heard the helicopter? Dmitri laid it on for Ralf, he has to be somewhere tonight. Hey, come on, I need you to open the door. Look, no hands.'

He was standing outside the third door along the corridor, the one between the bathroom and Tatyana's bedroom, holding up the tray and the case, one in each hand, and wearing an expression of mock-helplessness.

She walked towards him, slowly, trying to appear unconcerned at the same time as she felt her insides begin to shred. With a wide fixed smile on her lips she opened the door.

'After you,' he said.

The room was the same size as Tatyana's and boasted a similar four-poster bed. Curtains of dark green silk, tied back against the four posts, hung down from a canopy covered in the same material. Grace's eyes were drawn to the elaborately embroidered Tudor rose cushions propped up against the carved oak headboard. She imagined Tatyana on the other side of the wall, listening.

Gallagher closed the door behind him with his foot and carried the tray to a chest of drawers. Grace laid her bag and his jacket down on the bed. While he opened the champagne she walked to the window.

The helicopter was still there. She couldn't see clearly from this distance, but a light was flashing on the tail and she could hear the engine, though it was much quieter than before. The rotor blades were idling.

'Here,' said Gallagher.

He was standing behind her, holding a champagne glass over her shoulder. She took the glass, and his hand dropped lightly to her neck. She felt his breath on her ear.

'Everything OK?' he said. 'You seem tense.'

Now both hands were on her shoulders, the thumbs gently kneading her. His lips were on the nape of her neck, brushing her skin with the faintest of touches. She lifted her chin and rested the back of her head against his chest. He kissed her on the throat.

'Oh, everything's fine,' she said, hearing the catch in her voice and marvelling at how unlike herself she sounded. His lips were on her neck again, his fingers were gliding all over her. She closed her eyes and leant back into him. He bent over and kissed her on the lips, upside down.

'Let me have that,' he said, and took the champagne glass.

He led her to the bed. He sat down and placed his hands on her hips. He ran the tips of his fingers down to her knees, and then all the way up again, back to her hips, but this time underneath her dress. He took his time. She exhaled softly as his thumb made a little circular motion between her legs. He hooked his fingers under the elastic and began to pull down her French silk knickers.

'Just a moment, Mike.'

She clasped his wrists. He looked up at her, surprised.

'I need to freshen up. I'll be right back.'

'Mm.'

He put on a pained look. He kicked off his shoes and slid up the bed. He put the back of his head into his hands and came to rest against the big Tudor cushions.

'Promise you won't be long,' he said.

'I promise.'

She snatched up her bag and hurried out. She took a few steps down the corridor and dived into the bathroom.

She caught a glimpse of herself in the mirror as she strode to the window. Flushed and dishevelled. No change there then. She took the phone out of her bag and turned it on. She stood waiting for it to register, her fingers poised over the keypad. It seemed to be taking an age.

She thought of him lying on the bed, next door, waiting for her. Her pulse was racing. But then, why shouldn't it? Considering where she was. What she was about to do. But she had been calm enough a few minutes ago. Before he'd taken her into the bedroom. Before he'd touched her. More than touched. She was aroused, she couldn't deny it. Well, it wasn't her fault that her body had responded. She was hardly to blame that he seemed to know exactly what he was doing. *Wouldn't mind.* Too damned right she wouldn't mind. What of it? It was hardly shocking, in this day and age. It didn't mean she really was a tart. Damn, why was the phone taking so long to register? If she'd been a man, the positions reversed, no one would think twice about it. Where in Christ's name was this irrational guilt-trip coming from? Bloody hell, she hadn't even been brought up a Catholic . . .

The phone gave a *beep*. She hesitated. She knew what she had to do, but that didn't make it any easier. The helicopter was on the lawn. There could still be time. She thought of Jeanette's terror. It wasn't supposed to be like this. It wasn't their fault the whole thing had been screwed up. Use your discretion, they had told her. She was using it.

She typed in the word, those three simple letters. She watched them flash up on the digital display.

ACE.

Transmission would be instantaneous. She imagined the effect the little word would have, the sudden burst of activity, the frantic issuing of orders. Everyone would surely be in place by now. It wouldn't take long for them to get here. Not now they thought that Martinez had been positively identified.

She turned off the phone and put it back in her bag. She adjusted her hair in the mirror. Not long, but maybe long enough for Gallagher to ruff it up again. Strange, but she felt calm now. The calm before the storm, she supposed. Carefully she reapplied her lipstick.

She had left the bathroom and was walking back down the corridor when she heard the alarm bell ringing. It was loud, piercing, electronic, and it came from outside the front of the house. Somebody was shouting downstairs. She could make out the distinctive Russian inflection, but not the words. Through the small leaded windows in the hallway she saw lights flashing out in the drive.

The door to the bedroom opened and Gallagher appeared, in bare feet, his shirt unbuttoned. He glanced at her and she smiled back, trying to look both innocent and suggestive.

'Something's going on,' he said, frowning.

She didn't answer. The shouting voice downstairs had been joined by others. Someone, somewhere, was banging on a door. But it was for another, mechanical noise that she strained her ears. It was above them, loud and insistent but already fading away. The helicopter had taken off. Jeanette had already gone. Grace felt her smile freeze into place.

Damn, she thought. *Always did have lousy timing . . .*

8

They kept her waiting for four hours before they gave her the treatment. The room wasn't exactly a cell, but it was square, windowless, featureless, and even though the door wasn't locked it might as well have been. A uniformed officer brought her a coffee and a single biscuit when she arrived. She had no idea where she was, but the drive in the back of the blacked-out van hadn't taken long. No one had spoken to her since the men in balaclavas had burst into the bedroom and told her to get down on the floor. She always did what she was told when someone was waving a gun at her. She had had plenty of time since to prepare herself. She didn't know exactly what for, but she knew that it wouldn't be pleasant.

She was actually asleep when they came in, her body slumped into one of the plastic chairs, her arms cradling her handbag and her head propped against the corner of two of the identical blank white walls. It wasn't a deep sleep and she woke as soon as she heard the door open. She sat up, rubbing her aching neck, as they came in and took the chairs behind the room's only other piece of furniture, a plastic-topped table that looked – they all did – as if it had seen better days. Dent put his briefcase down on the table and busied himself for half a minute with taking out papers and spreading them on the desk. Bob Challoner crossed his legs and stared past her, as if the wall was the most interesting view in the world.

Dent closed his briefcase.

'Well, that was a grade one fuck-up, wasn't it, Miss Cornish?'

Grace might have laughed, had she been in the mood. The profanity didn't go with the quiet controlled tone, the smooth bland face. Dent looked and sounded like an old-fashioned BBC announcer, all white tie and tails behind the microphone, dead from the neck down. The impression of toothlessness, she knew, was dangerously misleading. She didn't say anything.

'Have you heard of George Tregear, Miss Cornish?'

Yes, she'd heard of him. The solicitor beloved of criminals and celebrities, she presumed, unless there was someone especially presumptuous masquerading under his name. She nodded.

'Oh good, so you do still have some contact with reality. That is comforting, Miss Cornish, very comforting. It may interest you to know that Mr Tregear is downstairs now and he's not very happy. I can't say I blame him. You see, the warrant we used to enter his client's house, although technically legal, was nonetheless somewhat dubious. Frankly speaking, it's a crock of shit. We know it and he knows that we know it and he's not very happy. Nor are we. I am going to have to spend most of the next few days covering my back, and when I'm not doing that I shall be covering my head. Mr Tregear, as I'm sure you appreciate, is very well connected and has the power to make life extremely uncomfortable for anyone his clients find disagreeable. Obviously when this operation began we had no idea that it would end with us presenting ourselves on the doorstep of one of those clients, but had everything gone according to plan we could have lived with it. It would have been worth the aggravation, let us say. But things have not, as you may have noticed, gone according to plan, and we are left with nothing but the aggravation. Have you any suggestions, Miss Cornish, as to what I should put in my report to the Home Office?'

She could think of a few comments, but none to which he would want to append his signature. She returned his cold stare and kept her mouth shut. She had dealt with enough bullies in her time to know when to avoid self-justification.

When he saw that she wasn't going to answer his eyes became, if possible, even colder. He leant back in his seat, took off his glasses and gave them a polish with the handkerchief in his top pocket. He took his time. He wanted to show her who was boss. She held his gaze and tried not to blink. After a minute or so he put his glasses back on. He produced a fountain pen from his inside pocket, unscrewed the top and began writing, slowly and deliberately, on one of the sheets of paper he had taken from his case. His body language couldn't have been clearer.

You don't exist. I wash my hands of you.

'Let's start from the beginning, shall we, Grace?' said Bob Challoner.

He continued staring at the wall. There was a touch of sadness in his voice, but she wasn't fooled. He wasn't hinting at sympathy but contempt.

'Oh, I see, you're going to go for that old variation, are you, Bob? Nasty cop, nasty cop?'

He swivelled his eyes to meet hers and she saw the anger flaring up in them. He'd been playing along with Dent's cool style but it really didn't suit him. She understood perfectly that he didn't want to interrogate her. He wanted to smack her in the face.

'Keep your smart-arsed comments to yourself, Grace. Just answer my fucking questions.'

'Fire away, Chief Superintendent.'

'The codeword Ace was only to be used in the event of a positive identification of Mickey Martinez. I would like to confirm firstly that this was clearly understood by you.'

'It was.'

'Yet no one even remotely matching his description appeared all evening. Can you confirm this?'

'I thought he was in the helicopter. I made a mistake.'

'The only person in the helicopter was the pilot. He stayed in the cockpit the entire time it was on the ground, we know because we had him under close observation. The only people who approached the helicopter were Orhan and WPC Dixon. They got in and the helicopter flew away. I do not understand how you could have made this mistake.'

'Is Jeanette all right?'

'Answer my question.'

'Tell me how Jeanette is.'

'No idea. We haven't heard from her.'

'But where did Orhan take her?'

'How the bloody hell should I know? We've got better things to do than chase bloody helicopters all over the shop, you know. I expect she'll turn up.'

'He might want to keep her on.'

'Don't you worry about Dixon, she can take care of herself. It's you I'd be worrying about if I were in your shoes. Now answer my question. How did you –'

'I don't know.'

'That's not good enough.'

'I made a mistake, that's all I can say.'

'A bloody expensive mistake.'

'What did you expect? The whole operation was put together on a wing and a prayer. Things have a habit of going wrong when you have to improvise.'

'Oh, I see, so it's our fault, is it?'

'I think there's enough blame to go around.'

'Something unforeseen happened, I'll grant you that. But you still agreed to go ahead with the operation.'

'Did I have a choice?'

'Yes.'

'Well then, I also had discretion to abort the operation if I saw fit.'

'And that's what you did, is it? You deliberately aborted it?'

'No. I used my judgement, and I made a wrong call, OK? These things happen when you're under pressure.'

'You're saying you couldn't handle the pressure?'

'You're putting words in my mouth. It was dark, I was confused, I made an innocent mistake. That's all there is to it.'

'I don't believe you.'

'Which bit?'

'All of it.'

He stopped talking for long enough to light a cigarette. He glanced around for something to use as an ashtray and saw the empty plastic coffee cup lying on the chair next to her. He got up slowly and came and stood over her.

'Let me tell you what happened,' he said, flicking his match into the thimbleful of cold coffee at the bottom of the cup and leaning against the wall so that his face was directly above her.

'If you know already, why ask me?'

'You bottled it, that's what happened. I didn't think you would, but you pulled the wool over our eyes. Came over as a proper big girl, proved all the nice things I said about you to Mr Dent here, made us all think you could handle it. You knew what the job entailed. You knew there might be more to it than window dressing. We all of us hoped it wouldn't come to that, but if it did you had to grit your teeth and go along with it. That was the deal. Only when push came to shove you couldn't hack it. Martinez not showing put a spanner in the works, I know, but you didn't have to make it a fucking hand grenade. All you had to do was act the part till morning, just go through the motions on automatic pilot, and that'd be it, your cover stays intact, no one in that house even knows there was a copper within five miles and the whole operation is uncompromised. Instead of which you bottled it. Because suddenly you're miss fucking prim and you decide you're too precious to put out. What did he want you to do, Grace, that had you reaching for the panic button? Ask you to suck him off and swallow it? Who are you kidding? You've had more dicks in your mouth than hot dinners.'

'None as small as yours.'

His hand flew up. She saw the fury in his eyes and flinched, but he caught himself in time. With evident reluctance he let his arm fall to his side.

'What's the matter, Bob? Knuckles still sore from the last beating you dished out?'

'Give it a rest, Grace,' he said, and suddenly sounded very weary.

It wasn't surprising. It was half past three in the morning. They were all red-eyed.

Bob walked back to his chair and slumped into it. Dent, who had finished whatever it was he was writing, must have exchanged a look with him. Grace saw the glimmer in his eyes. They weren't finished with her yet.

'I'd like to go home,' she said.

'You have some more questions to answer,' Dent answered.

'You mean you have some more questions to ask. I don't think I can answer them.'

'Operational questions. Much of it is routine.'

'Then it'll keep till morning.'

'I want to hear while the details are fresh in your mind.'

154

'Nothing's fresh in my mind right now. We'll all feel better for sleeping on it.'

'Sleep is not high on my list of priorities right now.'

'It should be. You're looking strained, Mr Dent.'

'Don't concern yourself on my account, please. What I want —'

'I know what you fucking want, Dent.'

The sound of her own voice shocked her. She had not intended to shout, still less to sound hysterical, but the raw emotion had burst up and overflowed before she could control it. Her words echoed shrilly in the little room. At least she had their attention.

'I know exactly what you want and as far as I'm concerned you can have it,' she said dully, her voice hoarse with exhaustion but back to its normal pitch.

She'd been through enough. She wanted it to be over.

'You want something to put in your report. An excuse. Not faulty planning, oh no. None of it could be your fault, could it? Much better to lay it at the door of some dumb, lowly female who probably wasn't thinking straight because it was the wrong time of the month, right? What you want is a scapegoat. Well, you're looking at her, OK?'

She stared at them in turn. They didn't say anything, but their eyes were alert.

'Write your report,' she said. 'Put in it whatever you have to. I'll sign it. I'm not a cop any more, I've got no career to lose. I'll sign it. Provided our earlier agreement stands.'

'It stands,' said Dent.

'Good. Then there's no need to keep me here any longer, is there? If you need anything else, ask me in the morning. Now take me home, please.'

She got to her feet and stood with her hands clasped in front of her, like a schoolgirl waiting to be dismissed by the headmaster. Dent had no intention of being hurried. He sat back and laced his hands together and stared at her, his chin resting on his fingers, for as long as he felt like.

'I'll arrange a car to take you back to London,' he said at last.

'I don't live in London. I don't want to go to London.'

'The debriefing isn't over yet, Miss Cornish. You'll spend tonight in the mews house. You'll be alone, the others have gone. We'll question you there and take you home tomorrow night. That's all that's on offer.'

'Then it'll have to do.'

Dent stood up and returned his papers to his briefcase. He nodded at Bob, as if formally handing over responsibility for the prisoner, and exited briskly.

'You might as well sit down,' said Bob. 'Car could be a while.'

'I'll stand.'

'Oh, do what you bloody like.'

There was something like affection mingled with the gruffness in his voice, but it was too late for that. Grace stared at him stonily.

The silence lasted until he had smoked his cigarette. He had either forgotten about the ashtray or, more likely, simply decided that he couldn't be bothered. He ground out the butt on the vinyl floor and immediately lit another.

'Back on forty a day again, eh, Bob?'

'Still the smug bitch who's kicked it, eh, Grace?'

'Pretty smug, yeah.'

'You should get yourself a badge.'

'I should get myself an air filter, hanging round you.'

'Should have thought I'm the last person you want to hang around at the moment.'

'Got a point there.'

He forced a chuckle. He leant back in his chair until it was resting on the two rear legs and put his feet up on the table. He gave her a long appraising glance.

'You're looking good on it, Grace.'

'Good on what?'

'On all this shit. Nice dress, by the way. You weren't wearing it this morning, were you?'

'Unlike you to be observant, Bob. No, I wasn't wearing it this morning, because it was hanging on a rail in Kensington. Gallagher sent me shopping and I sent you an e-mail telling you all about it. Remember?'

'Cost a bit, a dress like that. He must have liked you then.'

'Maybe.'

'I figured maybe you liked him too.'

'How'd you figure that?'

'The way you drove, threw off our tail. Like you preferred not to be found.'

'Ha ha. Had no choice. It was such a cack-handed tail you almost blew the whole thing there and then.'

'It was a balls-up, I admit. We weren't expecting you to leave London.'

'You weren't expecting a lot, were you?'

'I was expecting you'd make it easier to find you. Your directions took a while to work out.'

'They didn't provide me with headed notepaper.'

'Fair enough. We got it in the end, though. Got our people in place without disturbing anything, not an easy job in the middle of nowhere with nothing but a few trees for cover. Much easier in the city. All went like clockwork when the signal came. Couple of them tried to sneak off round the back by the tennis courts but we headed them off. A good clean swoop with no one getting hurt. Almost a perfect operation, except for the fact that it was a complete waste of time.'

'Don't start on that again.'

'I never thought you'd bottle it, Grace. Not you, of all people.'

'Afraid I've screwed up your promotion, Bob?'

'I've got my promotion, thanks. Don't change the subject, it's you I'm talking about. Why do I get the feeling that you're not telling me the whole story?'

'Save the grilling for tomorrow, will you?'

'I was only trying to pass the time, make some conversation.'

'This is your idea of conversation, is it?'

'All right, I'll keep quiet, if you prefer.'

'I prefer.'

He smoked another cigarette in silence. There was a knock on the door as he stubbed it out. Corliss entered.

'Car's here,' he announced brusquely, nodding in Grace's direction but trying not to catch her eye. 'Follow me.'

'It's OK, I'll walk her down,' said Bob.

Corliss looked relieved at being spared Grace's company. She followed Bob. They stepped out into a corridor and began walking towards a pair of heavy swing doors.

'Where exactly are we, by the way?' Grace asked.

'Nearest local cop shop. Place was deserted when we got here except for a desk sergeant. You should have seen the look on his face when the specials arrived, all that black Kevlar and enough kit to start a small war. They don't get too much call for that kind of stuff round here normally.'

'I should hope not.'

She followed him through the swing doors and down some stairs. A couple of men in plainclothes stopped in the middle of a conversation and stared at them as they descended. Grace felt their eyes boring through her as she followed Bob outside.

'Who are those guys?' she asked him, when they had stepped through the door. 'They with you?'

'Not exactly. Drug squad. Liaison. Why?'

'They were giving me the eye.'

'I'll warn them off.'

'What a gent.'

'You think so?'

'Christ no. If you were you'd at least offer me your jacket. It's bloody cold.'

Actually it was mild for the small hours of a September morning, but the radiators had been on at full blast inside and the thin material of her dress exacerbated the contrast. She was shivering by the time they reached the line of parked cars on the station forecourt. There were the usual marked and unmarked police vehicles, and, rather more grandly, a Jaguar and a silver Rolls Royce. At the end of the line was the same Toyota saloon that had picked her up at Waterloo on Thursday morning. It had the same driver too, she realized, as she spotted a familiar close-cropped head. Bob opened the rear door.

'Don't go talking to anyone now, Grace, you know the form. And stay in the house till we come for you.'

'You're not my superior officer now, Bob,' she said, her voice rising. 'Don't be so fucking patronizing.'

'Put a sock in it, Grace. Come on, we're all tired.'

'Oh, you too? Perhaps you could give me a clue as to what time I might expect you tomorrow? You want me scrubbed and brushed by eight o'clock or am I going to get a lie-in?'

'Couldn't tell you. Come on.'

'Where did you learn your technique? The Iraqi secret police? Come on, how about a rough idea? Morning? Afternoon?'

'Just stay in the house till we get there.'

'No thanks, I've had enough of being cooped up in that place. If it's a nice day tomorrow I might go for a walk. Might even go out to get some breakfast, and a toothbrush. Your gorillas only let me take my handbag, you see. All my stuff is in my suitcase, which is at that nice Mr Rostov's house, remember?'

'We'll send someone out for you.'

'No, I'll do it myself, thanks. If you want to talk to me you can ring me first and make an appointment. And if you want me to be there, make sure I'm given plenty of warning. I'll take the mobile with me if I go anywhere. You do still have the number, don't you?'

'Stubborn as a bloody mule, you,' he snarled.

She got into the car. He pulled his notebook out of his pocket and scribbled furiously. He tore off the page and thrust it at her.

'My mobile number. You go anywhere out the house tomorrow you ring me first. Got it?'

She didn't answer. He slammed the door on her. Bob rapped his knuckles on the front window and Ryan lowered it.

'Make sure she's locked in safely before you leave, Ryan,' said Bob sourly. 'Ball and chain would come in handy.'

Bob slapped the roof with the palm of his hand. Ryan rolled up the front window and almost immediately the car began to pull away. Grace settled in gratefully on the back seat. The upholstery was comfortable and the heater was on high. She peered through the windows and saw, without interest, rows of semi-detached houses pass by. They drove past a school, a park, over some mini-roundabouts, and through a big junction infested with traffic lights. She saw signs for London and the M4. It was quite a heavily built-up area but, unlike London at this or any other time of night, there were no other vehicles on the road. Ryan drove fast. He didn't speak.

'Still doing the strong silent act then?' said Grace, when she had grown tired of staring at suburbia by moonlight.

His head turned slightly. She couldn't see his eyes, but she knew he was looking at the smudge of her face in the driver's mirror.

'Thought maybe you wanted to be left alone,' he said.

'Would make a change.'

She laughed.

'Don't waste the effort trying to be nice to me, Ryan. It could damage your career prospects.'

'I doubt it.'

'Oh yeah, it'll be back to the army for you. The marines, sorry. You never did tell me how you got mixed up in this.'

'You never asked.'

'Tell me.'

'You want to know?'

'Why not? Pass the time.'

The car was slowing down rapidly. They were in the middle of a long stretch of open road, without a junction or traffic light in sight.

'Why are we stopping?' asked Grace, faintly alarmed.

The car ground to a halt. Ryan swivelled round in his seat.

'I never could do that cabbie's trick of talking through the back of my head. If you want to chat, get in the front.'

'Aye, aye, sir.'

She got out and came round to join him. He helped her click in her safety belt.

'I told you, Ryan, there's no percentage in being nice to me.'

'That's what I'm being, is it? Nice?'

'Sounds like you can hardly spit the word out. Afraid it doesn't go with your tough guy image?'

'What image is that?'

'Don't disappoint me, please. If you tell me you love opera or write poetry I might be sick.'

'Fat chance of that.'

'Good. So why are you being nice?'

'Because I think they're a bunch of wankers and they've got no business treating you this way.'

'Ah. I see. Carry on being nice, will you.'

'I also think they're fucking useless, the lot of them.'

'Yep, I think you've won me over.'

'And too thick to see what was staring them in the face. I know why you aborted the mission, and I know you were right.'

'You do?'

'Yeah.'

He eased the car into first and accelerated up through the gears to cruising speed. He was driving slower now, his attention shared between Grace and the road.

'It was down to timing, that's all. I was with them when the helicopter arrived. I had a pretty clear view of what was going on. I knew something was wrong as soon as I saw Jeanette coming out with Orhan. Thought she was hurt at first, she was stumbling around like she'd done ten rounds with him, then I sussed she was drunk. Not exactly how a high-class call girl behaves, is it? All I could think was to get her out of there. I told Challoner and Corliss, but they didn't want to know. Whole operation was dead in the water then, but they weren't going to admit to that, were they? No sign of Martinez and one half of the under-cover team liable to blow the gaffe at any moment. Called for drastic action in my view, and that's exactly what happened. Soon as you phoned in the call-sign I knew it was bullshit. Whole place had been under close observation for an hour and no one had come in or out. So unless Martinez had been hiding in the cupboard or disguising himself as the butler the whole time he couldn't have just been spotted, could he? No way. You were telling us to get Jeanette the hell out of there. Am I right so far?'

'It didn't work though, did it?'

'We moved two minutes too late. But it was the right idea.'

'You think so? Even though it screwed the whole thing up and warned Martinez to keep his head down?'

'There'll be other opportunities to get Martinez. The most

important rule is safety first. You knew that Jeanette couldn't hack it and you did what you had to do.'

'Don't be too hard on her. She was drinking because she couldn't face sleeping with Orhan. I'd have done the same.'

'Did you tell them this?'

'No.'

'Because you're afraid of what they'll do to Jeanette? Does she deserve your loyalty?'

'She deserves someone's.'

'And they think you're the one who lost her nerve? Ha bloody ha.'

'Thanks. Tell Bob Challoner.'

'I wouldn't waste my breath.'

'He's a good cop, you know.'

'He's an ambitious, ruthless shit.'

'Careful. He used to be my boyfriend.'

'I know.'

They were on the slip road coming on to the motorway. Overhead lights and a blaze of lorry headlamps suddenly brightened the car interior. Grace stared searchingly at Ryan's impassive profile.

'You know a lot for a chauffeur, don't you?'

'I've got eyes, ears.'

'Sounds like you'd have made a good cop yourself.'

'With Challoner as my role model?'

'You don't like him much, do you?'

'No. He's a man's man. But not my sort.'

'I expect you're surprised he was my sort.'

'No. Attractive and interesting women always pick wrong 'uns. Don't ask me why; that's the way it is.'

'Oh, I see. An expert on the opposite sex too, are we? Is there no end to your talents?'

'Don't get shirty now. You asked me a question, I gave you the honest answer.'

'You still haven't answered my first question.'

'What was that?'

'How you got mixed up in this.'

'Oh, that. You want to change the subject, do you?'

'Yeah, since you're asking.'

'All right. If you want to know. Dent asked for me. I'd worked under him in Bosnia. I was supposed to be going back to my unit but he asked if he could have me on special assignment for six months.'

'What happens in Bosnia?'

'All sorts of crap you don't want to know about and I'm not supposed to mention. Dent's background is military intelligence, though you've probably worked that out already.'

'I thought military intelligence was a contradiction in terms?'

'Yeah well, you said it. Dent talks a good game, but he's not much use in the six-yard box.'

'Why'd you say yes to him then?'

'Because he's not the sort you say no to. He made it sound pretty interesting too, didn't get round to mentioning the chauffeuring bit, funnily enough. I also thought if I was going to be in London it'd give me a chance to see my daughter, for a change.'

'How old's your daughter?'

'Eighteen. She's at Queen Mary's, law student. I haven't seen a lot of her in the last ten years. Or her brother.'

'What about your wife?'

'Divorced.'

'And did you get to see your daughter?'

'Not a lot. Dent likes having me at his beck and call. He enjoys all the trappings.'

'I still don't get why either of you are mixed up in a straightforward police operation.'

'Just a guess, but they didn't tell you too much about the set-up. Right?'

'Right.'

'Yeah, that figures. It's all on a need-to-know basis – that's their favourite expression, by the way. Completely obsessed with secrecy. I was with them for a month before I even found out the name of the outfit. It's AI 10, if you're interested.'

'AI?'

'Administrative Inquiries. Not Artificial Intelligence – that'd be too close to the bone. Don't ask me why it's AI 10, you can take it from me there isn't an AI 9 or an AI 11.'

'And what do they inquire into?'

'Corruption. That's why they're all outsiders. An intelligence man as boss, a copper from outside London as his number two, a customs man for a gofer.'

'Corliss?'

'Clueless Corliss, the same.'

'And you?'

'Poor bloody infantry. Gave me the bull about needing someone with my expertise about the place, but they haven't exactly used it. I'm not a copper and I'm not local, that's what they really cared about. Thank God my time's nearly up.'

'Hang on, is this why none of the girls were from London?'

'You're catching on.'

'They told me they hadn't been able to recruit anyone from the Met.'

'They didn't try. Word gets around too fast. They didn't want certain people to know they were up to something.'

'You mean coppers on the take?'

'Coppers, civil servants, customs, you name it. The money on offer's unbelievable, who wouldn't at least think twice? Imagine, you're on fourteen grand a year, stuck all day in the ferry terminal, and a guy comes along and says, "Here's two years' salary in a paper bag, now would you mind looking the other way for five minutes, please?"'

'I know. Tate told me that story at the interview the other day. Only he was talking about the Mexican border.'

'Right. They've got a bigger problem over there than we have over here, but that's only because everything's bigger over there. And we're much better at sweeping it under the carpet and pretending it doesn't exist. We like to think we're so incorruptible. Maybe we still are, relatively speaking, but for how much longer? They reckon the drugs economy is now the second biggest in the world. Might even overtake American GDP in a few years. Sorry if I sound like a public information film but I've had all this pumped into me till it's coming out of my ears. What chance have we got then? They want to flood us with crack they'll flood us with crack. All this talk about winning the drugs war, all that crap with the drugs czar, God help us, it's pissing in the wind. Cut one head off and ten grow in its place. Sorry, you probably know all this.'

'Yeah, I saw the same film. So Dent's remit is to tackle corruption, right?'

'Right enough.'

'So what's this operation about?'

'Good question. It's a fuck-up, that's what it's about. Dent acts like he's on the bridge of an aircraft carrier but the truth is it's a souped-up pedalo. There's him and Challoner and Clueless and that's basically the entire department, apart from a couple of spotty kids working in the basement of that building in Southwark who spend all day looking at computer screens. They're the ones who actually do the work, by the way, trawling through bank accounts, looking for money transfers, that sort of thing. Not doing a bad job of it either, from what I hear, though they're overworked and underfunded. It was them who made the connection between Gallagher and Martinez, and the rest, as they say, is history.

Gallagher hasn't even got so much as an outstanding parking ticket against his name, but Dent turned him into the number one surveillance target on three continents. That's why he got so excited when that phone intercept from Turkey came in. It was the first concrete lead on Martinez in years, and it all happened because he passed Gallagher's name to Interpol. That's why he couldn't resist getting in over his head. Dent didn't have the resources to mount an operation on this scale, but he was damned if he was going to let anyone else take the credit. He bullied, he smarmed, he licked every arse in sight. I know, I was driving him most of the time while he was yacking into his mobile. He got his way in the end too, and kept everyone else out of it, with the result you saw tonight. A thing like this takes months of planning, but it was all cobbled together in a week. Surveillance teams, police marksmen, the heavy squad, they all had to be bussed in from outside. No one knows anyone else, and they're all running around like headless chickens because Dent's terrified of leaks and he's issued strict orders that no one's even to name the target until the final briefing. The final briefing. That really was a joke, you should have been there. Naturally, you don't even get a mention. All Dent will say is that there may be some inside information.'

'So that guy who was waving a gun at me didn't even know I was on his side?'

'No.'

'I'm glad I did what he told me.'

'The foot soldiers were supposed to think that Gallagher was being tracked by a routine surveillance operation. Another total cock-up. The teams were kitted out as traffic wardens, council workmen, even a pizza delivery guy and a cycle courier. Not a great deal of use in the middle of the sodding country.'

'They went to all that trouble even though I was already on the inside?'

'The surveillance people weren't in the loop. They were part of some deception plan.'

'Deceiving who?'

'I don't know that. But I do know there are a lot of pissed-off coppers out there tonight.'

'Like the drug squad guys?'

'Oh no, they're loving every minute of it. They totally resent Dent, all the coppers, hate anyone who strays on to their patch. And they really loathe Challoner because they figure he's a turncoat.'

'Yeah, I know the way they think. But I can see there's logic in a set-up like this. AI 10 isn't such a bad idea.'

'Well, don't expect them to come to you for a testimonial. You're top of their shit list now, as if you didn't know. You ever want to see greased lightning try watching Dent passing the buck. He's the best.'

'What did all those coppers think they were doing?'

'Busting an illegal gambling operation.'

'It takes men in balaclavas and machine guns to do that?'

'No, but they help make Dent feel important. Ringing the doorbell doesn't make nearly enough noise. Especially when it turns out the doorbell belongs to Dmitri Rostov.'

'They knew who he was?'

'Oh, right away. Dent was even more full of himself than usual.'

'Who is Rostov?'

'He didn't give you a copy of his CV? Not that it matters. Put down anything you like – drugs, prostitution, smuggling, fraud, robbery, murder – he's up to his neck in it, though you couldn't say any of that publicly without getting slapped with a slander writ from that poncey solicitor of his. Rostov's exactly the kind of big fish they're desperate to net, but they can't get to him directly.'

'They think they can get at Rostov through Martinez?'

'And a fair few others besides. But where's the mileage

in nailing Martinez? He's only the middleman, all he's got out of running rings round the world's law enforcement agencies for the last ten years is the odd million here and there. Much better to let him keep his millions if he agrees to split on the guys with billions. It would mean plastic surgery, a life on the run and almost certainly a bullet in the neck one day somewhere down the line, but what's the alternative? Even if he had no intention of opening his mouth, do you think any of his friends would believe him?'

'I see. Well, I half see. How come they've got something on Martinez if he's so good at covering his tracks?'

'Because he didn't used to be. There's a murder rap hanging over him, though he doesn't know it. Fifteen years or so ago he killed a man in Las Vegas by the name of Jimmy Ramirez. We don't know why, but Ramirez was a drug dealer so we can guess. He also killed Ramirez's girlfriend, after first raping and torturing her, probably while Ramirez watched. She was called Paula, I think. Yeah, that's right, Paula Schultz. She had a twin sister, identified the body. Can't have been pleasant, I've seen the autopsy report. He'd used her lipstick to leave graffiti all over her naked body. Nice guy, Martinez.'

'What graffiti?'

'Bitch. Whore. Cocksucker. Nothing very imaginative. It gets worse, though. When they found the bodies she had Ramirez's dick in her mouth. Only it wasn't attached to Ramirez any more, if you get my drift. As I say, nice guy, Martinez. He was a suspect, but there were no fingerprints and no other evidence so he got away with it. But back then they didn't have DNA. A while back they ran tests on the semen stains on the girlfriend's clothing and made a positive identification. As Mr Tate put it so eloquently, he either sings or he fries.'

'OK. Huh. When we were at the hotel and Gallagher sent Jeanette on I assumed she was going to Martinez. Maybe she's better off with Orhan, God help her.'

'You still worried about her?'

'Yes. They don't know where she is and they don't care either. And if she does get away from Orhan in one piece she's going to have to face Dent. Do you think he'll haul her over the coals?'

'Depends what state she's in when she turns up. They might decide to make an example of her.'

'Why do they need her? They've got me, haven't they?'

'Yeah, maybe you'll be enough. And maybe they'll decide to be sadistic.'

'But why would they . . . I mean . . . ah shit, I can't think straight . . .'

'Are you all right?'

She picked her head out of her hands and glanced sideways at him. They were coming off the motorway on to the lighted Westway and his features were clear enough for her to see his concern.

'Tired,' she said, seeing the time on the clock on the side of one of the tall buildings. The luminous dials pointed to a quarter past four.

'I'll bet you're bloody exhausted,' he said.

She lowered her head into her hands again, glad to take the weight off her aching neck. Yes, she was tired. And hungry, and thirsty, and feeling chilly again despite the blasts of hot air from the heater. But that wasn't why she'd slumped so suddenly, her body so heavy against the seatbelt that she could hardly breathe. Simply, she felt overwhelmed. The accumulated tensions of the last few days and the raw undigestible mass of information with which Ryan had been feeding her had combined at last to fill her head to bursting point. A throbbing, violent headache was pummelling her brain; a lumpen listlessness, like the dropsy, had invaded every muscle and limb. She was done in.

'Take me home, please,' she mumbled.

The roads were empty apart from the odd pre-dawn lorry.

170

They were back at the mews in under ten minutes. Ryan unlocked the door and turned on the lights for her.

'Keys on the table,' he said. 'I was supposed to give you the lecture about not speaking to anyone, but I think we'll skip that.'

'Thanks.'

'Get some sleep, Grace.'

'Hey, Ryan –'

He stopped halfway through the door.

'Thanks for everything, Ryan. You know.'

'No problem.'

'Will I see you again?'

He thought about it for a moment. He gave a nod.

'Yeah. I expect so.'

Grace dragged herself up the stairs and into the room she had shared with Jeanette. Her last thoughts, when she had flung off her dress and crawled under the duvet, were of her former room-mate, but they were as fleeting as consciousness itself. Tonight, at least, she wouldn't be needing any pills. The instant she closed her eyes she fell into a deep sleep.

She woke to see bright sunlight streaming through the curtains. It took a minute to focus her eyes on the face of her watch and register that it was half past ten, but when she had calculated that that meant she'd been under for a solid six hours she felt a lot better. Better still when she had stood for five minutes under the shower and was dressed once more in familiar clothes, her own person and not a painted confection. Best of all after she had downed a mug of strong black coffee and filled the hole in her stomach with toast and cereal. The sunlight was so strong that it hurt her eyes to look at the shine on the kitchen floor. She went upstairs to get her sunglasses from her coat pocket and rooted around in the Karen Millen bag for the mobile. The brown envelope was at the bottom of the bag.

Funny, that. More cash than she'd ever had in her life and she'd completely forgotten that it was there. Would Dent demand it? On what pretext? Did she deserve it, did she even want it? She shrugged. She had better things to agonize over right now. She keyed in Bob's number on the mobile, snatched the house keys from the table and marched briskly out of the house. No point waiting around for the Spanish Inquisition.

Bob wasn't answering. He'd always been notorious for never having his phone switched on; he was somebody who called you, not the other way round. A curiously refined embodiment of his voice informed her that she had reached the call-back service for Chief Superintendent Challoner and invited her to leave a message. She did so, promising that she hadn't gone far. She walked down to Queensgate and bought a toothbrush, some face cream and a paper. Then she wandered into Hyde Park and found herself an untenanted bench. A beautiful morning, technically early autumn but the leaves still on the trees and the grass smooth as a cricket pitch. Couples arm in arm, some wobbling on rollerblades, dogs walking, kites flying, kids cycling. You could look at a world as picture-postcard perfect as this and forget what went on in the unsanitized parts. The parts where she spent too much of her life.

Grace put the paper down unread. Where was Jeanette? It was half past eleven. Unless Orhan had decided to extend her contract he would be finished with her by now. Unless she had the nerve to walk out, and without a pint of vodka to sustain her she probably didn't. How was Jeanette? Hung over, exhausted, frayed. No, probably much worse than that. Terrified, degraded, abused. Full of self-loathing, perhaps even suicidal. She'd been the joker of the pack, she'd kept them all buoyed up with her repertoire of innuendo and stream of laddish gags. *I'd shag him all right. That Gallagher? You mean he pays us? Christ, I'd pay him. Tasty, eh?*

172

For a Scouser. Wouldn't mind, eh girls? Wouldn't mind ... No jokes today, though. Whatever she'd woken up to this morning it wasn't a scene from the picture-postcard world.

Grace picked up the paper again and tried to absorb the headlines. The waiting was the worst bit, always was, but at least she had a better idea of what it was about this morning. She wasn't powerless, thanks to Ryan. They needed her co-operation if they were to get their alibis straight. In that case they would have to help her. She wouldn't sign anything until they'd agreed to track down Jeanette. If she'd already reported in then OK, no problem. But if they hadn't heard from her they would have to find Orhan and get her out. And if that burst her cover, so what? It was too late to worry about keeping up appearances.

She got up and stretched. She felt pretty good on her six hours, much more alert than her usual sluggish Sunday-morning self. Perhaps she should try overdosing on adrenaline more often. A picture of Rostov and Orhan flashed into her mind. Then again, maybe not. She thought of Gallagher, coming up behind her at the window, gently pressing against her. His fingers on her skin. *Wouldn't mind.*

She started walking, fast. That was what she needed, a brisk bit of exercise to chase the stiffness from her limbs, the unbidden thoughts from her mind. And that vague, uneasy, sensation of guilt. *So what's the point of that then?* she asked herself, her inner voice putting on a gruff no-nonsense tone even as she felt the colour flushing her cheeks. An automatic, physical response, that had been all. Reacting to some external stimuli, no exercise of the will involved. If he'd tickled her, wouldn't she have laughed? And if he hadn't told her Jeanette was in the helicopter would she have done anything at all to stop him taking off her clothes?

She snapped to a halt as she felt the mobile phone vibrating in her hand. It was ringing loudly and people were looking round, making her feel self-conscious. She veered off the path on to the grass and put the handset to her ear.

'Is that you, Grace? Are you OK?'

She slowed to a halt, the phone filling one ear, her hand closed over the other, an expression of total surprise spreading over her features.

'Grace? Are you there?'

She moved her lips. The sound that came out was tiny, a croak. She cleared her throat and tried again.

'Yes, I'm . . . sorry, I was thinking about you actually, Mr Gallagher.'

He laughed.

'A little formal this morning, aren't we? Did you have a bad night?'

'No. I mean . . .'

What did she mean? She had better get her head clear, fast. The last she had seen of him he had been going down-stairs to investigate the commotion. He had told her to stay in the bedroom.

'I didn't know where you'd got to,' she said. 'They didn't tell me anything, I was frightened.'

'I'm not surprised. Look, I'm really sorry about last night. It's hard to explain, but it was all some big dumb mistake, the police got the wrong people. Did they give you a hard time?'

'No, not at all. They . . . they asked me my name and what I'd been doing. I . . . told them I was with you, that was all, but they didn't seem interested. They wouldn't tell me anything else. I thought the least they would do was take me home, but all they did was give me a telephone directory and tell me to call a cab.'

'Assholes.'

'Yeah, my thoughts exactly.'

She gave herself a mental tick: *It's the details that count; nice touch.*

174

'I'm really sorry,' he said. 'I know I said that, but I'll make it good, OK. Where are you?'

'Now? Um, Hyde Park.'

'Great. Get a cab. Come right on over.'

A long pause. She stared into the distance, empty-eyed.

'Grace? Hurry, will you? We got a plane to catch.'

'Plane?'

'To Nice. Remember? We got to be at Heathrow at one. We're cutting it pretty fine.'

'But . . .'

But what? But nothing, if she was who she said she was. The fug in her head was clearing rapidly. Whatever else had gone wrong last night it obviously hadn't compromised her.

'That's not very long. I need time to pack.'

'I picked up your suitcase from Dmitri's. Come as you are. As long as you got your passport we can get anything else you need in France. And your driving licence, don't forget that.'

'OK. I'm on my way.'

She'd started walking already, back towards Bayswater. She could see plenty of cabs going past with their hire signs on.

'Where are you, Mike?'

'Same hotel. Same suite. Got to make some calls now, I'll see you very soon.'

'Hey, hang on!'

'Yeah?'

'Do you know what happened to Jeanette? I'm a bit worried about her.'

'Oh, she's fine, I guess. They got out before the police arrived. Maybe we'll see her tomorrow.'

'She'll be there?'

'Maybe. Ralf liked her. I've got to run. See you pronto, OK?'

'OK.'

The line went dead. She dialled Bob's number. After an interminable series of rings she got through to his messaging service again.

'Bob? Call me as soon as you get this. Gallagher rang, I'm meeting him at the hotel, then we're going straight to Heathrow. He doesn't seem to suspect anything. I don't know if I should be doing this, but . . . well, I am doing it. You'd better call me if you've got a problem with that.'

I don't know if I should be doing this . . . Who did she think she was kidding? Of course she shouldn't be doing it. She should be sitting patiently in the mews, waiting to get any unpleasantness out of the way and to carry on with her life. Go back to the routine minor work she knew how to do, not hang around with flashy playboys and major-league criminals. She should be going back to Guildford later, not Heathrow, Nice, who knew where? She was way out of her depth. What the hell did she think she was doing?

She was walking fast, head lowered, her body hunched and tense. Why wasn't Bob there? Perhaps he and Dent were at the house already. If not there'd be – what? half an hour? – for the phone to ring and someone to overrule her. She'd think of an excuse, be ready to cancel him anyway. Family emergency, mother seriously ill, cat stuck up a tree, anything would do. She could leave it till the last minute, ring him from the hotel lobby if need be. Should she leave the five grand there for him, wipe the slate clean? A tricky one, she'd have to think. But then what about Jeanette? Was that her problem? No, but . . . no time to work it out now.

A cab pulled up as she stepped out on to the pavement, disgorging an elderly couple not ten feet away. She had caught the cabbie's eye and was in the back even before he had been paid off. She gave the address of the mews house. Some stuff to pick up, she explained, and then down the motorway.

The house was empty. She'd known it would be. She tried the phone again. Still not there. Were there any other numbers? No, and it was kind of unlikely that Dent or AI 10 would be listed on Directory Enquiries. She ran upstairs to the bathroom, giving herself five minutes. Wash, brush, a dab of eyeliner, it would have to do. She was wearing her black skirt, white blouse, black tights. Smart enough for an interview but not exactly the working uniform. She took off the tights and pulled on a pair of black hold-up stockings. She held her eyes in the mirror. Working uniform. You know what that means? You sure? Think about it. You're not committed yet. Twenty minutes at least down the motorway, plenty of time for the phone to ring.

She checked her pockets, but she knew there was nothing of Grace Cornish in them. Leave her own battered handbag then, take the Karen Millen, the Grace Collins passport, driving licence and the rest. Did she need anything else? Her camel coat, in case the evenings got cold. She didn't have any time to waste. Twenty past twelve, forty minutes to get to the hotel and then on to Heathrow.

She ran out of the house. The cabbie could see she was anxious. In a hurry, love? he asked. Late, she said. Plane to catch. Somewhere nice? South of France. Nice, not nice. Ha ha, yes very nice.

His voice all casual and slow, her words a staccato rush, her breathing tight and shallow. She spread herself across the back seat, concentrated on filling and emptying her lungs slowly. Couldn't do anything about the blood sprinting through her head. The cabbie, thank God, had sensed that she didn't want to talk and closed his window. She laid the phone out on the seat and stared at it, willing it to ring.

The same route as before, Notting Hill, Shepherd's Bush, Goldhawk, Chiswick. Most of the traffic coming the other way, into London. They were on the motorway. The phone just sitting there, a silent lump of plastic. The cab ploughed on at a steady sixty-five, eating up the few remaining miles.

She saw the hotel, as before, approaching the junction. The last stage was agonizingly slow, waiting for a gap in the traffic at the roundabout, then long queues at the traffic lights. And all the time the big, unattractive building inching closer and closer. At last the cab turned into the hotel slip road, crawling over the speed bumps. She glanced at the meter. She extracted a fifty-pound note, discreetly, from the envelope in her handbag. A generous tip, but she couldn't be doing with faffing about waiting for change. The cabbie smiled broadly. Enjoy your holiday, he said.

She paused outside, staring up at the windows, as if she could possibly make out which room it was from here, as if it would make a difference. She pressed the recall button and listened to Bob's answering tape again. No point in leaving another message, there was nothing new to say. She was on her own.

She walked into the hotel. One of the receptionists noticed her but didn't look twice. The sudden rush of self-consciousness that was flooding through her was miraculously unsuspicious. She made her way to the lifts. One was waiting there, empty and open. She pressed the top-floor button.

Her stomach gave a lurch as the lift began to rise. Nerves or vertigo? The latter, unless she was kidding herself. She stared at herself in the mirror. Looking pretty relaxed, she thought, all things considered. She held out her hand, the palm flat and down. See, steady as a rock.

Out of the lift and turn right, she knew the way. But walking much slower today, no Jeanette to feed her anxiety. A long corridor, so time to think it through again, time to turn around and retrace her steps, leaving Gallagher none the wiser. She pictured him waiting on the other side of the door. Not in a towel, like yesterday, because they had

178

a plane to catch. What was it she'd thought before? *Stripped and ready for action.* Yes, well, that would come later, but not now. It would come, though, no point in avoiding the issue. She'd have hours on the plane to prepare herself. And maybe she would be able to slip away anyway, in Nice or wherever, and never even have to go through with it. Find out if Jeanette was OK first, then, if she was there, they could get out together. Impossible to make a hard-and-fast plan, but plenty of scope if she kept her wits about her and played it by ear.

She stopped outside the door. She was feeling a little hot. Not surprising, it was a warm day and she was wearing her coat. She stared long and hard at the phone, as if giving it a final chance. It didn't take it, so she turned it off and put it away. She took a deep breath.

And then another deep breath. She could feel her pulse racing. No, not nerves, but adrenaline. A touch of danger was no bad stimulant, so long as you kept a level head. *Remember who you are,* she told herself, *and who you're pretending you are. And remember you're only pretending.*

She knocked.

And waited, like yesterday, for what seemed an age. Maybe he was in the shower again, or on the phone. There was still time to walk away. All she had to do was turn around and –

'Grace, is that you?'

'Yes.'

The click of the door unlocking from the other side.

'It's open. Come in.'

She pushed open the door and almost walked into him. He was standing immediately inside the door, with a bottle of champagne and a fizzing glass in his hand.

'A bit early, I know, but what the hell?'

He topped up the glass and handed it to her. He picked up another glass from the table and saluted her.

'Here's hoping we don't get interrupted this time.'

'Yes. What exactly was all that about?'

'You tell me. Crazy guys, your police. But hey, let's not talk about that now.'

He put down his glass and came over to her, slow and easy. He smiled, but there was a predatory hardness in his eyes.

'Why don't you take off your coat?' he said.

He was wearing a black T-shirt and matching jeans. He didn't look like he was in a hurry.

'Didn't you say we had a plane to catch?'

'We do. But maybe not quite so early as I said.'

'Oh, really?'

He took the glass from her and came behind her. He slipped off her coat and draped it across a chair. He turned her by the shoulders to face him.

'I didn't want you to waste any time getting here,' he said.

'You're not wasting any time now, are you?'

She glanced down at his fingers, unbuttoning her blouse. His other hand had found the zip of her skirt.

'Never did see the point in hanging back when you know what you want,' he said.

She stepped out of her skirt. He picked her up and kissed her hard. She wrapped her legs round his waist as he carried her across the room. He lowered them both into the well of the sofa. She listened to his heavy breathing, in rhythm with her own. She lifted her hips as he pulled off her knickers.

'And I know exactly what I want,' he said, unbuckling his belt.

She pushed his hands away and finished unbuckling it for him. She yanked down his jeans and underpants and pulled him urgently towards her. She said:

'I want you too.'

180

9

The blinds were drawn so tight that only the tiniest sliver of natural light penetrated the room. The harsh white spill from the big spot lamp made the faces of the three men sitting around the desk seem bleached and characterless.

'As I see it, we have two options, neither of them attractive,' said Dent. 'I propose to state them for the record and then to open up the discussion. Agreed, gentlemen?'

The others nodded their approval. Dent cleared his throat and pressed the switch on the cassette deck on his desk.

'Record of a meeting held on Sunday, 16 September at 16.15. Present: Head of Department, DCS Challoner and Inspector Corliss. Postscript to Operation Ace. It would appear that at approximately midday, today, Grace Cornish was contacted personally by Michael Gallagher. He requested that she join him at his hotel and fly with him to France, as per the agreement made between them on Saturday. Cornish attempted to contact DCS Challoner by phone, but he was in a meeting and unable to take her call. She left a message stating that, entirely on her own initiative, she was intending to join Gallagher. A recording of that message is in her file. According to our inquiries, Gallagher and Cornish were both booked on today's 15.30

Air France flight from Heathrow to Nice, travelling first class. They are airborne as we speak. We are currently considering two options.

'Option one. We revive Operation Ace, officially suspended as of this morning. This would entail mounting a secondary operation, in France. As this is outside our jurisdiction it would have to be mounted on an unofficial basis and would be limited strictly to surveillance. There would be no possibility of action on French soil. In the light of this, the usefulness of such an operation in the event of Cornish being compromised must be questionable.

'Option two. We do nothing. I wish to state plainly at this juncture that it is not the policy of this department to abandon agents working in the field. At the same time it must be clearly understood that this policy can only apply to agents working under instruction.

'A third option has been aired in prior discussion: to inform the French authorities of Cornish's action and to suggest a co-operative venture. This option, although superficially attractive, must be discounted both for practical and political reasons. Firstly, Cornish's actions are unauthorized. Although we may assume that she will attempt to contact us again, we have no agreed communications protocol. The reputation for the competence of this department, already seriously undermined, may suffer permanent damage if we involve ourselves in a joint venture where we have no control over our own agent. Secondly, the French are notoriously prickly on issues of sovereignty and – quite understandably – may react angrily to any admission that a British agent, whether authorized or not, is working without agreement on their territory. Thirdly, we have no information as to the extent of the penetration, if any, of the relevant French official agencies by Martinez, Rostov, or any other criminal factions. As we cannot vouchsafe the security procedures of these French agencies, we cannot risk divulging information that may imperil the safety of Grace Cornish. I would therefore invite you, gentlemen, to consider options one and two only.'

Dent sat back in his chair, his eyes on Challoner. He ignored Corliss, as he usually did. The gap in rank, and responsibility, clearly defined his presence at the meeting as a token.

'We haven't the resources, even if we had the will, to commit ourselves to an extended operation,' said Bob Challoner. 'Seeing as it was me who introduced Cornish into the set-up I feel I bear an added responsibility. In my view she has put us to enough trouble already. She had no business agreeing to go with Gallagher. I won't buy any suggestion that she was worried about maintaining her cover. She's quick-witted enough to have come up with an excuse to fob him off, particularly in the light of Saturday night's events, which it's reasonable to suppose could have furnished her with sufficient reasons to decline his invitation. She could also have arranged to refund him his money, if that was an issue. Therefore I favour option two. I agree with you that the idea of abandoning an agent in the field sticks in the gullet, but Cornish is not, repeat not, an operative agent. This department is in no position to support freelance grandstanding. The situation might be different if WPC Dixon was still in the field, but I understand that she has now reported back to duty. For the record, Inspector Corliss might like to confirm this point.'

'Yes, sir. Dixon was discovered on the Albert Embankment by a police patrol vehicle at 04.30 hours this morning. She was unconscious. An ambulance was summoned and she was conveyed to St Thomas's Hospital. Acute alcohol poisoning was diagnosed. Her stomach was pumped. She briefly regained consciousness and became delirious, at which point she was given a sedative. She was carrying no identification. At approximately 13.30 hours she became conscious again. Shortly afterwards she borrowed a cell-phone and sent a text message to the operational number. I was sent to interview her. Dixon stated that she had been violently ill in the helicopter on Saturday night. That Orhan had verbally and physically abused her during the flight and had abandoned her. She remembered being in a cab. She thinks the cabbie threw her out after she was sick in his vehicle. She said she couldn't remember anything else. Apart from minor cuts and bruises and the aftereffects of alcohol she appears to be in reasonable condition. She discharged herself from hospital at my request and I accompanied her to the mews house in Bayswater, where she is awaiting further interrogation. She is officially on duty.'

'Thank you, Corliss,' said Dent. 'It would appear that standards of conduct in the course of this operation have fallen below an acceptable level. I agree with DCS Challoner's assessment that this department bears no responsibility for Cornish's actions. We cannot be expected to extricate her, should the occasion arise, from a situation which she has created for herself without sanction. Nor, as far as I can see, would there be any benefit in shadowing Gallagher. After last night's events I think we can safely assume that Martinez will have gone to ground for the foreseeable future. We can also assume that he will cover his tracks in his usual manner. As we have no interest in Gallagher except as a conduit to Martinez the value of continued surveillance at this juncture is doubtful. Given these circumstances, I am at a loss to understand Cornish's motivation in setting off on this wild-goose chase. Have you any thoughts on this, Bob?'

'Possibly, sir. Could be she's trying to redeem herself. She knows she screwed up badly, and she thinks this'll be a way of getting back into our good books. Maybe she's frightened that we'll go back on our word and refuse to stop the prosecution. She may also have been stung by my accusation that she bottled it. She's proud and very stubborn, and wants to show us that she really can handle it.'

'Mm. I suppose if Cornish keeps her ears and eyes open she may even learn something useful. Dmitri Rostov's got a place in the South of France, hasn't he?'

'Several, I believe, sir.'

'Gallagher took the last girl, Natalie, to meet Rostov, didn't he?'

'We're not sure. All she knows is that she spent an afternoon with some Russians on a yacht in Cannes. She didn't remember any names. It may have been Rostov's, but there's no way of knowing. The Riviera is crawling with Russians with yachts.'

'All legitimate businessmen, naturally. This Gallagher certainly seems to know some unsavoury people. If Cornish does hear something I assume she'll be able to communicate through the usual channels.'

'There's a problem with that, sir.'

'What problem, Corliss?'

'The phone isn't programmed to send or receive outside the UK. It can be reprogrammed, but Miss Cornish doesn't know how to do that. We didn't include it in the training, for obvious reasons.'

'Well, she'll have to find a payphone, won't she? You know, all this may actually have a beneficial side effect. We wouldn't use Cornish again, under any circumstances, but at least her cover is intact. Say that Gallagher sticks with the same pattern in future, hiring a girl every time he visits London. If we give ourselves a proper lead-in time, select and properly train the right operatives, we could get another crack at Martinez some time down the line. It might be wishful thinking, but from the flak we've been getting from Rostov's lawyer it appears that he thinks last night's raid was aimed at him. Not an entirely illogical supposition, bearing in mind the number of criminal tills he's got his fingers in. I'm willing to bet that it hasn't even occurred to anyone that we were really after Martinez.'

'You may be right, sir.'

'If I am, Bob, it may just be a question of waiting till the heat dies down before taking another pop at Martinez on the same terms. After all, there was nothing wrong with the basic plan, was there? No, the plan was sound, we simply had problems with the personnel. At least we know a little more about the people Rostov associates with. Is there any word on the German chappie, Bob?'

'Turns out he's Dutch, sir. Sammy de Boer. Owns night-clubs and strip joints in Germany and Holland. Suspected drug dealer, known to Interpol, but no convictions. He flew back to Schiphol this afternoon. I've asked my Dutch contacts to keep an eye on him. I mentioned the Rostov connection. They were very interested.'

'I bet they were. You didn't say anything about Martinez, I take it?'

'Not a word.'

'Excellent. Despite the monumentalness of last night's cock-up we may yet have some cautious grounds for optimism. Is there anything else on the agenda? Bob?'

'I think we've covered all the angles.'

'Good. Well, that about wraps it up then, gentlemen. In the case of WPC Dixon I shall be recommending a reprimand. In the circumstances that is sufficient. In Grace Cornish's case there's no avenue for disciplinary procedure and to invent one could prove legally unenforceable. Provided she makes a full statement on the lines she agreed last night immediately on her return from France I shall propose that we draw a veil over the matter. How long did Gallagher book her for?'

'Four days.'

'Then she should be back by Wednesday. I hope for her

sake she keeps her head screwed on. We all know that women find it impossible to separate sex from emotion. That's why the classic East German honeytraps were so successful. The Stasi's biggest successes came when they used male agents to seduce impressionable females. And that, gentlemen – not Mata Hari – is the paradigm.'

'Very succinctly expressed, sir.'

'Thanks, Bob. Miss Cornish has made her own bed, literally. Let her lie in it. Alert me the moment she makes contact, Bob. We need to get the paperwork tidied up on this.'

'I will, sir.'

'Good. If there's nothing else, I shall say meeting adjourned. At 16.32. Good afternoon, gentlemen. Take this to Harrington, will you, Corliss, and ask her to put Ryan on standby.'

Dent turned off the cassette recorder and ejected the tape. Corliss took it to the small office down the corridor where Sergeant Harrington worked.

'Type up these minutes as soon as possible, Harrington. And tell Ryan Mr Dent wants him now.'

'Yes, sir.'

Sgt Harrington spoke into the microphone fitted to her desk.

'Easy 5, Easy 5.'

'Easy 5,' replied Ryan's voice over the radio.

'HoD requests standby. Over.'

'Understood, Jackie. Over and out.'

Sgt Harrington turned back to her computer screen and opened a new file. She inserted the tape into her recorder, adjusted her earphones, and commenced the transcription.

Five minutes later Dent left the building. Ryan was ready and waiting at the wheel of the Jaguar. Dent was pleased it was the Jaguar. Ryan changed the cars around on a regular basis in accordance with departmental procedure, but neither the Toyota nor the Rover came near to the Jaguar's standard of comfort.

'Home, Ryan,' Dent ordered when he had settled down in the back.

Traffic was light, the journey to Notting Hill would take only about fifteen minutes. Plenty of time to make his calls. Dent took his phone from his briefcase and typed in his password. The phone was fitted with the latest MoD encryption software and was perfectly secure. He spoke first to the Commissioner. He explained the situation with the Cornish woman and outlined his proposed course of action. The Commissioner accepted his recommendation, as usual. Next he phoned the Minister and got through to his private secretary, who happened to be a contemporary from university.

'It's all a frightful balls-up, Reggie,' he said, 'but I think there's a chance we can still come out of it smelling of roses. The important thing is to pay no attention to the flak from the drug squad and all those other police sects. You'll have my interim report first thing in the morning. Can I depend on you?'

Reggie assured him that he could be depended upon. Reggie then changed the subject. He spoke about a forthcoming dinner at Claridges and the need to make a positive impression on a visiting Commonwealth dignitary. Dent agreed to be on hand to discuss his experience of bringing Balkan war criminals to justice before the Hague tribunal. They exchanged greetings to each other's wives. They hoped they would be able to do Glyndebourne next year.

Dent ended the conversation as they turned into Pemberton Gardens. He put away the phone and locked it into his case. The car pulled into a conveniently vacant parking bay outside his house.

'See you tomorrow, Ryan.'

'I'm not on duty tomorrow, sir.'

'Oh yes, of course. Your daughter's birthday party. See you the day after tomorrow then.'

'Actually, I was wondering if it would be convenient for me to take a couple more days off, sir. I've two weeks' leave due which I'm going to have to take before the end of next month.'

'I can't spare you for two weeks.'

'A few days is all I need, sir.'

'If I say report back for duty on Thursday, will that give you enough time?'

'Should be plenty, sir.'

'All right. If the leave is due to you then you must take it. We have all your contact numbers, I take it? Thursday it is, then.'

'Thank you very much, sir.'

It was part of Ryan's standing instructions to wait until Dent had entered the house. The moment the front door had closed he executed a swift three-point turn. He drove back the way he had come and was in Southwark again in twenty-five minutes. He went straight up to the top floor and checked discreetly that all the other rooms were unoccupied before entering Harrington's office. She seemed surprised to see him.

'What are you doing here, John? He's not come back for something, has he?'

Ryan shook his head. He removed some papers from the only other chair in the room and sat down.

'Don't worry, Jackie. He won't be throwing any more typing at you tonight.'

She pulled a face. She indicated her tape recorder.

'Thank God for that. I've only just finished this lot. They don't really understand the concept of weekends, do they?'

'No. I'm going to make some coffee. Want some?'

'That depends.'

'On what?'

'On what you want.'

She crossed her arms and stared at him stonily. It would have been a forbidding expression had it not been for the sly smile creasing the corners of her mouth. It would have come as quite a surprise to anyone in the department to realize that Sergeant Harrington had a profoundly irreverent streak and a mischievous sense of humour, but then again none of her superiors had ever made the slightest attempt to engage her in conversation. Harrington was a workhorse and a dogsbody, and, since she was the only woman in the building, also an all-purpose domestic. Not that her sex was much taken into account. Her plainness and her bulk had discouraged even the most harmless expression of flirtatiousness. No one could even be bothered to be civil to her.

No one except Ryan. None of the others would have even dreamt of offering her a coffee. Or of wanting to know her name. Theirs was the only relationship in the office where both parties were on first-name terms. She revelled in it, and he tolerated it. He had never liked his own first name.

'I want a favour,' he said.

'As if I didn't know,' she said. 'What favour?'

'I'd like to take a quick look at what you've been typing.'

'It's classified, John. You know I can't let you look at it.'

'I wonder. Is it technically classified until it's signed and filed?'

'Don't try and blind me with science.'

'It's important, Jackie. I wouldn't ask otherwise.'

'Why do you want to see it?'

'I need to know something. Out of curiosity.'

'You could get me into a lot of trouble.'

'Only if someone found out. And who's going to find out?'

'Humph.'

She stared at him in silence for a good few seconds, to make sure he understood that she disapproved. She pushed her chair back from the desk and stood up.

'Isn't it my turn to make the coffee? I shan't be long. Don't you go mucking about with my computer when I'm out of the room.'

'Would I ever?'

As soon as she had gone he sat down in her seat. The transcribed document was the only one open on the computer screen. He read it thoroughly. It took Jackie Harrington a remarkably long time to make two cups of instant coffee.

'I brought some biscuits too,' she said when she came back, bearing a tray. 'Afraid we're out of the chocolate Hobnobs.'

He nibbled on a plain digestive and took a few token sips of his drink.

'Sorry I can't stay longer, Jackie, I'm in a bit of a rush,' he said, putting down his three-quarters-full cup. 'I can't tell you how grateful I am.'

'For what?' she enquired innocently.

'For the coffee, of course,' he answered in kind.

He took the service lift down to the ground floor and jumped into the Jaguar. He checked his watch and did some calculations. He reckoned he could afford to give himself another two hours in town.

He drove north-west once again, following the same route he always took to Dent's house. This time, though, he turned off early at the Bayswater Road. He parked up in the mews and checked the other cars. None of them was familiar.

He let himself into the house using the second key he should have already returned. It was gloomy inside and the lights were all off on the ground floor. He climbed the stairs, slowly and quietly. The landing was also dark, but a strip of light showed under the door of the far bedroom. He knocked loudly.

'Who the bloody hell's that?' she demanded in a shrill voice.

He pushed open the door and showed her his face.

'Jesus, Ryan. What the hell are you doing going around like a cat burglar?'

She was sitting up in bed, the covers to her knees, wearing a nightdress and a cardigan over her shoulders. The bedside table was covered in packets of pills and cigarettes. An overfull ashtray had spilt some of its contents on to the floor. Her face was white. She looked dreadful.

'Mind if I sit down?' he said.

She nodded. The only chair was covered with her clothes. He sat down on the other bed, the one Grace had used.

'What do you want?' she said, clasping her knees with her hands, huddling herself up like the small frightened child she was.

'I need to ask you some questions,' he said.

'I already told Corliss what I know,'

'I'm not asking on their behalf, Jeanette. I want to know because I think it might help Grace.'

'Where is she?'

'France.'

'What's she doing there?'

'I think she went to rescue you. She thought you might be there.'

'Oh my God.'

She slumped forward, her head falling into her raised knees. Her voice was dull with misery.

'You mean she's gone with Gallagher?'

'Yes.'

'When?'

'This afternoon.'

'So if I hadn't been out of it this morning and had

reported in in time I might have been able to stop her. Thanks, Ryan, I feel really great for knowing this.'

'I want you to think hard, Jeanette. I know your memory's not going to be very clear, but try and remember, will you? Not for me, for Grace.'

'Remember what?'

'Grace said she thought Orhan might want you for another few days.'

'Yeah, well, when I puked up all over him he had second thoughts.'

'Grace thought she might run into you out there, in France. Did Orhan say anything about where he was going?'

'I don't know.'

'Think. Tell me anything he said.'

'I can't remember.'

'Think.'

'I'm trying.'

'Try harder.'

She hit her forehead with the heel of her hand. When that didn't help she lit a cigarette. She took a few deep puffs.

'Was there anything about a yacht?' asked Ryan.

'Yeah ... A boat, yeah, there was a boat. I ... damn, I'm trying to think. It was in the helicopter, when we were leaving the house. I was already feeling sick, and the engine was so noisy. He said – he wasn't talking to me – something like, "Maybe see you on the boat next week."'

'Who was he talking to? One of the Rostovs?'

'No. The blond guy.'

'Sammy?'

'Yeah. Orhan said, "See you on the boat. And the guy said, "No, I won't be there." And Orhan said see you ... someplace else then, some other name, I can't remember what.'

'That's not a lot of help.'

'I know, I know. Look, it was hard to understand Orhan at the best of times. He and the other guy were fooling around. They were joking about skiing.'

'Skiing?'

'Yeah, Sammy said, "Well I don't go there for the skiing," something like that – this was the other place they were talking about – and Orhan thought it was really funny. Then Sammy said he was glad they were all friends and hoped they'd have a good time on the boat. That was all. Honestly, I can't remember anything else.'

Ryan got up and walked to the window. He stared out across a row of high-walled narrow gardens, the spaces between the bricks lost in the late afternoon shadows.

'Are you Grace's friend?' he said quietly.

'Hang on, what the –?'

'Just tell me if she's your friend.'

Something in his voice stopped her protesting again. She nodded sullenly.

'Yeah, she's my friend.'

'Good. Because she's going to need all the friends she can get. Will you promise me something? It's very simple.'

'What?'

'Don't tell anyone that I've been here. Not a word to a soul. Promise?'

'Why? Are you doing something you shouldn't be doing?'

'Not yet.'

He got up. Jeanette stubbed out her cigarette.

'I really fucked up, didn't I?'

Ryan shook his head.

'It wasn't your fault. And don't let them convince you it was. Stand up to them.'

'I'd like to. The way Grace does. Is she going to be all right?'

'Yeah. She's going to be fine.'

He wasn't sure that she believed him, and he wasn't sure

that he believed it either. He checked his watch. It was coming up to six o'clock. Grace was already in France.

'I've got to go, Jeanette. Remember, not a word to anyone.'

From the mews he drove south, across the river again but this time headed west. He drove from Battersea to Wandsworth and parked in the forecourt of a small nondescript modern block. For the last five months, since Dent had recruited him, he had been living on the top floor.

It was nominally a two-bedroom flat, but the smaller bedroom was piled high with the motley collection of junk which he had acquired in different parts of the world during the last twenty years and which gave him the nearest sensation he thought he was ever again likely to get to domestic stability. That most of his stuff was in packing cases in no way lessened the illusion. The fact that it was there should he ever need it meant that he was happy to call the place home.

He lifted his two big heavy kitbags out from under some stacks of papers trussed in plastic bin liners and carried them through to the living room. He laid out clothes and equipment and made a preliminary selection as he rang Directory Enquiries and obtained the numbers of the ferry companies. He made a booking at the first attempt, securing a cabin on the ten o'clock sailing from Dover to Calais. He was going to be driving through the night and needed to get a couple of hours of decent sleep.

His next call was to the office. To his relief Jackie was still there.

'I've got to leave some numbers where I may be in the next few days,' he explained. 'Don't have them all at the moment, but I'll call you later on your mobile. Leave it switched on tonight, will you?'

'I'll switch it on now so I don't forget.'

'Thanks, love.'

He put down the receiver, gave it ten, and then called her mobile.

'Me again. I need to ask a favour.'

All office calls, incoming and outgoing, were automatically recorded, although no one except Dent was meant to know that. Fortunately Dent's own standards of security were rather lower than he customarily demanded, a fact for which his keen-eared chauffeur was especially grateful.

'You and your favours, John. I don't know.'

While she tut-tutted he asked her if she would be so good as to access the Criminal Records Bureau. He heard the click-click of the keys as she tapped into the online national databank. He knew that she had only low-level clearance, but he hoped that it would be sufficient to get him the intelligence he was after.

'I want the file on Dmitri Rostov, Jackie.'

'Oh, I don't need to go into records for that. The file's on my desk.'

He clenched his fist at his reflection in the mirror over the mantelpiece.

'Known addresses, that's all I'm after. Anything in the South of France.'

'Hang on a sec. OK. I've got an apartment in Cannes, a hotel in Nice it says he has a suspected interest in, a villa near Frejus—'

'The villa. Is there much information?'

'Quite a bit. Photographs. A floor plan. Looks like it comes from an estate agent's brochure. I'm not sure, my French isn't good enough. This is shared intelligence from the Interpol computer. Lots of photographs, diagrams. Tons of those. Think this is the floor plan of a boat. Yes, it is.'

'What sort of a boat?'

'A ruddy big one. Called the *Pugachev*. Listen to this: "The glass elevator conveys guests directly from the helipad to the VIP staterooms. There is sufficient parking space in the hold for four cars . . ."'

'A ruddy big one, as you say.'

'It says here it's being refitted. In Kiel, Germany. Hang on, there's another one. The *Anastasia*, a ninety-foot luxury racing yacht.'

'Where's that?'

'Moored at his villa, it says here.'

'Are you going to be at the office much longer?'

'An hour at least.'

'Wait for me, will you? I need a copy of that stuff.'

'What are you up to, John boy?'

'Just satisfying my curiosity. See you in an hour.'

It didn't leave him much time. He was going to have to be brutally short with his next call, a prospect that did nothing to relieve the symptoms of guilt he was already experiencing. He steeled himself and dialled his daughter's number. Her answering machine came on, which made it easier but made him feel worse.

'I'm sorry, darling, but something's come up and I don't think I'm going to be able to make tomorrow. I'm really, really sorry. I know you'll be disappointed and I know I'm letting you down again, but there's nothing I can do about it. I'll make it up to you. Promise. Have a good one. Love you.'

He was looking at the photographs on the mantelpiece as he spoke, painfully aware of how unconvincing he sounded. Ever since he could remember he had been letting down his family. His eyes lit on his favourite photograph of her. It had been taken on the beach when she was twelve, the last summer they had been together as a family. The holiday had been make-or-break, Jane had given him fair warning. She was sick, the kids were sick, even he was sick of never being there, of being the world's worst husband and father. It had been no good him telling her that his near-permanent state of absence had been part of the deal when she married him, because the deal had palpably got much worse as his career progressed. Hence the make-or-break, the last of her many ultimatums. It had been break.

Selfish and single-minded, how Jane had always described him. He couldn't deny it. Still, the single-mindedness came in handy.

He couldn't make his next phone call from memory. It took him a while to find the number, scribbled almost illegibly into the back of last year's diary. When an old woman answered he wondered if he'd got the right place.

'Could I speak to Johny, please?' he said slowly.

The old woman replied, not so slowly, in French.

'Is Johny there, please? Do you speak English?'

There was a thump as the receiver was thrown down at the other end. He heard the old woman's voice, in the distance, calling out. After a long pause the receiver was picked up again.

'Who is talking, please?' asked a young woman's voice in heavily accented English.

'I'm after Johny Suchet, please.'

'He's not here. Who are you?'

Her tone of voice was brusque, no-nonsense. He thought she sounded like a woman who could make life tough if she took against you.

'My name's Ryan,' he said.

There was a brief pause at the other end.

'You are Ryan? I know about you, Ryan.'

'If you're Anne-Marie then I know a bit about you too.'

'Well then, we know everything about each other.'

She laughed. He could picture her. She had been laughing in the photograph Johny had shown him, her pretty nut-brown face split from ear to ear, her huge almond eyes bright with merriment. Beautiful, isn't she? Johny would say, nudging him, grinning. *Elle est belle, n'est-ce pas? Oui, elle est très belle,* he would answer in his bad, clumsy French.

'Johny's out with the guys from his old unit tonight, he won't be back for hours. Can I get him to call you?'

'Can you give him a message? Tell him I'd like to see him. I need his help.'

'You are coming here?'

'I'm catching a ferry tonight. I can get to you by early morning.'

'You will stay with us?'

'I can't stay, I've got urgent business to attend to. You're at the address I've got here?'

'Rue Michel.'

'That's what I've got. Johny'll be there in the morning?'

'For you, Ryan, he will be anywhere you say. Come soon, I want to meet you.'

'I'm on my way now.'

It was almost literally true. The minutes were being eaten up, and another detour to Southwark was going to swallow up the last of his margin. He selected gear from both kit-bags and repacked it in one of them, leaving the rest of his stuff all over the floor. He opened his bedside cabinet and took out his passport and driving licence. He took off his shoulder holster and stowed his 9mm Browning in the bottom.

He went into his bedroom and pulled out the drawer at the bottom of the wardrobe. He lay down on the floor and extended his arm into the gap, feeling along the base of the wardrobe. His fingers brushed the holster of his spare gun. He left it in place. Tempted as he was, it was hardly sensible to take either of his officially-issued handguns into a foreign country. His fingers closed round a large brown envelope that was taped to the wood. He ripped it out.

Inside was a cellophane packet containing a roll of fifty hundred-dollar bills. He put the lot into his inside pocket.

He gave the flat a quick last check. Windows locked, answering machine on. He dropped the keys of the Jaguar on to the table and picked up the keys to his own Rover. He shouldered his kitbag.

Six hours later he was in France.

PART TWO

10

The sky, she could see, was a perfect blue, and the sunlight had a different quality, not just brighter – that went without saying – but much, much yellower. Even inside, in the cool shade, the whiteness of the sheets, framed in the stream of brightness pouring through the window, was almost blinding. She turned over in the bed, one eye open, the sun like a warm hand resting on her bare back. The other side of the bed was empty.

She pushed herself up by her forearms and squinted into the corners of the room. It was deeply in shadow and she could see nothing for the spots dancing in front of her eyes, but she sensed there was no one there. The door to the other part of the suite was open and she saw no sign of movement there either. She called softly.

'Mike?'

No, he wasn't next door. She flopped back on to the pillows, letting the drowsiness seep back. It was too warm, too delicious to move. She would lie like a salamander, all day, the soft deep bed her rock. And then, in the evening, he would come back.

The dullness in her head cleared. She rolled over and sat up, kicking off the sheet that was bunched round her shins, her only covering. Her eyes had adjusted, now she could see clearly the state of the room. She saw the empty bottle in the champagne bucket, the glasses on the floor, the glass they'd broken glinting at her from the bottom of the over-turned wastebasket. She remembered scrabbling around on the floor for the slivers of glass, him not helping much, quite the contrary, making her giggle, dragging her away, laying her down on the bed. Who needs a glass? he said, pouring the champagne over her, licking it out from her navel, emptying the bottle, his head travelling lower. Then her taking the bottle from him, reciprocating. Had they really done that, like the stars of their own blue movie? Oh yes, and more. She could feel the stickiness still on her belly, see the evidence of debauchery all around: the rum-pled sheets, the ripped condom packets and the heap of tis-sues on the bedside table, the clothes on the floor. Some of his clothes anyway. Hers were in the other room, mostly on the rug by the door where he had torn them off her the second the porter had gone out, hardly even waiting for the click of the closing lock. Sex on the rug, and on the couch, then up against the wall on the way to the bed-room, finally in the bed itself, though not before he had bent her over the back of the chair in front of the long wall mirror. Was there anywhere they hadn't done it last night, anything they hadn't tried? No wonder she had slept like a log.

She got out of bed and swayed giddily as the blood rushed from her head. At least she didn't have a hangover, which was something of a miracle considering the amount she'd drunk. There was a second empty bottle standing next to the one in the ice bucket, and she had a strong suspicion that there was the remains of a third somewhere next door. Her mouth felt dry, but there was no other evidence of alcoholic excess. Something to do, she suspected, with the price of the champagne.

She walked unsteadily to the en suite bathroom and contemplated herself in the mirror over the sink. In the unnatural light her naked body looked like raw veal. Her hair was a messy tangle, her eyes, last night's make-up unremoved and irredeemably smudged, like holes in a coal bucket. A good thing he wasn't around then, or he'd be demanding a refund. She poured a glass of water from the tap and slaked her thirst. She splashed more water over her face.

'Who's been a naughty girl then?' she said to herself in the mirror.

Naughty was putting it mildly, a seaside postcard reproof. Not the right word at all. She'd been a lot worse than naughty. Wicked, sinful, a scarlet woman. A whore.

She stared at herself in the mirror. She shrugged.

She removed her vampiric make-up and climbed into the shower. She washed away her sweat, and his, the smell of sex. So much for the escape routes she had lined up in her head yesterday. Find Jeanette, then sneak away, her virtue intact . . . Well, that had been blown out of the water before they'd even left England, back in the Concorde Suite. Of course she'd gone along with it, what else could she have done? And once the die was cast, she had had to play the part to the hilt. Hadn't she?

She finished in the shower and dried herself off. She put on the white towelling dressing gown that was hanging on the back of the door and walked through the bedroom on to the balcony.

She had no idea of the time but the sun was high. The silver glare of it on the sea was too much for the naked eye. Her sunglasses were in her coat, wherever that was. She turned away from the sun and caught a delicious waft of cool breeze. She could see the flags outside the hotels all down the promenade rippling with it. Far down below, outside her own hotel, uniformed porters were unloading luggage from an open-topped red Ferrari. She leant over the balcony railing and watched her sleek, half-naked fellow guests pass in and out. The cafés, the streets, the seafront and the beach hugging the long curve of the bay were all packed with sleek, half-naked people. Hedonism, like the sun haze, shimmered in the air. She closed her eyes against the brightness and faced out to sea again, tanning her face.

She thought: *I could get used to this.*

An image of Alan popped into her head. She pictured his face. It was an effort. Would she have preferred to be sharing that big bed next door with him tonight? She knew the answer to that even before she had finished asking herself the question. In her mind's eye she could see only Mike Gallagher's lean, muscular body.

Another thought: *Just what the doctor ordered . . .*

She heard a sound behind her. She stepped into the bedroom and saw movement in the other room. He called her name.

'Here,' she said, appearing at the bedroom door.

He was dressed in shorts, a T-shirt and sandals, towel over his shoulder, sunglasses perched on top of his head, his cellphone in his hand. He wasn't alone. A porter was wheeling a trolley in from the outside corridor and behind him came a couple of chambermaids carrying cardboard boxes.

'Figured you could maybe use some of this –' he said, waving the porter in. The intoxicating smells of fresh coffee and bread filled the room. The maids put the boxes down on the chaise longue. He indicated the mess in the room with an airy wave and suggested they come back later to clear up. He handed out generous tips from a wad of notes and the three of them departed, kowtowing furiously.

'How'd you like your coffee?'

'Strong and dark,' she said.

Like my men, she thought, but didn't say. It made her

smile, though. She watched him as he poured the coffee. His bare arms and thighs were beautifully tanned and smooth with muscle. Would he want to take her back to bed after breakfast? She could think of worse ways to pass the day.

'Sugar?' he asked.

She shook her head. He handed her a large cup of black coffee and a plate of croissants. She bit greedily into the soft flaky pastry, aware suddenly that she was ravenous. She smeared the croissant with one of the jams laid out on the tray, wolfed it down and started on another. He put the boxes on the floor and sat beside her on the chaise longue.

'I like a girl with a healthy appetite,' he said.

'You've got pretty healthy appetites yourself,' she answered. 'Have a nice swim?'

He smiled and ran a hand through his damp hair.

'The pool's great, you should try it.'

'I'll have to get a bathing costume.'

'Oh, that can be arranged,' he said carelessly.

He reached for one of the boxes and untied the red ribbon across the top. His fingers rustled in tissue paper for a moment before emerging with the strap of a yellow bikini top.

'*Voilà*. I wasn't sure about the colour, but it's easy to change if you don't like it.'

'I love it,' she assured him. 'Hope it's the right size.'

'I looked in your suitcase while you were asleep. I got all your sizes.'

'Even my hat size?'

'Maybe not that.'

'Glove?'

'OK, OK. Not all your sizes, but enough.'

'What's in the other boxes?'

'Eat your breakfast first. I don't want you to get jam everywhere.'

She finished her croissant and wiped her fingers on a napkin. He opened a second box and peeled back sheets of crepe before handing it to her.

'For tonight,' he said.

She lifted a red silk dress from the wrapping and held it up to her body. It was low cut, the material indecently thin, and, although it reached most of the way to her knees, it was slit on the right side almost to the hip. She gave a wry smile.

'Doesn't leave much to the imagination, does it?'

'That's the idea. I want every eye on you tonight.'

'Where are we going?'

'Same place I always go. A guy's got to earn a living, even when he's got better things to do with his time. The tough part is the living doesn't get any easier. It's a bad idea to make a habit of winning in casinos, at least as far as they're concerned.'

'Do they think you're cheating?'

'Worse than that. They think I know what I'm doing. Blackjack, I'm talking about. I only play poker in private with certain people I either know or know about, ditto backgammon. I've never bet a cent on a roulette table in my life and I'm not about to start now. Blackjack's my casino game, and it's an easy game, as I told you. Play it right and over time you'll beat the bank, but the percentages are so small it's not worth the effort. That's why good players count cards. You understand the principle of that?'

She shook her head.

'OK, I want you to understand this. I'll keep it simple. Twenty-one is the magic number. Pictures are ten, the rest are face value, the ace is a special case, either one or eleven. Best combination is an ace and a picture, twenty-one on the nose, blackjack. The more pictures in the pack, the better the chance you have of making a winning hand, so the higher you make your bet. The odds are constantly shifting, but if you can keep a count of what cards are gone you can shift them in your favour. You with me? Good. Of course, the casinos make it as tough as they can. They use multiple decks and just when you're getting on top it's always time for a shuffle. In the States these days they use continuous shuffling machines, which is the end for guys like me, but in Europe it's more sedate, for now at any rate. That's not to say it's easy. The dealers are taught to work fast, so there's not much time to calculate. There's constant distraction, pressure, talk, noise – you saw Saturday night. It's hard to think and you can't afford to look as though you're thinking. They see you thinking too much, they know you're counting and you're out.'

'How can you count so many cards? Have you got a photographic memory?'

'You don't try and remember every single card, you keep what's called a running count. You want a resumé? OK. Small cards have a plus value, big cards are minus. You're constantly adjusting the total in your head as you go along, but all you have to keep in your head is a simple plus or minus digit. When the count's against you, you lower your bet. And vice versa. You've got to make allowances for the number of packs, but essentially that's all there is to it.'

'They throw you out for doing that? It's using your nous.'

'Not the way they see it. But I don't get thrown out these days, because I'm good. Unfortunately, one of the ways I'm good is that I stop before I make real money. I always get out after certain time limits, win or lose. I make a pretty good living, but I never make a killing. With you around, though, I've got a chance. Who's going to be watching me when you're in the frame?'

'Isn't that a bit obvious?'

'You're right. Very right. You really are smart, Grace, and that's why I think this'll work. I know it's obvious, I found out the hard way. I remember this one time I was asked to

leave a casino in Vegas. I put it that way, sounds as though
they were asking politely. They weren't. I couldn't believe it,
I'd had this lady at the table with me, very smart like you,
and almost as beautiful, and the pit boss had been all over
her. She did a great job, I sat there quietly making a stash.
But they still spotted me, because if there's one thing these
guys care more about than sex it's losing money. It's easy to
forget that in a casino sometimes, because there's more testos-
terone in the air than a singles bar on a Friday night, but
the bottom line is that if it comes down to a choice between
losing your shirt and getting laid there's no choice at all.'

'Why do you want me dressed up to the nines then?'

'Ah ha. That's the double whammy. You're the eye-candy,
but you're also one half of the team. You look like the
dumb blonde, but I'm the one acting the part. Don't worry,
we'll practise this afternoon, at a low-stakes table someplace else.'

'Practise what?'

'Winning money. Even though it's a simple game there's
still a few things I've got to teach you. Basic etiquette, how
to lay a bet, how to split, what to say when the dealer
offers you insurance, et cetera. Think you can handle it?'

'I've no idea.'

'I have. You needn't get involved if you don't want to,
it's not part of our deal. But I think you've got what it
takes. I think you're a hell of an actress.'

'I am?'

She looked at him with big innocent eyes that belied the
sudden quickening of her pulse.

'Oh yeah,' he said, relaxing back against the arm of the
chaise and giving her a long frank stare. She felt herself
begin to blush.

'You think I'm a fake?' she said, with a throwaway laugh.

'No, but you're pretty good at faking it. Maybe the best
I've ever seen.'

210

She felt the blush spread up through her cheeks. The sooner she got outside and gave herself a covering tan the better.

'You mean last night?' she said, leaning into the back of the chaise and trying to mirror his nonchalance. He nodded.

'Yeah. Last night and this morning some too, wasn't it? I don't know, I had better things to do than check the time.'

He glanced around the room, as if looking for mementoes of their debauchery. There were plenty to be had, from the pile of her underwear on the floor by the door to the champagne bottle lying on its side on the rug. He turned back and gave her one of his subtle knowing smiles. Her neck tingled with goosebumps.

'Who said I was faking?' she said.

He thought about it for a moment.

'If you weren't, then maybe you should be paying me.'

'Maybe.'

Her handbag was on the table. She withdrew the thick brown envelope and dropped it on to the chaise, between them.

'Want to call it quits?'

His smile grew fainter, more enigmatic than ever. He blinked lazily. The tiniest of reflexes, it seemed characteristic of him, a man always relaxed, never hurried, almost preternaturally in control. Even at the height of passion – last night, this morning and whenever – he had given the impression of holding something back.

'You want to terminate the contract?' he asked, not quite serious, not quite amused.

'Maybe renegotiate the terms,' she answered. 'You uncomfortable with the idea?'

He opened his hands.

'What idea, exactly?'

'Of being with a woman you haven't paid for.'

His hands stayed open, the palms opened out towards her, the fingers splayed and rigid. He sat very still.

'You seem surprised,' she said.

'Who wouldn't be?' he replied. 'I never heard of a hooker who gave it away.'

'I've never been offered a partnership before.'

'Is that what I'm offering you?'

'You said I was one half of the team. Sounds like a partnership to me.'

'It does? So what are the terms?'

'Straight down the middle. Even split.'

'When I do the hard work?'

'When I give you the chance to make a killing.'

'Sounds like a hard bargain.'

'Is there any other kind?'

He laughed. It sounded genuine.

'Seventy–thirty,' he said. 'Unless you want to share the expenses?'

'Sixty–forty, unless you can find someone better.'

'Mm, I like your style.'

'I like yours.'

'I'm flattered.'

'It's not what I would have expected.'

'How do you mean?'

'Let's just say you're a cut above the average Scouser.'

'Hey, how do you know that?'

'What?'

'That I'm from Liverpool.'

'Isn't it obvious? Your accent.'

She laughed. He didn't join in.

'I've got a confession to make,' she said quickly.

'Yeah?'

'I've been talking about you. To a mutual friend.'

'I didn't know we had any.'

'Natalie. Don't tell me you've forgotten her already?'

'From your agency?'

'Yeah. When you booked me, Stan said Natalie had gone

212

with you last time. So I rang her to get the low-down. She said you sounded American but you were really English.'

'I told her I was from Liverpool?'

'You've got a British passport. She saw it when you went through Customs. Birthplace Liverpool.'

'Eagle-eyed, huh?'

'Yeah. She was kind of intrigued. So am I. When did you lose your accent?'

'That's a long story. What else did she tell you about me?'

'Girl talk.'

'Hey, come on. I've got to know.'

'She didn't go into details, she's very discreet.'

'You expect me to believe that?'

'Of course. And I'm very discreet too, that's part of the deal. But I'll tell you one thing she said that's for real.'

'What's that?'

'She said I'd earn my money.'

They exchanged a smile. He stretched and recrossed his legs. He stared past her shoulder, out of the window, screwing up his eyes against the glare of the sky. Thinking, apparently.

She took a deep breath. He seemed to have bought her explanation, but she'd had a nasty moment. Lucky she was such a smooth liar. She had been about to claim that she had noticed his passport details herself, but their passage through Customs yesterday would be fresh in his memory and she couldn't remember a moment when she might have had the opportunity. Putting the time-frame back a month or so was safer, and there was nothing unreasonable about two professional girls exchanging notes, was there? It didn't seem to have aroused his suspicions in any case. He looked very relaxed.

'Tell me something . . .' she said.

She didn't go on. She let the pause hang in the air, until he turned his head and looked back at her.

213

'Tell me, you ever have sex without paying for it first?'

'No. Sometimes I pay afterwards.'

'Don't avoid the question.'

'What is it you want to know?'

'Whether you ever have sex without paying.'

'No, I mean what do you really want to know?'

'Sorry?'

'You trying to put me on the psychiatrist's couch?'

'I'm just curious.'

'Am I paying you to be curious?'

There was a glassy edge to his voice, which she took as a warning to back off. She tried another tack.

'All I'm saying is that you don't have to pay at all. I bet plenty of women would love to swap places with me.'

'Didn't we go through this the other night?'

'We didn't get far.'

'There's no mystery about it. I like women, but I don't have time to chase them.'

'So it's convenience?'

'Sure.'

'You don't have a problem with relationships?'

'I don't have time for relationships.'

'And that's it?'

'Maybe.'

'And maybe not?'

'Maybe I like paying.'

'You mean you like to call the shots.'

'I won't deny that.'

'You think I won't give you what you want if you're not paying?'

She picked up the brown envelope and casually tossed it to his end of the chaise. The corner of one of the wads of fifties spilled out on to the leather.

'You trying to get yourself thrown out of the hookers' union?' he said.

214

'Hooker is such a cheap word.'

'I'm sorry. You're not cheap.'

She laughed lightly, as if to say, *the very idea* . . . He didn't respond. He looked at the money lying between them, and then back at her.

'You serious?'

'You're the expert on bluffing. Why don't you tell me?'

They stared at each other in silence, two poker faces vying for impenetrability. The silence lasted a minute, and would have lasted longer, had the ringing of his cellphone not disturbed it. He grunted into it.

'Hold on a second, will you?'

He put down the phone. He picked up the envelope and slipped the money that had half fallen out back inside. Carefully he closed the flap. He put the envelope into her handbag.

'OK, sixty–forty on any profits tonight. For the rest, I think we'll keep things as they are. Now, if you'll excuse me, I really must take this call.'

He carried the phone into the bedroom, picking up his laptop on the way. He closed the door behind him. Grace heard the key turn.

She had to put her hand to her mouth to stifle a giggle. She was astonished by her own audacity. She didn't know where this cool, incisive, erotically self-confident persona had come from, but the process of inhabiting it was exhilarating.

She got up and paced about the room. How much further could she take it? What if this scam in the casino worked out and they made a killing? The idea was almost unbearably exciting. What if he wanted to see her again? Her head was buzzing. She ought to calm down. She thought of Jeanette, of what she might be going through. It sobered her. She wasn't here for the kicks. She needed a reality check.

She sat down and drank another cup of coffee. She leant across the chaise and picked the three unopened boxes off the floor. The first contained a pair of high-heeled black shoes with a diamond-shaped diamanté pattern on the toe. A little too tarty for her taste, but probably perfect for the risqué dress. The second box contained a short white cotton dress with big buttons down the front that was obviously his idea of casual day wear suitable for this neck of the woods. A pair of plain cork-heeled sandals, banded together with a price tag still attached, had been placed in the bottom of the box. She turned to the third box, which was bigger and fancier than the others, decorated with black and gold diagonal stripes. She removed the lid and took out a tiny black nightdress, diaphanously thin and barely long enough to reach to her hips. There was more tissue paper underneath. She lifted it carefully aside and pulled out a black-and-red basque and a miniature thong. A pair of black fishnet stockings completed the ensemble.

Gallagher came out of the bedroom. Grace made a cat's cradle of a fishnet stocking.

'What kind of a girl do you take me for?'

'The kind I like.'

He came and sat on the raised arm of the chaise. He put down his phone.

'We've been asked to a party,' he said.

'Anyone we know?'

'A certain Mr Dmitri Rostov.'

'Oh yes, I do believe I've had the pleasure.'

'I do believe he'd like to.'

They exchanged the knowing smile of practised co-conspirators.

'Party's tomorrow,' he said. 'He wanted us to come over today but I said we were busy. So he said to come early, we can relax by the pool, maybe even go out in his boat.'

'He's got a boat?'

'He's got a fleet of boats. He loves his boats. Only time I ever see him go goofy and dewy-eyed is when he's talking about boats. You don't mind driving over, do you?'

'Of course not. Have you hired a car?'

'A Range Rover, they'll deliver it to the forecourt. In your name, you can sign the paperwork when it comes.'

'Ah, I would have enjoyed a Mercedes more.'

'Yeah, well, I got a good deal. You don't mind driving on your own, do you? I've got to see a guy in Grenoble before we go back, maybe have to meet up with you later.'

'No problem.'

'But I'll definitely be with you at Dmitri's. Don't think I dare leave you out on your own there. He liked you a lot.'

'He did?'

'Yeah. He wanted to make sure I'd be bringing you.'

'How flattering. Where's the party?'

'His place, about a half-hour down the coast.'

'Will there be anyone else there we know?'

'Well, yes. A Turkish gentleman. I don't think you two exactly hit it off last time you met.'

'I can't say I found him *sympathique*.'

'I'm afraid you probably won't like him much better this time. He dumped your friend.'

'Jeanette?'

'He was pretty mad at her, the way Dmitri tells it. Wanted to throw her out of the helicopter. Oh, don't worry, he didn't. Leastways not until they were on the ground. Seems she made a hell of a mess of Ralf's suit.'

'You mean she was airsick?'

'I think she was boozesick. Whatever, he decided to, er, dispense with her services.'

'I see. Where is she then?'

'Who knows? All I know is she ain't here. Look, I'm going to take a shower now, wash the chlorine out of my hair. Maybe you should think about getting dressed, then we'll get down to the casino in a little while.'

'Should I wear the dress?'

'No, no. That's for tonight. This is a dummy run. Make it casual. Like a tourist, whatever. I'm going as I am. See you in five.'

'See you.'

He went back into the bedroom. Through the gap in the door she watched him undress. He disappeared from view into the bathroom.

She rose from the chaise longue and picked last night's clothes from the floor. Her watch and earrings were on the telephone table in the corner. She carried all her things through into the bedroom.

She looked at the watch. It was half-past twelve. She looked around the room. Her suitcase was in the corner. Her bag, passport inside, was next to it. She walked to the bathroom and put her ear to the door. She heard the whoosh of the shower.

It would take her a minute to dress. In two minutes she could be in the lobby. There was a permanent queue of taxis outside the hotel, she could probably be in one before he got out of the shower. Say he took five minutes, then found she was gone. What could he do? Come after her to the airport? Then she would go to the station, find out where you caught the TGV to Paris, Eurostar back to London. She had five thousand pounds in cash, she could get the cabbie to stop at a bureau de change and then pay him to take her all the way home. She could do anything she wanted.

She stood quietly thinking it through, aware of the seconds ticking by, the tension growing in her stomach. Jeanette was out of it, Jeanette was safe. She had no reason to stay. No reason at all.

She slipped the white towelling robe from her shoulders

and let it fall to the floor. Naked, she contemplated the heap of clothes on the bed. Suddenly her legs were weak with nerves. No reason to stay. She could be back in sunny Guildford by the end of the day. She could be in her own bed tonight, alone. She could be Grace Cornish again tomorrow, and begin explaining herself to Mr Dent. She closed her eyes and took a deep breath.

She walked away from the bed. She opened the bathroom door. She saw his head turn to look at her through the Perspex shower box. She opened the door and stepped in.

She didn't say anything. She took the soap from him and lathered her hands. He tipped back his head against the tiles and let out a long contented sigh as her fingers slipped between his legs.

'What's this?' he said. 'The house special?'

She smiled. She pulled him towards her.

'It's the standard room service, sir.'

11

Ryan drove through the night, coming off the Autoroute du Soleil shortly after dawn, midway between Lyons and the coast. He had bought the biggest road map of France he could find on the ferry, but even at maximum scale it was hard to work out exactly which bit of twisty road went with which village. Nor, as he moved further away from the main highways, were the irregular signposts of much help, but, eventually, taking his bearings from the river valley to his left and the distinctive razor-back ridge to his right, he found the correct small road and, at the top of the hillside where it petered out, the correct village. The inside of the car was already beginning to bake in the early-morning sun as he slowly wound his way in low gear through a series of cobbled alleys that had been designed, if designed at all, with four-legged modes of transport in mind. Street signs were as rare as summer snowflakes, but fortunately all roads led into the village square, where the local épicier was obliging enough to break off from sorting through his aubergines and tomatoes for long enough to point out Rue Michel. Ryan decided he had had enough of clipping his wing mirrors. He parked in the square, in the shadow of a squat Roman church, and walked the rest of the way. As he turned the corner into Rue Michel he almost walked straight into Jean-Louis Suchet.

He was carrying a stack of empty beer crates, piled up so high in his thigh-thick arms that he couldn't see over the top. But Ryan didn't need to see his face to recognize him. He tapped him on the bicep, between the heart tattoo with Anne-Marie's name curling around it, and the small tricolor with the single word *legion* scripted beneath.

'*Salut*, Johny Silver.'

The beer crates clattered to the ground and Ryan felt himself lifted in a bear-hug so powerful that a full-grown grizzly might have blenched.

'Put me down, for Christ's sake, you don't know where I've been.'

Johny dropped him and took a step back, folding his arms and taking him in with a big appraising grin while Ryan ostentatiously rubbed his kidneys. Johny winked with his one good eye.

'It's not where you been I'm worried about, it's where the hell you think you're going,' he said in his fluent, bizarrely accented English.

He had been born in Marseilles, where he had picked up snatches of a dozen languages in the quayside bar run by his parents. Two years at sea, latterly under the command of a Glaswegian master mariner, had added richly to his store of profanity without much improving intelligibility. For six months afterwards he had travelled the United States, doing casual work to keep alive, before slipping quietly over the border and entering into a brief marriage of inconvenience with a fiery French-Canadian stripper. A brief stint on an Alaskan oilfield in the company of mono-syllabic oilmen, followed some time later by six months in the company of rather more loquacious Aussies on a Queensland sheep farm, had provided the finishing touches to his personalized phonetic brew. Somewhere along the line he had ceased being Jean-Louis and become Johny. He had also become a soldier, but that was another, longer story.

'Where I'm going now is to get some breakfast,' said Ryan, giving his friend a hand with the beer crates. 'Someone told me there was some lousy café down this part of town.'

'Lousy enough for you, my friend. Give me a hand with these and we'll go fill your belly.'

They stacked the crates up at the top of Rue Michel then walked back down. The road narrowed sharply, confirming Ryan's wisdom in ditching the car.

'You get much trade down here?' he asked.

'You'd be surprised,' said Johny. 'We get tourists all through the summer. Dutch and Germans, you Brits. Not French, though. The French don't give a shit about the countryside. But you guys can't seem to get enough of it. Here we are. Welcome to my little corner of Provence.'

He stopped in front of a charmingly rickety building which gave the impression that it might at any moment abandon the effort of holding up against the steep slope and tumble on down to the bottom of the road. Everything about it was irregular, from the uneven grey and white walls to the broad crooked steps which led up to the entrance via a lopsided terrace on which sat sets of stacked non-matching chairs and tables. A blue-and-white striped awning hung above the terrace. The words BAR JOHNY SILVER were stencilled into the windows.

'Too early for tourists yet, my friend,' said Johny, drawing aside the coloured bead curtains and showing Ryan inside. 'We'll have the place to ourselves for a while.'

The room was big and low-ceilinged and so dark that Ryan didn't notice the white-haired woman scrubbing the floor until he had almost tripped over her. Johny spoke to her in French.

'My mother,' he explained.

Ryan offered the old lady his hand and she took it firmly in both of hers, shaking it furiously. Her face split into a huge grin as she unleashed a patently welcoming but quite unintelligible torrent of words.

'She says she's very pleased to meet you,' said Johny.

'I think I got that.'

'She says it will be an honour for her to bring you breakfast. Take a seat, I'll tell Annie you're here.'

Ryan climbed on to one of the bar stools while the family dispersed. As his eyes adjusted to the light he saw the evidence of his friend's past lives posted in the photographs on the walls. There were shots of Johny, in uniform and out, against backgrounds ranging from white-capped mountains to deserts and tropical beaches. In one big framed photograph behind the bar he was sitting up in a hospital bed grinning and holding his thumbs up to the camera, despite the bandages that swathed his upper body and the entire left side of his face. Amongst the group of Frenchmen standing by the bed Ryan recognized himself, conspicuous in his British regulation camouflage jacket and green beret.

Johny reappeared in the doorway ahead of his mother and took over the heavily laden breakfast tray she was carrying.

'Let's go outside,' he said. 'Annie'll come down when she's dressed.'

Ryan followed him through the open door at the back of the bar on to a small secluded terrace. Johny set down the tray on a table underneath a pergola groaning under the weight of generations of creepers and climbers. High walls on either side masked them from the eyes of any neighbours.

'Here we can talk,' said Johny, pouring two coffees from a big earthenware pot. 'Why you here, Ryan? I'm pleased to see you, but it's not for a vacation, I guess.'

223

Ryan shook his head. He picked up one of the beer mats lying on the table and pointed to the Bar Johny Silver slogan.

'I see the name stuck.'

Johny laughed and scratched instinctively the fine mesh of scarring that ran most of the way down his left cheek.

'Thanks to you, Ryan, yeah. Though I don't have the limp no more. And I never did get myself a fucking parrot.'

Ryan shared the joke. It had been in the hospital in Sarajevo, maybe even on that visit commemorated in the photograph behind the bar, that Ryan had told his friend that he looked like Long John Silver. The injuries to his leg had been slight, but the very visible legacy of his facial wounds had enhanced an image which Johny obviously relished. A black triangular patch lay at a rakish angle over the empty pit where his left eye had once been. He had never been the kind of man you would want to run into down a dark alley. These days he'd have scared the wits out of most people in the best-lit alley in France.

'You're right, I'm not here on holiday,' said Ryan. 'Pity, though. This wouldn't be a bad place to spend some time. How long you been here now?'

'Nearly two years. Since my discharge. They offered me a recruiting job, you know.'

'Brave of them. One look at your mug and most recruits would run a mile.'

'They don't think like that in the legion. They like a crippled hero. You know about Captain Danjou?'

'The guy with the wooden hand?'

'Yeah. He died telling his men to fight to the last bullet, and they did. When they were out of ammo and there were only three of them left they fixed bayonets and charged, even though they were surrounded by thousands of fucking Mexican revolutionaries. Camerone day, when they parade the wooden hand, is the biggest event in the legion's calendar.'

'So you think in another hundred years they'll be parading your eye-patch?'

'You'll have to stick around for that. But I figured, what's the point of being in uniform if they pin me to a desk? Anyway, I never was much good at that shit. I'm lucky, Annie handles all that here.'

'While you lounge about and drink the profits.'

'Yeah, that's the deal. The sun shines and I get a good pension. What about you?'

'I'm not thinking of retiring yet.'

'Still with your old outfit?'

'No, worse luck. I seem to be on permanent training secondment these days. Maybe they think I'm getting too long in the tooth for active service.'

'Maybe they realize you're too valuable to risk any more. Who you training?'

'Officially, the police.'

'Things in England that bad, huh?'

'Not far off. You remember Dent, the spook who was liaising with your people in Sarajevo? He was in Kosovo after that, dealing with Albanian drug traffickers. Uncovered something nasty a bit closer to home and got put in charge of a new drugs investigation unit, lording it over the cops and the customs and everybody.'

'So you're training his people?'

'I'm driving his car. But I've got a few days off and there's some business I've got to take care of. Figured you might be able to help me.'

'Help from a one-eyed cripple? You must be hard up, man.'

'Yeah, must be. I need some hardware.'

'What sort of hardware?'

'The usual sort.'

'You figure I keep an armoury?'

'I figure you know people who do.'

'How you figure that?'

'The cousin you told me about, in Marseilles.'

'Oh, him. You got a good memory.'

'The way you told it, it was pretty memorable. Unless you were bullshitting.'

'No, it was all true. Unfortunately he's not going to be around for the next twenty or thirty years. He killed a cop.'

'Shit.'

'Don't worry about it. We got plenty of other cops. What do you need?'

'Automatic pistol. An Uzi would be handy too, anything in that line, I'm not fussed. AK47 would do. Plenty of ammo.'

'That all? Shit, I thought you was after a tank or SAM missile or stuff. You got cash?'

'Five thousand US dollars.'

'Cool. What else you need?'

'Some grenades would be handy.'

'Stun or fragmentation?'

'Both. Can you get hold of plastic explosives?'

'Not so easy. You starting a war?'

'I hope not. I got a list here. All this is just in case.'

'In case what?'

'In case I'm right.'

'You going to tell me what this is about?'

'Sure, if you let me eat something first. I'm starving.'

Ryan quickly demolished the plate of brioches and croissants on the tray before filling him in on Martinez, the Rostovs and the rest. He described how the honeytrap operation had been conceived, how it had gone wrong, and how Dent was planning to cover it up. Grace, he explained, had been hung out to dry.

'Nice people, huh?' remarked Johny when he had finished. 'Does this Grace realize she's on her own?'

'I don't know. More to the point, I don't think she really

understands the kind of people she's dealing with. Maybe she's rung in today. She wasn't able to get hold of anyone yesterday. She left a message, though, and she probably thinks someone will be keeping an eye on her.'

'But there won't be.'

'Oh no, there will be. Me.'

'Keeping an eye, huh? That why you need guns?'

'If I have to get her out I don't think they're going to come to the door carrying her luggage for her.'

'How many guys do these Rostovs have?'

'Don't know. There were seven or eight at the place we raided in England.'

'And you're going to blow them all away, like that?'

'Don't know what I'm going to do. Ask me nearer the time.'

'You're crazy, man. This ain't just any bunch of criminal psychos, this is the Russian mafia. That's about the meanest bunch of people on the whole fucking planet. You go in there shooting from the hip like Arnold Schwarzenegger in some dumb movie, they're liable to shoot back.'

'I wouldn't be surprised.'

'Shit, Ryan, you are one crazy sonofabitch. Lucky for me you are though, huh, or I wouldn't be here to tell you how fucking crazy you are. You want me to get you some guys?'

'Not the kind of guys you know. I prefer it if the psychos are all on the other side.'

'Won't be easy for us without back-up.'

'Us?'

'Yeah. Us. We. You and me. The old team. You got a thing against working with cripples?'

'Not me, no. But I reckon *she* might.'

Ryan pushed back his chair and stood as Anne-Marie came out on to the verandah. She was taller than he was expecting, but identical in every other respect save one to the pretty, elfin creature he knew from photographs. The difference lay in the beachball-like protuberance straining at the material of her dress. She must have been at least eight months pregnant.

'Sit down,' she said to Ryan, coming and parking herself on the arm of her husband's chair. She saw that Ryan's coffee cup was empty and tut-tutted her disapproval. 'You call this being *le patron*, Johny? You're not in the legion now, you know.'

'Worse luck,' Johny muttered back.

She cuffed him lightly on the head. They exchanged a few words in French. The tone was playful, but then he said something else and the mood changed. Both looked serious. He nodded thoughtfully as she spoke rapidly. They talked for a minute. Ryan understood nothing of the conversation but he picked up a name they both repeated: Marcel.

'Excuse us, please,' said Anne-Marie. 'My English is not so good.'

It sounded good to Ryan, although the copycat cadences of Johny in her accent might have tested the uninitiated. Whatever it was they were saying, it clearly satisfied them both. Johny climbed to his feet.

'I've got to make some calls,' he explained to Ryan. 'Annie'll take care of you.'

Annie poured Ryan more coffee from the jug. She sat down in her husband's place.

'He's gone to talk to a guy,' said Annie. 'He'll get you what you need.'

'The guy being Marcel?'

'Ah, so you understand more than we think. We must be careful.'

'Not really. Who's Marcel?'

'Not a very nice man. But he is my cousin. Johny says he told you about his brother, Didi.'

'The cop killer?'

'Yeah. Didi is famous, he's the tough guy of the family, but he has no brains. Marcel is an asshole, but he's scared of Johny and he'll get you your weapons.'

Ryan tried not to look surprised. Annie flashed him a mischievous smile.

'You don't tell your woman everything, Ryan?'

'I don't have a woman to tell.'

'What about the woman you came for? What is she called?'

'Grace. She's not my woman.'

'But you would like her to be?'

Ryan shifted uncomfortably in his seat. He opened his mouth to say something, then thought better of it. He shrugged and drank some coffee instead.

'You're going to a lot of trouble for her,' said Annie. 'She must be quite a woman.'

'Yeah. She is.'

'If she was your woman, you would tell her everything.'

'Maybe.'

'You are a cautious man, Ryan. If I did not know you better I would think you are scared of women.'

'What do you mean, if you knew me better? You don't know me at all.'

'Oh, but I do. I know everything Johny tells me, remember. I am very glad to meet you at last. I want to say thank you for a long time. Johny owes you everything and for me it is the same.'

'Johny doesn't owe me anything, Annie. I did it because of circumstances, that's all. I wasn't even thinking, and I certainly wasn't playing the hero.'

'Johny says you are either a hero or a madman. He doesn't know which one.'

Ryan grunted and drank more coffee. No one had used the word hero at the time, that had come later. Madman, though, was another matter. Get down, you bloody madman, one of his men had shouted at him. Come back, you bloody madman, another voice, much further off – Dent's, perhaps – had joined in. No doubt there was a streak of madness beneath his bluff, so very calm professional exterior. Why else would he be here?

'You don't wish to talk about it, eh, Ryan? That probably means you are a real hero.'

Trying to get my circulation going, that was what he'd said afterwards. It had been so bloody cold, a hell of a place to spend a winter night, crawling through the forest on a hillside above Sarajevo, the wind sounding like an avalanche crashing through the trees. The Brits had picked the short straw, the French had had the easier time, or so Johny claimed afterwards, getting to within a kilometre of the place in their vehicles and sheltering inside until an hour before dawn. The French had been stung, it was said, by accusations that they had been letting UN-indicted war criminals slip through their grasp. They had got there first and been all keyed up to move the moment Dent had given the signal. Which was the moment it had all gone wrong.

The house was isolated and in darkness, the suspect alone in there, according to intelligence. Well, they all knew about intelligence. It had been rank bad luck, though, that one of the men inside had chosen that precise moment to let out the dogs they'd also not got around to mentioning. And that Johny had happened to be standing without a stitch of cover in the space between the treeline and the house when the man's torch had picked him out. Which was when they'd discovered that one suspect, probably lightly armed, was in fact four, armed to the teeth.

Someone had shot the dogs and the first man, but by then the alarm had been raised. Ryan had just dragged himself into position at the back of the house, some way ahead of his men, when the fireworks started. He had seen the flash of muzzles at the windows, heard the Frenchman yell as he went down. He hadn't thought about it, he'd started running, with the cries of bloody madman his only encouragement.

He didn't remember too much about it, it had all been done on training, instinct, adrenaline. Back in the forest he'd been worried about getting the feeling back into his fingers, but that obviously hadn't been a problem. Afterwards he'd counted three empty magazines for his Heckler & Koch. He had no recollection of reloading, but he remembered nursing the barrel of the gun afterwards, enjoying the delicious seep of warmth through his gloves. He also remembered Johny's dead weight across his shoulders, the bloodstains that no amount of washing would fully remove from his white parka. A little later he had been taken to meet the French colonel, who had embraced him and used the word hero for the first time. Dent had been in the command vehicle too, busy talking into the radio. Whoever he had been speaking to had done his job pretty effectively. The reports that hit the papers described a clockwork operation. Mention had been made only in passing of light wounds received by one UN soldier. No mention at all of that soldier's career being finished.

Ryan watched Anne-Marie pouring him more coffee. There were compensations, though. If it came to a choice between this and the army would any sane man choose life in a barracks? Would a sane man choose that life in the first place? Not if Ryan's ex-wife was to be believed.

'Johny says you don't want him to come with you. Why?'

Ryan found it hard to look at her. The spotless blue sky, the riot of colour in the flowers drooping from the pergola, even the chipped glaze in his coffee mug, all suddenly seemed worthy of attention. He stared at them all in turn.

'Why?' she repeated, her voice quiet but insistent. 'Is it because of him, or because of me?'

He looked at her now. Her frankness demanded it.

Demanded the truth too. The fact was that at the back of his mind he'd always known that Johny would want to tag along. And he hadn't been planning on raising anything more than a token objection.

'You,' he said.

'The fact he can't walk so good, only got one eye, you don't care?'

'I'd take him with half an eye over anyone I know.'

'How is that? You were never in a war with him, apart from that time.'

'I know he's got guts.'

'Sure. There are plenty of legionnaires with guts.'

'Yeah. But when a man gets half his face blown away and comes through it like he did I reckon he's something special. So are you.'

'Not me.'

'Yes, you. There's a time to take risks and a time to say enough's enough. When's the baby due?'

'Ah, so that is it.'

'You think I'd take him away from you now?'

'It is not for keeps. I lend him to you.'

'But what if I can't bring him back?'

'Without you he wouldn't be here in the first place.'

'He doesn't owe me anything.'

'You know that's bullshit.'

'Maybe. But getting himself killed isn't my idea of a payback.'

'How do you think he'd feel if you got yourself killed and he wasn't there?'

'I'm not planning to get myself killed.'

'Nor is he. You can ask him, if you like.'

Johny had reappeared in the doorway. He came and stood behind his wife.

'I can get the guns, the rest might be a problem,' he said.

'Sounds good. Where do I go?'

'He'll call me. Cash up front, but you know that. He likes your dollars. Two grand, as a favour. Two AK47, two 35mm Beretta, plenty of ammo. If you want to get rid of them, he'll buy them back for a thousand; fifteen hundred if they haven't been fired.'

'Let's hope it's fifteen hundred then. Why do I need two of everything?'

'Ryan thinks you're going to get yourself killed,' said Ann-Marie.

Johny looked offended.

'You think I can't take care of myself because I'm a cripple?'

'Cut out the guilt-trip crap, Johny.'

'I got one eye, Ryan. That's enough to look out for you. Besides, you need me. Marcel won't sell to a stranger.'

'That's blackmail.'

'And how you going to find your way around when you don't speak a word of French? You try your crummy English down here, people going to look straight through you half the time.'

'All the time,' said Annie. 'We don't like dumb tourists here.'

'Especially dumb English tourists,' agreed Johny.

'Especially.'

Ryan sat back in his chair and adopted his most implacable expression. But there was no way he was going to stare even one of them out, let alone the pair. He might not know the language, but he knew a *fait accompli* when he saw one.

'Looks like I've got an interpreter then,' he said flatly.

To judge by Johny's beaming expression a casual observer might think he'd won the lottery. Annie looked more restrained, but her smile was confident and bright.

'They'll never know what hit them,' said Johny, laughing.

Ryan looked at their bright, trusting faces and hoped to

God that it was true. He tried to join in the laughter, but the knot in his guts wouldn't let him. He smiled weakly. He wanted to be worthy of their confidence.

The truth was he had never felt more scared in his life.

12

He stood in the casino letting his eyes adjust to the light. He glanced from table to table, looking for anyone he knew, anyone who might know him. There were some familiar faces, a couple of Arabs he had seen in London, a Greek he had seen everywhere, an Argentinian playboy whose name was familiar to people who read gossip columns. The Argentinian was playing blackjack, the others were at the roulette tables. There was a big crowd around the Greek, no doubt hangers-on hoping for an invitation to the yacht moored in the harbour. Their laughter lapped across the vast floor, invading the quiet corners where more anaemic habitués of the night sat hunched over modest and generally diminishing piles of chips. He walked slowly through the room, weighing, gauging, breathing it in. He loved this moment of walking into a place, any place, the ritual start of the evening, the moment when the pulse quickened, the senses sharpened, the buzz tingled through him. The moment he smelt the money.

Nowhere, not even in a bank, was money so visible, so quantifiable in stacks and rows and columns. He loved the look of the coloured chips, he loved to touch, and to hear the incongruously cheap plastic clink of them. The only sense it didn't cater for was taste, and not just literally. Even here, a world away from the neon brashness of Vegas, there was an indelible streak of vulgarity. But he liked that. He liked the bordello style of the place, the plush red drapes, the gilded ceiling, the Empire chairs and chandeliers. He liked it when the greed and lust of others were transparent.

He picked out his table, walked past, turned half around and checked it out from a distance, pretending to watch the Greek throwing away his money. Not the biggest table in the place but big enough, thick stacks of black and gold chips in front of each of the two players. The player on the right fat and florid, slow in his movements, clumsy fingers. The man next to him thinner, more impatient. The dealer young, not quite male-model looks, but handsome enough to keep up the standard of the house, which was high. All of the girls – this was France – very pretty indeed. This guy was fast and neat, competent. Sharp enough to be keeping an eye on the fat man. The casinos all said they loved high rollers, but what they meant was that they liked big losers. It was not a class to which he belonged.

He settled into the empty chair on the right of the fat man, the end of the row. Seven chairs were in a semi-circle round the table. Between the fat man and the thin man – his thinness was relative – was one empty place. The other empty places were more or less opposite him, perfectly placed. If they both suddenly became occupied then he'd have to start over, but he was patient and he was flexible. They were about halfway through the shoe, so he had a while to kill.

The dealer bade him good evening. He peeled some notes from his wallet. 'Thank you,' said the dealer. They only ever spoke English to him in European casinos, they could see straight away what he was, another stupid American tourist in his garish Hawaiian shirt and white baseball cap. The other players didn't give him a second look. They never did; not any more.

He remembered when he'd made the transition. A naive young twentysomething hitting Vegas as if he expected the town to notice, a cocky confident kid going nowhere but thinking he was somebody, wanting all the world to see how cool he looked in his five-hundred-dollar leather coat, his moves as slick as his hair, a bargirl's dreamboy. Finding his table then waiting till the count got high before making his move, fanning his fat roll and tossing it all down like it was no big deal, like he hadn't done worse things to get it than any of these suburban vacationers could even imagine in their cosy little dreams. Of course he'd been noticed, what was the point of being the coolest guy around if no one was there to see? People had come from other tables to stand behind the young dude with the big chips and the big easy manner to match. Hit me, son, he'd say to the dealer, a man twice his age and ten times smarter, and the dealer would hit him and the onlookers would laugh to see him rake in the chips. He didn't win every hand – who did? – but that night the cards kept falling into his lap. And all the while he was shooting the breeze with the busty Texan who'd come to watch him and tell him what a great guy he was, and making her laugh the way he said *Hit me, son*, playing it brasher and brasher because he was sure he was going to lay her after. They got to the final few hands and he forgot about the woman, and everything else, and quadrupled his bet. Crash went one hand, but what the hell, the odds were in his favour, so he came back for more. And suddenly he was winning, and the fat stacks came back his way, more money than he'd ever had in his life, and that was only for starters, because with what he knew and the way the cards were falling he could go on, and on, until he had enough to buy whatever he'd always wanted, which wasn't much, given the poverty of his own ambition in those days: a fast car, a gold watch, women. It was his for the taking, right?

Wrong. He'd known what was going to happen the moment he felt the hand on his shoulder. They'd sent a posse to escort him out, the pit boss with a face like a pit bull and two guys as wide as they were tall to encourage humility. Not that he'd been in the mood to argue. He'd been too stunned to utter a word. After they threw him out he just stood there on the sidewalk gaping up at the neon signs, like a kid barred from Disneyland.

He understood then that all that knowledge, everything the other Mickey had taught him, hadn't been enough. Nine out of ten for substance, but no marks for style or intelligence. But he had always been a quick learner. A year later he went back to the casino. He sat at the same table, couldn't spot the same dealer, but took time out to ask the pit boss some dumb question. He hadn't been made. It wasn't that he looked any different, not back then, it was the way he dressed and behaved. Relaxed and open, friendly but not cocky, sensible but not smart. Mr Ordinary, Mr Unexceptional. Like it said on the passport. Mr Gallagher.

Mr Gallagher turned to the fat man and whistled admiringly as he raked in another pile of chips.

'Hey, man, I like your style,' he said, giving it his biggest goofiest grin.

Hey, man, what planet did you learn to play on? Standing on soft fifteen with the dealer's nine against you? Lucky for you he drew a three and bust on a picture. But you don't stay rich in this game juicing on luck.

The fat man flashed his lips in a polite half-smile but didn't look up. The dealer glanced at Gallagher, who was now the first player on his left.

'I'm easy,' he said, and dropped a single chip on to the box. He arranged his chips into half a dozen piles. The dealer dealt.

He hesitated, as if he would. Hard fourteen against the dealer's five, a textbook stand, but he always liked to buy

238

himself an extra second at the start, to set the pattern. He tapped out a little rhythm with his fingers on top of two piles of chips.

'OK, I'll stand.'

The fat man was slow too. Good, not that he needed the extra time. He could count as fast as he could think.

He lost his chip. The dealer dealt again, and again and again. He pushed out one chip each time, winning a fair few hands playing his ordinary game but losing more. Leaking a couple hundred bucks an hour at this rate. Big deal.

A small-time loser, no one paying him the slightest attention. The fat man was still winning, amazingly enough, but they had come to the end of the shoe. The dealer shuffled and put his cutting card right near the end of the pack, just as Gallagher had noticed he'd done the deal before, when he was walking around sniffing the tables. Any dealer who cut near to the back was a card counter's best friend. This one had left him over three-quarters of the deck to play with, as good as it gets.

But this shoe wasn't good. The count was steady, nothing to get excited about. He played on automatic while he tuned up. It's like putting sunblock on over your brain, the other Mickey used to say, a matter of filtering out the shit. Think of the brain like a chest of drawers. Open this drawer, put in the information, close it up. Everything separated, one drawer like the trash can on a computer, learn to put what you don't need right in there and wipe the screen. It helped to have a near-photographic memory and a gift for numbers, but that was nature's bonus. Not that he'd known he could even do anything with it until Mickey had realized it for him. Mickey sitting in the diner that time arguing over the lousy bill with Jimmy Ramirez and the two chicks who said they were twin sisters, Ramirez saying no way was he going to split it three ways when he was the only one not going to get laid. It had looked like they might fight about it, but then he'd stepped in, said, 'Hey, Ramirez, how's about you pay twenty-five per cent, which is fair because you ate as much as both sisters, and we'll pay the seventy-five, which is thirty-seven and a half each, and that comes to so much, but add fifteen for a tip makes it this for you, and this for us, rounded up to the nearest ten cents, so how about it?' And Mickey afterwards saying, 'How'd you figure that so fast?' And throwing more numbers at him, like lobbing balls for him to catch, saying add this, divide that, and going faster and faster, and him not dropping any of them, and at the end Mickey laughing and slapping his back and saying, 'Hey, it's like *Rain Man*! I can see possibilities.'

The possibilities hadn't worked out quite as Mickey intended. He'd been a good teacher, though, you had to hand him that. There wasn't anything he didn't know about counting systems or variations in casino rules. But Mickey had wanted to be the main man, and a junior partnership was not his idea of a sound career move. Mickey hadn't liked it much when he'd told him, but a bottle of tequila later he'd seemed in a happier frame of mind. He remembered the way Mickey had lain slumped on the floor of the car, the empty bottle caressed in the curl of his fingers, the pitch-black endless empty desert road ahead. He would always remember that night, the brilliant stars, the sky as clear as his own mind. He had mapped out the life ahead of him that night and fixed the strategy. It hadn't included partnerships, though it was a rule he'd been breaking a lot lately. He'd broken it again tonight. He glanced up, took a mental snapshot of the room and lowered his head again, back to the business of rearranging his piles of chips. The fat man had started giving him sideways looks every time he beat out another rhythm on the chips, which was every time he laid a bet, but his annoyance was probably more to do with the fact that he didn't appear to be winning any more.

'Tough luck, man,' said Gallagher amiably, as the dealer raked in some more of the guy's money.

She was in the crowd watching the Greek. A lot of the women around the big roulette table were young and sexy, and most were as underdressed as she was, but she was still managing to get her share of attention. A man in a white tux was talking earnestly at her. Some jerk in Ray-Bans who had his arm round another girl's waist was trying to speak into her other ear. Everyone was in high spirits, yelling and applauding every time the Greek raked in another pile, which was just often enough to keep the tension racked. Perhaps the Greek would actually walk away with a profit in his pockets this time. Whatever, he'd be back to lose it again tomorrow. No one walked away with money from roulette in the long run; it was a game for gamblers.

He was no gambler. He was a professional.

'Dammit, I reckon you'd better top me up,' he said to the dealer, producing his wallet with a solemn air and laying another few small notes on the table, as if anyone cared.

The dealer passed across a handful of chips. His hand returned to the mouth of the shoe, primed to deal.

Gallagher sat upright on his stool and stretched his back. Two-thirds of the way through the shoe and a positive count of six. This was it. With one hand he reached up and took a firm hold of the peak of his baseball cap. Then with both hands he twisted it round through a hundred and eighty degrees until it sat back to front on his head.

'Time for some action,' he said to the dealer, and pushed out another whole chip.

The fat man didn't look impressed, but the wind had been taken out of his sails by a string of losses and he too was betting small. The thin man had hardly won a dime all evening. He collected up his few remaining chips.

'*Fini,*' he said, and turned to go. He stopped dead.

So did the fat man. Gallagher watched him look up from his money for the first time all evening, his eyes expanding at the sight of something that interested him almost as much.

Grace smiled at him as she sat down in one of the vacant chairs.

'*Bonsoir messieurs,*' she said, slipping one heel back under the chair, resting it against the bar and crossing her legs.

The fat man and the thin man stared at the hem of her dress as it rode up her bare thigh. The man in the white tux, who had followed her over from the roulette table and was standing over her shoulder, stared down her cleavage.

Gallagher stared too, tracing the swell of her hips and breasts through the tight dress, remembering the feel of her skin, the touch of her fingers, lips, tongue, the bite of her teeth. There were bright red marks on his shoulder and neck where she had savaged him, a wild animal with her legs wrapped round his waist, howling in his ear, the sweat and the water pouring off them both as he held her up against the tiled wall of the shower, his eyes a blur from the splashing in his eyes, the steam, the haze of heat and lust rising from them both. And now look at her: so relaxed and poised, her make-up perfect, not a hair out of place; so cool and sure.

His pulse quickened. He wanted her the other way again, now.

She opened her handbag and pulled out an artlessly arranged fistful of five-hundred-euro notes.

'*S'il vous plaît, monsieur.*'

Even the dealer's impassive face twitched. The thin man let out a low appreciative whistle. Gallagher swallowed the lump in his throat and laughed.

'You sure mean business, honey,' he said.

She glanced up at him without locking eyes and flashed

242

the most condescending of smiles. He couldn't help but be impressed. She had something all right: style, class, whatever you called it, in the sack and out.

'*C'est fou, c'est fou!*' said the man in the tux, sounding the worse for drink. '*Il faut jouer a la roulette. J'ai un systeme parfait.*'

'*Ah oui, c'est parfait,*' Grace agreed. '*Parfait pour se vider les poches.*'

The fat man laughed ingratiatingly. Gallagher nudged his elbow.

'Hey, what's she saying?'

'She say the way he play is best way she know to lose all your money,' the fat man explained in a thick, unplaceable accent.

Gallagher joined in the laughter. It was a good way to ease his tension. He blinked and focused on the baize in front of his eyes. The dealer had finished counting out her money and was in the process of passing over a huge stack of chips. Gallagher rearranged his own little pile and splayed his fingers over the shiny tops.

A well-groomed man in a smart blazer piped discreetly in the casino's colours had appeared at the dealer's side. Gallagher noted the gold pin in his lapel, the only sign of his position.

'Good evening, mademoiselle,' he said to Grace. 'Is it your first time with us tonight?'

He was considerably smoother than the average Vegas pit boss, thought Gallagher, but no less sharp.

'You know, I'm not really sure,' Grace replied gaily, turning to tug the sleeve of her companion but keeping her big blue eyes firmly on the pit boss. 'Marco, where was it Harry took us last time?'

The man in the white tux, swaying slightly from foot to foot, shrugged. No doubt it was immaterial to him in which casino he deployed his *systeme parfait*. Not so the pit boss.

A flicker in his eyes confirmed that the magic name of Harry had struck home. He even glanced across at the roulette table, where the crowd around the Greek was more boisterous than ever.

'Good luck, mademoiselle,' he said, with an unctuous dip of his chin.

'*Merci beaucoup, monsieur.*'

Gallagher rested his index and middle fingers on his left-hand pile of chips. Grace boldly shoved two separate stacks from her own pile out in front of her without counting.

'*Qu'est-ce-que tu fais?*' demanded white tux man. '*Les deux?*'

'*Mais oui, les deux,*' replied Grace nonchalantly.

'It seems like the lady's played before,' remarked Gallagher.

'I have,' Grace answered. She looked across at the four tiny stacks of chips he had remaining. 'Have you?'

The fat man's laugh was even more ingratiating than before. Gallagher watched him straining forward in his stool, pretending not to stare at the bas-relief of Grace's nipples where they pressed through her dress. It was not an outfit that had been designed to be worn with a bra. She hadn't flouted the designer's wishes.

The dealer gave Gallagher and the fat man two cards each. He dealt Grace four, two for each position. She had queen, nine and four, two against the dealer's five. The dealer waited.

'I think I'll probably stand on that,' she drawled, laying her hand flat behind the queen, nine.

Gallagher tapped the start of a little beat on his chips with one finger.

'Hit me,' said Grace.

The dealer turned a ten. Gallagher's finger didn't move.

'I think I'll stand on that too,' said Grace.

'You crazy, baby?' whispered Marco loudly in her ear,

standing close behind and leaning over her. 'Hey, come away with me, I know exactly what I'm doing.'

'That's what I'm worried about, Marco darling.'

She reached a hand up behind her and ruffled Marco's hair. He said something else into her ear, too quietly this time for Gallagher to pick it up. Grace rapped him lightly on the knuckles.

'Comme tu es méchant. Plus tard, Marco. Plus tard.'

Marco seemed very pleased with himself. He stood above Grace with his paws draped proprietorially over her shoulders as the dealer dealt himself another five to go with the first five, then went bust on six and ten. He paid out everyone at the table.

'Looks like this could be my lucky night,' said the fat man, winking at Grace. She smiled back at him sweetly.

'I think not, monsieur.'

Gallagher grinned. Not that he was amused. Marco was kneading Grace's shoulders with his thumbs. He seemed to be rubbing himself up against her, and she was laughing, and patting his hand and leg, occasionally lifting her head back to murmur something at him in low fluent French he couldn't quite catch.

He picked one of his small piles of chips and stacked it on top of another. He made his usual crummy bet of one chip. He saw Grace out of the corner of his eye inclining her head to the side as Marco planted his thick fleshy lips on her neck, like she was encouraging him, like she was enjoying it. He stared hard at the table. The fat man had made his bet.

'Now stop it, Marco, I've got to concentrate.'

Grace removed the hand that had slipped down over her breast and casually pushed out half of her chips. She bisected the pile with an exaggerated karate chop.

Marco made an exaggerated gesture of his own, slapping his forehead with the heel of his palm. Grace shrugged.

'What's it matter, darling? It's only money.'

The cards tumbled down on the baize in a blur of numbers and suits. Gallagher stared ahead, trying to keep his head clear of everything except the crunch of the numbers. He lost his bet. The fat man lost. Grace had eighteen and nineteen against the dealer's seven. Gallagher tapped his beat on the chips. The dealer pulled a ten and Grace doubled her money. The fat man and Marco whooped on her behalf. Half a dozen people drifted over from the roulette tables, attracted by the noise. The count was holding. Gallagher rearranged his chips again.

'Still want me to stop?' Grace demanded, slapping away Marco's roving hand again. 'Go with the flow, I say. Go with the flow.'

She pulled another brick of notes from her handbag, as large as the first, and tossed it on to the table.

'S'il vous plaît, monsieur.'

Marco groaned. The dealer glanced at the pit boss. He nodded.

Grace doubled her bet. One of the group behind her clapped. When the dealer gave her ace, queen and a pair of nines the rest joined in. Gallagher patted the table appreciatively with his left hand. With his right he flipped two chips and spread them under his index and middle fingers.

Grace didn't speak. She indicated she was splitting her pair and doubled up like a pro. She drew a king to the first nine and an eight to the second against the dealer's exposed seven. She won both hands. The count was falling. Gallagher halved his chip pile with his right hand and halved it again. Grace shrunk her bets.

She lost, and lost again, and her little knot of supporters groaned. The fat man had been cleaned out, it was just her and Gallagher with his pathetic one-chip bets against the bank. He pulled one blackjack for himself and silently cursed, but the shoe wasn't dead yet. On the last deal before the cut she redoubled her bet and scooped both hands. Even Marco managed to take his hands off her for long enough to join in the applause.

'The luck was with you, mademoiselle,' said the fat man, who had hung around to watch.

'Luck, monsieur? But I have a *systeme parfait.*'

Gallagher got up and left the table. He heard them laughing as he walked away, slow and easy, not looking back. He didn't want to look back. He could hear her laughter, and Marco's, and it stuck in his craw. He stopped briefly at a roulette table, watched a few spins, pretending to be in no hurry. Out of the corner of his eye he watched Grace walking away from the blackjack table, Marco half a step behind, the flat of his hand against her bottom. They disappeared from view amongst the thick crowd around the Greek. He cashed in his handful of chips and walked out.

It was still light outside, the bloody disc of the sun hanging low but strong enough to turn the watery horizon into a glassy glare. He put on his sunglasses and joined the ambling deep-tanned crowd. He was walking faster than anyone else. He made himself slow down. He was sticky, despite the breeze blowing in from the sea. He clipped on his earpiece and listened to his cellphone messages. The little boats were bobbing about in the harbour to his left; the big boats, including the Greek's top-heavy yacht, lit up like a Christmas tree, sitting serenely. He wondered, as he often wondered, the cost of a thing like that. Twenty million, thirty, fifty? What's the difference? As the man said, if you've got to ask, you can't afford it. Dmitri would have known. And if it had been Dmitri's he'd have wanted everyone else to know too. Which was why Dmitri was a dangerous man to be around. He complained all the time about the hassle he got, but what did he expect, thrashing about like a piranha in a goldfish bowl?

He put his earpiece away, feeling much twitchier than a

minute ago. A message from Dmitri, asking after Grace, which didn't matter, but also mentioning Orhan by name, which did. Dmitri was the most pig-headed peasant he'd ever met. He hadn't planned to change his cellphone number in France, but the raid two days ago in England had made him nervous. Dmitri would accuse him of paranoia, of course. He'd do what he always did with Dmitri, laugh it off and pretend it was no big deal, make his usual joke about hiding from the IRS.

He stopped suddenly outside a shop selling tourist garbage and sifted through the sunhats and cheap sunglasses. He was sure no one had recognized him in the casino but he went through the routine anyway. Twenty years of looking over his shoulder had made him the way he was. Only he didn't usually feel this edgy.

He entered the hotel through a side entrance and went straight up to his suite. It was empty. Well, he'd told her to take her time, and she'd done a good job of learning the rules so far. Most of them. An image of her with the jerk Marco flashed into his head. Maybe it was time to teach her the rest.

He carried his laptop through to the bedroom and set it up on the bedside table. He undid the Velcro fastener on the money belt he wore under his shirt and pulled the whole thing off. He took the hard disk from one of the compartments and fitted it into the machine. While he waited for it to boot up he unclipped the back of his cellphone and replaced the simm card with one of the spares he kept in the belt. He read off the number on the sticky label, memorized it and tore up the label. He connected the computer to the cellphone and pulled up a chair. He entered his password and ran his usual check. Then he dialled one of the servers he used at random. He looked through his current list of e-mail addresses and found two messages. He pasted them into a temporary work file, decrypted them and wrote replies, one to his bank in Bermuda, the other to Sammy in Amsterdam. Then he copied the work file on to a floppy disk and deleted it from the laptop. He put the floppy into his money belt. He yawned. This much concentration was tiring and he'd already had a busy night. He needed a vacation.

He laughed out loud. He was in a luxury hotel on the Riviera with a beautiful hooker who was up for anything. A hooker who had even wanted to give back her fee.

He looked at his watch again. Nearly a half-hour since he'd left the casino. A thought struck him, all the more unpleasant for being unexpected. What they'd taken from the casino was peanuts, sure, but how long would she have to spend on her back to earn that much? You could take a girl out of the cathouse and make her look like a movie star but the bottom line was that she was still a hooker. Who had ever heard of a hooker giving it for free?

He went next door and fixed himself a scotch on the rocks. The rich peaty burn of the alcohol in his throat helped soothe his irritation. It would take some nerve for her to walk out on him.

She had some nerve.

Not only nerve but brains and imagination. Of all the women he'd ever had, bought or gratis, not more than a handful could have done what she'd just done, and with such style. She had learnt his signals in a matter of minutes, and both this afternoon and evening her performance had been flawless. He had hardly even noticed her glancing down at the prearranged patterns he was making on the chips with his fingers. Every variation had come up in those two sessions and she hadn't blinked an eye. She'd been inventive too. It had been smart work attaching herself to the Greek's party and dropping his name, though letting that sweaty slob paw her all over was another matter. If he was one of the Greek's friends he must be stinking rich.

Maybe he too had a yacht in the harbour. Maybe he'd made her the kind of offer a hooker couldn't refuse. He hoped for her sake she had refused.

He refreshed his drink and brought it back to the bedroom. He tried to quell his restlessness, and the uncomfortable emotion gnawing away somewhere inside him. Jealous, was he really jealous at the thought of her being with that guy? You didn't get jealous over hookers, that was the point of them. If she didn't show then he'd book himself another. It was Monday, though, and he needed her in place for Wednesday. There was another problem too. He didn't want another. This one suited him fine.

You think I won't give you what you want if you're not paying?

No, it wasn't jealousy, but something was nagging at him. He sat down again in front of the computer and touched the keypad. The screensaver cut out. He clicked on his bookmarks. The name he wanted was at the top, just as it had been the first time he'd found it in the London directory: A for Amorous Liaisons.

The page loaded up, a tasteful blue background with the silhouette of a classical figure for a logo, classier than the usual. He clicked on *Gallery* and waited impatiently for the thumbnail portraits to load. Natalie's was in the first row. The face was blurred, most of them were, but he recognized the blonde ringlets. He scanned down the page. Three girls in each row, four rows, twelve portraits in all. That was one of the things he'd liked about the agency, it was small and selective. Grace's picture wasn't there.

He checked the rows again, though he was sure he hadn't missed her. He hadn't. She'd been there two days ago, he even made a comment to the boss of the agency about the poor quality of the shot. The photos of Grace he'd mailed over hadn't been much better, though at least in those he'd been able to see her face. But there was nothing at all there now.

He flicked along the rows, reading off the names one more time. Jeanette wasn't there either. Well, that wasn't so surprising. The agency advertised sophisticated, intelligent escorts, so what was a girl that green doing on the books in the first place? No sign either of Emily, the girl he'd booked three months ago, but the turnover at these places was pretty rapid. But not that rapid. Why wasn't Grace there?

Maybe she'd got something better lined up. He glared at his watch. Take a cab to the end of the promenade, he'd said, then pick up another outside the strip of bars and nightclubs. It couldn't take this long, there were always cabs. It was as easy to hire a cab as a hooker.

He disconnected the cellphone from the computer and dialled Amorous Liaisons. He got a ringing tone, then a recording of a familiar nasal voice telling him his call would be answered shortly and asking him not to hang up. He hung up. What was the guy going to be able to tell him anyway? According to Natalie, all the girls thought their boss was a slimeball. Grace wouldn't confide anything to him. Would she confide in anyone?

He double-clicked on his computer address book. He always filed the girls under their agencies, he had a few for Amorous Liaisons now. Maybe time to be moving on. He liked the girls but he didn't like the idea of them talking to each other. And he'd never liked patterns. He dialled the mobile number at the bottom of the page.

Another recorded message, but one he liked better. He loved the English accent on a girl, one of the reasons he was happy to combine business with pleasure and work out of London. He carried the phone out on to the balcony while he listened to the invitation to leave his name and number after the tone.

'Hi, it's Mike Gallagher, remember me? I sure remember you. Call me, will you, soon as you can?'

He gave her his latest number. He put the phone into his top pocket and rested his forearms on the balcony ledge. The cool, gentle breeze was refreshing. He took a deep breath and held it.

A door slammed inside. He wheeled round. There was a flash of red in the next room. And then Grace, running into the bedroom, laughing.

By the time he had walked in from the balcony she had kicked off her heels and flung herself on to the bed. Her eyes were bright with excitement and she was giggling like a schoolgirl. As he came over she rolled up on to her knees and tipped open her handbag. Thick wads of banknotes rained down on to the coverlet alongside an assortment of cosmetics.

'We did it, Mike,' she said breathlessly, before lapsing into another fit of the giggles. She ripped the band off one of the wads. 'Sorry, I know it's corny, but I've always wanted to do this.'

She flung the money over her head and collapsed back on to the bed, arms outstretched. The effect didn't really work as she intended. A few of the notes peeled off, but most stuck together and flopped back in a wedge on to her belly. It only made her laugh more.

He stood on the edge of the bed, looking down at her. He'd changed twenty thousand dollars for her, and they'd made well over half that again. Maybe thirty-two, thirty-three grand on the bed. She really did seem to think it was a lot of money. She looked genuinely thrilled.

'Why did you stop?' she said. 'We were on such a high.'

'Yeah. I guess you were.'

His eyes coasted up and down her body.

'You took your time. You have any trouble from the casino?'

'None at all. But I thought I was never going to get rid of Marco.'

'Yeah?'

He dropped on to the bed and planted his knees astride her. He leant his weight forward, his hands on her shoulders, his face over hers.

'Ouch, Mike. You're heavy.'

'I thought maybe you liked it.'

'You're in a funny mood tonight. Liked what?'

He took both her wrists and snapped them back over her head. He held her down with his left hand while with the other he grabbed the strap of her dress.

'This.'

He ripped the flimsy strap from her shoulder and yanked down the front of the dress, exposing her bare breast. He squeezed her nipple hard.

'Hey, Mike –'

'This what Marco did to you, huh?'

'Marco? Mike, I –'

'Ssh!'

He let go of her breast and pressed his hand over her mouth, clamping his thumb and forefinger against the hinges of her jaw. The laughter had fled from her eyes, which were wide with surprise. There was alarm there too, a look he hadn't seen in her before. He savoured it for a moment.

'Ssh, honey, and listen up. Maybe a few things aren't clear. While you're with me you don't flirt, and you most definitely do not fool around with any other guys, whatever the circumstances. They can look all they like, but that's all. You got it?'

He didn't release the pressure on her jaw. When she realized he wasn't going to let her speak she nodded.

'Another thing. I'm not in a funny mood tonight or any other night. OK?'

She nodded again. He took away his hand. She said:

'I was only –'

'Ssh!'

This time he had only to touch her lips with his fingertip and she knew to shut up.

'No ifs and buts, honey. I know exactly what you were doing, and it was smart work, you did it well. Too well, is all I'm saying.'

He trailed his finger down her chin, her throat, over her collarbone, her breast. He circled her nipple, gently this time, and stroked her, feeling her harden. He shifted his weight, still keeping her wrists pinioned, and pressed himself into her, letting her feel his own hardness.

'I didn't figure you for the jealous sort,' she said tentatively, as if afraid he would slap his hand over her mouth again at any moment.

'Don't give me reason to be. When I hire a girl it's exclusive.'

'For both of us?'

'Don't get smart.'

'I thought we were partners?'

'On my terms.'

He levered his weight off her and thrust his hand between her legs. He twisted his fingers through the shoelace-thin band of her thong and snapped it. He tossed the scrap of lace aside.

'You could always just take them off, you know,' she said.

He jerked her legs open. He lifted his hips. He undid his belt.

'You don't say.'

He clamped his mouth over hers and gave her a deep bruising kiss. She didn't respond. He pulled away.

'You going to answer that?' she murmured, her voice as still as her body.

The telephone on the bedside table was ringing. He leant up on his elbows and glared at it. It carried on ringing.

'Well?' she said.

He climbed off her. He slithered up to the head of the bed, his trousers snagged round his knees. He pulled them up as he reached for the phone. Grace swung her feet to the floor.

'Where are you going?' he said.

'Nowhere.'

'Good. I haven't finished with you yet.'

She sat on the edge of the bed, watching him. Her face ached where he had held her. The money and the contents of her handbag were still strewn over the bed. She began to collect it all up as she listened to him talk.

'Sure I got your messages. I've been busy.'

His voice was cool and controlled, but he was obviously annoyed.

'Now? Shit, you've got to be kidding me.'

He looked at his watch.

'Hold on, I'll have to make some calls . . . Yes, I will . . . No, the cellphone's a new number, I'll get back to you. I'll mail it to you. For Christ's sake, take some precautions once in a while.'

He slammed down the phone and swung round. His eyes strayed to her bare breast. Self-consciously she pulled up the broken strap of the dress.

'You'd better put something on. We're going out.'

'Where to?'

'Be ready to leave in ten minutes. Stay in here.'

He took his mobile phone out of his shirt pocket. He walked through into the other room and slammed the double doors behind him.

Grace stood up. She slipped off the remaining strap and stepped out of her dress. She kicked it away into the corner, it was no use to anyone now. She massaged her jaw again, and her wrists, which tingled unpleasantly from his grip. He had been aggressive, overpowering, every time they'd had sex. She wasn't going to pretend to herself that she hadn't liked it, or that she had been any less inhibited than he had been, but this had been different. She had seen something in his eyes that hadn't been there before. He had frightened her.

She crossed silently to the door, barefoot, naked. She knelt down. There was a key in the lock. She removed it carefully and peered through. She saw nothing. She pressed her ear to the hole and heard the faint murmur of his voice coming from over the far side of the room. Whoever he was speaking to he seemed not to want her or anybody else to know about it.

She eased the key back into the lock. One of the hotel bathrobes was lying on the nearest chair. She slipped it on, knotted the belt, and crossed to the open balcony door. She stepped outside.

There was a balcony outside each of the two rooms, a three-foot gap between them. She crossed to the edge and leant over. She could almost reach the railing on the other side. There was a lot of noise coming from down below, cars, laughter, music. She couldn't hear his voice. She hesitated. How badly did she want to hear what he didn't want her to hear?

Grace considered it for a moment. What if he came back suddenly into the bedroom and found her gone? Then he would know she'd been out on the balcony eavesdropping. Not even her natural flair for lying would be able to get her out of that one.

She ran back into the room on tiptoe, crouched down by the door and slowly, carefully, turned the key in the lock. It made the tiniest click. She hurried back to the balcony.

She swung one leg over the railing. It was about a hundred feet down to the hotel forecourt. Best not look down then. She kept her eyes fixed on the black iron top rail.

She swung her other leg over, resting her bottom against the edge of her balcony, her heels in the gaps between the rails, her toes in space. All she had to do was reach across and take a firm grip. It was easy, a ten-year-old could have done it. Her palms were liquid with sweat.

Grace stepped out into space. She pointed her toes at a gap in the railings opposite and lifted her foot high. There was a nauseous moment as she felt herself suspended over nothingness, then the ball of her foot came down hard on the other side. Pain seared through her big toe as she stubbed it clumsily against the stone. She grabbed for the top of the rail with both hands and pulled herself up hard against it, whacking her stomach with so much force that she heard the breath whoosh out of her. She stood doubled-up for a moment, blinking out the pain, then she levered herself up and swung her legs over on to the other side.

She was shaking. She slumped against the wall, in the gap between the window and the balcony rail, and took deep breaths to calm herself down. Her heart was beating furiously.

She could hear him. The balcony double doors were open, the lace curtains billowing in the soft breeze. She craned her neck and caught a glimpse of him through the lace. She drew back sharply and flattened herself to the wall. He was pacing the room as he spoke into the phone.

'Sure they'll be safe. Wise up. A guy like him doesn't want to start a shooting war, he's got too much to lose ... Yeah, I know, I know, but that's what he's like. He likes to catch people on the hop. The smart thing is to stay cool, act like it's no big deal. So what's the difference if he wants to meet at midnight, or even four in the morning? You got anything better to do?'

The question hung in the air for a few moments. Then he coughed. Grace held her breath. He sounded very near.

'Yeah, me neither. He says he wants to play cards.'

He laughed. The lace curtains parted. She saw his face in profile, staring out over the harbour.

'Who knows, you might get the chance to take some money off him legitimately, for a change. You lost enough at roulette on Saturday night, about time you hit a winning streak.'

He was standing six feet from her, his face three-quarters turned away.

'Sure he doesn't need the money. He does it for kicks, same as me. Said I should stay till the end of the week if I want to see some real action. I said I had other plans. I think he'd like me to leave the girl behind.'

He laughed again. She saw the tip of his nose as he turned his profile towards her. Another fraction and she'd be in his eye-line. She was already as flat against the wall as she could be. A car horn sounded in the street below, so loud she might have jumped, had she not been frozen stiff.

'Yeah, I already told him I was going to Deauville. Pity about Wednesday, I been having some fun with this one. Yeah, maybe I should get a substitute, that's not such a bad idea. There's that place our Dutch friend recommended in Grenoble. Maybe I should try some French pussy, for a change.'

The car horn blared out again. Gallagher pressed the phone tight against his head and put his left hand to his other ear. The noise persisted. He tried to talk through it, but the anonymous driver had his hand wedged down.

'Some asshole . . .' she heard him say, and the rest was drowned out by the noise.

He turned on his heels and walked back inside. If he'd tilted his head another inch to the right he would have seen her, but his hand was still flat to his head and his raised arm was blocking his eye-line.

The car horn cut out. She heard the murmur of his voice inside, but her ears were ringing and she couldn't make out the words. She didn't plan on waiting around for her ears to clear.

She crossed to the railing and swung her legs over. This time she didn't hesitate. She flung herself across the gap and vaulted the rail on the other side like a gymnast. She ran back into the bedroom and slumped into the nearest chair. Only then did she realize that she was holding her breath and her lungs were at bursting point. Her throat rasped as she drew in huge desperate gulps.

Her breathing steadied, though not her pulse. What would she have said had he seen her on his balcony? There was nothing she could have said, he'd have known right away what she was doing. Had she learnt anything to make the risk worthwhile? She presumed that he had been talking to Orhan about Dmitri. Dmitri wanted to play cards. So? What did she think she was doing? Why the hell hadn't she got out the minute she knew Jeanette was safe?

She knew why, but she wasn't sure she wanted to admit it. She glanced around the room. She saw the money on the bed. Her share of the profits would be – what? – four grand plus for a half-hour's work? She thought about the way she'd behaved in the casino, flaunting herself, using sex as a deadly weapon. And loving every second of it. She thought about the five grand in the brown envelope and what she'd done to earn that. She'd enjoyed every second of that too. So what did that make her then?

There was a reason why she had been sent to Gallagher and one reason only. The operation had been blown, but her cover was intact and she was on the inside. On the inside of what? Gallagher might be clean but his friends weren't. How much did he know? Maybe he blanked it out. Or maybe he was an accomplice, unwitting or otherwise.

She noticed his computer on the bedside table. With a shock she realized that it was turned on. He never left it on when he wasn't in the room. The personalized screensaver was working. She saw the outlines of hearts, diamonds, spades and clubs expanding and contracting.

She sat down in front of the machine and touched the pad. Instantly the screensaver cut out and she found herself staring at a single row of icons. An unusually uncluttered desktop; did it signify an unusually uncluttered mind? She pushed the idle thought aside. There was an Internet Explorer icon, a telephone connection shortcut, an organizer, a systems folder, a folder entitled Docs and the recycle bin. The laptop wasn't connected so she ignored the first two. She double-clicked on the organizer, clicked again on the planner and calendar. He didn't use either of them. She moved on to the address book. She checked under M for Martinez and R for Rostov. There were hotels, the numbers for Manila and Rome airports and, also under R, what sounded like two escort agencies. She flicked quickly through some pages at random and found the same pattern. Under some of the agencies were first names, some telephone numbers, no surnames. Her name and mobile had been filed under A for Amorous Liaisons, along with Natalie's and a girl called Emily.

She quit the program and entered the documents folder, or at least tried to. When she double-clicked a box came up, saying *Enter Password*. She hadn't the first idea, she wasn't even going to try to guess. She closed the box. There was unlikely to be anything in the system folder. Unlikely to be anything anywhere from the look of it, but she clicked on the recycle bin anyway.

There were two files in the bin, both untitled. She clicked on the first. It wouldn't open, but a box flashed up telling her it had been created today and deleted half an hour ago. She minimized the box, dragged the file out to the desktop and double-clicked. This time it opened. The file contained one cryptic line of text.

Confirm babe shipment. Switch Wednesday morning. Hotel Moulin Rouge. See you in Grenoble.

That was all. Wednesday was when her contract terminated. He'd talked about Wednesday on the phone a minute ago. That phrase, babe shipment, she'd seen that before. It had been in the transcript of Gallagher's taped conversation with Orhan that Dent had played for her. She had no idea what it meant. She would just have to keep her eyes and ears open to see what, if anything, happened between now and Wednesday. It was late on Monday now, she wouldn't have long to wait. She closed the message, returned it to the bin and opened the second file.

Instruction confirmed. Transfer of $3m from A74260800 to A15606813 Grand Cayman authorized with immediate effect.

She read the text again, slowly, giving it time to sink in. Three million dollars. An awful lot of hours at the card table.

'Hey, what's going on in there?'

She heard the rattle of the locked door at the same instant as she heard his voice on the other side. She jumped away from the keyboard.

'Open up!'

He was banging on the panels. Hastily she reached for the pad and dragged the file back to the recycle bin. She crossed quickly to the door.

'Grace, what are you playing at?'

Her hand closed on the key. She glanced back into the room. She saw the computer screen. The desktop background was clear blue. The screensaver was off.

'Hang on a second.'

If he noticed the screen he'd know she'd been at the machine. How long until the screensaver cut back in?

'I've got a surprise for you, Mike, but you've got to close your eyes.'

'What the –'

'I'm not opening the door till you promise to close your eyes. You promise?'

'We've got to be downstairs in ten minutes, there's a car coming. Open the damned door.'

'You've got to close your eyes.'

'For –'

'Please close them, Mike.'

'OK, they're closed.'

He sounded exasperated. He sounded as if he could get nasty again. She glanced back at the machine; still no screensaver.

'I'm coming. Eyes shut, remember.'

She loosed the belt and dropped the bathrobe from her shoulders. She unlocked the door. As she did so she felt a sudden surge of pressure from the other side. She jumped back as the door was flung open in her face.

'I don't know –'

His voice cut out when he saw that she was naked. For a second she glimpsed the anger frozen in his face, then saw it soften with astonishment. She watched his eyes travel slowly down her body. As long as he didn't notice the computer screen he was welcome to look all he liked. She took a step towards him.

'I thought you promised to keep your eyes shut,' she said.

'I thought I told you to get dressed,' he answered.

'Don't you want your surprise?' she said.

She took his hand and placed it round her waist. She curled her fingers round his neck and pulled his face down to her.

'What the hell are you playing at?'

It was the second time he'd asked that question, but this time there was no aggression in his tone. She heard the catch in his voice as she unzipped his fly and slipped her fingers inside. She pressed the flat of her hand against his shoulder and turned him, slowly, pecking his lips with little kisses, until his back was to the room. She steered him, backwards, towards the bed.

'You wanted to try the *spécialité de la maison*, didn't you?' she said.

The back of his knees brushed the bed. She undid his trousers and eased them down his hips. She pushed gently on his shoulders and he sat on the bed.

'We've got to go in ten minutes,' he said, but there was no resistance in his voice.

She knelt down. Behind him the screensaver still hadn't come on, but there wasn't the slightest possibility of him noticing now. She took him in her mouth. He gave a little moan as she circled him with her tongue. She broke away for a moment and glanced up into his already glazed eyes.

'Then ten minutes it'll be.'

13

She had expected that he would ask her to drive, but a car had been sent, a silver Rolls Royce with opaque smoked windows. People stopped to watch as they climbed into the back, even though the forecourt was the natural habitat of expensive marques. She had become used to turning heads now, but even so she found herself feeling self-conscious as he handed her into the back seat. What would anyone think, seeing them together? Some millionaire and his sleek wife, he in his fresh pressed linen suit, she in the chic silk dress she'd bought in Kensington on Saturday afternoon. A far cry, for both of them, from the display they'd made in the casino only an hour or so earlier. There was an ease about the way they were together that didn't say to the world – she didn't know why it mattered to her – a whore and her client.

There was something solicitous, tender even, in the way he held her. His arm was round her shoulder as he walked her from the lift. He slipped it around her again when they were together in the back of the car, and she nestled up against him for a moment, her head under his chin. He stroked her hair.

'Damn, but you're good,' he said quietly.

It was what he'd said up in the bedroom when she had finished with him, lying there with his heavy-lidded eyes and a lazy satisfied grin, his aggression all melted away. How easy it had been to disarm him. They had stayed upstairs for a lot longer than ten minutes, but he hadn't mentioned the time again. She had lain on the bed, indifferently naked, and discussed casually with him what she should wear while he closed down his laptop. She watched the screensaver cutting out as he touched the keyboard, all the time thinking: *You don't know how good I am . . .*

The laptop was on the seat beside him, along with his phone. She had brought her handbag and a silk shawl.

They drove out of the city and along the coast, the sea on their left. She saw the road signs flash past, mostly local but some for Toulon and Marseilles.

'We'll be coming back tonight, though he'll want us to stay,' said Gallagher.

'I take it we're talking about Dmitri?'

'He's got a thing about hospitality, like a lot of Russians. But after what happened last time I think we'll spend the night at the hotel.'

'You mean the police might turn up here too?'

'They could turn up any time when Dmitri's in town, here or anyplace. He thinks he's untouchable. But he isn't. Who is?'

His voice was very soft, he might have been speaking to himself. The interior of the car was solid black, she couldn't see his face. She reached across the leather seat, found his hand and took it in hers. She squeezed his palm.

'You sound tired,' she said.

'Feeling a little stale, maybe. Well, I'll be wide awake tonight. Got to be, when Dmitri's around. Don't think he'd mind so much if I came back to the hotel alone and left you behind. He was very insistent I bring you along. He wants to talk.'

'What does he want?'

'What do men usually want from you?'

His voice was calm, dispassionate. She pulled her shawl up around her shoulders. The air conditioning was going full blast.

'I'm booked up,' she said warily. 'Remember?'

'Till Wednesday, yeah. Maybe he'll invite you back after that.'

'Maybe.'

She wanted to match the coolness of his tone, but it wasn't easy. Lurid images of Dmitri were swamping her brain.

'And how would you feel about that?' she said.

'Why should I feel anything? No business of mine.'

'You didn't much like the idea of me being with someone else an hour ago.'

'Not while you're with me, no. But after Wednesday that won't apply. Being with guys is what you do, right?'

'I don't sleep with anybody, you know.'

'You don't? Maybe you're in the wrong line.'

It was unnerving, staring into the darkness where she thought his face might be. There were cars ahead on the road but none coming towards them, so no prospect of an enlightening wash of headlamps. She looked out of the window towards the sea, at the pale silver crests of the waves.

'Maybe I'm stale too,' she said.

'You don't like what you do?'

'Would you?'

She heard his laugh, faintly, above the hum of the aircon. Coming out of the darkness it had a sinister sound.

'There's something different about you, Grace.'

'So you said.'

'My apologies for repeating myself. I'm sorry you don't like what you do. You're good at disguising it.'

'Oh, I don't necessarily dislike it all the time,' she said tentatively.

She didn't know what tone to adopt. It was a big disadvantage not being able to see his face. Impossible to gauge his mood from his voice.

'You got enough put by to retire?' he asked.

She smiled to herself. Not an unreasonable question, if she were really who she said she was. She thought about the reality, her overdraft, the gruesome totals on her credit cards.

'Not quite,' she said airily.

'I'm pleased to hear it. I'd like to see you again.'

'You've got my number.'

'It's all right to call you on that?'

She thought about it. She supposed the line would be cut off as soon as she handed back the phone, if not before.

'Sure.'

'What about your boss?'

'My boss? Oh, Stan. I work for myself, thanks.'

'He's cool about you making private arrangements?'

'He doesn't own me.'

'He'd be sore if you quit, I guess.'

'He'd get over it.'

'You'd be hard to replace. I'm surprised he doesn't make more of you.'

'In what way?'

He didn't answer for a moment. The sea had temporarily disappeared from view. She watched the car's headlamps flash over a wall of sheer white rock running parallel to the curve of the road.

'Lousy photos on the website,' he continued. 'Your choice or his?'

'Nothing to do with me.'

'You checked it lately?'

'No.'

'You ever check it?'

'Why should I?'

'Maybe you should. Seems strange to me there's no mention of the fact you're fluent in several languages. Some French or Russian guy in London on business, doesn't speak much English, would love to have you as a dinner companion. That's a nice easy way to rack up a big commission. Easy money for you too.'

'I don't tell Stan everything about myself.'

'Where were you before Stan?'

'Why are you asking?'

'Curiosity. Who did you work for before?'

'I've been around and about. You checking up on me?'

'Is there anything to check?'

'I'm just an ordinary working girl, Mr Gallagher.'

'Don't think I'd go along with ordinary. Sharp turn coming up. Hang on to yourself.'

She clung to the armrest as the car veered off the main road and swung into a series of tight hairpins. The road was narrow and uneven enough to trouble the silky suspension. The car didn't slow down.

'Maybe he learnt to drive in a tank,' said Gallagher.

'Our chauffeur?'

'Yeah. Hey there.'

She heard the click of the intercom switch on the panel behind the driver's head.

'Slow down, Mickey,' Gallagher said in English. 'We want to arrive in one piece.'

'Sure, Mickey,' replied a thick, distorted voice, laughing.

The Rolls Royce braked smoothly. As they rounded the next curve Grace caught a glimpse of the sea again. The road straightened out and began to dip.

'Is everyone around here called Mike or Mickey?' she said.

He laughed.

'He's Misha at home, but there's already a Misha at the Rostovs. So I call him Mickey and he reciprocates. The two Mickeys, our little joke. We're almost there now. You see the lights?'

She saw them, a cluster of bright yellow lights up ahead. They were travelling on a smooth surface now. She saw a sign flash past, announcing a private road, access *interdit*.

'Oh good,' she said, not thinking about it.

Thinking instead of the voice she'd heard on the intercom. Such a metallic rasp that it was hard to tell the accent. Maybe Russian, maybe something else, Mikhail or not. She heard Tate's voice in her head. *Mickey and Mike, a couple of regular guys . . .*

'Sounds like there's a party going on,' said Gallagher. 'Dmitri likes to party.'

He had opened his window a fraction. She heard music in the distance, loud but unidentifiable. In any case she wasn't listening. Her brain was churning. Her stomach too, she felt quite nauseous. It couldn't be, but then again why not? What better disguise for a man wanted by half the world's law agencies than a chauffeur, a man with a built-in reason to be everywhere he needed to be but to stay in the background? Everyone had been thinking in terms of plastic surgery and flamboyant disguises. Wasn't it somehow inevitable that the truth would be more mundane?

She remembered what Ryan had said in the car on the journey back to London. No one had come in or out of the place all night. So the only way Martinez could have been there would have been if he'd disguised himself as the butler. Maybe Ryan had stumbled unwittingly on the truth. Only for butler, read chauffeur.

The car was slowing down. Up ahead was a high fence and an equally imposing gate. There were lights behind the fence, dotted at regular intervals up the hill, to their right, and all the way down to the sea, on their left. The gate swung open automatically. A camera swivelled on a metal stalk, following them in.

'It's quite a pad,' said Gallagher.

She could see that. The house was floodlit at the front and back, marking the parameters of a low but immense edifice that seemed to climb on at least three distinct levels, like rice terraces, up the slope of the hill. Palm trees marched in well-ordered pairs along the broad, straight drive, ushering them into an expansive oval courtyard dominated by an ornate baroque fountain. Between the house and the sea, flat on another scooped terrace, was an Olympic-sized swimming pool. There were a few heads in the water, but the score or so of guests were clustered at one end, where white-jacketed waiters slalomed between them with trays held high. As the car slipped noiselessly into a waiting berth between another Rolls Royce and a couple of huge shiny motorcycles everyone at the poolside turned to look. A shadowy figure in the middle, it could have been Dmitri, half raised an arm in salute.

'Should I have brought my swimming costume?' Grace asked.

'Not strictly necessary,' Gallagher answered, with a dry laugh.

The engine cut out. She reached instinctively for the door handle.

'Wait,' he said.

She raised an eyebrow. It was bright enough now, courtesy of the fluorescent spotlights illuminating the shrubs and statuary around the courtyard, for him to be able to read her expression.

'If we're going to make an entrance, let's do it right,' he explained.

The driver's door opened. A moment later Gallagher's door was opened from the outside. He got out. The door closed after him. Grace waited.

Her door opened smoothly. She saw the legs and torso of a tallish, well-built man dressed in a single-breasted grey suit. She lifted her left leg and deposited her foot daintily on a glassy flagstone. She eased herself out of the back seat.

Gallagher was waiting for her but she didn't look at him as she took his arm. Her eyes were glued to the face beneath the black peak of the chauffeur's cap. The broad, slightly fleshy face of a man near to forty, tanned, a little coarse. The long nose had been broken once. The moustache beneath was thick and dark. The black peak was so low over his forehead that she could hardly make out his eyes, but she sensed him staring back at her. She felt the nape of her neck prickle.

'*Spaseeba*, Mickey,' she said.

He pulled his head away, as if taken aback by her familiarity. A sliver of light penetrated beneath the black peak and for a second she saw the look of surprise in his black, slightly hooded eyes. Then he lowered his head again. She paused, almost out of the car, waiting for him to speak, wanting to hear his voice again. He didn't oblige.

'Come on now,' said Gallagher.

He steered her towards the swimming pool. Behind her she heard the car door slam.

She glanced back and saw the shine of the peaked cap above the shadowy face. He was about the right age, right sort of height and build as well. She could sense him staring at her.

'Something the matter?' Gallagher asked.

'Oh no,' she answered quickly. 'He looked familiar, that's all. I wondered where I'd seen him.'

'In England probably, at Dmitri's. He's usually around.'

Usually around. She turned the phrase over in her head. Could there be a more perfect cover for someone who needed to be at the centre of things, and yet remain unnoticed? She shivered.

'Cold?' he asked, guiding her to the top of some steps and leaving his arm round her shoulder.

'No, not at all.'

How could she be cold on a night as warm as this, so little breeze, the air thick as an English greenhouse at midday? It wasn't the temperature that had got to her, but the sudden icy flow in her veins. If she were right then this man with his arm around her now, this man with whom she had been more intimate in the space of two days than she had been with anyone in her life, must be much, much more than a disinterested third party. Mickey Martinez was supposed to be his friend, so if her hunch was right and he was the chauffeur then they were both acting a part. Could Mike be Mickey's friend and not understand what kind of a man he was? Was it really credible that he should breathe the same air as any of these people and remain untainted? Of course not; only naivety could have made her think otherwise. Naivety or something worse. She glanced across at Mike Gallagher's so perfect, sculpted profile. Had she allowed herself to become infatuated by this man?

He inclined his head towards her as they reached the bottom of the steps and kissed her lightly on the neck. So tender now, what woman could resist him? The brutal streak he'd shown back in the hotel room had been an aberration. His lips brushed her ear.

'Don't let Dmitri bully you,' he whispered.

'I won't,' she murmured back, standing very still for a moment, wanting to feel the touch of his lips on her flesh again, and despising herself for wanting it too, feeling suddenly ashamed by her own desires, by the memory of the pleasure she had taken from this man, the pretence that she had only been faking.

'Mike, so good to see you. Good to see you again too, Grace.'

Dmitri was approaching, beaming. A waiter followed, bearing a tray with two full champagne glasses. He stood back while Dmitri hugged his guests, Gallagher first, then Grace.

He kissed her on both cheeks. She smiled and didn't avert her face from the strong smell of something pickled on his breath. His hands squeezed her hips.

'So very, very good to see you,' he repeated, taking his time before withdrawing his hands. 'This time no police, I promise.'

He snapped his fingers and the waiter presented the champagne. Dmitri touched Gallagher's elbow.

'They're all here already,' he murmured, jerking his head towards the guests. 'They seem nervous. What have you been telling them?'

'I don't need to tell them anything, Dmitri. Maybe they heard about you on the grapevine.'

Dmitri smirked. He began to speak again but his words were drowned out by a sudden high-pitched screech from the direction of the pool. He swivelled round and yelled in Russian.

'Learn to behave or I'll put you both across my knee.'

A rumble of male laughter came from the guests. In the centre of the pool there was a flurry of splashing and two dark heads pulled apart.

'I see you started without us,' Gallagher said.

'Not true, my friend,' said Dmitri. 'You are the main event.'

A group broke away from the other guests at their approach. Grace recognized Orhan, but not the two men alongside him, both short and powerfully built, with similar dark hair and thin moustaches. Orhan paid no attention to Grace. He nodded at Gallagher.

'Ali, Tony,' he said, indicating the two men. 'Ali speak no English.'

273

'Italiano?' asked Gallagher.

The heavier looking of the two, Ali, grunted.

'Mi fa molto piacere conoscerLa,' said Gallagher, switching to Italian and offering his hand. *'Ho sentito molto di Lei.'*

Ali replied and the two men conversed in Italian. It seemed that Gallagher was, once again, effortlessly fluent.

'Come with me,' said Dmitri, flinging an arm around her shoulder. 'Let's leave these guys to talk for a while.'

Reluctantly Grace allowed herself to be steered away. Gallagher glanced across but didn't break off from his conversation. He seemed not to mind her being taken away.

'You want food?' asked Dmitri, walking her towards the poolside. 'There is pig. You see?'

A whole pig was being roasted on a spit fifty yards away, in front of a spacious glass-fronted white summerhouse.

'Real good pig, wild boar,' said Dmitri proudly. 'Flown in today from Poland, very good.'

'I'm not hungry, thanks.'

'You want more drink? Here is all the champagne in the world. One day I fill the pool with it. You like champagne?'

'I prefer it in a glass.'

'Good. I have special bottle, maybe we drink together later?'

'Well, I don't know Mike's plans.'

'Don't worry about Mike. I want to talk with you, but later. Now, I want you to meet other important English guest.'

The people gathered at the poolside parted respectfully at Dmitri's approach. Grace recognized Misha Rostov, but no one else. The dozen or so men were mostly in their forties and fifties, uniformly thickset, all dressed in shorts and T-shirts. There were also seven or eight women, all conspicuously much younger and scantily dressed. Most had distinctively Slavic cheekbones. They were all very pretty.

Dmitri airily acknowledged the respectful greetings of his

guests but he didn't stop. He carried on walking, his hand resting heavily on Grace's shoulder, towards the summer-house, in front of which was a row of sunbeds and loungers. Tatyana, her characteristic bored expression in place, was reclining on one of the loungers, apparently not listening to the animated chatter of the dapper, bald little man seated next to her. Tatyana was wearing a white-and-gold silk kimono. Her companion was the only guest present wearing a jacket. White linen, but a jacket nonetheless, and close-fitting enough to make him visibly damp around the armpits.

'Tatyana you know,' said Dmitri, pushing Grace forward. 'Meet my lawyer, George Tregear. You have probably heard of him, he is most expensive, is best lawyer in England. This is Grace, young woman I tell you about, George.'

The lawyer jumped smartly to his feet. The face was familiar. Grace remembered seeing him interviewed on television.

'Charmed to meet you,' he said, thrusting his hand out to enclose hers in a loose clammy grip. 'Absolutely charmed.'

There was an empty champagne glass in his other hand. From the sound of him it wasn't the first glass he'd emptied tonight.

'Good evening,' said Grace, politely reclaiming her hand.

'Please entertain ladies, George,' said Dmitri. 'I have important business, excuse me please.'

Yuri, the shaven-headed man who had been at the house in England, had appeared at Dmitri's elbow, clutching a small black box. Dmitri led him away, talking rapidly into his ear.

George Tregear brushed the fabric of the lounger on which he had been sitting.

'Do sit down, Grace. I'll grab another chair.'

He wobbled off with an unsteady air. Grace sat down on

the lounger. Tatyana turned her head, slowly, appearing to notice her for the first time.

'Same dress as last time, I see. Maybe you need to increase your prices, so you can afford a decent wardrobe.'

'Perhaps you'd like to take me shopping tomorrow. Or do you only go out after dark?'

George Tregear reappeared with a canvas chair, which he plonked down noisily between the two loungers.

'Don't mind if I butt in, I hope, ladies?' he said cheerily.

'Nothing could give me greater pleasure,' said Grace.

'Nothing?'

The lawyer guffawed. He winked suggestively.

'I dare say I could think of something, my dear young lady, that would give you very considerable pleasure.'

'I'm already spoken for, I'm afraid. My apologies, Mr Tregear.'

She withdrew her hand from his for a second time. She lay back on the lounger, deliberately edging away as she stretched herself out. The lawyer didn't seem unduly perturbed.

'Please, please call me George. I absolutely insist. No formality here, you know, we're not before the beak now.'

He seemed to find this remark very funny. He snorted into his empty champagne glass. When a waiter appeared silently from nowhere and filled it up he snorted into it again.

'I gather I almost had the pleasure of meeting you last weekend, Grace. Fortunate in the circumstances I was late for dinner, eh?'

The waiter was offering the champagne bottle to Grace. She covered her glass with her hand. Tregear was chuckling contentedly to himself.

'It wasn't very pleasant, no,' said Grace idly, aware of the sudden quickening of her pulse, the rush of thoughts going into overdrive in her brain. 'Was that empty place at Dmitri's on Saturday meant for you then, George?'

'Yes. Jolly lucky my plane was delayed, eh? Couldn't believe it when we arrived, saw all the lights, helicopters, coppers. Coppers couldn't believe it either when they saw me. They couldn't work out how Dmitri had got me there so soon, poor souls; didn't realize it was sheer chance I happened to be on my way already. You should have seen their faces. Most disgraceful case of police harassment I've ever seen, I told them. Dmitri's going to sue the pants off them, and quite right too. They'll settle, I expect. Pity, really. The publicity would serve them right.'

'A pity you weren't in the house then, George,' said Grace. 'If they'd arrested you too, you could have sued on your own behalf.'

'Good God, I hadn't thought of that. Ha, ha, yes. You didn't train to be a lawyer, by any chance? Fall by the wayside, or something?'

'Which wayside would that be, George?'

'Oh, you know. There are more rewarding ways of earning a living than poring over dusty old law books, you know, if you have the assets – which you most certainly do. More rewarding, I dare say, for all parties concerned.'

He had inclined himself towards her again. He breathed hoarsely, attempting a drunken man's version of *sotto voce*.

'I don't suppose you've got your business card on you by any chance, have you?'

'Not taking bookings, I'm afraid. Why don't you try over there?'

She indicated the poolside, where Yuri was assembling all the girls in a line. He was shouting at two dark heads bobbing in the water. The same two, Grace assumed, who had been splashing about before.

'Oh, that,' said Tregear, giving a dismissive wave. 'That's the house menu. I'm more of an *à la carte* man myself. Though I dare say I could make the odd exception, if push came to shove.'

He was leaning forward in his chair, suddenly alert, staring past her into the pool. The two girls were climbing out by the steps at the shallow end. They were both naked.

'I say! What will they do for an encore?'

The other girls were all stripping off too, some eagerly, some bashfully. The men greeted the exposure of naked flesh with wolf whistles and roars of approval. Most of them were brandishing their wallets. It looked like they were laying bets.

Yuri clapped his hands smartly for attention and the chatter died away. Someone turned off the music, a scratchy recording of Russian gypsy songs that had been blaring out from speakers attached to the summerhouse. Dmitri appeared at the edge of the pool. He walked down the line of girls, holding the black box open towards them, showing whatever was inside. When he had reached the end of the row he held the box up and twisted it round in his hand to show everyone else. Grace caught a glimpse of something flashing as Dmitri spoke.

'What's he saying?' asked Tregear.

'It's a diamond necklace,' said Grace. 'Apparently it's worth fifty thousand dollars.'

'If he paid more than five for it then I'm the Pope,' remarked Tatyana acidly.

Yuri passed Dmitri something else. Dmitri held it up in his left hand, for all to see. He made a show of indicating that it was heavy, then held out both fists in front of him.

'Necklace. Stone.'

Yuri produced a large transparent plastic bag. He undid a plastic zip and held the bag open. Dmitri put in the necklace and the stone and Yuri closed the zip.

'Sealed, watertight,' announced Dmitri proudly. He tapped Yuri on the shoulder.

Yuri took the sealed bag and began walking towards the far end of the pool. Dmitri spoke to the girls.

'What's he saying now?' demanded Tregear impatiently.

'I think he's telling them that there are no rules,' explained Grace hesitantly, only half able to hear. 'Yes, he says it's winner takes all. The first one to get to the top of the diving board with it gets to keep it.'

'Good heavens, you mean it's a race?'

'Apparently.'

'It is unique race,' said Tatyana tonelessly.

'How's that?' asked Tregear.

'It is the only competition in the world where the winner also gets the booby prize.'

'Really? And what is the booby prize?'

'She gets to fuck Dmitri.'

The lawyer staggered to his feet.

'I think I may need to take a closer look at this. If you'll excuse me, ladies.'

Neither Grace nor Tatyana attempted to detain him. He made his way to join the other men, who were spreading out on either side of the pool. Yuri had thrown the plastic bag into the deep end. There was no sign of Gallagher or the two men he had been introduced to earlier.

Dmitri had been given a starter pistol. He pointed it into the air and fired.

A great shout went up from the men as the girls hit the water. One girl leapt straight out again, clutching her elbow and screaming in pain. Two of the others never made it out of the shallow end, stopping to trade insults and blows as their bodies became tangled up in the confined space. The rest ploughed on doggedly to the deep end, churning up great geysers of water. A few of them seemed barely able to swim. Two heads, one blonde and one dark, streaked out in front.

'Let's hope the blonde wins, for Dmitri's sake,' said Tatyana. 'She is tall with nice legs, that one. Not too skinny, a nice round bottom. Exactly his type. The same as our friend Gallagher. What is it he likes doing with you, by the way? You were going to tell me.'

'I was?'

'Oh yes. In England you said you had not slept with him yet. I expect now you have done it many times. Tell me what he likes in bed.'

Another shout went up from the crowd by the pool as the blonde emerged at the far end with the bag between her teeth. The brunette was right behind her. The pair of them raced for the diving board.

'Why do you want to know?' asked Grace casually.

'I am curious. All his women are blondes, but they are not the same type. Some of them are even older than you. I wonder what is it about you that turns him on. I do not think it is your brilliant conversation.'

'Perhaps you'd like me to give you lessons.'

'You think I have anything to learn from you?'

'If you don't, why are you asking so many questions?'

'I ask one question. You don't give me the answer.'

'Perhaps I'm not the person you should be speaking to. Why not ask him yourself?'

Gallagher was walking towards them, minus his erstwhile companions. He looked to be in a good mood.

A groan went up from a section of the crowd as the brunette grabbed hold of the blonde's ankle and yanked her back just as her hand was closing over the top of the diving board. The blonde lost her balance and fell back heavily on to the concrete. The brunette snatched the plastic bag from her and scrambled to the top of the ladder. She bounced joyfully on top of the diving board, waving her prize above her head for all to see.

'So, the Georgian wins,' said Tatyana. 'Poor Dmitri.'

Gallagher came and sat down between them, in the canvas chair Tregear had brought over earlier.

'Seems like I missed out on the fun. I only caught the tail end.'

'I'm not sure if fun's the right word,' said Grace.

The blonde was still lying on the concrete at the bottom of the ladder. A couple of the waiters picked her up and set off with her towards the main house. Gallagher chuckled.

'A bit of horseplay. She'll be fine. How you been keeping, Tatyana?'

Tatyana condescended to raise one pencil-thin eyebrow.

'*Comme çi, comme ça.* Did you have money on the Georgian?'

'No, nor on any of them. You know me, I only bet on certainties.'

'I see. Then you intend to take more money from Dmitri?'

'Whatever's going free.'

'Nothing is free with Dmitri. But you know that already.'

'Oh yeah. I know that already.'

He smiled, but not with any warmth. Tatyana mirrored his glassy expression. She stared past him.

'Now he brings his new girlfriend. What a pity she has such fat thighs.'

Dmitri approached, his arm round the shoulder of the Georgian girl, who was looking very pleased with herself. Her soaked hair hung shapelessly and her naked, slightly plump body glistened with drops of water. She clutched the plastic bag tightly to her bosom. Gallagher stood up.

'Well done,' he said to the girl in Russian.

She flashed her teeth at him.

'A favour please, my friend,' said Dmitri boisterously.

'Sure,' said Gallagher.

Dmitri pointed to the Georgian.

'Take Maryam up to the house for me, will you? When you are ready. She deserves champagne treatment. I need to talk with Grace, OK?'

'Sure.'

Gallagher sat down again. He turned to Grace.

'Be good now,' he said casually.

Grace stood and the Georgian girl sat down in her place. Gallagher snapped his fingers and a waiter appeared with champagne. Another arrived with a towel. She seemed to be enjoying the attention.

'This way – come, my dear,' said Dmitri, pushing his way between Gallagher and Tatyana and beckoning Grace to follow.

Gallagher didn't look at her as she squeezed past. Nor did Tatyana, but she opened the side of her mouth.

'Try and keep your legs together, my dear,' she murmured sarcastically.

Dmitri had set off for the summerhouse. Grace trailed in his footsteps and found him waiting by the double glass doors, holding one open for her.

'Sit down. Make yourself comfortable. You want champagne now? Some drink?'

'I'd like a glass of water, thanks.'

There were half a dozen canvas chairs arranged around a table. She chose one and made herself comfortable. The air in the summerhouse was close. She picked a magazine from the pile on the table and fanned herself while Dmitri fiddled around with the bottles and the ice bucket on the sideboard.

Dmitri brought her a glass of iced sparkling water. He took a step back and looked her up and down, quite openly and in his own time. Grace sipped at her water self-consciously. Dmitri smiled.

'He has good taste. Always makes good choice.'

'You mean Mike?'

'When he comes, I say, "Come alone, I give you pick of my girls," but he refuses, always. He brings his own women, and all are tasteful, very beautiful. You are most beautiful.'

'Thank you.'

'I know him two years now, this he does every time. I know him before, but I invite him my home two years only. He did not speak Russian then. He took lessons before his first time. Very impressive.'

'He seems to be a talented linguist.'

'He travels much. It is easy, when you have English, to be lazy, but he is hard worker, and quick learner. Mike makes life easy. It is good to speak in your own language when you do business. Then no misunderstandings. You say you speak French. Some German?'

'Only a few words.'

'You want to learn better?'

'I don't know. I've never thought about it.'

'Think about it now. German is useful to me.'

'Useful for what?'

He picked out one of the other canvas chairs and lowered himself into it. He twisted himself round to face her.

'How old are you?' he asked bluntly.

She laughed.

'Do I have to answer that?'

'Ha! Waste of time asking, women always lie. Tatyana pretends she is twenty-six. I know she is thirty-one but she thinks I don't know.'

'She doesn't look thirty-one.'

'She doesn't look twenty-six either. How long have you been a prostitute?'

Grace took a long sip of her water.

'I'm not sure I want to answer that either.'

'A prostitute is good for five years, six years, I say. More when she looks after herself, keep off drugs, but I say ten years maximum. You know this. You see old whores, skin like animal, thick paint, disgusting. What kind of guy pays such a woman? For my girls a man pay two hundred, three hundred pounds the hour. For that the girl is fresh, is healthy, is young. Over thirty, I say forget it. How much you charge?'

'That depends.'

'I see. You play cat with mouse with me. You are clever. You charge what market will bear. That is sound business sense, very good. I say you are top of the range. I pay three hundred for you.'

Grace sat rigidly, knees together, hands tightly gripping the glass in her lap. He, by contrast, was looking very relaxed. He leant back in his chair, one ankle crossed over his knee, his hands clasped behind his head, assessing her physical attributes at his leisure.

'You have good body. You work out?'

'A little.'

'I would like to fuck you.'

She said nothing. He tipped back his chair and crossed his hands over his tummy, smiling at her like a corrupt Buddha. She wanted an excuse to look away. She lifted her glass to her lips and drained it, slowly, her eyes fixed on the ceiling.

'You are thirsty,' he said, getting up. 'Give me your glass.'

He took her glass to the sideboard and topped it up, adding a large cube of ice.

'Warm here,' he said. 'In a minute I take you to the house.'

She took the glass. He was still standing over her. She glanced up and met his eyes plainly.

'*Spaseeba*,' she said.

She took a deep breath, and continued speaking in Russian.

'As you say, it's important to have no misunderstandings. I can't sleep with you, I'm afraid. I have a prior engagement, which doesn't expire till Wednesday, and I make it a strict rule never to break a contract. Besides, my client is a very jealous man.'

There was a long moment's silence. She thought he must be angry, despite the broad self-satisfied smile, but when he laughed it sounded like he was genuinely amused.

'Very good,' he said, sticking to Russian. 'I admire professionalism, it makes business much easier. That's why I asked you here. I have a business proposition to make.'

He returned to his chair. He had adopted a much brisker air. In English he sounded slow, sometimes even buffoonish. In Russian he spoke crisply, precisely, and, needless to say, fluently. It was as if he was another person entirely.

'Tell me if I'm speaking too fast or if you don't understand anything.'

'I'm a bit out of practice, but I understand you.'

'Your Russian is good. That's why I want you. You see those girls out there? They all work for me. They're all young, no more than twenty-two, twenty-three, some still in their teens. Myself, I like a woman who's a little older. I prefer intelligent women too, another reason to like you. But when a man hires a whore brains don't figure much on his checklist. Young girls are at a premium, and I have a limitless supply. These girls tonight are mostly Russian, but I get them from all the old Soviet republics, the Baltics, Balkans. They'll do anything to get to the West, earn real money, and I give them the opportunity. I get visas, papers, even passports, and I arrange transportation. Then I set them up in a nice place, in Amsterdam, Munich, Paris, London. My business is multinational, you see, I'm an apostle of globalization. All this costs money, a lot of money, so they must work hard to repay me. They do, most of them, but business is slow sometimes, and there's a lot of competition. You saw the guys Orhan brought along?'

'Tony and Ali?'

'Yes. They're Albanians. Very tough customers, these Albanians, but not very subtle. They've been flooding Western Europe with girls, especially London. London's crawling with Albanians, did you know that? Now they don't care, they'll put anything on the streets, no matter her age or looks. Doesn't make sense to me, but they don't see it that way. The problem is it depresses the market, and we had a little dispute with them a while back, not very pleasant but these things happen. That's why they're here now, so we can smooth things out, all be friends. The Turk has been very helpful, I must say.'

'Does the Turk work for you?'

'No, he's a friend of Mike, but we've got interests in common. He can speak to the Albanians in their own language, and that's why he's been useful to me. The same applies to you. There's really no reason why us and the Albanians can't live together, you see, and I think they understand that now. I'm a peaceful man, I want to make a living, like we all do. As far as I'm concerned, they can bring over all the cheap tarts they like. I'm operating at the other end of the market. You want another drink yet?'

'I'm fine, thanks.'

He got up and walked to the sideboard. He half-filled a tall glass with ice and poured in a stiff measure of Stolichnaya. He carried his drink over to the glass doors and pointed outside.

'My only problem is the girls. They're all young and good looking, sure, but they're immature. Immature and ignorant. Most of them don't even have any manners. I'm paying a fortune to put these girls in beautiful apartments, in Kensington, Park Lane, wherever. I surround them with beautiful things and they act like peasants. You see the girl who won the necklace – Maryam? At dinner last night she sat picking her nose all the way through. I'm not kidding. Then some of the others started belching and they all thought it was hysterical. Couple of them even threw the bread rolls at each other, like kids. I say to them I want them to be like Tatyana, but Tatyana is such a cold, stuck-up bitch that's not what I really want at all. No, I don't want them to be like Tatyana. I want them to be like you.'

He was staring at her intently, gauging her reaction to

his words. The only reaction she was capable of was stunned surprise.

'Those girls are only any use as whores, but there are better ways for an intelligent woman like you to make a living. Come and work for me, Grace. I'll pay you very well, more than you make now, much more. You want a Porsche, a Ferrari? I can get you one of each. Two of each, what the fuck do I care? You'll live only in beautiful places. I have villas in Spain, Italy, Greece, all over. Come and see my chateau in the Dordogne, it's got two hundred rooms. I bet not even Buckingham Palace has got two hundred fucking rooms. I bring my girls to these places and you teach them to be classy and sophisticated. Teach them how to act like an English lady. That's why I want you. Because you can teach them exactly how to please the kind of clientele I'm after. Three hundred an hour is just the introductory rate. I've got girls who with a bit of polish could charge a thousand. And I know where to find the men who'll pay that much too. Plenty of them. What do you say, Grace?'

What could she say? Teaching etiquette to prostitutes was not a career move she had ever contemplated before. She felt something heavy – a stone in a plastic bag perhaps – drop through her stomach.

'I think I'd quite like a drink now,' she said.

'Let's have it up at the house. We can drink to our partnership. No need for you to go back to England when you finish your current engagement. Come and stay here, we'll talk it through in detail. Don't mention this to Mike, by the way. As you say, he's a very jealous guy, though it's no bad thing if I make him agitated. We're having a little game tonight, you see, so it's good to get under his skin. He has too good a poker-face already, much too much of an advantage. You will come and watch?'

'I didn't think you liked spectators.'

'What makes you say that?'

'Last weekend you played behind closed doors.'

'Oh, that was different. Tonight I want a big atmosphere, lots of excitement, like a real casino. It'll give you an opportunity to take a closer look at the girls. You'll have a lot of work to do with them, I won't pretend otherwise.'

'I'm really not sure –'

'I am.'

His interruption was curt. She didn't attempt to go on. She read the steely insistence in his eyes.

'I'm very sure. Don't worry about your pimp. Any trouble, I'll fix it.'

'He's not my pimp.'

'Sure he's not. Consider it taken care of. When I make my mind up, it stays made up. It is that simple. Now come along. It's late, and I can't keep my guests waiting any longer.'

He swung open the double glass doors and beckoned for her to come.

The party by the pool had broken up, only a few waiters remained behind to clear up. The floodlights round the pool had been turned off. Yuri, who must have been waiting outside the whole time, appeared with a torch. He walked ahead of them, flashing the beam at the ground to point the way.

'Ah, some breeze at last,' said Dmitri. 'That is good. Perhaps you will come sailing with me later this week.'

'I'm not a very good sailor, I'm afraid.'

'You will like sailing with me. Tomorrow I'll show you my yacht. You and Mike will stay the night. I promise there will be no more interruptions from the police.'

She laughed with him, even though it was the last thing she felt like doing. Of course there would be no interruptions from the police, she knew that better than he did. She knew she was entirely on her own.

Suddenly she felt a long, long way from home.

14

The house had been built in the 1920s and must once have been full of art deco features. The original design survived in the doors and the stained-glass windows, but in little else. The furniture and fittings were an incongruous mixture of the antique and the cutting edge, of Louis Quinze and tubular steel. It ran through Grace's mind that it wasn't just Dmitri's working girls who lacked a touch of class.

The huge living room at the front had been transformed for the night into a casino. There was a roulette table, around which the girls were already gathered, betting excitedly with piles of gold-wrapped chocolate coins, while members of Dmitri's entourage encouraged and petted and condescended to them in turn. Some of the men were shooting craps in the corner and there were even a couple of one-armed bandits. But there was no doubt where the focus of attention lay. In the centre of the room, beneath a glittering ormolu chandelier, was a round table covered with green baize. Five men were already seated. Yuri, who had walked into the house with them, stepped forward smartly and positioned himself behind the remaining empty chair.

'Good evening, gentlemen,' said Dmitri.

He walked around the table, in his best lord-of-the-manor mode, acknowledging them in turn.

'Tony, Ali, so glad you could stay.'

He patted the two Albanians on the shoulder. Behind them stood another Albanian, a classic-looking heavy wearing the regulation dark suit and Ray-Bans.

'Ralf, my friend, you ready to lose some money?'

Orhan grunted. He murmured something to Ali, who was sitting next to him.

'Speak English only during game,' said Dmitri, moving on. 'Or maybe my lawyer will think we are cheating him.'

George Tregear gave a glazed smile.

'Bit out of my league here, I know, but what the hell, I'll give it a go.'

Dmitri slapped him on the shoulder.

'We are all out of our league here. Maybe we give Mike our money now, save ourselves the trouble of handing it over later.'

'Where's the fun in that?' said Gallagher casually. He glanced up from the table, but not at Dmitri. He was staring at Grace. 'We were beginning to wonder if you were going to make it, Dmitri.'

'Important business, my friends. I apologize for delay. We will start now, OK?'

He sat down. Yuri pushed in his chair for him.

'OK,' said Gallagher.

Grace was standing inside the door, where Dmitri had left her.

'You don't look too comfortable there,' said Gallagher mildly. 'Take a seat.'

'Yes, take a seat,' echoed Dmitri.

She looked around the room. Everyone was by the roulette and craps tables except Maryam, who was sitting by the window with a large glass of champagne, looking pleased with herself, and Tatyana, who was reclining on a chaise longue reading a magazine. Grace took a step towards one of the comfortable armchairs on the other side of the room, by the fireplace.

'No, no,' said Dmitri. 'Sit here, you bring me good luck. Yuri, chair.'

'Maybe she doesn't want to watch,' said Gallagher.

'Maybe you are afraid she bring me luck,' replied Dmitri.

Yuri brought a chair. Dmitri patted the seat.

'Sit, Grace, by me. My lucky mascot.'

Grace hesitated. She glanced at Gallagher. He shrugged.

'Sure, let him enjoy your company for half an hour. After all, I'll be enjoying it the rest of the night, won't I?'

He looked pointedly at Dmitri, but Dmitri's attention was on Grace. She sat down in the chair, behind and to his right. George Tregear was on her other side.

'Perhaps you'll bring me a spot of luck too, my dear,' said the lawyer.

The white-jacketed waiters appeared. One laid down a tray of unopened card packets. Another produced a rack full of coloured chips. A third took orders for drinks. Gallagher was the only player to decline.

'He likes to keep his head clear,' explained Dmitri to Tregear. 'He is dangerous man, take care.'

'Well, I'm only here to have a bit of fun, in all honesty,' said Tregear. 'Don't expect I shall be taking it too seriously.'

Orhan leant across and said something to Ali, who laughed.

'English only,' said Dmitri, rapping his knuckles on the table.

'You said after game starts,' said Tony darkly. 'He speaks no English.'

'OK,' said Dmitri, suddenly conciliatory. 'Mike, explain house rules. Then, Tony, you tell him.'

'Mike can tell him, in Italian.'

'Then what about George? He has no Italian.'

'It's the bloody tower of Babel,' said Tregear jovially. 'Ah, thank God for that.'

The waiter had arrived with the drinks. He handed Tregear a large brandy.

'Dealer's choice?' asked Tony.

'Texas Hold'Em, but Dmitri's betting rules,' said Gallagher. 'No blinds, it's a straight ante, one hundred dollars.'

'I like it simple,' said Dmitri.

'Cards dealt the usual way, two in the hole, first round of betting, then three more rounds, flop, Turn and River. No checking on the first round.'

'Maximum bet?'

'Pot limit. We keep it modest, you see, a nice, friendly game. Otherwise Dmitri could throw in the keys to his yacht and blast us out of the water.'

'Not all of us,' said Tony quietly.

'But I would never throw in yacht,' protested Dmitri. 'Some things too precious.'

'Dmitri, you'd bet your grandmother,' Gallagher told him. 'He show you his latest toy, Tony?'

'No.'

'She's a beauty, and I say that as someone who doesn't give a damn about boats.'

'How big?' demanded Tony.

'Size not important,' said Dmitri. 'You want big yacht, I show you big yacht, in Cannes I have *Pugachev*, forty metres, three decks. This is *Anastasia*, much smaller but many times more beautiful. I show you later, you will love her.'

'Not tonight.'

'Tomorrow.'

'Not tomorrow.'

'Another time. You will love her.'

'Maybe. But I didn't come here to talk about boats. That it, Mike?'

'No looking at mucked cards. No betting light, it's limited to what you bring to the table. Buy in for new chips any time you like, but once the hand's begun, *finito*.'

'I'm not sure I understand that,' said George Tregear. 'What if the other chap raises and I've got no money left?'

'Then anything bet after that goes into a side pot. Even if you win the hand, you get none of it.'

'That sucks,' said Tony.

'House rules,' said Gallagher.

'My house. My rules,' said Dmitri.

Gallagher looked at Tony.

'You OK with that?'

'OK.'

'Ali OK with that?'

'Yeah, he's OK.'

'I know Ralf is OK. You OK, George?'

'Haven't understood a word you've said. Never mind, I expect I'll pick it up as we go along.'

'Yeah? Well, it's your money. Want to cash in, Dmitri?'

Dmitri lifted his hand and rubbed together his thumb and forefingers. Yuri came across and drew a massive wad of hundred-dollar bills from his inside pocket. Dmitri scooped the packs of cards off the tray on the table and Yuri laid the money in its place.

'Twenty thousand,' said Dmitri.

The Albanian in the suit appeared between Tony and Ali. He opened a slim silver attaché case and offered it to them. The case was filled with bundled hundred-dollar bills.

'We'll take twenty each,' said Tony, adding to the pile.

Orhan and Gallagher both reached into their waistbands and came out with fistfuls of cash. Dmitri was counting out chips. The red and blue chips were round and marked 100 and 500 respectively. The green and white chips were rectangular, marked 1000 and 5000.

'It's all a bit rich for me,' murmured Tregear, reaching

into his inside pocket. 'Will you take sterling? Think I've got about four thousand here.'

He handed over an envelope stuffed with fifty-pound notes. Dmitri produced a calculator and worked out the exchange rate before passing Tregear a stack of red and blue chips. He pointed to the packs of cards on the table.

'Someone want to choose?'

Tony leant forward and stared at the dozen or so packs. They were all identical, with red or blue backs. He picked out the red packet nearest to him, broke the seal and fished out the pack. He scratched off the cellophane and discarded the jokers. One of the waiters took them away, along with the rest of the packs. Another took the tray of money, which he placed in clear view of everyone on the sideboard.

'Mind if we take a closer look?' said Tony.

Dmitri indicated that he should be his guest.

Tony handed the cards he'd chosen to Ali, who spread them expertly in a fan. He picked out a handful at random and held them up in turn to the light. Tony, meanwhile, had produced a small magnifying glass and was scrutinizing the aces.

'Careful guys, these Albanians,' said Gallagher amiably, leaning back in his chair and looking round the table. 'Guess we'll talk among ourselves. You play any poker, Grace?'

'Cards aren't really my forte, Mike.'

'Oh, I wouldn't say that, a mean blackjack player like you. Poker's easy. You just got to know when the other guy's lying.'

'And how do you know that?'

'In Dmitri's case, it's when his lips move.'

Dmitri laughed.

'Mike is still sore. I won big from him last month. He not like people take money from him.'

'I not like people take anything from me,' said Gallagher softly.

The two Albanians had finished examining the cards.

'Everything OK?' asked Gallagher.

'Sure,' said Tony.

'No need to worry. Dmitri's games are straight. It's everything else about him that's crooked.'

Dmitri forced a smile.

'Cut for deal,' he said brusquely.

Gallagher drew the high card. He shuffled and offered the pack to Orhan, who cut for him.

'Ante in, everyone.'

'I think you'd better talk me through this, if you don't mind,' said Tregear uneasily.

The sight of a hundred thousand dollars thrown casually on to the table appeared to have had a sobering effect on him.

'Sure,' said Gallagher. 'You make your best five, same as seven-card stud. Difference is the five in the centre are community cards, meaning they're shared. Make any combination you like with the community cards and what you got in the pocket. That's it.'

Gallagher dealt two cards to each player. George picked his up and stared hard at them. The others lifted the corners of theirs with their thumbnails.

'And now the flop.'

Gallagher dealt five more cards into the middle of the table, face down.

'Yours, Ralf.'

Orhan threw in a red chip.

'George?'

Tregear hesitated. He blinked at his two cards.

'Do I have to bet?'

'You can fold.'

'Oh, what the hell,' he said, with a heavy show of bravado.

He added his chip. The others followed suit and Gallagher

turned over the first three cards in the middle, the two red queens and the jack of clubs.

'Will you look at that? You gonna bank on the nice ladies, Ralf?'

The pot held eleven hundred dollars. Ralf chucked in a red and a green chip, doubling it.

'You in, George?'

'Why not, seeing as it's the first hand?'

He matched the bet. So did Dmitri. The Albanians and Gallagher all folded.

'This next card is called the Turn, George. Don't ask me why.'

Gallagher turned over the fourth card; the two of diamonds.

'That help you, Ralf?'

Orhan didn't answer. He threw in a green chip.

'A thousand to stay in, George.'

Tregear looked at his modest pile.

'It does tend to dwindle awfully fast,' he observed sadly, before contributing another thousand.

'Faster still, my friend. A thousand, and I raise another thousand.'

Orhan tossed in a thousand. Tregear, after a long, sweaty pause, did likewise.

'Good man, George,' said Gallagher. 'You hung in this far, eh? This is called the River. Again, don't ask why.'

He turned over the fifth card, the seven of diamonds.

'OK, folks, it's showdown.'

'Check,' said Orhan.

Tregear looked at Gallagher.

'What does that mean?'

'He checks the bet to you. You can bet, if you like, or you can check it to Dmitri. If he doesn't want to bet then you can all look for free.'

'Oh no, I don't think that's any good at all,' said Tregear. 'I raise a thousand.'

He pushed a stack of his chips forward confidently. Dmitri beamed at him.

'Very good, my friend. Now let's see.'

Dmitri estimated the pot with a glance.

'I raise ten thousand.'

Orhan didn't flinch. He pushed forward the rest of his chips.

'See you. And raise.'

Tregear looked down at his reduced pile of chips.

'What do I do now, Mike?' he asked.

'You can see him for what you've got and they make a side pot. Or you can fold.'

Tregear didn't take long to think about it. Quietly he turned his cards over.

'As I feared, too rich for me,' he murmured apologetically.

No one paid him any attention. All eyes were on Dmitri. He pointed to the chips piled in front of him.

'At least I don't have to count them. Now you put in twenty thousand . . .'

He opened his palms, consigning himself to the fates with a gesture.

'And now I cover it.'

He pushed out his chips with a flip of the hand.

'So?'

Orhan flicked over his hole cards, revealing two diamonds.

'Flush.'

Dmitri nodded.

'Not bad. But full house better.'

He revealed a queen and a seven. Orhan sat back with a scowl.

'Unlucky, Ralf,' said Gallagher. 'And lucky Dmitri.'

'Never mind, my friend,' said Dmitri, scooping up the pot with his big fleshy hands. 'It is early days. Your deal, George.'

Tregear cleared his throat uncomfortably.

'I think I'm a little out of my depth here. Feeling some-what the worse for wear too, to be honest. Sorry to be a party pooper, but would you mind if I called it a night and turned in?'

'Of course not, my friend. Yuri, cash in his chips for him.'

Tregear pocketed his money and slunk away wearing a chastened expression. Dmitri crooked his finger at Maryam and the Georgian came to the table. Grace overheard him whispering loudly in her ear.

'Go with George. Make sure he gets five-star treatment.'

Maryam looked none too pleased at the assignment. She turned for the door reluctantly. Dmitri slapped her across the bottom to speed her on her way.

The deal passed to him. Orhan had cashed in another twenty thousand. Tony summoned the man with the attaché case.

'Want to raise the ante?' Dmitri enquired generally.

'Ante's fine as it is, thanks,' replied Gallagher.

'I guess you want to see which way the wind blows.'

The wind was definitely blowing Dmitri's way. He didn't win every hand, but he seemed to win the big ones. The deal passed rapidly round the table. The Albanians played impatiently and glowered whenever any of the others – it was usually Dmitri or Gallagher – seemed to be taking too much time.

'It's too damned noisy round here,' said Tony, throwing down his cards after losing another big hand.

Dmitri swivelled his neck and bawled down at the other end of the room, where the girls were whooping at the spinning roulette wheel.

'Shut up!'

The noise of their chatter ebbed away.

'Want me to get rid of them?' said Dmitri.

'Wouldn't be a bad idea,' said Tony. 'But not the redhead.'

Dmitri snapped his fingers.

'Lara. Here.'

A tall, green-eyed girl with a mass of luxurious auburn curls came over. She couldn't have been more than eighteen.

'You want her?' said Dmitri.

Tony looked the girl up and down. He liked what he saw. She stared back indifferently.

'I got to get back tonight.'

'Take her with you. Send her back tomorrow. At your leisure.'

'Yeah?'

'Yeah. Ali too. Tell him make choice, any choice.'

'He's got his wife and kids with him at the villa. Maybe not such a good idea.'

'Another time then.'

Dmitri spoke brusquely to Lara. She went and sat down in the window, where Maryam had been earlier.

'Return in good working order, please,' said Dmitri, cutting the cards for the next deal. 'Now let's play.'

Yuri had cleared the other end of the room. The game continued more or less in silence.

Tony lost another big hand. The man with the attaché case started to come forward but Tony waved him away.

'Enough. You got a good deal out of me already, Dmitri. No need to skin me alive.'

'Ha. Deal good for everyone, Tony.'

'Yeah, I guess so.'

The Albanians cashed in their remaining chips. They had lost the best part of a hundred grand between them. Most of it had fetched up in front of Dmitri. The Albanians didn't seem especially bothered. They went round the table, shaking hands and saying their farewells.

'I see them out,' said Orhan, rising from the table. 'But I come back.'

'Sure,' said Dmitri. 'Take your time. We'll be here.'

Tony collected Lara and they all left the room. Yuri saw them out. The waiters were by the roulette table, picking up empty glasses and discarded chocolate wrappers. Only Dmitri, Gallagher and Grace were left at the poker table. Tatyana was still reading her magazine.

'Seems like the party's on its last legs,' said Gallagher. 'You want to call it a night?'

Dmitri looked ostentatiously at his watch.

'What's the matter, Mike? No stamina?'

'Maybe we should be getting back to town.'

'Stay.'

'I told you, I can't stay. Too much to do.'

Gallagher looked at Grace.

'Maybe if I don't get you back by Wednesday, you'll turn into a pumpkin.'

'Might be a good thing,' said Grace. 'My glass slippers are killing me.'

Gallagher laughed. He leant back in his chair and stretched.

'You want a drink?'

Grace shook her head.

'Think I will. How about you fix it for me? Jack Daniels, on the rocks.'

'I will have same,' said Dmitri. 'Why not?'

Grace got up and walked to the sideboard, which resembled the drinks counter at her local supermarket. The sideboard was next to the chaise longue. Tatyana looked up idly from her magazine.

'At last, a job suitable for your talents, my dear.'

Grace ignored her. She took two tumblers from the rows of empty glasses and filled them with ice. She opened one of the half-dozen bottles of Jack Daniels and poured in generous measures.

'Not like you, my friend,' said Dmitri, taking one glass from Grace. 'You never drink and play.'

'I thought we'd stopped.'

'Ralf comes back.'

'You want to play with three?'

'Why not?'

Grace carried the other glass round the table. Gallagher indicated for her to put it down on the table next to him. He slipped his hand round her waist.

'If we're going to play some more, maybe you'd better stick with me. My turn for some luck.'

She sat down in the chair vacated by Tony. He moved his own chair closer, his hand not straying from her waist.

'How'd you like the sound of Deauville?' he said to her, speaking softly, leaning in close.

'Sounds good,' she said.

She was aware of Dmitri staring at her. She kept her eyes down on the table. Gallagher's fingers trailed up her back. He stroked her neck.

'I promised to see a guy in Grenoble tomorrow night, but what the hell. He can wait.'

Dmitri shuffled the cards noisily. He banged the pack down on the table.

'Let's play, Mike.'

'There's only two of us, Dmitri.'

'You got my lucky mascot, Mike. You scared?'

'What did you have in mind?'

'One card.'

'No.'

'One card each. Come on.'

'No way.'

Dmitri threw a handful of chips on to the table.

'Twenty thousand.'

'I said no way.'

'I pay three to two.'

'You're crazy.'

'No, that ain't crazy. This is crazy: I pay two to one.'

'Two to one?'

'You win, I pay you forty thousand. Final offer. You shuffle, I don't care.'

Gallagher's fingers brushed the chips in front of him. He was the only one, apart from Dmitri, not to have bought further chips, but there wasn't much more on the table than he'd started with.

'I quit now I'm still ahead,' he observed neutrally.

'I take fifty from you last month.'

'What goes around comes around, Dmitri.'

'Shit, man, you call yourself a gambler?'

'I never gamble, I play odds.'

Gallagher picked up the cards. He shuffled thoroughly. He glanced at Grace.

'Cut it, will you?'

Grace cut the pack. Gallagher fanned out the cards. He laid his hand flat on the table.

'Fifty–fifty's lousy odds. But I like the stake.'

Dmitri laughed.

'You mean you like taking my money.'

Gallagher turned over his hand, offering the pack. Dmitri leant forward, both elbows on the table. He lowered his right arm, slowly, like the arm of a crane, and pointed his forefinger down at the cards. He waved his finger gently from side to side, as if it were a divining rod.

'Shit or bust,' he murmured.

He pulled out a card from the middle of the pack and flipped it over. The ten of spades. He eased back into his chair, a complacent smile on his face. He winked at Grace.

Gallagher placed his finger on the pack and scraped his nail lightly along the backs. He stopped suddenly and flipped over a card. The eight of clubs.

He didn't react. Neither did Dmitri. After a pause Dmitri said:

'Double or quits?'

Gallagher frowned.

'You won, Dmitri. What the fuck you talking about?'

'I give you second chance. Double or quits.'

'Double what? I don't understand.'

'Is simple. Now I have sixty thousand. Sixty my stake. Against what you have.'

Gallagher indicated his small pile of chips.

'I got three, four thousand. You expecting me to cash in and match you?'

'Oh no, Mike. House rules. Only what is at table, remember?'

'I told you, I got four thou, max.'

'Oh no, Mike. You are very rich man.'

Dmitri leant forward over the table. He smiled at Gallagher, and then he turned his head, slowly, and winked again at Grace.

'I want only what you have at table, Mike.'

It took Gallagher a few seconds to realize what he meant. Not so Grace; she understood immediately.

'You're crazy,' Gallagher said.

Grace hardly heard him. His voice sounded tiny, inaudible over the pounding of the blood through her head. She sat rigidly still, unable to take her eyes off Dmitri. She registered his lips moving. She had to concentrate to pick up the words.

'. . . I understand contract expire Wednesday. So what is left? After this one day, one night. Against this, and your four thou max, I stake sixty thousand. Pretty good deal for you, I think.'

'You're crazy.'

'Yeah, Mike, sure I'm crazy. Women expensive, you tell me about it, but even me, I never pay so much before. But this time I make exception. For very exceptional woman.'

Dmitri smiled at Grace and touched his fingers to his lips.

'Very exceptional woman,' he repeated, blowing her a kiss. 'You are flattered, I hope?'

Grace didn't move a muscle.

'What is it with you, Dmitri?' Gallagher was saying. 'Why do you only want what other people have got?'

'Why? Why is simple, my friend. Because I have everything else.'

Dmitri glanced at Grace.

'He hesitate. He must like you very much. That is good sign. I know you must be very good, very good. So then, Mike. You want my money or not? Twenty-four hours of pleasure against sixty thousand dollars. How many women you buy with that, my friend?'

'I expect you know the answer to that better than me, Dmitri.'

'I give you pick of my girls tonight. For free. You pick any one you like. Maybe you even want Tatyana?'

Tatyana threw down her magazine and leapt off the chaise in one sudden movement, eyes blazing. She marched straight to the door.

'Where the fuck do you think you're going?' snarled Dmitri in Russian. 'Sit down.'

Tatyana didn't answer. Her hand closed on the door handle.

'I said sit down!'

Dmitri snatched up his glass from the table and hurled it at Tatyana. She squealed in pain as it struck with tremendous force between her shoulderblades. She staggered, lost her balance and tumbled to the floor. Dmitri casually snapped his fingers at Yuri.

'Put her back. If she tries to get up again without my say-so, break her fucking arm.'

Yuri grabbed Tatyana under the arms and hoisted her up. She looked stunned. She hung like a rag doll as Yuri dragged her back to the chaise.

'I don't want your woman, thanks, Dmitri,' said Gallagher quietly.

'But you want your money back, no?'

Dmitri laughed. He leant forward and pushed the pile of chips in the middle of the table into a heap, like a child making a sandcastle.

'How bad you want it, Mike? What you got to lose? Four thou against sixty? Shit, man, maybe I am crazy.'

Gallagher said nothing. He stared at Dmitri. Grace put her hand on his sleeve.

'Can we go please, Mike?'

Her voice was so hoarse it was like a squeak. The plaintiveness in it made her wince.

Gallagher turned his head towards her. His tanned handsome face was as expressionless as a waxwork. His clear blank eyes fixed on her for a moment, and then he looked away again.

'We can make more than sixty thousand, Mike,' she said quickly.

'It's not about money,' he said.

His hand closed on his pile of chips, the four thousands' worth. He flicked over his wrist and held out his closed fist.

'What are you doing, Mike?' said Grace quickly.

He didn't answer.

'I said, what are you doing?'

'Making a living,' he said.

He opened his hand and let his chips fall into Dmitri's sandcastle.

'You've no right,' said Grace.

'I haven't?'

Those empty eyes turned to her again. She felt the chill from them spread through her.

'What you gonna do?' he said. 'Hire a lawyer?'

She felt her face burning. The quiet mockery in his voice was unbearable. All of it was unbearable. She wanted to scream, she wanted to hit him, she wanted to run, and keep on running, until she was home, far away, anywhere but here. But she had no strength. She watched, in appalled fascination, as his hand slid across the table to the pack of cards.

'Guess it's my turn to draw first,' he said.

Dmitri nodded.

Gallagher touched a card with his forefinger and drew it back slowly over the baize. He lifted the corner with his thumbnail and took a peek. His face gave nothing away.

'So?' said Dmitri.

He was trying to look as unconcerned as Gallagher, to sound as casual. But there was a catch in his voice.

Gallagher flicked over the card. It was the jack of hearts.

Dmitri raised an eyebrow.

'Not bad. Not bad at all. Odds in your favour, my friend. Two to one. Not so good, from here.'

'Not so bad, from here,' said Gallagher.

Dmitri hunched forward over the table. He poked a finger at a card, and then at another. He hesitated, then closed his eyes and stabbed suddenly into the centre of the pack. His hand came away, dragging two cards. He released the downward pressure on his fingers and one card dropped away. He steered the other to the edge of the table. He tapped a beat on it with one finger. And then he flipped it over.

No one spoke, or moved a muscle. Every eye in the room, even Yuri's, even Tatyana's, was on the card. They might have been statues, all of them, fixed for all time on that same coloured picture, that crowned curled head and black beard.

The king of clubs.

15

There was a film in front of her eyes. She could see the outline of the card but the picture was a coloured blur. She blinked, and thought she saw the scowling face move.

The king of clubs, mocking the one-eyed jack.

Sleepwalking must be like this, she thought. You move, breathe, even talk, but it's not you doing it. Whoever it's happening to, it can't really be you. Please God, let it not be me . . .

'Yuri, call Mikhail. Have him bring the car round.'

Dmitri's voice sounded tiny, like he was in another room. But he wasn't. He was sitting opposite, grinning at her, practically licking his lips, like a cartoon cat in a dairy. He spoke in Russian. She had to strain to understand the simple words.

'Take Grace down to *Anastasia*. See she is comfortable. Tatyana, you go too. Get all your shit out of the cabin. And make yourself scarce before I arrive. That goes for the crew too, Yuri. Get rid of them. All except Yakov.'

Yuri was talking into his mobile. There was a scrape of wood against wood as Gallagher rose from his chair. He laid a hand on her shoulder.

'Not my lucky night,' he said. 'I'm sorry.'

Sorry? She stared up at him with her unfocused eyes. He was pale, tight-lipped. He sounded and looked choked. He did seem sorry about something. Sorry to have lost her or sorry not to have taken Dmitri's money?

'I'll maybe call in a few days when you're back in London,' he was saying, squeezing her shoulder. 'Be good to see you again. We made a great team.'

She had thought so too. She hadn't realized she was quite so disposable.

'She won't be going back to London,' Dmitri said to Gallagher. 'She's too valuable. From now on she works for me.'

The fingers kneading her shoulder froze. Gallagher said:

'I see. And when did you arrange this?'

'Just now, by the pool.'

'I see.'

The pressure lifted from Grace's shoulder. Gallagher patted her on the head. The gesture was affectionate. It didn't match the coldness in his voice.

'Neat work, babe. You could go a long way. Thanks for the hospitality, Dmitri. Maybe Mickey could run me into town when he gets back.'

'Mickey's going to be busy for a while. Ask Misha.'

'I take you,' said Orhan, who had reappeared at the door. 'If it's over.'

'Oh yeah, it's over,' said Gallagher.

He walked to the door. Casually he jabbed a thumb at Grace.

'I'll have her stuff taken down to the lobby. You can get it picked up some time. Goodnight, everyone.'

'Better luck next time, my friend,' said Dmitri.

Gallagher didn't answer. Orhan cashed in the chips he'd left at the table and followed him out of the room. Dmitri turned to Grace.

'Go with Yuri, please. I have some things to take care of. I will be along soon.'

Grace stood. She was surprised to find that her legs would take her weight. There was no feeling in her limbs. She seemed to be floating, but the sensation was not a pleasant one. She picked up her bag and walked to the door.

Tatyana had got up from the chaise. Grace couldn't see her eyes. She had put on sunglasses.

'Follow me,' said Yuri.

Tatyana walked out briskly. Grace followed, in a daze. She trailed them down the long hallway, past the art deco relics, to the open front door. A car was pulling out of the courtyard, Orhan's she presumed. At the bottom of the steps the silver Rolls Royce waited, engine purring. Yuri was holding the rear door open for her.

She got in. Yuri closed the door after her and got into the front. The car pulled away. Tatyana was sitting on the other side of the wide rear seat, staring out of her window. She didn't speak.

They drove out of the courtyard and turned down a paved, narrow track. The big car went slowly round the sharp zig-zagging bends. It went down the hill, past the swimming pool, towards the sea. Grace caught a glimpse of the high fence that surrounded the property, the metal mesh glinting in the spotlights that studded the perimeter.

The road flattened out. Gentle white breakers rolled towards a narrow strip of moonlit beach on their left. Up ahead was a wooden jetty. Small lights hung from the tall mast of the boat that was moored to it.

The car stopped. A moment later both rear doors were opened. Grace stepped out and Yuri closed the door after her. The door on the other side of the car banged shut.

Grace glanced across. Tatyana had started walking towards the boat. The driver, Mickey, was still standing by his door. Could he really be Mickey Martinez? It didn't seem so important any more. Grace saw the white blur of his hands, lying flat on the roof of the door. She couldn't see his face by the dim light coming from the boat, but she knew that he was staring at her. The thought of those unseen eyes boring into her back as she walked on to the jetty should have made her nervous. But she was past nerves.

The boat was long and sleek, quite low in the water, much smaller and much less ostentatious than she would have expected. The hull was gleaming black, the rest of it spotless white. A small, moustachioed man in immaculate whites stood amidships, by the gangplank, welcoming them aboard. She remembered seeing him at the house in England. Tatyana brushed past him and disappeared below.

'Take her to the cabin, Yakov,' instructed Yuri. 'See she has anything she wants.'

Yakov gave Grace a crooked smile and led her towards some steps. He indicated for her to go down. She hesitated a moment, as if she had a choice. Yuri was on the jetty. Even without his lumbering presence there was no escape that way, past all Dmitri's other cronies, over the barbed-wire fence. She thought of old PoW movies. Were there guards with Alsatians, watchtowers with searchlights? How far would she get if she flung herself over the side and started swimming? She had noticed a rubber dinghy with an outboard motor tied to the stern. Maybe she could try and make a getaway in that. The image flashed through her brain and was gone in an instant. She knew it was all idle fantasy. She went down the steep wooden steps.

Her instinct was to duck her head, but it was unnecessary. The ceiling was eight feet at least, and the sleek modern furnishings, a carefully co-ordinated arrangement of cream and natural wood, gave the room more of the feeling of a swish docklands penthouse than a boat. It wasn't her cup of tea, but someone around here had taste. Not Dmitri, she assumed.

She followed Yakov down a thickly carpeted corridor towards the stern. There were doors to either side of her, all shut. The door at the end was ajar. Yakov pushed it fully open and stood aside to let her pass.

It was the bedroom to complete that swish penthouse experience. A parquet floor, wall units and a desk in gleaming walnut, a king-sized bed, a fridge and small bar within comfortable reach of the head, the wall opposite the foot dominated by a giant widescreen TV, chest-high speakers on either side. Above the desk there were photographs of this boat and of another, a vast luxury yacht with a multi-tiered superstructure like a wedding cake. There was a close-up of Dmitri on the bridge, one of those Russian officers' naval caps, smothered with gold leaf, sitting on his head like an outsized pancake.

There was an adjoining door to an en suite bathroom. Tatyana was in there, taking things out of a cabinet. Her Louis Vuitton handbag and an open matching suitcase, as yet empty, were on the bed.

'You like drink?' asked Yakov in halting English. 'Wine, coffee, food?'

'I'd like some water, please,' said Grace.

Her tongue and throat were stone dry. The room was fully air-conditioned, very cool, but she could feel the sweat trickling down her face.

'You want shower? Plenty towels. I bring. Two minute.'

He pulled a conspiratorial face and nodded towards the bathroom, indicating that he would wait until Tatyana had departed. He was used, no doubt, to the etiquette of evicting former favourites. He slipped away discreetly.

Tatyana came out of the bathroom. She dumped an armload of cosmetics into the open suitcase. She opened one of the fitted wardrobes and lifted out a fur coat and half a dozen dresses. She folded them loosely and laid them in the suitcase. She emptied a drawer of her underwear and filled the case to bursting point. Grace stood by the door watching, a reluctant trespasser.

'This wasn't my idea, you know,' she said.

Tatyana ignored her. The suitcase was so full it wouldn't shut. She pulled out a cashmere sweater and made sufficient room for the zip to close. She emptied her handbag and pushed the sweater into the bottom. She refilled the handbag, making the sides bulge with her purse, her lipstick, her mobile phone and other accessories. She went back into the bathroom and closed the door.

Grace glanced over her shoulder. The corridor was deserted. She walked quickly to the bed and thrust her hand down the side of Tatyana's bag. She found the mobile, a hi-tech toy scarcely bigger than a ten-pack of cigarettes, and transferred it to her own handbag. She heard the toilet flush. She walked back to her old position by the foot of the bed.

Tatyana came out of the bathroom, her appearance changed so utterly that Grace did a double take. Her hair was short, almost cropped, still blonde but quite reddish. Her former head of hair, her silky platinum mane, was resting on the wig block she had cradled in her arms. She took off her sunglasses and put them into her handbag.

'I lasted three years,' she said, not looking at Grace. 'If you want to last as long, learn to be what he wants you to be. Forget about being yourself.'

She sounded matter-of-fact, like an older relative dispensing from the fount of wisdom. So cool, thought Grace, that you almost didn't notice the strain in her eyes.

Yakov came in with a bottle of Perrier and a glass on a tray, a big white towel draped over his arm.

'Bring my case,' said Tatyana, shouldering her handbag and marching out.

Yakov put the tray down on the desk. He laid the towel on the bed and picked up the suitcase.

'Mr Rostov arrive ten minutes. Please take shower.'

Was the shower an invitation or an order? Grace wondered. Did Yakov have standing instructions to oversee the preparation of sacrificial lambs? His oily unctuousness would have been quite at home in a Third World brothel. And that, she thought, irrespective of the showroom-brochure surroundings, was more or less where she found herself now.

Yakov struggled out with the heavy case. He closed the door after him.

Grace sat down on the bed. There was a horrible, gnawing sensation in the pit of her stomach, not helped by the gentle rocking of the boat. She was breathing fast, almost hyper-ventilating. She felt giddy, she felt sick. She felt like she was drowning.

She gripped the edge of the bed. She had to clear her head, she had to think. What about the dinghy? She could say she needed a breath of air, yes, that wouldn't be sus-picious, an innocent stroll along the deck. Then, when nobody was looking, hop in and away. Away where? Even if she could start the outboard motor, even if they were so dozy they let her start it, how far would she get? It was the middle of the night, she'd probably plough into the nearest rocks. In that case, best head straight out to sea, but what then? It was a beautiful, clear Mediterranean night, but it wasn't much use having the stars to guide you if you didn't have a clue where you were going.

No, escape tonight was pure wishful thinking, even without taking into consideration what they would do if they caught her. So then, better come up with a plan B, and quick. Sorry, Dmitri, it's the wrong time of the month. Sorry, Dmitri, I'm feeling whacked, mind if we give it a miss? Sorry, Dmitri, I've got to get home urgently, my mother/cat/budgerigar is on the critical list. Sorry, Dmitri, you're ugly and your breath stinks and looking at you makes me want to heave. But we can be friends, if you like . . .

She got up and began pacing the cabin. Sitting made her too aware of the motion of the boat. She still felt enervated, but there was enough adrenaline pumping through now to sustain her. Enough fear.

She poured herself a glass of water, drank it down thirstily and poured another. She carried it to the nearest porthole and drew aside the curtain. A little light from the boat spilled on to the jetty. She could see the glow of a cigarette, a shadowy figure, Yuri she supposed, walking slowly up and down. There was no one else about.

She snatched up her bag and marched into the bathroom. She looked in vain for a lock on the door, and had to settle for closing it firmly instead. Tatyana's phone was already switched on. She sat on the edge of the bath and dialled Bob's number. Her heart sank as she listened to his recorded message.

'Damn you, Bob, why are you never there?'

She bit her lip, regretting the querulous rise in her voice. He was probably tucked up in bed, where any sensible person would be at this time of night. And it wasn't his fault she was where she was. He hadn't told her to come. No one had.

'Look, I'm on Rostov's boat in the South of France. It's a complicated situation, but I'm stuck here. I'm going to get away as soon as possible, but it may be tricky. Bob, I think you've got to get on to the French police and work something out. I think I've identified Miguel Martinez. Repeat, I have a possible ID on Martinez. Rostov has a chauffeur, Mikhail, known as Mickey, I think it could be his cover. It sounds far-fetched, I know, but check him out, will you? You can't call me but I'll try and get through again soon. This is important, Bob, I may be on to something.'

She could only hope she didn't sound as hollow as she felt. Yes, she might be on to something, but all she really wanted was for the Seventh Cavalry to appear on the horizon. And the chances of that happening weren't going to improve if her only contact with the outside world remained stubbornly incommunicado.

She put the phone back in her bag. She checked her appearance in the mirror. She didn't look too bad, which was some kind of a miracle considering the way her insides were churning. She reached into the bag and found her lipstick. She hesitated. Was she really going to tart herself up for him? The thought was repellent. What was the alternative? She stared in vain for an answer at her reflection.

It was no use trying to stand on her rights. She was going to have to sleep with him. Perhaps if she played along, perhaps if she did whatever he wanted and gave him a good time, then he might drop his guard and loosen the leash and she'd have her chance to get away. Yes, there must be something she needed, something she had to get herself, shoes, clothes, anything. She would ask to be taken into town tomorrow, and take it from there. He wouldn't be suspicious, not if she convinced him she was loving every minute of being with him. All she had to be was what he thought she was anyway, for one night.

It made her skin crawl. She thought of him touching her. She thought of lying underneath him, feigning pleasure. Well, it wouldn't be the first time. It was just that she'd never done it with a mafioso before.

It occurred to her that if she had got through to Bob he might have asked her to stay put. They'd probably been trying for years to get someone on the inside of the Rostov organization, and now here she was, about to share the bastard's bed. You couldn't get much more inside than that, could you? Bob might even have ordered her to stay. Whichever way she looked at it, she was going to get screwed.

She felt the anger surge inside her. It was a good feeling. She could have done with it up at the villa. She should have screamed and stormed and stamped her foot. She should have insisted that she wasn't a commodity to be traded on a whim. Only she'd been too numb and shocked, and much too intimidated. Too late to do anything about that now. She'd have to bite her lip and get through it. At least, according to Tatyana, it wouldn't last long. What was the worst that could happen? Dmitri was a big slow slob of a guy with an over-inflated ego to match. She knew enough to handle that, didn't she?

She fetched the towel from next door, undressed and removed her watch and jewellery. She took off her make-up and got into the shower. It was a space-age cylindrical unit with an opaque frosted-glass door that slid open and shut noiselessly. She put on the shower cap Tatyana had left behind and immersed herself in the powerful jet. The blast of steaming water invigorated her. She soaped herself all over, then turned up the pressure to maximum, until the stinging needles of water made her face numb. She turned it down, and stood with head bowed, enjoying the tickling sensation of pleasantly warm water trickling down her body. For a few blissful moments she almost succeeded in forgetting where she was.

Reluctantly she turned off the water. She remembered coming out of the shower yesterday, clinging to Gallagher, flushed and tingling all over, returning his kisses, sharing his lust and wanting him back inside her, knowing that she had never let herself go with such abandon in her life, and never would again, and not giving a damn, just living the moment in a way she had never thought possible, without so much as a millisecond's thought to the future, or to the past. She had surrendered utterly to physical sensation. And now, like a character in an old morality tale, she was paying the price.

She slid open the shower door and stepped out, pulling off the shower cap and freeing her unruly hair. Blinking water from her eyes, she took a step towards the chair, reaching out a hand to grasp the big white towel. She pulled up, noticing suddenly that her clothes were missing. At the same instant she saw out of the corner of her eye that the bathroom door was open. She snatched up the towel and wrapped it round her body, tying it above her breasts.

'Dmitri, what are you doing?'

She glimpsed him through the door, sitting on the edge of the bed. He glanced up at the sound of her voice, then returned to what he had been doing. He was going through the contents of her handbag, which he had tipped out on the duvet.

'Dmitri . . . ?'

Her voice died away as she saw that he was not alone. Yuri was by the desk, on which her clothes were carelessly piled. He was running her dress slowly through his fingers.

'Sit there,' said Dmitri, jerking his thumb towards the head of the bed.

She remained where she was in the doorway, too surprised to react. Dmitri saw that she wasn't moving and a scowl flashed across his features. He nodded at Yuri.

Yuri put down her dress and crossed to the bathroom door in two long strides. His hand reached out so suddenly that she didn't even have time to flinch. He grabbed a handful of her hair and gave it a sharp savage twist, half yanking her off her feet and propelling her down to the other end of the bed. She gave a yelp as she fell across the pillows.

Instinctively she pulled her knees up into her chest, compressing herself into as small a space as possible. Feeling bewildered and terrified in equal measure, she watched the two men going through her possessions and tried to make sense of what she was seeing. Yuri was holding her dress up to the light, pinching the seams between his finger and thumb. Dmitri was examining her lipsticks. The rest of her make-up had already been pulled apart and scattered over the bed.

'What is this?' he demanded suddenly.

Her eyes were still smarting, she had to blink out the tears before she could make out that he was holding up a folded scrap of paper. She could just see that there was something written on it.

'I don't know,' she said faintly, and meant it.

He unfolded the paper and thrust it towards her.

'Phone number,' he said.

Yes, she could see that now. It was a phone number she had learnt by heart. So why hadn't she thrown the paper away?

'Perhaps this will refresh your memory.'

He was holding up Tatyana's phone, showing her the display. He pressed the recall button.

'Familiar?'

She couldn't read the display, but she didn't need to. He walked over to the desk, where there was a phone and fax machine. He punched in the UK code, consulted the paper and copied the numbers. He flicked a switch and she heard the loud, tinny, ringing tone. There was a click, and then Bob's voice:

'You've reached the answering service of Detective Chief Superintendent Challoner. Leave your message and the time of your call after the beep.'

Dmitri slammed down the phone. He walked over to her. This time she remembered to flinch.

The first blow glanced across the side of her head. With his left hand he grabbed her hair and wrenched her face up towards him. His second, third, and fourth blows hit her full in the face. After that she lost track.

She tasted blood. Her face was wet with it. When she breathed in she could feel blood bubbling in her nostrils. She heard a pathetic, whimpering sound and took a few moments to understand that it was her making it. She was so dazed she hadn't realized that he had stopped hitting her.

318

She sat up against the headboard. Her left eye, the one that had been blacked a week ago, was throbbing, and her entire face felt as if it had been stung by bees. Her arms too were covered in bruises from her feeble attempts to shield her head. She saw his faintly ludicrous, roly-poly figure leaning against the bar. She had had no idea of the man's brute power.

He filled a glass with ice and poured in vodka. He tipped the glass to Grace in a mock salute.

'Good enough for the Iraqi secret police.'

It was as if he had emptied the ice from his glass and clapped it to her spine. The chill spread through her as a picture formed in her head, the connection obvious, only she hadn't made it till now. She remembered marching through the car park, bickering with Bob as he opened the door of Ryan's car for her. And she remembered the rather grander vehicle parked a few bays along, the sleek Rolls Royce with its blacked-out windows.

'My driver, Mikhail, knew he had seen you before. He was waiting for Tregear at the police station when he saw you come out with this Challoner. He heard you arguing, he heard what you said. He did not know you, of course, he was at the airport waiting for Tregear when you came to the house. And then he was waiting for Tregear at the police station when you came out. He said Challoner ordered you to go home and wait for him. He said it was obvious you were working for him.'

Dmitri drained his vodka and banged down the glass. He made a cradle with his hands and flexed his fingers. She heard the knuckles crack.

'I knew you were too good to be true. How many English whores speak fluent Russian? Very clever idea, though. I didn't think your police were that smart. So then, what have you learnt about me so far? And what did you tell your friend Challoner on the phone?'

He took a step towards her and she recoiled, pressing her elbows together and burying her face between her arms. She held her breath as she felt the bed heave with his weight. She sensed his lumbering bulk and braced herself.

'There, there, my pretty spy.'

His hand was in her hair again, but not roughly as before. He was stroking her. His voice had a nursery tone.

'Don't be alarmed, I'm not going to hurt you again. Not unless I have to. You're intelligent enough to know the score. All you have to do is tell me the truth. It'll be easier for you, easier for me. We got a deal? I said, we got a deal?'

She winced as his fingers tightened on her hair. She had been too numb with shock to do anything except cower for the last few minutes, but the sharp fresh tug of pressure on her scalp had the effect of bringing her brain into focus. If, as he had so thoughtfully pointed out, she had enough intelligence to know the score, then she'd better start using it.

'Dmitri, listen to me, I'll tell you everything, anything you want to know, but please believe me, I'm not working for Challoner. He's putting the heat on me, but not in the way you think. That's why I had to ring him, but it wasn't to talk about you, he doesn't even know I'm here –'

She yelped as he jerked back her head. She saw him draw back his arm, his hand closing into a fist.

'Just ask yourself one question, Dmitri, before you start on me again. One question, then if you don't like the answer you can hit me all you like. We got a deal?'

She was hardly in a position to bargain, but she saw the flicker of hesitation in his eyes. She seized her chance. She spoke fast, in English. Her Russian wasn't good enough to match her speed of thought.

'It was Mike who booked me, remember, through my agency. He was offered a load of girls. How could I have known he was going to book me? I'd never heard of him

320

till the agency rang on Saturday morning. And even if I had known somehow, how could I have guessed he was going to introduce me to you? That's my question to you, Dmitri. Even if I am some kind of spy, how could I know he was going to lose me to you in a game of poker? How in God's name could I know?'

His fist was still primed to strike. But he hadn't moved. She gave him all the wide-eyed innocence she could muster.

'It was my bad luck Challoner was there the other night. He knew what I was right away, took me away for what he called special interrogation. He's a corrupt bastard, they all are, but he's one of the worst. He's got friends in vice, he made some calls, checked me out. His friends have been hassling me, threatening to report me to the Inland Revenue. I've never declared any of my income from escorting, you see, they've got me over a barrel. I'm already sleeping with one cop to keep him quiet. Now Challoner wants a piece of me. That's what it was about on Saturday night, in the car park. He told me to be ready for him the next morning, said he was coming straight round, and unless I put out for him he'd be on the phone to the Revenue. What choice did I have? But Mike called me again; I had to come here with him. I rang Challoner from the airport, he was really furious, but he said he wouldn't report me if I made myself available Thursday. That's why I rang him. I had to, don't you see? He's not going to like being stood up twice, I don't know what I'm going to do. I'm just an ordinary working girl, Dmitri, I don't know anything about you, or spying, you've got to believe me ...'

Her voice was shaking. There was a liquid sheen before her eyes, she felt the hot tears run down her cheeks.

'I don't know what Mikhail thinks he overheard, but I swear he's got the wrong end of the stick. How could I be working for Challoner or the police? Look at me. Do I look like a fucking cop?'

Even when she had been a cop she hadn't looked like one. Then what chance of even a fleeting resemblance now, as a quivering half-naked wreck of a woman with a bloody nose and eyes as swollen as a stream in flood? She had one hand pressed against her cheekbone, so raw from his blows that the slightest touch was agony. It wasn't so hard, making herself cry.

She felt the mattress spring back as his weight was lifted from the bed. She opened one damp eye and watched his blurred figure moving about the room. He seemed restless, fidgety. He picked up the cellphone.

'This is Tatyana's. What were you doing with it?'

'She left it behind. It must have fallen out of her bag, it was here, on the bed. My own phone's not working. I'm sorry, I didn't think it would do any harm to use hers, I was going to give it back. I told you, I needed to make that call.'

She was amazed at how easily the lies came tumbling out. She had gone from stunned confusion to a pitch of dissembling in the blink of an eye. She heard the conviction in her voice and could almost have believed it herself. Dmitri tossed the phone on to the desk, where Yuri had piled up her clothes.

'Anything?'

Dmitri's question was delivered in a murmur. Yuri shook his head.

'Clean,' he murmured back.

Grace saw that he had broken the heels off her shoes. She understood now. He had been looking for bugs. A chill ran through her as she remembered Corliss's explanation of how they had considered fitting a tracking device to the mobile phone, but decided against it for unspecified practical reasons.

'Maybe you're telling the truth,' said Dmitri quietly.

The breath caught in her throat as he loomed over her

again. Instinctively she covered her face with her hands. He grunted.

'And maybe you're not.'

She shivered as his hand brushed the top of her head. But he merely patted her hair.

'We'll find out soon enough, one way or the other. Put her in the crew's cabin, Yuri.'

He pushed back her head and pulled her hands away from her face. She sensed that he wasn't going to hit her and didn't resist. He stared down at her dispassionately.

'Sorry, my dear, you'll have to sleep on your own tonight.'

He ran a finger across her nose and wiped away a smear of blood. He laughed to himself, a nasty, mirthless sound.

'All of a sudden you're not looking so pretty any more.'

16

The grounds were surrounded by six kilometres of high fence, topped with barbed wire. It didn't seem to be electrified. There were floodlights at regular intervals, but the main security cameras were mounted by the main gate and on the outside of the house and there were plenty of gaps. Only the ground-floor windows were barred. In addition to the main entrance there was a set of French windows giving on to a patio at the back and two side doors, one on either side of the extensive kitchen. The fence along the north side of the property ran along the crest of a hill. On the west side it ended abruptly at a vertical section of cliff face some twenty metres high. The east side looked more promising. The ground undulated irregularly as it dropped to sea level and the fence followed the little dips and rises, petering out finally at an outcrop of sea-washed rock.

'Too dangerous to go round by the rocks, too slippery and far too exposed,' said Johny. 'But fifty metres in, between those olive trees, there's a blind spot. Cut the fence, then you could work your way unseen up to the hedge round the swimming pool. I don't know if there's motion detectors, but what'd be the point? So much wildlife around here they'd be going off ten times a minute. Get to the pool

324

and from there it's easy to follow the wall on the far side of the courtyard all the way to the house. The front is covered with creepers, should be easy to get a hold, swing up to one of those first-floor balconies. I got a glass-cutter. No problem.'

'What if we set off an alarm?' asked Ryan.

Johny grinned.

'We shoot first.'

They had the firepower. A Beretta automatic apiece and two AK47s, Bulgarian paratrooper issue, wherever the hell Johny's cousin might have dug those up from. He hadn't offered the information and they hadn't asked. The meeting, in an abandoned barn near Marseilles, had been conducted in near total silence. The cousin had counted the money and nodded. They had inspected the guns and nodded back. Then they had transferred the guns, wrapped in a greasy old sleeping bag, from the boot of his car to theirs and both parties had driven off their separate ways.

That had been four hours ago. Now it was late afternoon and they were a hundred and fifty miles down the coast, stretched out on a flat piece of rock a stone's throw from a perfect blue sea and slowly roasting in the sun. They hadn't come for the sunbathing.

Ryan stared at the plans Jackie Harrington had printed out for him in London. There was a second fence, clearly marked, running about fifty metres in from the main fence and shadowing it all the way around the property, in the same rough horseshoe shape. It was only about shoulder height, no problem to climb, but it worried Ryan. Suddenly he pricked up his ears.

'Ssh! What's that?'

'I don't hear nothing.'

'Yes you do.'

They were a hundred metres from the outer fence, keeping their heads down so as not to attract any attention.

They couldn't see much of the house from where they were, but they could see the road that led up to it, the only way in. They both lay very still and listened carefully. The faint noise of barking came to them on the all too gentle breeze. Ryan snapped his fingers.

'Of course, dogs. He had dogs in England, bound to have them here. I'll bet you they run free at night, between the two fences. See the gate on the road, by the inner fence? They must close that at night, after they let the dogs free.'

'We better get some steaks, smother them in tranquillizer shit.'

'I don't think that'll be necessary. As you say, there's a blind spot, but it's not anywhere round the perimeter. It's there –'

Ryan casually jerked his thumb out towards the sea. Johny groaned.

'Shit man, you expect me to get my feet wet too? It's OK for you, you got gills for lungs. I can't hardly swim.'

Ryan laughed.

'Yeah, that could be a problem. I'm going to go down to the shore for a minute, check a few things. Keep an eye out here, will you?'

Ryan was wearing baggy shorts and an ill-fitting T-shirt, a white sunhat and dark glasses. He looked like any pale-skinned Englishman abroad, and certainly no more worthy of note than the two boys perched on the long ridged tongue of rock to his left, their legs and fishing lines hanging over the edge a few feet above the water. He was grateful for the boys and hoped that their failure to catch anything wouldn't discourage them. The nearest public beach was ten minutes away and they hadn't seen anyone else since arriving. It was far too hot for rambling. Only mad dogs and Englishmen went strolling on days like this.

He walked down to the water's edge, picking up a handful of pebbles as he went and tossing them out at the waves.

He could see plenty of pebbles there already beneath the surface, the water was very clear. Although the rocks around where he stood were sharp and jagged, the bottom looked smooth and the slope away from the shore was gentle. The sea was warm and inviting, perfect for an invigorating evening swim.

He walked towards the villa, measuring the distances with his eye. He could see the masts of the boat moored at the jetty, but not the hull or the jetty itself, which were obscured by trees and the curve of the shore. Impossible to gauge accurately without knowledge of the currents, but he thought he could do it in fifteen minutes. How long it would take Johny, or any inexperienced diver, was anyone's guess, and, as with any team, he'd only be able to go at the pace of the slowest. Fifteen minutes was a lousy enough response time anyway. Idly Ryan picked up a few more pebbles and tossed them out at the breaking waves.

He had trained with his squadron several times along this very coast, as well as off Corsica. The last time they had come in on a couple of powered submersibles, rugged little underwater craft that could manage a steady five or six knots even with a stick of heavily armed frogmen aboard. He could have done with one of those now, not to mention the firepower that came with it. Johny was a landlubber, it wasn't worth the risk of dragging him along. No, if he went in that way it would have to be on his own. He would have to figure out another way of getting his back-up in place. He wondered how good the security was around the villa. It hadn't been too hot in England, but they might have tightened things up since then. On the other hand, they might have grown more complacent, thinking that lightning was unlikely to strike twice. Well, it was unlikely. He certainly wasn't planning to go in unless he had to. He had been trying since yesterday to think of the circumstances that might compel him, and to remain relaxed about it at the same time.

He turned around without glancing towards the villa and walked back to the secluded spot they'd chosen for a base. The car was parked off the nearest dirt track, a good kilometre away, and they had lugged all his equipment up to here. He had slept about two hours in the last twenty-four and needed rest badly. But he would need to send Johny back into town first, and that meant keeping watch on his own for another few hours.

Ryan picked up his rucksack and walked up towards where Johny was sitting, halfway up the slope, in the shade of a stunted tree. Ryan took out his diminished roll of hundred-dollar bills.

'What do you need?' asked Johny.

'A boat,' said Ryan. 'Small speedboat. Rubber dinghy with an outboard would be perfect, but whatever you can get.'

'Should have asked Marcel.'

'I didn't think of it till now. Dumb of me, seeing as it's my line, but there you go. As I told you, I'm making it up as we go along.'

'I'll need a trailer to get it back.'

'Is it a problem?'

'Hell no. You can't hire that stuff round here, where can you? I better leave now, before everyone shuts up for the night.'

When Johny had gone, Ryan took his spot in the shade of the tree. It was a passable hide. A sleeping bag, blankets and towels, one laid on top of another, marked out a comfortable enough spot on which to lie, the feet hanging down the slope, only the neck and head in line with the crest. Johny was an old soldier and had his priorities right. He had strung up a net between the tree trunk and a gnarled, arched length of root from beneath which the rocky soil had eroded away. Through gaps in the leaves and grasses that filled the net Ryan could see the outer gate, a hundred metres away, and the front of the villa. There was a perfect vantage point only a little higher up the slope, from which he would have been able to take in the whole property, but it was too exposed. He would go up there only after dark.

He settled down and unpacked his rucksack: two pairs of binoculars, one of them night-vision, his cellphone, suncream and insect repellent, some bread and cheese, water, half a thermos of warm coffee. He swapped his floppy hat for something similar but in jungle camouflage. A potentially long wait stretched ahead: the rest of today, all of tomorrow, maybe the first part of Wednesday. The tickets Gallagher had booked from Heathrow to Nice had been one-way and there was no indication of when or how they planned to return to England. Ryan's plan, inasmuch as he had one, was to stay and observe until such time as Grace was safely on a plane, a train or a ferry home. He would only try and get her out if it seemed she was in obvious danger, though how he was going to assess her degree of safety, like just about everything else, was not a question to which he had an obvious answer.

He took the first pair of binoculars, standard issue in a matt black finish and with hooded lenses to cut out the risk of a telltale sunflash. He poked the lenses carefully through the netting and swept what he could see of the house and grounds. The only activity was down by the swimming pool, where half a dozen young women were splashing around noisily. He could hear their faint squeals of laughter. Two men on sunloungers, dressed in swimming trunks, were watching them. One looked as if he might be Mikhail Rostov. Photographs of the Rostovs and known associates were included in the file Jackie had given him.

He scanned the poolside in vain for the bald head of Yuri Andropov. Few names had been attached to the fuzzy long-shot photographs of the assorted heavies included in the file, but his had come not only with a name but a full service record, courtesy of Russian intelligence. A former Soviet paratrooper with twelve years service, decorated and promoted to sergeant on the battlefield after rallying his company and leading a successful counter-attack against ambushers in Afghanistan. Johny had counted six heavies so far, excluding the waiters and household staff. He said they looked like standard-issue thugs, the kind popstars and celebrities like to pack behind them to advertise their self-importance, the kind you buy by the metre. Ryan wasn't so sure. If Andropov had trained them then life could get difficult.

There'd be the Rostovs plus at least seven guns. Maybe more if the chauffeur and the rest of the staff were more than hired help. He thought about those odds. Two years he'd spent as an instructor down in Poole. Two years of delivering the same spiel to each new batch of trainees. He could do that speech in his sleep, as easily as strip down an M16. First thing, lads, is you forget everything you've read about us. And forget about what you've seen in the movies. Those of you who make it are going to be the best-trained soldiers on God's earth. But you're not going to be Hollywood action heroes. You're not going to be supermen, hurling yourselves through windows, firing from the hip and mowing down dummies too slow to shoot back . . .

Everything he'd ever learnt, and ever taught, had stressed the importance of teamwork, good equipment, good planning. And here he was, thinking of rolling up with nothing more than a couple of spare clips in his pockets and a one-eyed landlubber for back-up. What kind of a superman did he think he was?

The door of the summerhouse opened and a blonde woman stepped out. Ryan felt his heart skip a beat, but even though it was too far away for him to be able to make out the features he knew at once that it wasn't Grace. The hair was too blonde and too straight, and even though she was of a similar height and build there was a lazy quality about the way she walked, and an unsubtle hint of provocativeness in the way she swung her hips, that wasn't Grace's style. She peeled off a robe to reveal a red bikini and stretched out in the sun in a corner away from everyone else. The men on the sunloungers watched her every movement. She paid them no attention, immersing herself in a book.

The sun beat down. It was hot even in the shade of his tree, but nowhere near as hot as some places Ryan could mention. He thought of Honduras and the Syrian desert. He remembered chemical warfare training in Oman, the sensation of being boiled alive in his protective suit, the sweat pouring off him in pints and gathering like rainwater in his boots. Some minor tourist-level glazing wasn't going to bother him, though he could have done without the pleasant sense of drowsiness that was its natural accompaniment. Thank God the mental side of his training had been as rigorous as the physical.

So far he hadn't seen any sign of Gallagher. Maybe he'd taken Grace somewhere else, maybe this whole thing was a wild-goose chase. Ryan hadn't seen Gallagher in the flesh yet, but he knew him from the photos in the file. The picture of him lying by the pool, that Cheshire cat grin splitting his handsome tanned face as the pretty blonde rubbed his back, was ingrained in his mind. He kept seeing Grace in the blonde's place, and kept trying, not always successfully, to block it out. He didn't like the tug of the heart he'd experienced a moment ago when he'd seen the blonde by the pool, the tiny moment of hope, followed by the dash of disappointment. He wasn't an emotional man, he was quietly proud of his iron self-control. He wasn't used to feeling jealousy. But Grace had got under his skin, and he didn't know whether to resent or enjoy the sensation.

Plenty of unimagined pictures lingered in his mind. He'd

thought her quite attractive when he saw her for the first time, even with the black eye, but nothing more. He was quite blasé about having pretty women in the back of his car. He'd already driven Jeanette to her interview earlier that morning and been impervious to her flirtatiousness. But something in Grace's manner had impressed. He remembered her snapping a salute at him in the car park of the hotel by Tower Bridge, and that same bold look in her eye when he'd caught the two of them drinking in the bar. Jeanette had tried it too, but one cold glance had been enough to call her bluff. The next morning, when the three women had come out to meet him, he had been secretly pleased that Grace had been the one to get in the front with him. He remembered her being in the car again on Saturday night. The scent of her perfume had still been in the car the next morning and was sharp in his memory. He remembered the firm grasp of her hands on his arms as he had taught her on the blue mat in the garage. Of course she couldn't match his physical strength, but mental strength was another matter. Their eyes had locked as they went through the sparring motions and he had glimpsed her toughness. He had caught himself thinking: *This one can cut it . . .*

He wasn't the only one who'd been impressed. He remembered Dent in the back of the car, extolling her virtues on the phone to some nameless apparatchik at the Home Office. They'd all known she was the one who would make it work, the only one with the qualities to make the trap close. And afterwards they hadn't been able to wash their hands of her fast enough.

The same thoughts recirculated in his brain as the long afternoon dragged on. There was precious little activity except by the poolside and not a single car entered or left the property. It worried him that there was no sign of Grace, but at the same time it was a relief that she wasn't at the point of danger. He had read through some of the thick sheaf of material on Dmitri Rostov coming over on the ferry and hadn't found it comforting. The front of business respectability he showed to the world may have been, as yet, legally unimpeachable, but the number of rivals and former associates who had died or simply disappeared in the course of the last twenty years meant that he was unlikely ever to win the Queen's Award for Industry.

Shortly after eight o'clock Ryan heard the ringing tone of his mobile through his earpiece. It was Johny, telling him that he was back at the parking place, mission accomplished. Although Ryan was reluctant to leave his vantage point there was no choice. He hurried back the half-kilometre along the shore and helped Johny wheel the trailer to the water's edge. The small grey rubber dinghy fitted the bill exactly, although the engine was puny in comparison to what he was used to. He checked it out, topped up the petrol from the jerrycan Johny had brought and headed along the coast, away from the villa, for a five-minute test. Then he slowed right down and took it for a stately chug back up towards their camp. He moored the dinghy in the lee of the rock where the boys had been fishing earlier.

Johny was already back up at the hide. He shook his head to indicate that nothing was happening. Ryan made a pillow out of his kitbag and settled down to sleep. He went out like a light.

It was dark when Johny woke him with a touch on the shoulder. Ryan was alert immediately.

'Something's going on,' said Johny. 'People been arriving in cars, including a blonde woman. They're having some kind of party.'

Ryan followed Johny back up the slope and took the night-vision binoculars, though there were so many lights on around the pool he almost didn't need them. He saw the women clustering at the shallow end of the pool and heard Johny whistle.

'Hey, man, it must be a Playboy party.'

Ryan had moved the binoculars so quickly over them he hadn't realized they were naked. Johny nudged him.

'She one of those nudey babes, Ryan?'

'No way.'

He didn't even bother to check them out. He swung the binoculars rapidly from left to right and took in the men standing on either side of the pool, then ratcheted up the magnification and homed in on the cluster of people sitting around the summerhouse.

And there she was, next to the blonde he'd seen earlier, a small middle-aged man between them. His view was blurred and washed with green, the figures like humanoid shapes in an alien landscape. But he knew it was her, despite the spectral limitations of the viewfinder. He confirmed as much to Johny. The man she came with, Johny told him, had gone into the house with some other men who'd arrived earlier.

Ryan suggested to Johny he get some rest, but he said that he didn't want to miss anything. In truth there wasn't much to miss. They watched the naked girls swim their race, but after that the swimming-pool party broke up and drifted off to the house. Grace and another man emerged from the summerhouse half an hour later and went up to join them. It was almost midnight.

Another half-hour passed and the Turk, Orhan, came out of the house with three men and a young woman he hadn't seen before. Orhan walked the men to a car and stood leaning in at the window, talking to them, for a good ten minutes. Then he waved them off and went back into the house. Five minutes later he reappeared with another man in tow. It looked like Gallagher, but where was Grace? Orhan and Gallagher got into a red Audi and drove out of the compound.

The Rolls Royce drew up in front of the house. A thickset man came through the door, followed by Grace and the other blonde.

'You'd better bring the car up to the road,' said Ryan.

Johny ran off, and Ryan tried to work out how long it would take him to make it to the road, and how far ahead the Roller might have got, but he realized almost immediately that the calculation was redundant. He whistled and Johny came back.

'They're going down to the sea,' Ryan explained. 'Wait here.'

The beach in front of the house was invisible from where they were. Ryan snatched up his binoculars and hurried down the slope. There was a lot of moonlight, he was able to pick his way quite comfortably across the broken ground. He realized he might be visible from the house, but felt he had no option. He sensed that something significant was going on.

Fifty feet short of the fence he found a low rise from which he could get a clear view of the shore. The sea was breaking noisily on the rocks so close by he could feel the spray in his hair. He threw himself flat on the rock and watched the Rolls Royce stop in front of the jetty. The chauffeur and the thickset man opened the rear doors for the women, then shut them together. The chauffeur got back into his car and the others went up to the *Anastasia*.

Ryan knew all about the *Anastasia*, he had the design in his file. She was a ninety-foot sailing yacht, built originally as a luxury Atlantic racer. The previous owner had run a Formula One team, and there were cuttings in the file of famous drivers and beautiful models lolling on the deck, shot by paparazzi. Ryan felt his heart sink. If *Anastasia* was about to head for the open sea he wasn't going to get very far following in his pathetic rubber dinghy.

But there were no signs of her getting underway. The

only crewman visible was the one who arrived at the gangplank and showed the two women down below. The thickset man – he was convinced by now it was Yuri Andropov – remained on the jetty. Ten minutes later the other woman re-emerged, followed by the crewman in whites, who carried a heavy suitcase to the Rolls Royce. The car drove back up to the house, the woman inside.

A short time later another thickset man, shorter than Andropov, came down in the Rolls Royce. Ryan was fairly sure it was Dmitri Rostov. He spoke to his man on the jetty and they went down into the *Anastasia* together. Half an hour later Rostov came out on his own and was driven back up to the house.

Ryan tried to make sense of what he'd seen. Grace was on her own apart from the crewman and Andropov. He'd never have a better opportunity to get her out, but was there any reason to think she was in danger? He lay still on his rock and carried on observing, feeling acutely powerless. The thought that the boat might set sail and leave him stranded continued to nag at him.

But nothing happened. The night dragged on slowly. Johny came down to relieve him, but he was too keyed up to sleep. A little before dawn they relocated to a more secluded spot a hundred metres further back from the fence. They could see only part of the boat and jetty, but at least the approaches were visible. Reluctantly Ryan agreed to snatch some sleep. He extracted a promise from Johny that he would wake him the moment he spotted anything unusual.

Ryan slept all through the morning and missed nothing. The only activity, Johny assured him, had been by the pool. The same pattern continued through the afternoon. Ryan endlessly rechecked his equipment. He had wondered about taking the dinghy out to get a closer look at the boat, but had decided that that would only be drawing attention to himself. Grace was probably sunning herself on the deck. The shadows were lengthening, there wasn't too long to go now. Tomorrow she'd be safely back in England.

It was just after eight o'clock when he heard the sound of a vehicle coming up the private track. He put down the unappetizing snack he'd been munching and scrambled back up the slope to the first hide. He was in time to see a brown Range Rover go through the gates and up the drive to the house. It must have been expected. Two men came out of the house and walked into the courtyard to meet it. Ryan studied the distant faces through his binoculars. He couldn't be certain, but he thought that he was looking at both Rostov brothers.

The Range Rover stopped in front of them and a slim dark man got out. This time Ryan had no doubts. It was Gallagher. The three men spoke to each other. They seemed agitated, there was a lot of waving of arms from the broader of the Rostovs, Dmitri. Dmitri followed Gallagher as he walked round to the other side of the car and opened the passenger door.

A woman with long blonde hair got out. For a moment it looked like Grace and Ryan felt a slight shock. It wasn't Grace, although there was something familiar about her. She was too far away for him to be able to see the expression on her face, but he could tell that she was nervous from the hunched way she held her shoulders. Dmitri Rostov took a step towards her and she flinched. And then he hit her across the face.

The woman stumbled and fell. And in that instant the spark of recognition, like a camera flash, shot through Ryan's brain.

Calmly, much more calmly than he felt, he took the mobile phone from his top pocket and called Johny. Through the binoculars he watched Gallagher helping the woman to her feet. She was clearly in some distress.

Gallagher held her head in his chest and patted her hair with one hand while with the other he waved away Dmitri Rostov.

'Ryan? What's up?'

Johny sounded eager and alert. He had probably seen it all happen from his position down by the shore.

'Get your kit ready,' said Ryan quietly, glancing up at the still bright sky, calculating how long he had before darkness fell. 'We're going in.'

17

The crew's cabin was long and narrow, like an extension of the corridor outside. Besides the three double-bunks the only furniture consisted of two bolted-down hard chairs and a small table. The walls were bare and there was only one porthole.

Grace had watched the sky lighten through the porthole. She had lain all night on the lower bunk nearest the door, a crewman's blanket pulled up to her chin for warmth, dozing fitfully but never dropping off for long. Each time she woke it was with such a violent start that the prospect of falling to sleep again seemed as miserable as the burden of consciousness. She had tried to find a comfortable sleeping position, but it wasn't easy with her left wrist chained to the bottom rung of the bunk ladder.

She might have bought herself some time, but there wasn't a lot she could do with it. It hadn't just been the fact of being handcuffed, but the casually brutal way in which Yuri snapped them on, that confirmed the change in her status from guest to prisoner. The bruising and blood on her face were almost immaterial; Dmitri doled out that kind of treatment to the women around him irrespective of position.

The porthole was up against the jetty and she could see next to nothing. She had no idea of the time, though the day, if anything, had seemed to pass even slower than the night. She was hungry, and thirsty, and her bladder was fit to burst. She felt like a medieval prisoner tossed into the oubliette.

Only she hadn't been forgotten. Dmitri would be back, in his own good time, his fists primed for another interrogation. She had deflected him, no more, she wasn't going to let herself cling to any illusions. Her instinct back at the dinner table in England – was it really only three days ago? – had been sound. She'd have been a lot better off playing the dumb blonde.

She went over it all in her head, again, trying to work out where she was most vulnerable. How convinced would Mikhail the chauffeur be when Dmitri relayed to him her version of the conversation in the car park, and how much would it matter? Well, that would depend. The opinion of Mickey the chauffeur wasn't going to be the same thing at all as Mickey the criminal mastermind, Mickey the ruthless killer. She hoped fervently she was wrong on that account. Did it matter, either way? If they had any doubts, wouldn't it be safest to kill her anyway?

She pulled instinctively at the steel bracelet round her wrist. She felt like an animal tethered for slaughter, and the gruesomeness of the image filled her with terror. Self-pity flooded her brain. Even if, by some miracle, the handcuffs were to snap open, she would be too feeble to make a run for it.

She pulled herself down the bunk, until the chain was slack and her feet were hanging over the edge and she was almost comfortable. Very deliberately she slowed her breathing. She had to quell the nausea in her stomach and steady her nerves. She'd been in a worse spot than this before, she told herself, and still come through. She remembered what

340

she usually tried to forget: the terror of being bound and blindfolded in the cottage in Derbyshire; the journey in the car to the place where the man – she never named him, even in her head – had planned to kill her; the strength she had found from somewhere to defend herself; the unguessed-of strength of her own will to survive. She wasn't a passive, helpless thing, to be snuffed out like a candle, then or now.

Some strength had trickled back into her veins. Her pulse seemed steady. There was no point mapping out a plan of action when there was no scope for manoeuvre, but she could map out a plan of attitude. Too late to be the dumb blonde, maybe, but she could play bewildered. If she appeared to be accepting her lot then it would only confirm her guilt, but getting strident would cut no ice either. She would be pathetic, frightened, unthreatening. Not a tall order, in the circumstances.

She could hear voices. She strained to see if there was any movement out on the part of the jetty visible through the porthole, but the faint sound wasn't coming from there. The voices were outside her door.

She swung her legs over the side of the bunk and sat up, her head hunched into her shoulders to avoid the mattress springs above. She cleared her throat.

'Hello, is somebody there, please? Please?'

Her voice sounded weak and hoarse. Good, at least she wouldn't have to try for her effects. She strained her dry throat again.

'I said, hello? Can you hear me?'

She rattled the ladder for emphasis. The bedframe gave a hollow rasp. In the long pause that followed she heard the metallic noise fading away. She assumed that whoever had been outside must have gone, but then the door swung open suddenly and Yuri poked his head round.

Grace pulled the blanket up to her collarbone, not that

he appeared to be interested in her near nakedness. His eyes were hard and unfriendly.

'I need to use the bathroom, please,' she said, in her best little-girl-lost voice.

He frowned, as if the request had been delivered in some outlandish dialect, and not Linguaphone-polite conversational Russian.

'You'll have to wait,' he said gruffly.

'I can't!'

He shrugged and began to close the door. Grace heard Tatyana's voice on the other side.

'Don't be an idiot, Yuri. What do you think she's going to do?'

Yuri growled and swore. Tatyana swore back.

'OK, OK,' he muttered in English, coming back into the room and pulling a key from his pocket. He released her wrist from the handcuffs and left them dangling from the ladder. She followed him out into the corridor, clutching the bathroom towel to her breast.

Tatyana was walking away towards the master cabin. She glanced over her shoulder at Grace but didn't meet her eyes. Yuri pushed open a door.

'Be quick. And don't lock it. You make me kick it in, I'll kick you in too.'

She didn't doubt it. She found the light switch and closed the door. It was a tiny bathroom, about a quarter of the size of the one in Dmitri's cabin, with barely enough room for a toilet, a shower and a sink. She faced herself in the mirror above the sink.

Not a pretty sight. A black and yellow bruise, another one, coming up round her left eye, smears of congealed blood on her cheek and above her lip. She washed it off with soap and water. Removing the blood was easy. A pity she couldn't wash away the strained and haggard look in her eyes.

She gulped down a few cupped handfuls of the water. It tasted metallic, probably not meant for drinking at all, but she was desperately thirsty. Her head ached. She found some aspirin in the medicine cabinet next to the sink and swallowed them gratefully. She searched through the other shelves. The crewmen were obviously a functional lot, not given to leaving helpful pairs of nail scissors or other potentially useful sharpened objects around. There wasn't even a packet of safety razor blades. Just toothpaste, mouthwash, sticking plasters, a lip salve and a small tin of Vaseline.

'Hurry up,' said Yuri through the door.

'I'm sorry, I've got terrible diarrhoea,' said Grace.

He didn't answer. Nor did he bother her again. She took her time, and when, finally, she emerged, a good five minutes later, he said nothing at all. He merely indicated with a nod of his head that she should go back to her cell.

'Wait,' said Tatyana's voice behind them.

Grace turned round.

'Take this –' said Tatyana, her habitually neutral eyes filled with something approaching sympathy.

Grace looked down at the white bundle in her hands. It was a silk dressing gown. She murmured a barely intelligible thank you, too surprised to come up with anything more fulsome.

But Tatyana had gone anyway, with a characteristically imperious toss of the head that implied that the resumption of her former status was complete.

'Would you mind, please?' said Grace, once she was back in the crew's cabin.

Yuri affected not to understand. She unfolded the dressing gown and held it up, making it obvious. He didn't react. His eyes were too glassy to give any hint at his thought processes, but she could guess what was going on. Could he really be bothered to exercise his power and humiliate her?

343

Not enough. He turned his back on her, in a manner which might have been disdainful had he considered her worthy of his disdain. She took off the towel and put on the dressing gown.

'Thank you.'

She sat down. He came over and held out his hand. Reluctantly she offered her wrist. He took it and reached for the handcuffs. He was neither rough nor gentle, merely indifferent. She stared at his face, wanting to make eye contact. He didn't oblige.

'Please don't put it on so tightly,' she said meekly. 'My wrist is very sore.'

He didn't answer. He snapped shut the cuff.

'Could I have a glass of water, please? I'm thirsty.'

She smiled sweetly. How could anyone so childishly polite be a threat? Not a flicker disturbed his robotic expression. He walked out and banged shut the heavy door. Somehow she didn't get the feeling that he was on his way to the galley to look for the nearest Evian bottle.

But the handcuff was a great deal looser round her wrist. She felt around it and pressed the little finger of her other hand up under the tendons. She got it in between the skin and metal to the first joint without any difficulty. She flexed the wrist. It was still tight, but it might be possible. She studied the span of her hand, which seemed suddenly to have acquired a boxer's breadth.

She lay back on the bed and tried to keep calm. She went over in her head what she had learned. Yuri and Tatyana seemed to be the only people on the boat. If Tatyana was around then it was a safe bet that Dmitri wasn't far away, but she didn't think he was on board now. He was a man who filled space, wherever he was, and she hadn't noticed anything in the manner of the other two to suggest the boss was about. Yakov might be somewhere, but that was less of a problem.

So what else did she know? Yuri kept the key to the handcuffs in his shirt pocket. A pretty casual place to keep it, a deft pickpocket could have lifted it with no trouble. Unfortunately that skill was absent from her repertoire. So was escapology, but she could give it a go.

She glanced out of the porthole. The light was less bright, maybe the afternoon was drawing in. Or maybe the sun was behind a cloud and it was still morning. She doubted it, but without a watch she couldn't know. All she could do was lie and wait. She closed her eyes. She tried to sleep, but she was too keyed up. She made herself breathe slowly, in time to the gentle rocking of the boat.

The cabin was getting gloomy. There was a red tinge around the porthole. Would they come for her after dark? She could have five minutes or five hours to wait. Bob would have got her message by this morning at the latest, perhaps the cavalry was on its way even now. She let the thought blow away as fast as it had come. For all intents and purposes she knew she was on her own.

She stared at the springs and the mattress above. She stared, and stared. The moment came when the metal coils were submerged in shadow. She sat up and swung her legs over the side of the bunk.

It was not quite pitch dark, but she couldn't see into the corners. A dim light was on outside, on the jetty. She listened and heard nothing. She should wait until the middle of the night, she knew, but it might be too late by then. She could at least see if she had a cat in hell's chance of working it.

She felt for the towel, which she had carefully rolled up when she put on the dressing gown. She opened it and retrieved the jar of Vaseline from its hiding place. She dipped in two fingers to the bottom and smeared a great dollop over her wrist. She worked it in under the metal bracelet and all the way up to the thumb and finger joints. Then she braced her feet against the ladder and pulled the chain taut.

She pressed her thumb and little finger together and made her hand as cylindrical as possible. She wedged her spare thumb behind the lock on the bracelet and began to push, leaning back at the same time and pulling from her shoulder. The bracelet tightened against her skin. She felt the pressure, and the movement of the slippery metal over her flesh. An agonizingly slow movement, but a real one. The bracelet was almost up to the base of her thumb. She gritted her teeth and pulled.

The pressure was intense. It was like having her hand crushed in a vice, and she was the one applying the force. She couldn't do it, the nerve-endings screaming at her brain were making her slack off. She wanted to ignore everything and try harder but she couldn't. Her hand was on fire. She heard herself hissing pain.

She yanked the metal back down over her wrist. Gingerly she touched the throbbing flesh above. If she hadn't been able to get it off before she wasn't going to manage now. Her skin was swollen and horribly raw.

Miserably she slumped back against the pillow and curled her knees into her chest. She told herself that she'd try again later, but she knew it wasn't going to work. She felt the disappointment, like a physical weight, in her gut. Had she really kidded herself she might get free? The more she thought about it the more idiotic the notion seemed. With the towel she rubbed away the excess Vaseline from the handcuffs. She stuffed the tin under the mattress and hoped they wouldn't find it.

The cabin had become pitch black. She stared at the glow around the porthole as if it were a desert mirage. Time passed. She closed her eyes. At some stage she must have gone to sleep.

She woke suddenly. She was alert instantly, and very

afraid. She saw for an instant a spill of light over by the door and then it was snuffed out. Someone had come into the room.

'Who's there?'

Her voice was a tiny croak, her throat as dry as sandpaper.

'Be quiet,' said Tatyana softly.

Tatyana? Grace was too stunned to speak. She sat very still as the other woman felt her way into the room. The frame of the bunk trembled. Grace felt the mattress dip as a body settled in beside her. She caught a whiff of strong perfume.

'Where are you?' Tatyana whispered.

Grace felt a hand touch her arm.

'What do you want?' she whispered back.

'I want to help you.'

'Why?'

'Because they're going to kill you.'

Grace felt her stomach float free, the way it did before the plunge on a rollercoaster ride. She could hardly speak.

'How do you know?' she managed eventually, in a voice that was more breath than sound.

'They're going to wait for a few more hours, until the middle of the night, and then they're going to take you out to sea and get rid of your body. I overheard them talking up at the house, Dmitri and Misha. I have been thinking about it ever since, and now I have decided that I am going to help you escape.'

'But why?'

'Why are they going to kill you, or why am I going to help you? They are going to kill you because you work for the British police and I am going to help because it will be my turn too some day. I was surprised to learn you are police, almost as surprised as they are. I did not think the English were so imaginative.'

347

'What makes them think I'm police?'

'Please, there is no time to pretend. We have to get out of here.'

'What do you mean, "we"?'

'I'm coming with you. Take my hand, please. You must show me where the lock is on your handcuffs.'

'Yuri's got the key.'

'No. I've got the key.'

Grace felt Tatyana squeeze her left arm. Awkwardly she reached for her hand and guided it down to the old-fashioned cylindrical lock.

'How did you get the key?'

'Yuri is asleep, with half a bottle of vodka inside him. There's no one else on the boat.'

'What about Yakov?'

'At the house.'

'Why are you coming with me?'

'I've told you, I will be next. I know too much. When he tires of me again, like he did yesterday, he may put me out like an old horse to pasture. Or he may decide it's easier to put me to sleep. I don't think I'll wait to find out. Dmitri is a very strong believer in euthanasia. The lock is stiff.'

'It's a powerful spring. Twist the key hard.'

'I will. But first you must promise to help me.'

'How can I help you?'

'You must put me on a witness protection programme. You have such a thing, like in the States?'

'I don't know. I suppose.'

'They will kill me unless you protect me. I will be valuable, I know much.'

'Look, can we just get out of here?'

'You must promise to help.'

'OK, OK, I promise.'

The handcuff snapped open with a loud click and Grace snatched away her aching wrist. She grabbed hold of the ladder and pulled herself to her feet. Her legs felt weak, though whether that was from fear or simple stiffness she couldn't tell. The best thing to do, in either case, was to get moving fast.

'Where's Yuri sleeping?' she whispered.

'In the living quarters, at the table.'

'Has he got a gun?'

'He's always got a gun. What are you going to do? Maybe we can steal a car.'

'No, we'd have to crash through the gate. Too noisy. We'll sneak out past Yuri, take the dinghy. As long as we can start the motor.'

'That is also noisy.'

'There must be paddles. We'll get out to sea first.'

'Are your people nearby?'

'What people?'

'Dmitri said you are in contact with the police. He said they must be watching.'

'No one's watching.'

'Then where are we going to go?'

'We'll worry about that later. Let's get out first.'

'But where can we go? I do not believe your people are not here. They would not leave you on your own.'

'Trust me, Tatyana, I'm on my own. We'll find a British consul, we'll be fine. Have you got money?'

'Yes.'

'Good. You lead the way. You know it better than me.'

'OK.'

'What's the time?'

'About midnight.'

'You ready?'

'Yes. I am ready. Thank you, you have been most helpful.'

Grace heard the heavy click of the door. She walked towards the sound. Suddenly there was another click and bright light flooded the room.

Grace flung her hands up to her face to protect her eyes, but too late. The harsh white light was dazzling. She stumbled, horrified, towards the door, spots dancing before her eyes.

'What are you doing?' she gasped.

She could see Tatyana at the door, incongruously dressed in a chic striped dress and knee-length white boots, and beyond her the unlit corridor, and figures moving towards her, dark and shadowy like some slumbering nightmare beasts. And she heard Tatyana's cool sharp voice, restored to its normal pitch, the hoarse stage whisper switched off as clinically as it had been put on.

'No problem, she's working on her own.'

Dmitri stepped into the room. He patted Tatyana on the shoulder.

'Well done.'

Tatyana shrugged. She glanced, almost apologetically, at Grace.

'You know how it is,' she murmured. 'No hard feelings.'

'No hard feelings at all, bitch,' said Grace, and punched her in the face.

It was a Pyrrhic victory. She'd never in her life punched anyone, and she was surprised at how much it stung her knuckles, but at least she had the satisfaction of seeing Tatyana hit the floor, the complacent sneer well and truly expunged from her lips, before Yuri, who had followed Dmitri into the room, flung her back with tremendous force against the wall.

Whether it was her skull cracking against the wall or whether he hit her again she never knew. But the lights went out as suddenly as they had come on.

18

They took her into the lounge at the stern, that dazzling penthouse room in cream and wood. They sat her on a canvas chair in the middle of the room and cuffed her hands behind her back. Still dazed from the blow to her head, she offered no resistance. Not that resistance was an option. Yuri drew the blinds over the portholes. Dmitri sat at the long dining table, glaring at her, his hands clasped over an automatic pistol fitted with a silencer. She told herself that they wouldn't kill her here, he was only trying to scare her. As if she needed scaring.

She heard the door open and footsteps behind her. A man walked past, stopped and looked back at her. There was no expression in his face, and she found that more frightening than Dmitri's knotted anger. One glance from him was enough to make the thickness in her head dissolve. She remembered the blankness of that look, the cold eyes hanging above her, the weight of him pinning and hurting her. Her lips moved, though hardly any sound came out.

'Hi, Mike.'

Gallagher didn't answer. The tiniest smile lifted the corners of his mouth, but she was aware now of how meaningless his smiles were; of how transparent his charms ought to have appeared to her long before now.

'Nice friends you've got,' she said.

'Let's talk about your friends,' he said.

'Could I have some water, please?'

He ignored her.

'It was a neat set-up, but how did you know I would lead you to Dmitri?'

'I didn't.'

He shook his head. He picked up another canvas chair and planted it in front of her. He sat down, very close, so that their knees touched.

'Still want to play innocent? Don't. Dmitri's not the patient type.'

'You don't say.'

She shrugged. They could threaten, bully, beat her. No doubt they would, but she had to try to buy time. They all knew what would happen when they had finished with her, Mike included. His mere presence confirmed that the question of his complicity was one of degree only. She wanted to kick herself for ever thinking it could have been any other way.

'Let's be frank, Grace,' he said softly, leaning in and resting his hands on her knees. 'Dmitri doesn't like people poking into his business. And I don't like being used.'

She glanced down at his hands, at the fingertips pressing lightly into her flesh. His thumbs were making gentle circular movements on the inside of her thighs. She wanted to laugh.

'So you don't like being used, eh, Mike?'

'Don't get cute.'

'I'm kind of short of options here, Mike.'

'You got plenty. We need to know a few things. Play ball and Dmitri'll be nice to you.'

'You mean he'll only kill me once?'

'Hey now, what's with the paranoia? Why would anyone want to kill you? You're a lot more useful alive, you know that. More useful in a lot of ways.'

He leant in very close and practically breathed the words into her ear. His fingers travelled lightly up her legs, disappearing beneath the hem of her dressing gown.

'What's the matter, Mike?' she breathed back. 'Is there a shortage of hookers all of a sudden?'

He nuzzled her ear. She felt his tongue lap gently against the lobe.

'I said, don't get cute.'

He bit her ear, suddenly and savagely. She yelped and tried to twist away, but he grabbed her head in both his hands and held her fast. She felt his hot breath on her face.

'You fuck around with us you'll wish you could only die once. Answer my questions or I'll take the fucking gun and blow your fucking head off right here, you understand?'

He didn't raise his voice, he didn't have to. She felt the chill of his words all the way down her spine. She gave a tiny nod, all the movement she could make against the pressure of his hands.

'That's better. No games, no pretence, no shit, OK? We know who you are, we know how you set the whole thing up, we know it all. You got a problem accepting that? Still want to try and act wide-eyed and cute? Fine. Maybe we can speed things up here. Hey, don't go away now.'

He released her and stood up. She flinched instinctively as he came behind her but he didn't stop. She heard his footsteps receding down the corridor, clipping the smooth wooden deck.

Dmitri banged his gun down noisily on the table. Grace turned to the sound, as she was meant to. He began tapping an impatient rhythm with his fingernails on the barrel. Grace lowered her eyes.

She heard Gallagher returning, accompanied by lighter

footsteps. Gallagher's shoes came into sight, followed by a pair of woman's ankle boots. The woman seemed unsteady on her feet. She slumped into the canvas chair.

Grace looked up. For a moment she didn't recognize the white, terrified face. *God, is that how I look?* she thought, but even as her mind mulled the question she knew that this woman's fear was on a different scale. Her eyes were corpse eyes, frozen wide.

'No shortage of hookers I can see,' Gallagher said laconically.

Suddenly the pale face, and its frame of straight blonde hair, seemed horribly familiar. The woman was huddled into the canvas chair, her eyes swivelling round the room, looking frantically for anything to alight on except Grace's face.

'I think you two have already met,' Gallagher said. 'Where was it now? Ah yes, a mews house in Bayswater. You had such an interesting talk about me, I understand. Care to renew your acquaintance? Come on, babe, don't be shy, say hello to Grace.'

He grabbed a clump of blonde hair in his hand and twisted it hard. The woman yelped and blinked back tears. The tiniest murmur passed her lips.

'Hello, Grace.'

'Hello, Natalie.'

Grace attempted an encouraging smile but Natalie wasn't looking at her. She had screwed shut her eyes. Her shoulders shook with silent sobs.

Gallagher sighed.

'Hey, don't go all quiet on me. The least a guy can expect for a couple hundred bucks an hour is a little conversation. Don't you agree, Grace?'

'Leave her alone.'

'Who are you now, her big sister? She was very talkative before. Least she was once she got going. I was puzzled, you see, I needed the answers to some questions. She claimed she knew nothing about you, never even heard your name before, and there you were telling me you were such good friends. Fact, all I had to do was mention you and she started acting guilty. Same way as your pimp did when I called to book her yesterday. I ask a simple question about you and all of a sudden he gets confused. The same with Natalie here. Kind of intriguing. I thought all hookers were natural liars. Maybe you could give her some lessons. And you're not even a hooker.'

He came round to her. He put his hands on the arms of the chair and leant over till his face was only inches above hers. He spoke softly.

'Maybe she could take lessons in other departments too. I got her to blow me before we came out, but frankly the service just wasn't the same quality.'

'Thanks for the testimonial.'

'They teach that stuff at police college? I got to admit, your people did their homework. Makes me the big sucker, huh? I never could work you out, though, there was always something about you bugging me. Maybe you're not so smart, after all, offering to give it away for free.'

'I'll know better next time.'

'Oh yeah, and so will I. My own fault, using the same agency too many times, making patterns. Obviously I was getting complacent. Hey, thanks for the warning, Grace.'

'No problem, Mike.'

'That's better. Nice and friendly again. Perhaps we can have that talk now. I ask you the questions, you give me the answers, straight, no bullshit. How's that sound?'

'Could I have some water first?'

'Yeah, you asked that before. What's the matter, they not been looking after you? I'll tell you what. I'll be nice to you, and you be nice to me. How's that for a deal?'

He walked over to the table and opened a small cabinet

above where Dmitri was sitting. Dmitri had the gun cradled in his lap, as if it were a cat.

'Why you waste time?' he demanded brusquely.

Gallagher shrugged. He produced a bottle of mineral water from the cabinet and poured a glass.

Take all the time you like, thought Grace. *As long as you're talking, I'm still breathing . . .*

Gallagher brought over the glass and put it to her lips. She tipped back her head and swallowed eagerly.

'Thirsty, huh? Let's talk, then you can have some more. OK?'

She nodded. As he carried the empty glass back to the table she saw Natalie's head move. She had opened her eyes and was staring at her imploringly. Her lips framed a word.

Sorry.

Grace smiled encouragingly, but Natalie had closed her eyes once more. Gallagher pulled up another chair and sat beside her.

'Mike?' she whispered.

'Mm?'

He inclined his head towards her, looking faintly amused at her conspiratorial tone. She glanced at Natalie.

'Let her go. She doesn't know anything.'

'Sure she can go, as soon as we're finished talking.'

'Thanks, Mike.'

She had spoken loudly enough for Natalie to hear. She hoped she'd be naive enough to believe it, but it looked as if she was no longer capable of taking anything in: her face was tightly screwed up and her head was rocking gently back and forwards. She was making a tiny whimpering sound.

Gallagher had settled back in his chair. Languidly he crossed his legs. He might have been a guest at a cocktail party, quizzing her on her social itinerary. It seemed he was chief interrogator, with Dmitri's reluctant approval.

'One more time now,' Gallagher began. 'How did you know I would lead you here?'

'It was a lucky guess.'

'Oh yeah? You saying your people go to all this trouble on some kind of hunch? Come on, babe, you can do better than that.'

'They intercepted a phone call.'

'You see, you can do better. What do I keep telling you, Dmitri, about unsecured telephones? For Christ's sake, man, use encrypted e-mails.'

Dmitri glanced up sharply. He looked surprised, and angry.

'Why you give me this shit again?' he demanded, banging the gun down on the table. Grace flinched. The barrel was pointing directly at her.

'I give you this shit because you're careless,' Gallagher snapped back. 'You talk all the time on the phone, I seen you do it, I heard you do it, for Christ's sake, mentioning names, mentioning places.'

'You use phone. I use secure line.'

'There's no such thing as a secure line, how many times have I got to tell you? Sure, I use the phone, but I change the numbers around, and I never use names, So then if something does get picked up it means jack. For fuck's sake, Dmitri, this is fucking elementary.'

'Who the fuck you are, you tell me how to run my fucking business?'

'You want to run a fucking chat-line, Dmitri, go right ahead and publish your number in the FBI directory. I'm telling you this stuff because I keep telling you this stuff and you don't fucking listen. And because you don't fucking listen you got a fucking undercover cop on your fucking boat.'

'Why the fuck she here then? Because you bring her.'

'And why you think she tags along with me? To meet the tooth fairy?'

'She with you because you are weak link, Mike. You say it yourself, you make pattern, they know you are the guy thinks with his dick.'

'Yeah, and what were you thinking with when you tried to recruit her? Seems like they got you figured too.'

'Who the fuck you think you talk with? You think I pay you, you give me this shit?'

'Somebody's got to give it to you straight. I'm telling you how it is, OK?'

'You don't tell me how it is. I tell you how it is. You shut the fuck up. Shut the fucking whore up too.'

Natalie's sobbing was no longer silent. She was rocking in her chair, her hands pressed to her ears, shaking and making an animal, bleating noise. Gallagher turned away in disgust.

'Shut her up yourself.'

Dmitri crossed to her in two strides and struck Natalie across the face with the back of his hand. She gave a gasp as her head snapped back, and stopped crying. But only for a moment. As soon as Dmitri turned away from her she started screaming.

'Shut up.'

Natalie's answer was to scream louder. A dam had been burst. Terror flooded out of her.

Dmitri jabbed the pistol butt hard into the back of her head. Natalie screamed louder. Dmitri swore in Russian.

'You finished with her?' he demanded.

Gallagher shrugged.

Dmitri placed the barrel of the gun against Natalie's temple and pressed the trigger.

There was hardly any sound, just a puff like a sharp exhalation of breath. The long silencer quivered and a fine red spray fanned out from the side of Natalie's head. Her body gave one grotesque convulsive twitch, then slumped into a heap at Grace's feet.

Grace stared in horror at the lifeless round eyes. She saw

358

the dark thick blood mixed with flecks of brain and splintered bone, pumping out of the hole in the side of the head and forming a pool around her bare toes. She vomited.

She heard the men shouting at each other but she couldn't make out the words. Her brain was frozen, her whole body too, apart from her insides, which were emptying of their own accord. She gasped for air. She tried to spit out the foul taste, but more kept filling her mouth.

Her head was jerked back suddenly. She stared, wide-eyed and uncomprehending at Dmitri's furious contorted face. It took her a moment to realize that the hard thing pressing into her face was the barrel of the gun. The fingers of his other hand were curled tightly round her hair.

'No fucking bullshit,' he snarled at her, and then, in Russian: 'Why did they send you to me? Talk.'

There was no saliva in her mouth. All she could taste was the bile.

'Talk.'

She tried to speak but gagged on her own sick. There was nothing left inside to throw up, she was choking on dry spasms.

'She can't talk with the gun in her mouth,' she heard Gallagher say. 'Jesus, Dmitri, what the fuck you doing, man?'

She couldn't breathe, the black sensations overwhelmed her. She fainted.

She was unconscious for seconds only, but it felt like she was coming out of deep sleep. She stared sluggishly at the man who was shaking her by the neck with one hand and slapping her face with the other but couldn't understand what he was saying to her. She felt something against her feet and when she looked down she saw that she was touching the dead woman's mangled skull. Sticky wet blood seeped between her toes. Natalie's torn dress had fallen from her breasts, revealing livid weals of blood all across her torso. They must have tortured her earlier. Grace felt her gullet contract, but she was empty. As empty as Natalie's eyes.

'Don't hit me, please,' she said.

Her face was so numb, her tongue so swollen, she could hardly speak the words. She hardly heard them either, above the roaring angry torrent, in a language or languages she could no longer comprehend, coming out of Dmitri's mouth. She wondered why she was bothering to speak at all. Maybe it wasn't her speaking, the voice sounded so small, so far away. She saw Dmitri raise his hand to strike her and closed her eyes against the blow. It never came. She waited for long, agonizing seconds, bracing herself against the pain. But the hand that touched her next was light, almost gentle.

'It's all right,' said Gallagher. 'He's not going to hurt you. No one's going to hurt you. Here, drink this.'

He poured a full glass of water slowly into her mouth. She gulped it down. It tasted salty, but at least it washed away the bile.

'No one's going to hurt you,' he repeated. 'All you have to do is answer a few questions, then we'll get you cleaned up.'

Cleaned up? As if the state she was in was the result of some unfortunate social accident. As if the woman at her feet was merely dead drunk, not dead.

'If you want me to keep him off you, you got to tell me what you know. OK?'

She wanted him to keep him off her. She nodded.

Dmitri was back in the corner, sitting sullenly at the head of the table while Misha was speaking urgently into his ear. Misha had taken the gun from him.

'Look at what a mess you made of the floor,' she heard Misha saying to his brother in Russian. 'Someone's got to clean this shit up.'

360

All of a sudden they were obsessed with domestic hygiene. It was surreal. How much of a mess would they make when they killed her too?

'We want to know what your orders were,' Gallagher was saying, standing over her. 'Why were you sent after Dmitri?'

They wouldn't kill her here, then. No more blood on the smooth shiny deck. How very inconvenient for them, to have to dispose of two bodies. Would they shoot her too? Or slit her throat, or strangle her, or club her like a baby seal? What did it matter? She felt nauseous inside and numb outside.

'Come on, babe, I need you to meet me halfway,' said Gallagher. 'Tell me why your people are so interested in Dmitri.'

She was feeling drowsy. She was wrecked, all she wanted was to close her eyes and obliterate consciousness.

'They're not interested in Dmitri,' she said slowly, picking the words with care.

The fake smile disappeared from his face.

'Don't do this to yourself,' he said.

'They're not interested in Dmitri,' she repeated obstinately.

He sighed, pretending he was sad. If this was the best he could pretend it was enough to make her wonder how she'd ever believed him, about anything.

'They want Mickey Martinez,' she said.

Her head slumped forward. There, she'd said it. Perhaps they'd stop hitting her now. Leave her to sleep, to die, in peace.

She could hear a deep rumbling sound. It took her a few moments to realize that it was laughter. It was a noise that sounded like it should come from the throat of a bear, not a man.

She lifted her head. Gallagher wasn't laughing. He was standing exactly where he had been a moment ago, immobile, stone-faced. The noise was coming from Dmitri in the corner. His body shook with it.

'They want Mickey Martinez? What the fuck they want with Mickey Martinez?'

He was laughing so much he could hardly get the words out. Grace stared at him. What was so funny about Mickey Martinez? None of the others was laughing. Yuri and Misha were as impassive as Gallagher. No, that wasn't true. Gallagher's eyes, his whole face, had come alive again. He was leaning over her, one hand resting on each of the arms of her chair, his lip curled back in a sneer, his expression one of pure distilled venom.

'Shut up, Dmitri,' he said, and then, to her: 'You lie to me, I'll break your fucking neck with my bare hands.'

She didn't flinch. Weariness had settled on her like a lead weight. She could no longer summon up enough energy to be intimidated.

'I'm not lying,' she murmured flatly. 'They've got a tape of Orhan talking to you on the phone. About the poker game you played Saturday. Said Martinez was going to be there. Why they sent me to you, so you would lead them to Martinez.'

'You're lying,' said Gallagher.

'No,' said Dmitri.

He had stopped laughing. He had got up from the table and was walking across to Gallagher. Misha tried to lay a hand on his sleeve but Dmitri brushed him off. He squared up angrily to Gallagher.

'She's not lying, look at her. You want me to tell you advice, my friend? You want to know about unsecured phone lines, that kind of shit? Go on, you tell me what you want to know.'

'Shut up, Dmitri.'

'Maybe it's time you listen for a change. Or maybe it's time I stop paying for your shit advice.'

'Shut up, Dmitri, I've got to talk to the girl. I don't have much time.'

'How much you give her? She look asleep already.'

'There's plenty of time.'

'You give her too much.'

'You're the one said get her out of here.'

'Don't tell me you fucked up again?'

'It's under control. No problem.'

'No problem? Sure. She want Mickey Martinez, sure, is no problem to me.'

'She's lying.'

'Look at her. You think she's brave enough to lie? It's like George Tregear say. They got nothing on me, so why they make fools of themselves on Saturday, break into the house like the fucking Iranian Embassy? I thought maybe they want to scare me, but that's too dumb. No, she's not lying. Maybe it's time my so-called friends learn to be careful.'

'Shut up, Dmitri.'

'Hey, you still awake?'

Grace gasped as Dmitri grabbed her by the hair and jerked back her head. She was awake, just. Her eyelids, her limbs, felt ridiculously heavy. She wondered what drug they had put into the water. She stared blearily into Dmitri's mocking malevolent eyes.

'You got plenty time to sleep later, baby. Talk to me now. What you want with Mickey Martinez?'

Plenty time to sleep. Yes, she knew what that meant. Sleep and never wake up, buried and forgotten, she and poor Natalie together. Why they'd given her the drug. So she could fade away, no trouble to anyone.

'Fuck you,' she said through numb lips.

He hit her across the face, but there was no force in the blow. He was actually laughing as he hit her. It was a rasping, unpleasant sound, but he sounded genuinely amused.

363

Her head slumped forward. She found herself staring down at Natalie's half-naked body, at the streams of blood flowing across her face, her breasts, her belly. No, that wasn't right. Grace blinked. Her head was fuzzy, but she understood now. The red lines on her body weren't blood, they were lipstick. The lipstick spelt out words. She mouthed them aloud.

Judas. Whore. Liar.

'I say, what you want with Mickey?' Dmitri was saying. 'You want to ask him something, go right ahead, be my guest. This could be your last opportunity.'

'I think it's time you shut up, Dmitri,' said Gallagher quietly.

She blinked again, and the cloudy film in front of her eyes dissolved for a moment. She stared at Gallagher and registered his uneasiness. And his transparency. How easy it was to see through him, now. Dmitri was still chuckling to himself. She wanted to laugh too.

'Hi, Mike,' she said. 'Or would you rather be called Mickey?'

She was laughing, she couldn't help it. It was the drug, she had no control over her body, her limbs were rubber, her brain was so much jelly. She had to laugh because it was all so stupid, because she had left that message on Bob's machine telling him that Mickey Martinez was Mickey the chauffeur. She had been so wrong, and she had been so right. He had been under their noses all of the time. The truth had been too obvious, too easy to grasp. And here she was, staring it in the face. Too late.

'What are you going to do with that three million in the Caymans, Mike?' she murmured when she had stopped laughing. 'Get yourself some babe shipments?'

She heard him talking at her. No, more than talking, yelling, screaming. She saw vaguely his furious contorted face and was puzzled at how she had ever thought him attractive. She closed her eyes. He was shaking her. She could feel her head rocking backwards and forwards, but it wasn't enough to keep her awake. She was going to sleep now. She needed to sleep now.

She needed to die.

19

The dinghy sped across a calm mirror-flat sea on a course parallel to the shore. The night was starry and bright, visibility was good. The only other vessel in sight was the yacht, stationary at its moorings half a kilometre to starboard.

'Ready,' said Johny over the throaty growl of the engine.

Ryan tensed. He was hanging half out of the dinghy on the port side, his hands gripping the bow, his right leg slung over the stern, his left held straight with the foot trailing in the water. It couldn't have been easy for Johny, steering with such a lopsided load, but he was holding a pretty straight course. Ryan heard the noise of the engine fade as Johny decreased the throttle. The plan was to drop to a couple of knots when they were abreast of the yacht, but only for a moment.

'Go,' said Johny, and whacked the rubber hull with the flat of his hand to ensure that Ryan got the message.

Ryan released the rope and dropped into the water, pushing himself away from the vicinity of the lethal propeller blades with a couple of firm kicks. He heard the engine, momentarily loud in the water, as it revved up again, and then he heard nothing. He sank into the silent inky blackness.

It was eerie and not silent at all; his breathing, like that of a hundred-a-day man, rattled through his head. The compressed air tasted metallic and cold. The water was cold, too, even through his wetsuit. He began to move his arms and legs, geeing up circulation. He was carrying little weight, he wasn't falling very fast. He held his wrist tight to his mask. Gradually, through the pitch darkness, he began to make out the phosphorescent dials on his gauges. He levelled out at seven metres and checked his bearings. The shore was directly north north-east and it was ten minutes before midnight.

He was sure that the dinghy had been spotted from the yacht. There had been someone posted, either at the jetty or on the boat itself, ever since Grace had first gone on board. But Ryan had to assume that a one-man dinghy minding its own business as it crossed the bay hadn't aroused any undue suspicions, and that he hadn't been seen going into the water. If he was wrong then he might as well quit now. He tried not to think about being wrong. He started swimming.

He settled quickly into a steady, even crawl. It didn't take long to find his rhythm, even though he could see or hear nothing. He trusted to instinct, and to his training. He was used to coming in from much further out, more often than not by parachute, a far hairier proposition than gently slipping over the side of a slow-moving dinghy. He was also used to coming in the easy way, on a powered submersible with a squad of men honed by the toughest training on God's earth and sea to watch his back. It was no use pining for what he didn't have. He had Johny, he had a gun that appeared to be in working order in the bag strapped to his belly, a knife strapped to his leg, his own strength and guile. Above all, he had the unexpected on his side. It was his best hope.

There would be at least six men on the boat. The other

Rostov, Mikhail, had joined his brother and Gallagher when they had taken Natalie on board. The chauffeur and the skinhead paratrooper, Andropov, were sharing the watch. The sixth man was the only member of the crew they had spotted. Maybe there were more crewmen below who'd managed to stay out of sight for the whole of last night and today, but that didn't seem likely. There were at least a dozen others up at the house, but none of them had been anywhere near the yacht, so far. He was guessing that if they were up to something bad then they would want to involve as few people as possible. Dmitri Rostov's mistress, the platinum blonde, was the only other person who might be around. She had been on and off the boat several times today. He doubted that she would be dangerous, but he would nevertheless have to take her into account.

He stopped to check his bearings, treading water while his eyes adjusted to the dials on his gauges. He had been underwater for only minutes, but it felt like much longer already. With all the senses distorted it was not surprising that time played strange tricks. It was lucky that he had never suffered from claustrophobia.

He swam on in the darkness. Sometimes, when he peered upwards, he caught a pale flush of something, as if milk had been spilt into the water. The hint of moonlight at least confirmed which way was up. Even the pull of gravity, in the featureless dark, felt illusory. He counted the strokes in his head as he pushed on towards the land, trying to dull his anxiety with method.

It had been over an hour now since they had taken Natalie down to the yacht. Before that she had been in the house, and, from the state she was in when she emerged, barely able to stand on her own two feet, it was clear that they hadn't been gentle with her. It was equally clear that Grace was in terrible danger. He had wanted to go in the moment he had recognized Natalie, but it had been too light. Johny had said to hell with it, they should take the dinghy straight up to the yacht at full throttle, all guns blazing if necessary, relying on the shock of the unexpected. Only the paratrooper and the crewman had been on board at that time, so it might have worked, but it was probable that someone would have ended up getting killed. The problem, as ever, was guaranteeing that it was the right someone. Losing Johny in order to get Grace was not a trade he was prepared to make. And then what would have happened to Natalie? No, this had to be the better way, he told himself as he ploughed inexorably on through the liquid blackness. At least both women would be together. If they were still alive.

His fins brushed against something. He stopped swimming and let himself sink. Almost immediately his feet touched the bottom. He let himself drop all the way down into a crouch, then pushed up from his haunches.

His head broke the surface. He was fifty metres from the shore and about the same distance from the jetty, which was to his right. The currents had been stronger than he'd realized. He could see the lights on the yacht mast, and a spill of light from one of the portholes. He raised his mask to get a clearer view. He couldn't see anyone either on the deck or the jetty.

He replaced his mask and slipped back under water. He swam towards the jetty. As he drew near he could see the yacht's lights reflected on the surface. He felt his way between the wooden piles of the jetty and, once he was safely in the middle, came up to the surface again.

There was no sign of life on deck. The yacht and its dinghy were bobbing gently in the near-flat sea. Ryan hooked his arm through one of the struts attached to the piles and eased the top half of his body out of the water. Even had there been anyone on deck they wouldn't have seen him amongst the shadowy mass of the jetty's substructure. He undid the Velcro fastenings on his belly bag.

He opened the heavy-duty zipper and felt inside for the zip to the second, inner bag. It was completely dry inside, not so much as a drop had penetrated the double seals. He wiped his hands on the scrap of towel he had stuffed in earlier. His fingers brushed over the butt of the gun. He pushed his hand in deeper and found the mobile phone. He switched it on. When he had heard the muffled electronic bleep he pulled out the phone and cycled through the keys blind, punching out a self-explanatory text message – *boat*. Johny's number was the first on the address list. He sent the message and waited. Within thirty seconds the LCD flashed up briefly. The reply was an even terser *OK*. Ryan put the phone back into the bag and zipped it up again. So much for the easy part.

He refitted his mask, adjusted the regulator and dropped again under the water. He followed the nearest pile all the way down to the bottom and started swimming towards the yacht. It would be safer to come at it from the port side, he reckoned, because that way he'd be able to keep an eye on the jetty.

He reached the hull in a few strokes and felt his way under the keel. There wasn't much of a gap, despite the yacht's shallow draught. He came up, slowly, by the stern.

As soon as his head broke the surface he heard voices. He darted in, as close to the hull as he could, although he couldn't see anyone. The voices were above him, on the deck. They were too soft for him to be able to make them out, but he didn't think they were speaking English. He heard a metal clang. He was right by the stern, between the propeller and the big grey dinghy. There wasn't much light, but he could make out something moving above him. The ladder fixed to the stern began to tremble.

He ducked back underwater and kicked off in the

direction of the shore. He raised a hand and felt his way along the thick rubber bottom of the dinghy. He clasped hold of the ladder next to the engine mount and pulled himself up, slowly, keeping the outboard motor as a shield between his head and the yacht. The motor was in the up position, with the propeller out of the water. He slipped off his mask and peered through the gap in the mounting.

There were three men on the deck. Two of them were talking quietly. The third was standing on the bottom rung of the ladder. He had hooked a foot over the rubber curve of the hull and was dragging the dinghy towards him. He said something to the others and they stopped talking.

The men on deck bent down and picked something up. It was heavy, they were having trouble manoeuvring themselves to the top of the ladder. The other man, by now with one foot in the dinghy, was hurrying them impatiently. They all spoke in Russian. It was too dark to see any of their faces, but Ryan guessed that the man giving the orders was one of the Rostovs. Mikhail he assumed, unless Dmitri liked to do his dirty work himself. One of the men on deck was tall, the other was shorter but heavily built. He looked like the paratrooper.

Ryan was no more than a few feet away, but he was completely invisible. He watched with cold disgust as they went about their business.

The object they were handing down was a human body. It was wrapped in sailcloth and tied with rope, but the form was unmistakable. The body was limp, and it hadn't even been well wrapped. The pale pathetic blur of a foot was visible sticking out at one end.

Ryan's first instinct was to reach into his bag for the gun. The moment passed. All he would have succeeded in doing was alerting the others on board, not to mention everyone up at the house. Reluctantly he let his hand slip back into the water. He waited to see what they would do next.

They got the body into the dinghy with difficulty. They seemed to be handling it with care. Ryan's heart jumped. Did that mean she was alive? Was it Grace, or was it Natalie? Whichever it was, where was the other? It didn't seem as if they were going to bring anyone else out. The paratrooper had climbed back up the ladder while Rostov and the other man stayed in the dinghy. The paratrooper leant easily over the rail and lit a cigarette. Ryan tried to stay calm, but he had lived for too long amongst the dregs of human life to be able to keep his emotions at bay. It was obvious what they were going to do with the body, and death was not a prerequisite for disposal. He imagined the woman in the sailcloth, coming to as the water filled her lungs, kicking out helplessly in her terror. He imagined Grace, spiralling down into the depths.

The dinghy trembled in the water as the men moved down it. A shadowy figure filled Ryan's view. He dropped out of sight. There was a loud click and the outboard motor began to swing down into the water. He pulled down his mask and submerged.

He swam towards the bow of the dinghy. He heard the loud roar of the motor as it started and felt the water vibrating behind him. There was no time to think any more, time only to act.

He pushed a hand up out of the water and felt for the hard front section of the rubber hull. The dinghy was already starting to drift. He hooked one hand up and laid it flat against the bow while with his other hand he sought for a secure grip. He only had seconds, he could hear and feel the increasing vibrations of the engine. His fingers closed on a mooring ring attached to a nylon loop. He grabbed it with both hands just as the throttle began to open up.

He twisted himself to his side and curled his knees up into his chest, keeping his feet far away from the propeller.

If he'd stretched out fully it would have trimmed his toes. The engine was still warming up, but already the pressure was forcing his face mask into the bridge of his nose. He disengaged a hand and ripped it off. No matter, he wasn't planning on swimming back. He put his hand back in the loop and held on.

The dinghy picked up speed. He could hear a roaring in his ears, feel the churning water all around him. It was like being in an exploding jacuzzi. He gripped the nylon loop harder, felt it burning into his palms. The rushing water was clawing at his regulator. If he lost that now, he was done for. She was done for. He bit harder on the rubber, gasping in air. His whole body was shaking. His arms were being levered from their sockets.

The dinghy was at full throttle. It was impossible to keep his knees bent. He tried to extend his legs slowly, to keep his legs apart and his feet away from the propeller. He knew there wasn't much leeway. At full stretch his body was flush to the rubber bottom, his belly and chest pressed up into it by the massive force of the water. The dinghy was rising and falling with the waves and every time it fell it thumped him. He could feel the breath being pummelled out of his lungs as fast as he could gulp it in. His body ached all over. He felt as if he were trapped on some insane underwater rollercoaster. He hung on grimly, like a spent boxer waiting for the final bell. His brain was a blur, full of nothing but the sound and fury of the water.

Suddenly the dinghy slowed. He was so disoriented it took him a moment to realize what was happening, but the loss of momentum was dramatic. He couldn't hear the motor, it was either idling or off altogether. He opened his eyes to the salty water, but there was nothing to see. He drifted with the dinghy in the black sea.

He'd had no real sense of time, but the dinghy couldn't have been going for more than a couple of minutes. Surely they'd want to get further out to sea before getting started? Expecting the throttle to open up again at any moment he pulled his right wrist out of the loop and flexed it in a blissful moment of release. He reached down quickly and pulled off his right fin. He was surprised it was still on his foot, the other one had been torn away. He quickly checked the belly bag and the sheath strapped to his leg. It was all in place. The loop had become twisted round his other wrist. He started to readjust his grip, then stopped as something brushed against his knuckle. The moment passed, and he had almost convinced himself that he had imagined it. Then someone's hand touched his.

The man up there must have been as shocked as he was. His fingertips froze in place, spread across the back of Ryan's hand. Ryan reacted first.

He thrust his other hand out of the water and grabbed hold of the man's wrist. With all his strength he snapped it through a hundred and eighty degrees. The man tried to exert counter-pressure but he was too slow. There was a split-second as he fought desperately to keep his balance. And then he crashed down into the water.

Ryan clung on to the man's wrist as the water exploded all around him. He felt himself sinking, borne down by the man's momentum. He felt the bulk of the man knock against him, and flung his arms around him. The man kicked and lashed out blindly. He grabbed at Ryan's head and clawed at his breathing apparatus. Ryan took a breath and let go. There was an explosion of bubbles. Ryan's hand closed on the man's throat.

He had both hands around the throat. The man's hands were over his, scratching, trying desperately to get a grip. No chance, Ryan thought with grim satisfaction. The two of them sank slowly, locked in a lethal embrace. Ryan ignored the man's feet, slamming repeatedly but weakly into his shins, and redoubled the pressure. The man gave a last violent shudder and went limp. Ryan held on for a long count of ten to make sure.

A terrible thing, death by drowning. He had seen it happen to one of his best friends in a training exercise that went wrong. He still came out in a cold sweat sometimes thinking about it. But not this time. He thought of the body lying wrapped in sailcloth a few feet above. He wasn't going to lose any sleep thinking about this sodden husk of dead flesh.

He grabbed his tube and took in a mouthful of oxygen and sea water. He placed both hands under the man's back and pushed them both up towards the surface. They rose slowly.

The corpse broke the surface first. Ryan poked his head up cautiously and took in a deep draught of fresh air. He heard a voice, thin and anxious, calling over the water.

'Mickey? Mickey . . . ?'

The dinghy was ten metres off. The man on board, Mikhail Rostov, had a flashlight. Ryan watched it flickering wildly over the black waves.

It had all happened so quickly that Rostov probably didn't have a clue what was going on. This Mickey hadn't even had time to call out. Rostov might only have heard the splash.

Ryan felt for the buckle across his chest and unclipped it. He slipped the harness off his shoulders and released his oxygen tank. He shoved the tank underneath the corpse, wedging it under the dead man's pullover, to give him extra buoyancy. His mouth was dry and tasted of salt. He made saliva to moisten his throat. Then he let out a loud, desperate shriek.

'Mickey?'

The torch beam flashed towards him. Ryan took a deep breath and submerged. He waited, treading water, directly underneath the body, until he sensed the vibrations intensify around him. Now he could hear the faint chug of the outboard motor. Rostov must have seen the body; any second now and he'd be reaching out to try and save his friend. It would be easy enough, Ryan reckoned, to wait where he was and ambush the second man exactly as he had the first. But he needed this one to talk.

He kicked off in the direction of the engine noise. He reached up a hand and felt the bottom of the dinghy. He came up at the stern.

The motor was idling in neutral beside him. He could hear Misha Rostov calling, his voice more high-pitched and urgent than ever. He could dimly make out the human shape moving in the bow. The flashlight was pointing down into the water.

Ryan felt for the diving ladder at the stern. There were three slim metal rungs. He grasped the top one with his left hand and hooked his toes round the bottom one, crouched and ready to spring. With his right hand he unfastened the clip across the top of the sheath. He drew his knife.

He heard Rostov grunting. He pulled himself slowly out of the water until he was high enough to see into the dinghy. He could make out the man's bulk in the bow. He appeared to be reaching into the water for his dead friend. Ryan tensed.

He heaved himself out of the water and tumbled headlong into the dinghy. He hadn't meant to fall so wildly but his foot had slipped on the ladder. Rostov reacted far faster than Ryan had anticipated.

There was a blinding flash in the darkness and a thunderclap in his ear. He felt the pressure of the bullet as it seemed to part his hair and smelt the sudden whiff of the cordite. At the same instant his body thudded into his target and the pair of them collapsed into a heap of limbs on the deck. Ryan was on top. The thought of keeping this one alive had vanished the instant the shot had gone off.

Ryan thrust his knife hard into the centre of the squirming body.

He heard the man's shocked gasp at the same moment as he felt the warm sticky blood spreading over his knuckles. He had buried the knife to the hilt in the soft belly. He whipped it out and Rostov rolled on to his side, bent double with both hands clutching the gash in his midriff.

Ryan ignored him. He felt around on the wooden decking for the gun and threw it down the other end of the boat. He also found the flashlight.

The sailcloth-bound body was stretched out in the middle. He had felt it beneath him when he had fallen into the boat and there had been no reaction. He knew beyond any doubt that whoever was inside was dead. A lump of ice solidified in his heart.

A chain and a small anchor were secured round the waist. Ryan thrust his knife into the canvas covering the body and ripped it open lengthways.

Long blonde hair tumbled out. Fury and terror consumed him simultaneously. He shone the torch and saw the black congealed blood, the hideous gaping hole in the side of the head. He saw Natalie's blank staring eyes.

Along with the revulsion he felt something he was ashamed of, but couldn't help. He felt relief. Gently he covered the bloody head with the torn cloth.

The man in the bow groaned. Ryan shone the torch into his face and confirmed that it was Misha Rostov. He recognized the bulbous nose and moustache from the file.

Rostov tried to push him away as he yanked up his head by the hair, but he had no strength. Ryan shone the torch into his eyes.

'What have you done with Grace?'

The only answer was another moan.

'Grace – where is she?'

Rostov murmured something in Russian. Ryan pressed the tip of the knife against his throat.

'Speak English.'

Rostov shook his head.

'No English,' he muttered thickly.

Reluctantly Ryan decided he believed him. Rostov's eyes were filled with as much fear as pain. It would have taken more courage than he had ever possessed to lie now.

Ryan took a moment to think. If he had no further use for him then the sensible thing to do was tip him overboard and have done with it. It would be merciful to slug him first. Ryan wasn't feeling merciful.

He thought again. Two men had left in the dinghy. If there was a lookout on deck then he would expect two men to be coming back. Ryan calculated rapidly. He had no idea what they'd got planned for Grace, but he knew that time was not on his side.

He unzipped his waterproof bag and took out a roll of heavy-duty masking tape and one of half a dozen pairs of plastic handcuffs. Rostov was clutching with both hands at his wound and it took Ryan a few moments to master his last desperate outburst of strength. The man would be dead soon anyway, but Ryan wasn't taking any chances. He wrenched the arms behind the body and snapped the wrists together. He bound the ankles with the masking tape, then used some more over the mouth as a gag.

He cleaned the blood from his hands and reached back into the bag. The pistol was loaded, the silencer was fitted. He pulled out the phone and called Johny. There was an earpiece attached to the phone. He tugged off his hood and fitted it while he waited for Johny to answer, then he unzipped the top of his wetsuit and wedged in the phone above his collarbone.

'I need back-up, now. I'm out at sea in a dinghy.'

'What the hell you doing there?'

'I'll explain later. I'm no more than a kilometre out, I reckon. You didn't hear a shot, did you?'

'No.'

'Good. I'm coming straight in now. The dinghy's expected, it should be no problem. Use my engine noise to mask your own approach. I want you to get as close as you can, cover the shore and the jetty. I'll take care of the yacht. You see anything, yell. I'll have the phone on the whole time. When I give you the word, come in and take me off. Warn me before you start any shooting, if you can. You copy?'

'Yeah, I copy. Something's been happening down there. A car came to the jetty, some people left.'

'Male or female?'

'I couldn't see. I think two people.'

'Fine. We'll worry about it later. I'm coming in now. No talk unless necessary.'

Too much talk already for his liking, but he had to risk the unsecured phone, there was no other means of communication. But if the equipment and the preparation fell some way short of what he was used to, at least his improvisation appeared to be bearing fruit.

He found a black peaked cap by his feet and put it on. It must have belonged to Mickey, the man he'd drowned. He dragged Rostov up into a sitting position in the bow, then stationed himself in the stern and shifted the engine out of neutral.

He couldn't see the yacht clearly, but there was plenty of light coming from the big house up on the hill. He opened up the throttle and steered towards his mark. The engine was much more powerful than the one Johny had hired, and he squeezed every drop he could out of it. There were a few vessels in the distance showing lights, but otherwise the sea was deserted. He had to trust to luck that he wouldn't hit a stray buoy. He didn't have time to trust to anything else.

The lights of the yacht appeared out of the darkness. He didn't slow down. No need for caution if, as he'd said, the dinghy was expected. He headed for the narrow gap between the boat and the shore and slewed to a halt through ninety degrees in a burst of angry foam. He cut the motor.

The dinghy bobbed up and down in the quietening water. Ryan crouched in the stern, both hands clasped round the butt of his pistol, covering the yacht. Nothing stirred on deck. He dipped his chin and whispered into the phone.

'Johny, in position?'

The answer, equally soft, came through the earpiece.

'Got you covered. All clear from here.'

Ryan pulled the mooring rope out from under Rostov's legs and tied it to the bottom of the yacht's ladder. He climbed slowly, one rung at a time, hauling himself up with his left hand, the pistol in his right. He stopped mid-way up, his eyes level with the deck, and took everything in.

There were no surprises, it was exactly as he had memorized it from the photographs and the plans. The whole deck was in his line of sight. The LCD displays on the impressive array of navigational equipment in the wheelhouse were blinking at him discreetly, but there was no sign of life. The hatch to below decks was directly in front of him. A bright spill of yellow light lit up the polished deck all around it.

He waited. Whoever was down there must have heard him coming. He wanted to see if there'd be a welcoming committee. Half a minute passed.

He felt the slight tremble in the deck at the same instant as he heard the heavy tread on the steps. A head began to appear out of the hatch, the features illuminated by the light beneath. Ryan ducked his head and slipped one rung down the ladder. In the instant before dropping out of sight he recognized the paratrooper. Good, he thought. Tackle the hard man first.

The paratrooper spoke in Russian. He sounded confident. His voice had an almost jokey tone.

Ryan hung down from the ladder by his left arm, thinking that it was probably a good thing he didn't understand Russian. His pulse and breathing were calm. The gun felt cool and heavy in his hand.

The paratrooper spoke again. This time the voice had an upward inflection. Not anxiety, but a hint of wryness. Maybe he was saying something like, *Come on, guys, I know you're there, so why won't you answer?*

Ryan was still wearing the drowned man's cap. He thrust his head up to the top of the ladder.

The paratrooper was about a metre away, in the act of leaning forward to grasp the handrail. He was alone. He checked when he saw Ryan. Although Ryan was in shadow he must have realized something was wrong. He thrust his hand inside his jacket.

Ryan raised the pistol and fired. The gun kicked heavily in his hand, emitting a muffled thud, like a distant backfire. The paratrooper crashed to his knees. Ryan felt the man's breath on his face as he let out a gasp, half pain, half shock. The man had fallen side-on and for an instant Ryan caught a clear glimpse of his features underlit by the glow from the hatch. He saw the fear in the wide-open, glistening eyes.

Ryan placed the tip of the silencer against the bridge of the nose and pulled the trigger.

The paratrooper jerked backwards as the bullet exploded into his brain. What remained of his head slumped to his side and he was still.

Ryan hung on the ladder, motionless. He detected neither sound nor movement below. He didn't glance over his shoulder. He was relying on Johny to cover his back.

He eased himself up on to the deck and crouched down by the paratrooper's body. He ignored it. He wasn't immune to horror, by no means, but he had seen enough wounds, whether inflicted by himself or others, to be practised in indifference.

He stared into the hatch. The steps down were steep. He could see a chair, the edge of a table. It was well lit, there was a sheen on the polished floor. He watched closely for shadow, any sign of movement. The only sounds came from the gentle creaking of the boat.

He grabbed the paratrooper by the ankles and dragged the body away from the light. He left it lying in shadow against the wheelhouse and returned to the hatch. Again he crouched down in silence. No sounds came from below.

He climbed down into the boat. His bare feet made no noise, either on the steps or the smooth floor. The room was empty, but a glass and an empty bottle of water on the table suggested it had been occupied recently. He stood with his feet spaced comfortably apart, the pistol in both hands, covering the door at the other end of the cabin.

The door was open, the corridor beyond brightly lit. It was as deserted as the cabin. Ryan crossed the floor.

He smelt disinfectant. The floor became sticky under his toes. He glanced down but saw no sign of what they had been trying to cover up. But he could guess.

He stepped into the corridor. There were six doors leading off it, all of them closed. He knew the layout by heart. Port side were the crew's cabin and the captain's cabin. The door between them was a shower room and lavatory. To starboard were the galley and the guest cabin. The master cabin was the door at the end.

He checked the guest cabin and the galley first. Neither was locked, but the door levers were heavy and a bit creaky. He opened them carefully. Both rooms were in darkness and there were no signs of occupation. He crossed the corridor. The crew's cabin was also empty. He opened the door to the captain's cabin.

The lights were on. In front of him was a single bunk.

A man lay on it, propped up against a pillow and reading a magazine. He had earphones on and was whistling softly to music. When he saw Ryan he turned his head slowly, apparently unconcerned. Too late he realized his mistake and tried to sit up.

Ryan grabbed him by the throat and rammed his head back hard against the wall. The man opened his mouth to cry out and Ryan thrust the silencer between his teeth.

'Make a sound and I'll kill you.'

The man froze. His eyes were two pools of terror. His face was ashen. There was no movement at all in his body. He didn't even seem to be breathing.

'You speak English?'

The man couldn't have spoken, even had he been capable, with the gun in his mouth. After a moment he nodded. Ryan withdrew the gun from his teeth and stepped backwards, keeping him covered the whole time. He felt for the door with his spare hand and shut it.

Ryan recognized the man from his white uniform. It was the crewman who had welcomed Grace on board yesterday.

'What's your name?'

'Yakov.'

'OK, Yakov. Tell me what I want to know and I won't hurt you. Piss me off and I'll kill you. Understood?'

'Yes,' Yakov murmured.

'Where's Grace?'

Yakov tried to speak. His voice caught in his throat. He shook his head.

'The Englishwoman. Where is she?'

Ryan held the gun an inch from Yakov's chin. He found his voice.

'I don't know.'

'Then you're no use to me.'

Ryan pressed the tip of the silencer into the soft flesh under the chin.

'I know nothing, please. They make me stay here, I see nothing.'

'Who makes you?'

'My boss. Mr Rostov.'

'Dmitri Rostov?'

'Yes.'

'Where is he now?'

'I don't know. In cabin.'

'Who's with him?'

'I been on my own since hours. I don't –'

The rest of his sentence was muffled by a choking fit as Ryan thrust the gun hard into his throat. Ryan watched the sweat pouring down his face. He smelt the whiff of bile in his sour heavy breathing. He wasn't lying.

Ryan grabbed him by the collar and jerked him over on to his side. He offered no resistance at all. Ryan unzipped his belly bag and pulled out more plastic handcuffs and the roll of heavy tape. He cuffed Yakov's wrists behind his back. He tore off a long strip of the tape and wrapped it twice round his head, covering his eyes. He tore off a second strip and covered the mouth. Then he bound the feet to the foot of the bed. Yakov was docile. He lay stretched out on the bed, as stiff as a board.

Ryan walked softly to the door and eased it open. The corridor was empty, as before. He adjusted the earphone and dipped his chin to the cellphone.

'Check.'

'Roger.'

Johny's voice was the faintest murmur in his ear. Ryan walked on down the corridor on tiptoe.

He reached the door at the end and put his ear to it. The door was solid, he heard nothing. He contemplated the heavy door lever. None of the doors so far had been locked, but what if this one was the exception? If he tried it and it didn't budge then it would only alert Rostov to the fact that someone was trying to barge in. He had a better idea.

He walked back to the crew cabin. Yakov hadn't moved an inch, but his body tensed as he heard Ryan's footsteps and the black-taped eyes swung towards him. Ryan let him sweat for a few moments before ripping the other piece of masking tape from his mouth.

'I need you, Yakov. Do exactly as you're told and you won't get hurt.'

Ryan unbound his feet and yanked him up by the shoulders. He laid the barrel of the gun against his cheek as an ungentle reminder while he explained to Yakov exactly what he wanted.

'I understand Russian, so don't try and piss me around. You got it?'

Yakov gulped. Even if he thought that Ryan was lying he was unlikely to dare take the risk.

Ryan grabbed him by the collar and marched him into the corridor. They stopped outside the master cabin. Ryan knocked sharply on the door.

There was no answer. Ryan knocked again. An irritated growl came from the other side. Ryan pressed the tip of the gun into Yakov's cheek.

A stream of Russian gushed out of Yakov's mouth. Ryan caught the name of Yuri, the paratrooper. Ryan had told Yakov to say that Yuri needed to talk urgently. If pressed, Yakov was to say that he had spotted an intruder down by the rocks.

Whatever Yakov said it worked. There was a moment's pause, and then Ryan heard the sound of a heavy lock turning. He shoved Yakov down on to the floor.

The cabin door started to swing open. Ryan kicked it in hard.

The door flew into Dmitri Rostov's face. Rostov staggered back into the room. He tried to shout out something. Ryan silenced him with a kick to the stomach.

Rostov collapsed on to the floor. Ryan grabbed him by the wrist and twisted it hard, forcing him to roll on to his stomach. Ryan dropped down, his knee in Rostov's back. Rostov tried to push himself up. Ryan whacked the back of his head with the butt of the pistol.

Rostov's head slumped forward. Ryan had another pair of plastic handcuffs ready. He snapped them on, then grabbed the black tape from his bag and bound the ankles tightly. Rostov wasn't moving.

The door had swung half-closed again. Ryan opened it, giving himself a clear view all the way down the boat to the stern. He checked on Yakov. He was lying in a crumpled foetal heap, a frozen ball of terror. Ryan tore off another strip of tape and gagged him.

Ryan gave the master cabin the once-over. One glance as he came in had been enough to confirm that Rostov was alone, but he went through the motions anyway. He checked behind the bed and in the large floor-to-ceiling closet. There was nowhere else to hide. Except the bathroom.

The door to the en suite bathroom was closed. Ryan flung it open. The bathroom was small and neat and empty. Ryan pointed his gun at the laundry basket in one corner, the shower cubicle in the other. The air was damp and an extractor fan was humming quietly.

Ryan walked back into the cabin. Rostov hadn't stirred. He was wearing a towelling robe and slippers. His hair was damp from the shower, and from blood where the pistol butt had broken his skin. More blood was trickling out of his nose.

'I'm with the man,' Ryan said into his mouthpiece. 'Be ready to take me off.'

'Roger,' Johny answered.

There was a drinks cabinet in the corner. Ryan took a long slug of fizzy mineral water to wash away the taste of sea salt. He carried the bottle over to Rostov and emptied the rest over his head.

Rostov groaned. Ryan dragged him up into a sitting position against the foot of the bed. Rostov opened his eyes and stared at him blearily. He said something in Russian.

Ryan kicked him in the face. It wasn't a hard kick, more of a flick with the bare sole of his foot. It was just a warning. Ryan saw him looking at the other warning, the gun in his hand.

'You want money?' said Rostov, in English.

'I want you to answer one question.'

'I can pay whatever –'

Ryan kicked him again, harder.

'One question. Where's Grace?'

The question seemed to astonish him. His piggy eyes expanded into saucers of bafflement. He made a surprised noise, almost a snort of derision.

'Who pays you, you are police?'

This time Ryan drove his heel into Rostov's stomach. Rostov spluttered indignantly.

'Hey, why you keep kicking me? Give me a chance –'

Ryan dropped to his haunches in front of him and jammed the tip of the pistol into Rostov's neck.

'You want a chance? OK, you've got one chance. Tell me where Grace is and I won't kill you. I've killed three of your people tonight. I couldn't give a shit whether I make it four.'

So far, Ryan had to admit, Rostov had been doing a pretty good job of keeping up a front. Now there was a flicker of uncertainty in his eyes.

'That's right,' said Ryan, staring at him, his face close enough to feel the other man's breath. 'Your brother's dead. Your chauffeur's dead. Yuri Andropov's dead. We're talking a lot of dead people, not counting poor Natalie. Yakov's tied up outside. My people are surrounding the boat. No one's going to rescue you. Now, do you want to live?'

Rostov tried to stare Ryan out. Rostov blinked first. He spoke quietly.

'How do I know you won't kill me anyway?'

'You don't. But if anything happens to Grace I can guarantee I will. Where is she?'

'I don't know –'

'Then I'll kill you now.'

Ryan stood up. He aimed the gun between Rostov's eyes.

'Wait! They took her. I have information.'

'Who took her?'

'Gallagher. His friend the Turk.'

'Where did they take her?'

'I don't know.'

'Then I kill you.'

'No, wait! I find out. I tell you I have information.'

'I don't give a fuck about your information. Where is she?'

'I need book.'

'What book?'

'For address. In safe.'

'Safe? What safe?'

'On wall. Behind picture.'

'Over the desk?'

'Yes.'

Ryan walked to the desk and unhooked the big photograph of Rostov in his yachting cap from the wall. A small combination safe was in the wall.

'Seven-eight-nine-zero,' Rostov said unprompted.

'Is it alarmed?'

'No.'

Ryan mimed speaking into his mouthpiece.

'I'm going to open a safe. If it's alarmed or trapped in any way, kill Rostov.'

'I tell you, no alarm!' Rostov squealed.

Ryan opened the safe. There wasn't much in it: a wad of

five-hundred-euro notes, some keys and two soft-covered exercise books, one red and one black.

'Red book.'

Ryan pulled it out. After a moment's thought he pulled out the wad of money too. A lot quicker than filling out an expenses form, he reflected, stuffing the cash into his waterproof bag.

He flicked through the book. It was filled with Russian and Latin script. Ryan waved a page in front of Rostov's eyes.

'What is this? Names and addresses?'

Rostov nodded.

'I own many houses. I cannot keep them all in my head.'

'They took her to one of these?'

'Yes. Further back. Turn page.'

Ryan flicked through the pages.

'There. Stop. It's a chalet, near Grenoble.'

'Grenoble? Why are they taking her to Grenoble?'

'He give her drug. Maybe they drive for a few hours, she has to wake up, I don't know. Was his idea, all his idea. He kill other girl as well, was nothing to do with me. I can help you, I have important information.'

'How do I find this place?'

'There is map. In back page, you see?'

Taped inside the back page were two large-scale road maps, one of central and southern France, and one of northern Italy. They were both dotted with marks and comments in red felt-tip.

'What does this say?'

A long line had been drawn across the map from the crudely drawn star next to Grenoble into the margin, where something had been scribbled in Cyrillic script.

'It say two kilometres from main road. Take the sign for restaurant, Le Coq d'Or. First house on hill track.'

'That's all it says?'

'Why you think I lie? I help you, I tell you. You want, I can phone them.'

'You're not phoning anyone.'

'Why you think I cheat you? You need me, I have important information.'

'What information?'

'Good information. You are police, yes? I know who you want. I know you want Martinez.'

'I want Grace.'

'Then you will find Martinez also. He is Gallagher, I can prove it. You will win big promotion. I have papers, but not here, up at house. Let me call, they send papers, we make deal. Let me phone. Yes?'

Ryan unzipped his bag. He shoved in the red exercise book and pulled out the roll of tape. He was done here. All that remained was to get Yakov back to his cabin, safely out of sight, and ensure that both he and Rostov were properly secured. He spoke into his microphone.

'Take me off. Now. You copy?'

'Roger.'

Ryan clamped the tape between his teeth. He stood astride Rostov, grabbed him under the arms and hoisted him to his feet. He dragged him across the floor and dumped him into the swivel chair in front of the desk.

'We make deal?' asked Rostov.

Ryan tore off another long strip of tape.

'Close your mouth.'

Ryan wound the tape three times around Rostov's lower face. He secured his feet to the base of the chair and checked that he was thoroughly gagged and immobile. Then he grabbed Rostov's jaw and twisted his face towards him, making him meet his eyes.

'Yeah, I'll give you a deal. I'm going to this place in Grenoble now. If I'm too late, I'm going to come straight back and twist your fucking balls off. Then I'm going to shoot your fucking brains out. You like the sound of that deal?'

He held Rostov's gaze for long enough to let him know that he meant it. When he heard the hum of the approaching outboard motor he let him go.

Ryan walked out of the cabin. He slammed the door shut behind him.

The tinny whining noise of the motor touched a brief crescendo before it began to fade again. In another minute the sound had gone altogether. The only noise in the cabin was the soft whirr of the extractor fan next door.

Slowly, carefully, Tatyana stepped out of the shower. She closed the opaque plastic door of the cubicle behind her and walked softly to the bathroom door. She pulled her bathrobe off the hook on the back and slipped it on as she took in the situation.

She had heard most of it from inside the shower. She had just turned off the taps and had been about to get out when the sounds of the man bursting in and overpowering Dmitri had frozen her rigid. She had stood, utterly still, as the man had come into the bathroom a few moments later. She had seen nothing through the plastic, or he would have seen her too, but she had felt his eyes, reaching into every corner. If he had noticed her sandals, lying under the sink where she had kicked them off, they hadn't registered. Her clothes were in the laundry basket. He had gone next door and she had allowed herself to breathe again. She had breathed very slowly.

She put on her sandals. She pulled a towel from the rail and quickly rubbed her damp hair. Dmitri saw her out of the corner of his eye. He swivelled the chair awkwardly round towards her. He made a whimpering sound through his gag.

Tatyana took a step into the room. She glanced up at the

wall, saw the open safe. Dmitri's splutterings became more urgent. She touched a finger to her lips.

'Sssh!'

She stepped past him and opened the door. The corridor was deserted. She walked down towards the living quarters, checking all the doors as she went. Yakov was lying on the bunk in the captain's cabin. His arms were bound and his feet taped to the steel frame. He turned his taped eyes at the sound of the opening door. She saw him shake. She closed the door again and continued on her way. There was no one else below.

She climbed the steps up on to the deck. She watched the sea, and then the house. Everywhere was deserted. The guards had been told to stay in the top part of the grounds, away from the beach. No one disobeyed Dmitri. She had been present when Dmitri had phoned in his instructions, before sending her in to talk to Grace. She hadn't disobeyed him either.

She saw Yuri's feet sticking out beside the wheelhouse. She didn't feel the need to check on the rest of him. She had heard the man telling Dmitri how he had killed him, and Misha and Mickey. Extraordinary, then, that he hadn't killed Dmitri too. Why shoot the small fry and leave the big fish free? Some scruple, perhaps, about killing an unarmed, helpless man? Even police of the undercover variety, the class to which she presumed this man belonged, were bound by a degree of propriety quite alien to the men they pursued. There was no honour among thieves, nor among blackmailers, pimps, extortionists, murderers. Had their positions been reversed, Dmitri would have done what the policeman had only threatened to do and blown out his brains without a moment's hesitation. Following a suitable interlude of torture and humiliation, of course. At least, for all his other faults, Dmitri could never be accused of inconsistency.

She walked slowly to the stern. It was very gloomy, she didn't think that she could be seen from the house. In any case, she doubted that anyone up there would dare to spy. Outside the grounds was another matter. She supposed that the police might still be keeping the yacht under surveillance. Perhaps, if they spotted her, they would come and investigate. Something about all this didn't add up, but she didn't propose to hang around long enough to find out what.

She peered over the ladder at the stern. The dinghy was bobbing gently at its mooring rope. A figure was huddled up in the bottom. She was surprised. She had heard them carrying out the girl's body and had supposed it safely at the bottom of the sea by now. She climbed down the ladder to investigate.

She stubbed her toe against something in the bottom of the dinghy. She bent down and felt an anchor and chain. There seemed to be a lot of stuff around. She found a big piece of canvas, a jerrycan at least half-full with liquid, a gun, a torch. She shielded the tip of the torch so that only a little light would spill, and turned it on. She shone it at the inert figure at her feet. It was Misha.

He was trussed up like Dmitri and Yakov. The only difference was that he wasn't moving. She felt the great wet patch in his shirt and saw by the torchlight that her fingers were red. She washed off the blood in the sea.

Misha groaned.

She almost dropped the torch overboard. She recovered herself and shone the torch in his face. One eye was open. He groaned again.

'Water.'

His voice was very faint, very dry. She saw that the black tape with which he had been gagged was hanging loose. The policeman had been slacking. Doubly so, if had believed that Misha was dead. With the amount of blood he had lost, it was a miracle he wasn't.

'Water,' he hissed again.

'I'll get some. In a moment. Tell me what happened?'

'Tatyana?'

'Yes, it's Tatyana. What happened to you, Misha?'

'Tell Dmitri it wasn't our fault ... please, tell him we ... we felt something under the dinghy, we thought it was junk, stuck to the bottom. We stopped and ... and they jumped us. A submarine, I think they came from a submarine. Many of them, out of nowhere. Tell Dmitri, please tell him, there was nothing we could do. Nothing ...'

His voice cracked and trailed away into silence. She pointed the torch at him again. His eyes were closed and he didn't seem to be breathing at all. It was as if he had been saving up all his reserves to make his little speech of justification and the effort had finished him.

She put down the torch and picked up the gun. She had never fired one in her life, but she was pretty sure she could, if she had to. She presumed it was loaded. She found the safety catch and clicked it on and off a couple of times, as she had seen Dmitri do. She put the gun, which was small but unexpectedly heavy, into one of the deep bathrobe pockets. She climbed back up the ladder.

She walked back down into the boat, conscious of the weight of the gun knocking against her hip. She walked purposefully. She hadn't been sure what she was going to do when she came out of the bathroom. She was sure now.

She went back into the master cabin, this time keeping the door open to ensure that she could watch the rest of the boat. As she walked in Dmitri began jerking about in his chair and whining at her through the tape over his mouth. She was glad that the policeman had done a better job of gagging him than he had Misha. She ignored him.

Her suitcase was in the bottom of the closet, hastily packed with the clothes she had thrown in yesterday when Dmitri had told her to clear out for Grace. Too many clothes, the case was bulging. She carried the bag to the bed and tipped its contents out on the duvet. She slipped off her robe and put on the first underwear she saw, red panties and a violently clashing white bra. She pulled on blue jeans and a yellow T-shirt and slipped her sandals back on. She sorted quickly through the rest of her clothes and made an instant selection. She chose one summer dress, one skirt, her good linen jacket and a warm woollen top. She dropped in her jewellery box and purse and put her make-up bag to one side. She left out the rest, including her favourite Versace outfit. Sacrifices had to be made.

She walked over to the desk and reached across Dmitri's head. He was bobbing up and down dementedly in his chair, as much as his bonds allowed him, which, reassuringly, wasn't very much at all. She glanced at him and saw how his eyes were bulging and his face had turned lobster pink. He appeared to be having difficulty breathing through his nose.

She reached a hand into the safe. She pulled out the keys sitting at the back. She didn't know which one she wanted, but there were only half a dozen. She carried them all back to the closet.

It was amazing how much noise Dmitri was able to make through the layers of thick black tape. He sounded like a muzzled dog, ready to tear away from the leash and rend some poor soul to pieces with his teeth. It wasn't hard to imagine, at this moment, which soul he had in mind. Even though he was helpless it was still an unnerving sound. Tatyana worked quickly.

There were four small catches at the back of the closet, difficult to get at. On the two occasions she had watched Dmitri struggle with them she had wondered why he went to so much trouble, first hiding the key in the decoy safe, then making the real one so inaccessible. She had said as much to him. *Who would ever dare rob you?* Who indeed . . .

All four catches clicked and the back panel dropped down. Behind it was a solid metal safe door. She began trying the keys in the lock. The second one opened it.

The safe contained five transparent plastic bags and half a dozen large rectangular display boxes. The boxes contained gold coins, too heavy to carry around. She left them where they were. She carried the bags over to the bed.

The bags were sealed with heavy zippers. She opened one and emptied the bundles of hundred-dollar bills on to the bed. She made a quick calculation. About a quarter of a million dollars, she reckoned, which made sense. Dmitri loved round numbers. Four bags filled with dollars to make a neat million. The fifth bag contained a heap of five-hundred-euro notes. She'd have plenty of time to count them later.

She put the loose dollar bundles in the bottom of her suitcase and laid the four unopened plastic bags on top. She covered them with a couple of her T-shirts and closed the bag.

'Do shut up, Dmitri. It's like listening to a two-year-old having a tantrum.'

She unthreaded the towel belt from the bathrobe and laid it over her shoulder. Then she took the gun out of the pocket. That shut him up, temporarily anyway.

'You think I'm going to shoot you? No, no, far too noisy, far too messy and horrible. I saw what happened with that poor girl. Yakov was squeezing the blood out of his mop for ages. At least they got rid of her. You'll be pleased to hear that your people did something right tonight. There's only one body in the dinghy, and it belongs to that idiot brother of yours. Or did the police take the girl's body with them? Yes, that's possible, I hadn't thought of that. What kind of police do you suppose they were? Maybe they weren't police at all – did you think of that? Misha thought they came in a submarine, but he always did have a childish imagination. Unlike you.'

She put the gun down on the bed and picked up the empty plastic bag. She walked over to him.

'I don't want you to think this is about revenge, Dmitri. You probably think it is, but I'm not sufficiently naive for that. I don't care about all the times you've beaten me up, or humiliated me. It comes with the territory, I accept the losses along with the profits. You should be proud of me. You're always saying how Russians need to learn to think like capitalists. So there you go. I don't even care about you sending me away to make room for Grace. She's very pretty, or at least she was till you started knocking her about. And she had guts, I thought that even before you found out who she really was. Actually, I rather liked her, and I certainly didn't enjoy having to betray her. But I had to. It's a question of survival. Same as this. Sorry, Dmitri, but you know how it goes. Once you got free you'd come after me, and you'd find me, and you'd kill me. Maybe your people will come after me anyway, but there aren't so many of them left now and they'll probably have better things to do with their time. That's the thing about power vacuums. People quickly forget what caused them when they're so busy trying to fill them up. Even if you are remembered, you won't be lamented. Sorry if that sounds brutal, but that's what I have to be now. At least it'll be quick. Goodbye, Dmitri.'

She pulled the plastic bag down over his head. He tried to jerk himself out of the way but she was much too quick for him. She zipped the bottom of the bag hard up against his Adam's apple, as far as it would go, and sealed the plastic to his skin with the towelling belt. She knotted it with difficulty, fighting to make a loop as his head shook violently from side to side. At least his whining was so muffled now she could hardly hear it.

She finished tying the knot and stepped back out of the way of his thrashing skull. He had already sucked in all the

397

air in the plastic bag and it had collapsed into his face. It had also completely steamed up; she could hardly make out his features at all. It was quite amusing. He looked like an out-of-order parking meter. His head was barely moving at all now. He seemed to have acquired a violent twitch in his legs.

She picked up her make-up bag and walked into the bathroom. She examined herself in the mirror. There was a small yellowish bruise under her right eye, where Grace had punched her, but it didn't look like it was going to come up too badly. She powdered it lightly. She applied some mascara and a smear of dark red lipstick. Only the basics, she wasn't out to attract anyone's attention tonight. And not for a while yet, if it came to that.

She snatched the biggest towel from the rail and returned to the cabin. She packed away the make-up bag, threw the gun in on top and closed the case. Dmitri had stopped moving. A much quicker death than he deserved, she thought. Certainly much quicker than the one he would have given her.

She left him without a backward glance, dragging the suitcase behind her. It wasn't heavy, but it was awkward. It took her a while to get into the dinghy, taking the rungs of the ladder one at a time, the weight of the case threatening to pull her other arm from its socket. She laid the case down in the bottom of the dinghy and felt around for the torch. Misha was in the bow, his head and upper torso slumped over the side. She grabbed him by the knees and hoisted him, like a wheelbarrow. It was fortunate that he wasn't a big man. Even so, it took all her strength to tip him over the side.

She sank back into the dinghy, breathing heavily. When she had recovered herself she threw the anchor and chain overboard too. She laid the towel down where he had been lying, to soak up the blood. As far as she could tell, she hadn't got any on her clothes, and she wanted it to stay that way.

She unscrewed the top of the jerrycan and confirmed that the liquid inside was petrol. She didn't know how much was in the engine already, but she'd have quite enough now. It would take her fifteen, twenty minutes, to get along the coast and into town. After that, a taxi to the station, safer than the airport. Paris maybe, it didn't much matter. Her passport was in her purse, not that she'd need it, so long as she stayed within the EC. And when she wanted new papers, she'd be able to pay for them. She'd have to get to Zurich some time soon, to make arrangements about the money, but after that she'd be free to do what she wanted. And she had all the time in the world to work out exactly what it was she did want.

It took her a couple of attempts to start the outboard motor, but there was no one's curiosity left to arouse. She kept the engine low, though, as she eased away from the yacht and headed towards the headland. The moon was full and the night clear, but she didn't want to plough into any rocks or do anything stupid. Only when she had a good kilometre between herself and the yacht, and when she could clearly see the bright city lights along the coast, did she dare to open the throttle.

She headed for the lights.

20

He drove alone to Grenoble in the Range Rover. Ralf sat on his tail the whole way in the red Audi.

He liked to do his thinking driving through the night alone. It reminded him of the old days. Old and simple days. He never regretted anything, but he sometimes missed being himself. The ease, the smoothness he showed the world, had been learnt the hard way. The effort of deception was exhilarating some of the time, but it was wearing him down. Perhaps he would have been happier if he'd stayed rough and raw.

Happier but a lot poorer. He was thirty-six years old and he had never had to do what his father would have called an honest day's work in his life. Nor would he ever. What did happiness have to do with it?

How the real Mike Gallagher would have envied him. The only thing that had ever excited him was money. As the level in the nightly bottle declined so the sums would fill out, the dollar signs lighting the blank holes that were his eyes. *We're gonna make the big time, kid,* he would say, speaking the losers' language he'd picked up in a thousand bars. He'd said it so many times the words must have dug a groove in his brain. But the man did have some talent, before the booze blitzed it. He'd learnt how to play the casinos from the inside, as a dealer, making it to pit boss before the drink, or the drugs, or the itchy fingers – depending on which version he was telling – had finished him. The wonder was that in all the years he'd been playing his hustles and cheap tricks he'd never been busted until the night the two of them had shared a cell.

A friendship had been born that night, on one side anyway. Mike Gallagher had liked the idea of Mickey Martinez. *The kid has potential*, he would tell people, *the kid has guts*. Well, the kid thought the same way, but how the older guy – his senior by only two years, though it looked like twenty – got the idea into his head was anyone's guess. What he wanted was an audience. In a cell whose only other occupants were a couple of brain-dead smackheads, the kid was the sole contender.

He'd learnt almost everything there was to know about Mike Gallagher in that one night. How he had never known his father and wished he'd never known his mother. How he'd grown up in Toxteth, a poor part of Liverpool, how he'd had ambitions to make it as a rock star, or as a foot-baller – *that's a soccer player to you, Yank* – but had fallen in with the wrong crowd and let his talents go to waste. At sixteen he'd lied about his age and experience and got a job emptying ashtrays in a casino. One glimpse of the tables and he'd been hooked. The manager had seen something he'd liked and had taken him under his wing. *Same as I'm gonna do for you, kid*. Only what Mikey was going to tell Mickey was a whole lot more useful than learning how to deal cards from a shoe. He was gonna teach him the way to beat the bank at blackjack. Fool's gold, said one of the smackheads, waking for long enough to contribute to the conversation. It was the kind of talk you heard all over town.

But what Mikey taught him, starting there in the piss-sour cell, was the real thing. It wasn't rocket science, simply logic. The fact that he could do the math in his head without thinking, as they discovered the afternoon in the burger bar, was nature's bonus. That was one of the things he'd never been able to figure out about Jimmy Ramirez. Jimmy had seen for himself how he could do the numbers in his head without even thinking about it. So how had he thought he'd be able to get away with slicing off a percentage without being made? A guy that dumb deserved everything coming to him. And the chick, too. Any chick who ran out on him and into the arms of someone as dumb as Ramirez. Any chick who tried to screw him, period.

The speedometer needle had crept up to over a hundred. He took his foot off the gas, eased back to within the speed limit. Ralf, in his mirror, dropped down to match him, as he'd been instructed. It was no time to attract the attentions of a speed cop. He relaxed his grip on the steering wheel, sat back in his seat, made himself calm. It wasn't easy. He was tired, and he was getting hungry, and he wasn't enjoying the thought of how much he still had left to do tonight.

The light from a neon sign washed over the interior of the car. In the mirror he caught a glimpse of the blonde head lying on the back seat, the white skin blanched even whiter, almost the colour of the hair. She was wearing one of Tatyana's wigs. One of Tatyana's fur coats too, enough to fool casual prying eyes that might see a woman asleep in the back of a car. She was flat out across both seats, her knees pulled up to her stomach, one hand in front of her face. She could have been a baby, sucking her thumb.

He thought of that other night, driving through the small hours with another comatose passenger sprawled on the back seat. The difference was that Mike Gallagher had drunk himself into a stupor unaided, as he had done most nights, and most afternoons too. It had gotten so bad that he had

402

tried talking it over with him, had even suggested that he should seek some help. A waste of breath. Mikey sober was every bit as stubborn and a whole lot less friendly than Mikey drunk. In fact, it was probably easier dealing with him when he'd got a bottle in his hand, same as a kid with an armful of candy. It had made it easier to kill him too.

The idea had come out of nowhere, a flash of inspiration, not calculation. That came later. He had listened time and again to the same drunken complaints, the apportioning of blame for a screwed-up life to everything and everyone but himself. *I could have been a contender*, he used to say, thinking he sounded like Marlon Brando, and not just another slurred drunk. *I could have been a contender, if only people had shown some faith in me. Do you know what it's like to be all alone in the world? I've no one, no family, no friends, only you. If I fell under a bus tomorrow no one would notice . . .*

Mike Gallagher was wrong about many things, but he was right about that. He walked out of this world with the clothes he stood up in and an empty bottle of tequila clutched to his belly. No one noticed. The Mike Gallagher who was lying four feet under in the Nevada desert, that punks' graveyard, was forgotten even before he took his final breath. The irony was that the Mike Gallagher who took his place had become everything he'd ever dreamt, and much more.

The timing had been perfect. Poulson, the customs creep whose debts he'd sold on to his friends over the border, had gone missing, and the word was out he'd done a deal with the Feds. Then there was the little matter of Ramirez and the Schultz girl. There was no evidence connecting him to their deaths – damn right there wasn't – but the way he heard it the other Schultz girl was going to testify that she'd overheard him threatening Ramirez and her sister. Which was bullshit, and his attorney swore any judge would throw it out, but why take chances? So he had slipped Mike

Gallagher's British passport and green card into his pocket and skipped over to Mexico for six months. Mikey had been talking about going south to try a change of air and had the visa arranged. The passport photo hadn't looked much like him, but nor did it much resemble the real Mike Gallagher. They were roughly the same build and colouring and that was enough to get him past the bored immigration officer. In Juarez he had soon found someone to give the photo a makeover and make his new identity flawless. To anyone who questioned his accent he gave the same answer the real Mikey had always given: *Been over here so long, man, I gone native . . .*

It was only as he began to grow into the role that he realized how useful it was. Mike Gallagher was clean. The charge for passing the stolen cheque, the reason they'd wound up sharing a cell, had been dropped for lack of evidence. There were other advantages too. He found out that British citizens didn't pay tax on gambling profits. So he began the process of putting himself beneath the radar screen of the IRS. He hired a British accountant and lawyer, got himself domiciled in the Bahamas and moved around the Caribbean for the next few years. He had money from the deals he'd made with Ramirez, and, even better, solid-gold contacts. The cartel was pleased with the gift of Poulson, and didn't seem to hold it against him that the guy had cut a deal. They weren't too worried about his testimony – with good reason, as it turned out – and they'd gotten a big payback out of him in the nine months or so he'd been working for them. By way of a thank you they'd asked him to help out with a new angle they'd been working on, shipping cocaine through the Caribbean by speedboat. There'd been some trouble with the Colombians, who were already working the patch, and he had been able to smooth it out. His negotiating skills won him respect. When the Colombians wanted to offload some stuff into Europe they hired him as an intermediary. He discovered that London was a cool place to hang out, even if the casinos weren't to his taste. But he used them anyway, because being a professional gambler was the perfect front. He showed his face – his new face, subtly improved by a Mexican surgeon's knife – and acquired a new kind of reputation to go with it. He stopped trying to beat the big casinos at their own game and played along with them instead. He wasn't one of the really high rollers, but he dropped enough to ensure he was welcome wherever he went. And enough to justify to any policeman or border guard who might care to peek in his bag the large sums of cash with which he habitually travelled. Very occasionally, for fun, he might go someplace he wasn't known and count the cards and prove to himself he could still do it, but it was strictly for fun. The sums he won were too small to justify the effort. He preferred to play poker, in private, knowing he could always make enough to cover any losses at the blackjack table. And the money he made from his deals covered everything.

He became a big traveller and found there were plenty of cool places Mickey Martinez had never even heard of. As Mike Gallagher he learnt about them. Mickey Martinez quietly faded away. It was a name to open doors, but it was a name without a face. Not many people knew that the two were one and the same, but unfortunately the ones who did were the kind who would sell their grandmothers for loose change. He'd always known it wouldn't last for ever and the plans he'd made to disappear had been put in place long ago. Only he wasn't ready for it to happen yet. During the last year he and Ralf had put together a pretty neat operation. Small, discreet, and very profitable. Not the kind of profits a man like Dmitri Rostov would think it worth getting out of bed for, but that was the point. A guy like Dmitri had to do everything big, he couldn't help splashing in the pool. He, on the other hand, had always managed to stay submerged. Until now.

The woman made a sound, something between a sigh and a moan. He slowed right down and swung round in his seat to check on her. She was still flat out, her face twisted into a grimace. He figured she was having a bad dream. The drug did that to them, he'd seen it before.

His phone rang. He fished it out of his pocket and heard Ralf's voice.

'You all right?'

'Why shouldn't I be?'

'Why you slow down?'

'Nothing important.'

He pressed down on the pedal. The speedometer climbed smoothly back up to ninety. Ralf's headlamps receded briefly in the mirror before catching up again.

'How much further?' Ralf demanded.

'Another hour. Don't call me again, OK?'

He dropped the phone back into his pocket without giving him a chance to answer. He was sore with Ralf. No names, no places, no times, those were the three simple rules for any telephone conversation, no matter how secure the line. So why mention the name Mickey Martinez? No reason, he'd just been bragging that he was in the loop. More worrying was why Ralf's phone was being tapped in the first place. It didn't look like the operation was compromised at his end, or they'd have picked him up, but it could only be a matter of time. The question was, could they proceed with the current shipment or should they quit now? The difference to him would be about two hundred thousand dollars. Not enough to take any risks for, but too much to throw away for nothing. He needed to know what the woman knew. For 200k it had to be worth waking her to find out.

She was showing signs of coming round by the time he

reached the ski lodge. He saw her in the mirror, squirming on the back seat, once or twice lifting her head clear of the upholstery and half opening her eyes before slumping back, like a drunk incapable of pulling herself together. He wanted to bring her round and get this over with as fast as possible. He had thought she hadn't known anything and by the time he'd realized his mistake he'd given her the drug. It should be wearing off soon. Dawn had already broken. He couldn't afford to waste more than one extra day.

Sammy was waiting outside the lodge when he drove up, shivering in the cool morning air and pulling on a cigarette. He would have heard the engine and come out to wait. The lodge was so isolated, especially out of season, you could virtually guarantee that any car approaching must be visiting. The other big advantage from the security angle was the huge double garage. Sammy rolled up the door for him and he drove straight in. He indicated for Ralf to park outside.

The other half of the garage was occupied by another Range Rover, identical in every respect to his own. He walked round it and checked the details while Sammy closed and locked the garage. The copy of the hire firm's sticker was slightly out of place on the rear window, but he noticed it only because he was looking. The number-plates had already been attached and it looked ready to go.

He walked to his own vehicle and opened the rear door. The woman must have been pressed up against it, her head flopped straight out, the yellow-white hair spilling down to the ground. Sammy gave a little laugh.

'You still want to question her? It looks like you already beat the hell out of her.'

She didn't look good. He'd cleaned her up before setting out, but it needed more than tissues to wipe away the bruises and scratches Dmitri had given her. Her nose had bled again, leaving a thick congealed smear above her lip.

'Can we take her to the basement?'

'Sure. I've got a room ready. What did you give her?'

'Rohypnol. Let's get her inside and let Ralf in. We need to talk.'

He grabbed the arms and Sammy took the feet. They carried her through the connecting door into the basement. Three doors led off the corridor. All of them had heavy bolts on the outside. They took her through the third door into a small windowless room that smelt faintly of antiseptic. They dropped her on to the narrow iron bed and he took out of his pocket the handcuffs he'd removed from her earlier. He pulled her arms out of the fur coat. Underneath she was still wearing Tatyana's spare bathrobe, knotted round her waist. Sammy watched quizzically as he pulled her wrists together over her stomach and snapped the cuffs back on.

'You think she's going some place?'

'No, but I've got things to ask and I don't have time to ask politely. Got some rope?'

Sammy went next door and returned with a length of nylon cord. Gallagher stood on the bed and looped it round the cluster of water pipes that ran along one wall below the ceiling. Sammy heaved the woman off the bed and propped her up against the wall while he ran the rope between her wrists and pulled her arms up taut by the chain. He tied a knot and told Sammy to let her go. She slumped down, her entire weight supported by her manacled wrists. Her eyes stayed shut, but her face twisted into an expression of pain.

'You want to wake her now?' said Sammy.

He shook his head.

'She'll be ready when I'm ready.'

He whipped the wig off her head and tossed it on to the bed. He took a small key out of his pocket and handed it over.

'For the cuffs. Get rid of them before you dispose of her, will you? Dmitri says they're Russian police issue, we don't want to leave tracks.'

'I never leave tracks.'

'I know. No one else is here, right?'

'Only Ilya. I sent the others away for the night.'

'Good. Don't tell Illy more than he needs to know.'

'She is police? Illy will enjoy that. For a cop she is pretty.'

'I've seen her look better. Come on, let's find Ralf.'

They slammed the heavy door after them as they left. Through force of habit Sammy shot the bolt.

The metallic clanging sound hummed faintly through the air. The single bare light bulb hanging from the ceiling swung gently. It was the first thing Grace saw when she opened her eyes.

It was the only thing she saw. Her vision was blurred, her eyes so filled with water she could see only the white glare. Black waves were pounding through her brain. The light was overwhelming. She closed her eyes and darkness rolled over her. She opened them again and the light seemed to swim towards her. Consciousness flickered and her brain tried to crush it out. The nausea that came with it was unbearable.

Some part of her body was on fire. The moments of consciousness brought with them fierce stabs of red-hot pain. She opened her mouth to cry out and heard the tiniest muffled noise. Her tongue tasted something vile and she began to choke. The terrible pain in her limbs became unbearable. Hot tears gushed down her cheeks. Her body shook with sobs. Each convulsion intensified the agony.

She screamed through every nerve. She didn't know who she was or where she was. She craved oblivion.

She remembered sensing movement, she remembered the smell of leather upholstery. She had been in a car. Or was it a boat? Someone had put a lock on her brain. Half-formed impressions swirled briefly into focus before disappearing into the empty spaces between her ears. She closed her eyes tight to shut out the glaring light. She wanted darkness to smother her. But even with her eyes screwed shut the pain was still overwhelming.

She opened her eyes and felt the tears gush out of them. She stared blankly into a square, grim room. The walls were grey breezeblock, the concrete floor a shade lighter. She could feel the bare concrete through the soles of her feet. She felt the same hard coldness against her back. Was she naked? She sensed her cheeks flush with embarrassment, and then she wanted to laugh. Something terrible was happening to her and she was worried about her appearance.

Something terrible was happening. The thickness in her head began to clear. She realized she was hanging against the wall. Her arms were stiff and numb, but her wrists pulsed with agony. An image of crucifixion flashed before her eyes. A surge of horror, like an electric charge, jolted through her brain. She kept her eyes open. She looked around.

No, she hadn't been nailed to the wall. She saw the rope hanging from the ceiling, the way it had been looped around the handcuffs, the livid red weals on her wrists. No wonder the pain was so intense. Her legs were hanging uselessly and her whole weight was being supported by her crushed hands. She tried to straighten her legs. There was no feeling in them, her thighs were jelly. She gritted her teeth and pushed down from her knees. At once the terrible searing pain receded.

Her skin was raw and her arms ached abominably but the relief was intense. She eased the metal, tight against the bones in her hands, away from her chafed skin. The sensation was almost blissful. She shook the sweat out of her eyes. Her brain and body felt slow and sluggish. What had happened on the boat was beginning to come back to her. She had been drugged. She remembered the sickening feeling of losing consciousness, the terror of thinking she would never wake up again. And now that she had woken up it was impossible to resist the thought that perhaps it would have been better if she hadn't.

She looked around the small grey room. She had been in enough cells to know one when she saw one. In the corner was a chipped enamel sink and, next to it, a lavatory bowl without a seat. There was a rickety hardbacked chair; no other furniture apart from the bed. She knew she didn't want to look too closely at the stains which covered the mattress. She stared in bafflement at the fur coat and the blonde wig for a moment, and then she recognized the distinctive colour of the hair. Briefly she wondered if Tatyana had also been brought to this place and then the penny dropped. Her heart gave a jump. If they had been trying to disguise her then did it mean they were afraid of being seen? Being seen by whom?

The fog in her brain was dissipating, driven away by fear and adrenaline. The fact that she wasn't dead meant they needed her for something, and as long as they continued to need her they wouldn't kill her. The longer she could stay alive the more chance she had of being rescued. What else did she have to hope for?

She did not want to die. If they put a gun to her head, like poor Natalie, what could she do? But if they cut her down and tried to drag her to some dark corner and kill her there she would kick and scream and resist with every ounce of strength left in her. She did not want to die.

She was shivering. The room was very cold. She cast a covetous eye at the fur coat. She was not entirely naked, as she had thought, but the robe Tatyana had given her didn't offer much in the way of warmth. Were they trying to hurt or just humiliate her? It was hard to see any reason other than simple cruelty for stringing her up so painfully. The door and lock looked solid. An unwelcome thought kept breaking in on her. Was it a cell? Or was it a torture chamber?

Why torture her? She tried to remember what she'd told them in the moments before the drug had knocked her out. They had been going to kill her, she had known it with an icy certainty. What was it they still wanted to know? She knew what they had done to her already and she could guess what they might do. Did she have strength left to resist?

Her head was clearer but it ached abominably. It was hard to concentrate when every muscle and joint had been racked to breaking point. She had a raging thirst. This wasn't how they planned to kill her, was it, by leaving her to starve and thirst to death? Much more of this and she'd be begging for a bullet.

She gritted her teeth and mouthed a silent curse. No, she didn't want to die. All she had left was the will to live, she mustn't give up on that. She had always lived by her wits. If there was any chink in their armour she had to be sharp enough to spot it. That was how she had survived the last time someone had tried to kill her. Hadn't she been every bit as helpless then as she was now? Even if there was only going to be a chance in a million, she had to go for it.

She heard voices outside. They were muffled but coming nearer. How was she going to play this? Act unconscious? No, if they were going to wake her then they wouldn't be gentle about it. Maybe act slurred then, not let them know that the drug had worn off. Would that buy her time or make them mad? How could she know? Did she have a better idea? No.

She heard a metal bolt being drawn. She didn't want to look, but she couldn't help it. Her head turned in slow motion towards the sound.

The man she had thought of as Mike Gallagher walked into the room. Another man she hadn't seen before, small and bald with dark hooded eyes, came in after him, carrying her suitcase and her handbag.

He put the suitcase down carefully in the corner of the room and the handbag on top of it, like a hotel porter. He even hovered by the door, as if expecting a tip, though there the analogy ended. When he bent down his leather jacket opened and she glimpsed a pistol dangling in a shoulder holster. There was a big black-handled knife in a sheath in his trouser belt. He caught Grace's eye and grinned crookedly. He stood with both hands in his pockets, openly appraising her.

Mickey Martinez carefully laid out the fur coat on the mattress before sitting down on it. He was dressed smartly but casually in dark trousers and a bottle-green polo-neck sweater. He looked like a catalogue model, immaculately groomed and unnaturally relaxed. He had a glass of red wine in his hand. He took a long sip while he watched the other man stare at Grace, and studied her reaction.

'OK, Illy,' he said.

The man caught Grace's eye again and licked his lips. His tongue darted in and out like a small lizard's. It was such a repulsive gesture she wanted to look away, but she forced herself to meet his gaze. She didn't want to show fear in front of these people.

The man called Illy went out and closed the door after him. Martinez stared at her dispassionately.

'You must be cold,' he remarked.

He took another sip of his wine. He waved a thumb at her suitcase.

'I'm sure you've got some warm clothes in there. Let's get this over with quickly, then I'll let you clean yourself up and put something on.'

'That's big of you.'

She had meant to sound defiant, but her voice, so parched and cracked, came out as a squeak. Martinez's expression-less eyes met hers.

'There's an easy way and a difficult way of doing this, honey. Let me tell you about the difficult way. What happens is I say, Fuck it, why waste my breath talking with someone who doesn't have the sense to know what's good for her? I've got a nice hotel waiting for me the other side of Lyons, so say I drive over, rest up for a couple of days and forget all about you. Frankly, I'm dog-tired right now and the idea sounds pretty cool. The consequences for you, though, are not so good. You saw the way Illy was looking at you? Let me tell you about this place. It belongs to Dmitri, though you won't find his name on any piece of paper and he's never set foot here in his life. Illy's the caretaker, you might say, and Sammy's the guy he answers to. You met Sammy at Dmitri's, right? Between them they sort out Dmitri's woman problems, and boy, does he have woman problems. There's a hell of a lot of chicks in Eastern Europe desperate to get to the West and Dmitri's only too happy to oblige. He's got a lot of establishments to fill and turnover is high. Amsterdam, Hamburg, wherever, he's there. Sammy handles Dmitri's establishments in northern Europe. It's a very sophisticated operation, they should teach it in Harvard Business School. Only not all the girls are quite so happy when they get to Sammy and he explains the terms and conditions. Travel's an expensive business, you see. Dmitri has to make a big outlay upfront to get the girls over, and he doesn't like to be out of pocket. A hard-working girl can pay him off in two or three years, but for some reason not all of them think that's fair. That's where Illy comes in. Look on this place as a rehabilitation clinic. A girl might think she's got better things to do than lie on her back and make money for Dmitri, but by the time Illy's finished with her she knows she's deluding herself. She also knows that

414

anything a john asks her to do can't be half as bad as what Illy's done to her. Illy loves women, don't get me wrong. He loves women so much he can't get enough of them. But he likes hurting them too. He really, really enjoys it. Am I making it clear enough for you? You're pretty tough, I reckon, Grace, but do you have any idea what it's like to be raped by a sadistic psychopath? If you don't want to talk to me, I can guarantee you'll be finding out real soon.'

He finished his wine and put down the empty glass on the chair. He yawned and gave her one of his hard meaningless smiles.

'Alternatively you can talk with me and I'll keep him off you. I can't promise you a rosy future, but I can promise you a painless one. I'll find out what I want to know either way. It's your call . . .'

Grace tried to swallow down the lump in her throat. She knew that he wasn't exaggerating. She had seen Ilya's eyes.

'What do you want?'

'We're going to play a little word-association game, you know the kind of thing I mean? I mention a word and you tell me everything that comes into your head. It's very simple.'

'Can I have some water?'

'You're always asking me for water. Shit, the room service in these places must be terrible.'

He took the empty wine glass to the sink and filled it with water, smiling to himself at his own joke. He took the glass over to Grace and put it to her lips. It tasted metallic and tepid. She lapped up every last drop. He put the glass down on the chair and rearranged himself on the bed.

'You ready?'

She nodded.

'OK, here we go. Babe shipments.'

'I read it on your computer.'

'My files are locked. How did you get the password?'

'I didn't. I fished the files out of the trash can.'

'Oh yeah, I see.'

He touched a finger to his forehead and gave her a salute.

'Got to hand it to you, babe, that is smart. How did you get into my computer?'

'You left it on the other night in the hotel, in the bedroom. You went next door to phone.'

'Yeah, you're right. That was careless. And that's when you read about the three million?'

'It was in the other e-mail.'

'That was all there was in the trash can?'

'Yes.'

'I see.'

He laughed.

'No wonder I didn't notice, I was kinda distracted. Where'd you learn to do that? You sure you're a cop?'

'I'm not a cop.'

'What are you then? Don't tell me you're a frigging customs officer.'

He laughed louder.

'Jeez, how much duty you charge on a blowjob?'

'I'm not a customs officer.'

'What are you? An out-of-work actress?'

'I'm a private detective.'

'Private? Yeah, I guess it is. A private dick. Now that is funny.'

His laughter peaked and trailed away into a dry, mirthless cackle. It was odd watching him laugh; the face stayed resolutely immobile, free of lines and creases. The expressionlessness, she realized, was the result of plastic surgery. No surgeon's knife, though, could have disguised the heaviness around his eyes. Suddenly he was looking grey and tired.

'A private detective, huh? What's your real name?'

'It's Grace.'

'Collins?'

'Cornish.'

'Uh, huh. You work out of London?'

'Guildford.'

'Where?'

'Surrey. South of –'

'I don't care where it is. Let's cut the crap. When did you last report in?'

'On the yacht.'

'With Tatyana's phone. Yeah, so I heard. What did you report?'

'Babe shipments. Your real identity. I should have reported in yesterday. They'll be looking for me now and if they can't find me they'll come looking for you.'

'You don't say?'

'They'll offer you a deal, Mike. Or do you prefer Mickey now? They don't want you, they want what you know. And if you don't do a deal with us you'll be extradited back to the States. And then you'll fry.'

'Shit, I knew I should have paid that parking ticket.'

'I'm talking about Jimmy Ramirez and the Schultz girl.'

'Wow, you people have got long memories. They died, right? Was nothing to do with me.'

'They've got your DNA. Your semen on the girl's dress. They didn't have the technology then, but they do now. A top DEA agent told me in person. Be nice to them and you might get life without parole. Sorry Mike, nothing to spend your three million on in there, except lawyers.'

'That would be a shame.'

He got up and walked over to her. He placed his hands against the wall, one on either side of her head, and leant in close to her. She smelt the wine on his breath.

'I've got a lot more than three million, baby, and I'm not planning to spend a dime on lawyers. You say if you don't report in they'll come looking for you. They ain't been looking yet.'

417

'I wouldn't count on it.'

'I'm counting on nothing. Playing the odds. I think you're lying. No, I'll rephrase that. I *know* you're lying. You didn't know I was Mickey Martinez until last night. I remember your face when you realized, a couple hours ago on the yacht. It was sudden, like *hey bingo!* You didn't even suspect it before then, so no way did you report it.'

'They knew Mike Gallagher would lead to Mickey Martinez.'

'That's right, and I'm very grateful to you for bringing it to my attention. As of tonight Mike Gallagher has retired. Maybe it's a bit sudden, but it's not unexpected, so bye bye, Mikey. You had a good run but now it's over. Would you like to say hello to his replacement? Or rather, *Adios,* Mikey and *Buenas dias,* Juan. Juan Antonio Cruz. Funny guy, Juan, met him in Madrid a few years back when I was doing a favour for my Colombian friends. Juan's not with us any more, sadly, so I figured he wouldn't be needing this –'

He whipped a red EU passport out of his back pocket and flashed the photograph at her. She caught a glimpse of his tanned, too-perfect features. Even in a passport photograph he managed to look good.

'I'll be making some cosmetic adjustments, to be safe, but there's no hurry. I don't think they're going to be looking for anyone matching Mike Gallagher's description in the next two days, whatever you say. That's all I need. Two more days, one more shipment and I'm out of here.'

'I told them about the shipments.'

'So you say. Well, maybe you did, and maybe you didn't. But I'm kind of coming round to thinking that even if you did it's no big deal. You see, I don't think you've got any idea what's going on. No idea at all.'

'I know you've got another babe shipment today.'

'Actually, it'll be tomorrow. I had to postpone it for reasons you may appreciate. But that's not my point. What

I'm getting at is that it doesn't matter what you said when you reported in because you don't know what a babe shipment is, and neither do they. You got anything to say to that? Babe?'

He didn't wait for her to answer. He walked over to the door and pulled it open.

'*Adios, amiga.*'

'Of course I know what babe shipments are. You think we don't know about this slave trade in Eastern European women? It won't matter what name you're travelling under when they intercept the next one.'

'Nice try, baby, but that ain't it. The babes Dmitri ships in are nothing to do with it. I use this place because Sammy runs it. My partners are Sammy and Orhan, you see. We're just borrowing some of Dmitri's facilities. "Babe shipment" is our shorthand for a little operation that utilizes an infrastructure that happens to be in place already. Dmitri wouldn't be too happy if he found out about it, but, hey, who's going to tell him? I guess my secret's safe with you. Sorry, I'd love to stay and talk with you a while, but I'm clean out of time. You too.'

He stuck his head out into the corridor.

'I'm through here. Turns out she didn't know anything.'

He turned back to her. He snapped his fingers, as if suddenly remembering something.

'Oh, that promise I made. You know, about keeping Illy off of you? I'm real sorry. I asked nicely, but you know how it is. It's not every day you get the chance to make out with a real-live snitch.'

He touched the tips of his fingers to his brow in a farewell salute.

'Too bad you had to waste my time. Try not to scream more than you have to. It only encourages him.'

He waited, perhaps to see if she would respond. She looked down at the floor. She didn't think she had enough strength in her voice to tell him what she really thought, and she didn't want to give him the satisfaction of seeing her weakness.

She heard his unhurried footsteps disappearing down the corridor. He had left the door open. Somewhere in the distance another door slammed, and then, from somewhere even further away, she fancied she heard the sound of a car engine. Then silence.

Her brain was numb. She didn't want to think about what was going to happen to her. She could think of nothing else.

She felt the wall behind her with the back of her skull. If she swung her head back hard enough could she knock herself out? She still felt nauseous, maybe there was enough of the drug left in her system to at least partially anaesthetize her. No, there wasn't. The paralysis was in her thoughts only. Every nerve in her body was keyed up and alive. Whatever they did to her, she would feel it, every agonizing moment. Why hadn't they disposed of her along with Natalie? At least that had been quick. This was not going to be quick.

She was alone and she was going to die. No one knew where she was, there was no rescue party. She would be dead, when? An hour, two hours? Why didn't they get on with it? She should try and blank it out, think of positive things, at least deny them the satisfaction of seeing her fear and humiliation. She wanted to think of something positive, uplifting. An image of a green field, a sunny day, came into her head. It dissolved. What was the point? Her brain could not get a grip. She had lost the will to survive.

Her body slumped. Her legs were too weak to hold her, she was taking her whole weight again on her red-raw wrists. The pain was horrible, she heard herself moan softly. She opened her throat to scream but she didn't have the energy. Her eyes overflowed. She tasted the salt of her own tears.

She had no idea how long she hung by her wrists, enduring her own private Calvary. Time had no meaning in that windowless, airless room. Some amount of time passed. Then she was no longer alone.

She sensed movement and looked up. Ilya was at the other end of the room, crouched down by her open suitcase. She hadn't heard him come in. He was wearing soft black shoes, black trousers, a black vest and leather jacket; executioner's colours.

He was rummaging through the suitcase. She saw her clothes being carelessly tossed around. There was nothing that interested him. He emptied the contents of her handbag into the case, but nothing caught his eye there either. The brown envelope with the money Gallagher had given her was no longer there. He threw some clothes that had spilled on to the floor back into the case and closed the lid. He turned his head towards her and showed his teeth.

It might have been either a grin or a snarl. She suspected the effect was the same either way. She felt the ice spreading out from her spine even as another spasm of red-hot pain began in her wrists.

He got up off the floor and shuffled towards her. His movements had a furtive quality, like those of a small animal wanting to shield itself from view. A small, lethal animal. His eyes were as dead as a snake's.

He said something to her, in a thick tobacco-rich voice. It was only when he repeated what he'd said that she realized he was speaking English.

'Pretty lady.'

He said something else she didn't catch. It sounded like Russian, but the accent was too dense for her to penetrate. He showed her his teeth again. She thought of animal fangs. Slowly he raised a hand and stroked her lightly on the face with his knuckles. She shuddered and turned her face away from the rotten smell of his breath. He laughed. She screwed shut her eyes. Suddenly she felt asphyxiated. Her chest heaved as she tried to gasp in air. She was hyperventilating. She heard his laughter over her rusty wheezing.

She presumed he was mocking her, but when she dared to open her eyes again he was no longer in front of her. He was standing by the bed, playing with Tatyana's wig. He held it at arm's length, admiring it. And then he tried it on.

It was a perfect fit. He seemed delighted. He put on the fur coat and did a mincing walk into the middle of the room. He swung around with a hand on his hip and pouted, like some camp female impersonator. He clearly found the whole thing hilarious.

He spoke to her again, though whether it was in English or Russian she couldn't tell, the impenetrable accent was distorted even more by his rasping laughter. He seemed to be asking for her approbation. He did a twirl for her benefit and flicked a strand of platinum hair away from his face in an exaggerated, coquettish gesture. It was surreal. Should she humour him? She tried to smile, but she couldn't manage it. She felt overwhelmed by contempt.

He strutted around the room in fur coat and wig, a killer pretending to be a clown. He started to tell her something then cut himself short. He ran excitedly to her suitcase and examined the pile of things he had emptied into it from her handbag. He gave a whoop of delight as he found her hand mirror. He held it at arm's length and gazed at himself approvingly, fluttering his eyelashes and blowing kisses at his reflection. He carried the mirror over to the chair, propped it up and stepped back, trying to get a view of himself in full. He clapped his hands together with delight.

A slow, heavy handclap sounded from the door. It was

accompanied by a low sardonic laugh. Ilya jumped back from the chair and wheeled around angrily.

Orhan was standing at the door. Ilya hissed something at him and the Turk shrugged. He had a bottle of whisky tucked under his arm. He removed the cap and raised it to his lips. Before he took a swig he murmured something, half-aloud. Grace heard a word that sounded like transvestite.

Ilya erupted furiously. He ripped the wig from his head and hurled it into the corner. He threw open the fur coat and fumbled for the gun in his shoulder holster. Orhan whipped a knife out of his belt. For a moment it looked like they might be about to kill each other. Perhaps they would have had not Sammy come suddenly into the room.

Sammy knocked down Orhan's knife arm and came between them. He yelled at Ilya in Russian and at Orhan in English, switching between the languages effortlessly in mid-sentence. At least his Russian was easier to understand than Ilya's.

Don't be a fool, he was saying, *there's enough of her to go round*.

Reluctantly Ilya put away his gun. Orhan carried on muttering under his breath.

'Shut the fuck up,' said Sammy.

He turned to Grace and acknowledged her with a wry smile.

'Seems like you're in demand, babe,' he said, in his near-accentless English. 'I hope you won't take this the wrong way, but I'm surprised. When we met last week I thought, Hey, that's one sexy lady, I wouldn't mind a ride on that myself. But you're not exactly looking your best this morning. Even so, both these guys are anxious to have some fun with you. What am I supposed to do? It's tough trying to be a good host these days.'

He patted both men on the shoulder and spoke to them

briefly, in English and Russian. He invited them to shake hands. They did so, grudgingly.

Sammy pulled a coin from his pocket and showed it to them, both sides. Orhan shrugged. Ilya reluctantly shrugged his agreement. Sammy tossed the coin.

'Heads,' said Orhan.

Sammy showed them both the coin. From the thunderous look on Ilya's face it seemed that Orhan had called correctly. Ilya snatched off the fur coat and tossed it into the corner. He stomped out without looking at Orhan.

Sammy followed him to the door. He indicated Grace.

'Don't knock her around too bad now, Ralf. Who knows, I may change my mind and feel like a piece later.'

He showed Orhan his right hand and opened and closed it four times, spreading wide the fingers and thumb. He didn't need to explain. He was giving him twenty minutes.

Sammy went out and closed the door. Orhan walked across the room towards the bed. He didn't seem to be in a hurry. He took a sip of his whisky. He placed the bottle down on the chair. Only then did he turn to Grace. He walked towards her, holding his knife up to the light. He stopped a foot away, and pressed the tip of the knife against her neck.

'You ever hear of a Colombian necktie, bitch?'

Every part of her was still. She wasn't even breathing. It was one thing to accept the certainty of death philosophically; quite a different matter altogether when the moment actually came. The Turk was baring his teeth at her the way Ilya had, but in his case there was no mistaking the ferocity of his intent.

'Colombian necktie is what happen to bitch who snitch. I slice you from here to here –' he drew the flat of the blade rapidly across her throat – 'and pull out your bitch snooping tongue, like this.'

He thrust his own tongue out at her as far as it would

424

go. She recoiled from the reek of whisky on his breath. A whimper escaped her lips. She couldn't help it.

A self-satisfied smile spread across his face. She watched him watching her, enjoying her fear. She remembered the look of terror on Jeanette's face after she had been with him, when there had been no question of him actually doing her any harm. He was going to do harm now, and when he was finished there would be another one waiting to take over, like the other half of a sadistic tag team.

'But first we have some fun, right?'

He raised the knife and sliced through the rope securing her to the water pipe. She slid down the wall on to her haunches, clutching her hands to her bosom. Even though the handcuffs still pinched her wrists and every muscle in her arms ached abominably, the sensation of relief was almost exquisite. It didn't last long.

He twisted his hand through her hair and yanked her towards the bed. She was dragged across the floor on her knees. He sat down on the bed and let her go. She collapsed on to the concrete floor, breathing heavily. She listened to him drink down more whisky and smack his lips. He banged the bottle down on the chair. Then she heard the sound of him unbuckling his belt and unzipping his fly. The bedsprings creaked as he lifted himself off the mattress and dropped his trousers.

'OK, bitch, let's see if you're as good as Mickey says.'

He seized her by the hair again and dragged her face up to his groin. He was holding the base of his semi-erect penis with his other hand and thrusting it towards her mouth. He didn't have to tell her what he wanted. He pulled her head down by the hair and forced himself against her lips.

She kept them pressed shut. She couldn't. She would rather die. He pressed the sharp edge of his knife against her skin. She knew that he would cut her throat without a second thought. The terror of death overwhelmed her. She opened her lips.

'Don't let me feel no teeth, bitch.'

She took him in her mouth. He tasted of sweat and salt and when she breathed in through her nose she almost gagged from the stink of him. She screwed shut her eyes and forced down the nausea in her gullet and the revulsion in her mind. So Mickey had recommended he try her out. She could picture him saying it, casually throwing the words away as he sauntered off to his warm clean hotel bed in Lyons. She kept the image in her head. It gave her strength.

'Oh yes, baby, that's good.'

She wasn't actually doing anything. He was pulling her head back and forth. He was fucking her in the mouth. She looked up at him. His head was tilted back, both eyes shut, a fat smile on his lips.

She raised her hands off the floor and laid them on the mattress between his thighs. She flexed her fingers. She had some feeling in them again. She grabbed a piece of the mattress and screwed it up tight. Feeling and strength too.

He gave a sigh of pleasure and loosened his grip. His eyes were shut tight.

She eased her forearms up between his thighs and cupped his testicles in her hands. She stroked him gently with her thumbs and he gave another moan. She counted to three. She snapped shut her hands and squeezed his testicles with every scrap of strength she possessed. She bit into the head of his penis so hard that her teeth met. There was a moment of suspended shock, and then he roared like a wounded elephant.

A massive blow to the side of her head sent her reeling, but she kept her teeth clamped shut and clutched on to his balls with furious concentration. He struck her again and this time her head snapped back, releasing him. She fell to her side and he crashed down off the bed on to the chair.

Her head hit the concrete hard and her ears rang with breaking glass. She smelt and tasted whisky at the same instant as her face touched the floor. She had let go of him and he was rolling away from her, clutching his savaged groin. Half stunned from the blow to the head she tried to drag herself away from him along the floor. She was crawling through whisky and broken glass. Her bound hands knocked the broken neck of the bottle and sent it spinning round.

She saw him reach up to the bed for his knife. He crawled towards her on his knees, his face distorted with agony and fury. He slashed at her with the knife and she slithered away, through the glittering broken glass. He grabbed her by the ankle and pulled her towards him. She kicked at his groin with her other foot and he hunched forward to protect himself. He had lost his balance, he was falling towards her. She was on her side, staring at the crazily spinning bottle. She grabbed it with both hands and thrust it blindly upwards. Her head snapped back into the floor as he collapsed on top of her.

She almost passed out. Her head was roaring and she could hardly breathe. The weight of him was crushing her into the ground. Her blurred eyes swam into focus and she glimpsed her hands trying to push away his smothering bulk. She was covered with blood. She heard herself cry out, with rage, with pain, with terror. Somehow she slid out from under him and rolled across the floor.

Her head banged against the iron bedstead. She rolled up into a sitting position and leant against the bed, clutching her knees to her chest. She was shaking all over. Tears were pouring down her face. There was blood everywhere.

Orhan was lying on his back with his head twisted towards her. The top of the broken bottle was sticking out of the side of his throat. Blood was flooding out of the wound, spreading all around his head like a liquid halo. He looked grotesque with his trousers down by his ankles and the bloody mess of his groin. His hideous staring eyes looked as if they were popping out of his head.

Grace felt the bile rise in her throat. She choked it down. Though every limb was weak and trembling she forced herself to her feet. She staggered across to the sink.

She washed the blood from her hands and filled them with water. She drank them dry and filled them again, and again. She splashed her face and watched the bloodstained water drip into the enamel. A pity she hadn't been able to wash away the foul taste in her mouth as easily. She was becoming aware of pains all over her body. She picked a dozen tiny pieces of glass from her skin.

Her mind was clearer now. Spasms of terror and revulsion were pulsing through her head, but she forced them back, like the bile in her throat. She was alive, she had a chance. She had to take her chance while she had it.

The pool of blood had reached the bed. She had never seen so much blood, nor realized a human body could hold so much. She stepped around it as she walked unsteadily to the door. Her fingers closed on the handle and she mouthed a silent prayer. If the door were locked then she was finished anyway. The others would come back and find his body and kill her where she stood. Slowly, hardly daring to hope, she turned the handle.

The door opened. She pushed her head out slowly and peered into a bare and gloomy corridor, lit by a single weak bulb. The corridor was deserted.

She closed the door again and leant against it for support. She screwed up her face in concentration as she took deep, slow breaths. She needed to be clear in the head, she needed to think. Twenty minutes he'd said, and that had been a good five minutes ago. She had maybe a quarter of an hour. She didn't have a clue where she was, but wherever it was she had to get out. She wasn't going to get very far like this.

She skirted round Orhan's body and stepped between his legs. She went through his trouser pockets and fished out a wallet and a set of car keys, but no handcuff keys. The only other pocket was in his shirt and that was empty. She gritted her teeth and ran her hands under his shirt. He didn't have a gun. She pulled her hands free from the hot sticky body with disgust.

She hurried across to her suitcase, stopping only to pick more glass out from between her toes. She found her passport and driving licence lying amongst her cosmetics. No doubt they had been planning to dispose of the whole lot along with her body. She threw her papers and the car keys into her handbag. Even if she found his car could she drive it with her hands manacled together? She pushed the question to the back of her mind. She had about ten minutes.

Orhan's wallet was stuffed with euro notes. She dropped the money into the handbag too. She struggled into her jeans and flat sandals. She couldn't take the bathrobe off because of the handcuffs. She knotted the belt tightly.

With Orhan's knife in one hand and her handbag in the other she stepped out into the corridor. At the far end, to her right, was a flight of stairs. She walked on tiptoe.

She passed a half-open door and glanced inside. It was an empty cell, identical to the one she had just left. She carried on walking and came to another door. This one was bolted from the outside, but there was a square hinged shutter at eye-level. She lifted the shutter and found herself staring into another identikit cell. Two women were on the only bed. One, a brunette, was stretched out under a blanket with her back to her. The other, a young blonde, dressed only in a torn T-shirt, was sitting on the bed with her knees clasped to her bosom. Although she was staring directly at the door she made no reaction to the sound of the shutter. Her eyes were utterly blank.

Grace replaced the shutter and carried on to the stairs. Her first instinct had been to unbolt the door and let the women out, but how far were they going to get in that state? It was more likely that they'd end up spoiling what little chance she had. Better to get out herself and then send for help. She was right, she knew she was right, but she couldn't help feeling guilty. The blonde's empty eyes haunted her. She was a pale, thin slip of a thing, no more than a teenager.

There was another door at the foot of the stairs, but this one wasn't bolted. She felt a draught of cold air blowing in over her toes. Eagerly she pushed at it, but it was locked. She climbed the stairs.

Another closed door at the top: it was so dark she had trouble finding the handle. She turned it gently, murmuring another silent prayer. It was unlocked. She opened it a fraction and light spilled in on her. She froze. She could hear voices.

She was trembling all over. Her heart was pounding and she was breathing in short shallow gasps. Her knees felt as if they might buckle at any moment. She clung to the wall for support, while she fought to banish the terrors welling up inside her head. A minute passed, two minutes. She was acutely conscious of the precious time slipping away, but there was no help for it. She needed to plumb her soul for courage.

She was calm again. The voices she could hear had a tinny quality. They also sounded very excited. She opened the door another few inches and confirmed her suspicions. The voices were coming from a television set that had been turned up loud. Cautiously she poked her head through the gap in the door.

In front of her was a narrow hallway. The walls, the

430

floor, the ceiling, were all in dark-stained wood. Hanging on the wall to her right were a pair of skis and some ski poles. To her left, at the far end of the hall was a big solid door, an assortment of heavy boots piled up beside it. It looked like the main door to the building. Somewhere on the other side of it, only yards away, was Orhan's car.

She eased herself out into the hallway. It was very gloomy, but daylight was visible through a glass panel over the top of the door. She hugged the left-hand wall as she inched along. The wall opposite was solid and ran all the way to the main door, but on her side it gave out after a few yards. As she approached the corner a large open-plan room hove into view. She crouched down and listened, but could hear nothing over the loud television voice. It was a French football commentary.

She peered around the corner. The room was huge, the ceiling at twice the normal height. A railed gallery ran all around it at the upper level, with numerous doors leading off, presumably into bedrooms. The staircase was right beside her, and, immediately beyond it, an open door leading into a kitchen. The television, a massive plasma screen set into the wall, was in the far corner, facing her.

Between her and the TV was a huge white sofa. Ilya and Sammy were both sitting on it, watching the match. All she could see was the backs of their heads.

It was very dim. All the curtains in the room were drawn. Some light came through the kitchen door, and some more from upstairs, but the only light in the room itself was coming from the TV.

The front door was thirty feet away. The bright light outside gleamed like a beacon. All she had to do was cross that space. No, it wasn't all. What if the door were locked? Even if it was open, wouldn't they hear her? And if they didn't hear her, wouldn't they feel the draught? It might be sunny outside but the skis told her she wasn't going to find a sandy beach. And if she did make it, they'd hear the car engine and come after her. Every thought that ran through her head was charged equally with opportunity and risk. There was no way of embracing one without the other.

She dropped to her knees and crawled into the open. It wasn't easy, with both hands full. She kept her wrists as far apart as possible, the chain taut between them, to prevent any clanking. There was a dining-room table and chairs between her and the sofa. It would help shield her for some of the way should one of them chance to glance round.

The floorboards were battened down firmly and didn't creak. She was halfway to the door when the noise from the TV suddenly cut out.

She glanced round. The image on the screen was frozen. She heard the two men's voices, then Ilya stood up. He pointed a remote-control device at the screen and the image began to fast forward. The match they'd been watching was a recording; it had reached half-time.

Ilya handed Sammy the remote and walked round the sofa. He disappeared for a moment behind the table. He clattered into something and swore under his breath. Sammy laughed.

'Put the light on,' he said in Russian.

Ilya reappeared in Grace's eye-line. He was no more than ten feet away; if he so much as glanced in her direction he had to see her, no matter the darkness of the room. But as he walked he was bending slightly away, rubbing his knee with one hand. He headed into the kitchen. As he turned the corner he extended a hand behind him and flicked a switch. Bright light flooded the room.

Grace's eyes swam. Her whole body had broken out in an icy clammy sweat. She felt the knife slipping through her nerveless fingers. It clattered gently on the wooden floor.

The noise shook her to her senses. She glanced around

frantically, trying to take everything in at once. The back of Sammy's head still faced her, he hadn't heard the knife. Ilya was in the kitchen, humming tunelessly to himself. She pulled herself up into a crouch and measured the distance to the door.

Her heart sank. The door was chained and bolted at the top and the bottom. They would hear if they didn't see. She had to find a hiding place. If she went back the way she'd come she might cross Ilya coming out of the kitchen. She took a tentative half-step towards the table. A big white tablecloth was hanging halfway down the sides. Perhaps if she crawled into the middle they wouldn't spot her. She noticed Ilya's black leather jacket on the back of the nearest chair. His shoulder holster was hanging down beside it.

It was ten steps to the door, two steps to the gun. She didn't hesitate.

She dropped the knife and bag and threw herself at the chair. She grabbed hold of the gun butt with both hands and yanked it free of the holster, trying to get a firm grip with the right hand while feeling for the safety catch with her left. She found the catch but her hand was shaking so badly her finger slipped on it. She became aware of movement out of the corners of both eyes.

She swung the gun towards the sofa and dropped into a crouch, as she had been taught during her handful of sessions at the police firing range. Sammy was on his feet and was coming round the sofa towards her. She couldn't see if he was armed. She could hardly see anything at all, her vision was a blur. Her sweaty finger found the catch again and this time she heard the satisfying heavy sound of a click. She pulled the trigger.

The gun bucked and reared in her hand and there was a flash of red flame. At almost the same instant there was a noise like a thunderclap and the huge TV set imploded in a shower of glass. Sammy disappeared behind the sofa.

She staggered backwards, partly from the recoil of the gun, partly from pure shock. Ilya was coming out of the kitchen, a tray full of beers and glasses balanced in his hands and an expression of stunned amazement on his face. She waved the gun in his direction and fired again.

Another tongue of flame belched out of the barrel, making the gun squirm in her hand like a metal eel. The effect this time was not quite as spectacular but it was no less dramatic. The bullet punched a hole in the wall a foot from Ilya's head, throwing up a puff of white plaster. Ilya squealed and threw himself on to the ground. The tray crashed down beside him, spewing beer and broken glass in all directions.

Grace ran to the side of the sofa and pointed the gun at Sammy. He too was lying on the floor, shielding his head with his hands. He saw the gun pointing at him and yelled at her, his eyes popping open and shut frantically. She swung the gun round to cover Ilya and he started shouting too. The ringing in her ears was so intense that it took her a few moments to make out what they were saying.

'Don't shoot! Don't shoot!'

She had been stepping backwards, pointing the gun at them alternately, keeping both in view. She was at the point of an equilateral triangle, about fifteen feet between each of them. That was much too far apart for comfort. She aimed the gun at Ilya and waved him towards Sammy.

'Over there. Now, or I shoot!'

Her voice sounded loud and confident. Too damned right it did. She was on such a high of adrenaline she felt as if she could fly. She could feel the trigger pressing into her finger. One move from either of them and she would shoot them both without a second thought.

'Hands on your head. Now.'

Ilya scuttled across the room to join his friend. He looked completely stunned. Sammy, on the other hand, seemed to be recovering his composure. He had put his hands on his head, as ordered, but unlike his friend he wasn't trembling. She knew exactly what he was thinking. He was working out how he could get the gun off her.

She took a couple of steps towards them. She stopped ten feet away, far enough to deter them from trying to rush her, close enough to give herself a pretty good chance of hitting them, even with her shooting skills. They were side by side now. She kept the gun mostly on Sammy.

'Undo your trousers.'

They didn't move. She lowered the gun until it was pointing at Sammy's groin, closed one eye and took aim.

'Either drop your trousers or I'll shoot your dick off.'

She meant it. He knew that she meant it. Both men undid their belt buckles and flies and dropped their trousers.

'Now, hands on head.'

They did as they were told. She breathed a little easier. With their trousers round their ankles they weren't going to be doing anything in a hurry.

'Who's got the key to the handcuffs?'

Sammy didn't answer. She pointed the gun at Ilya.

'Him, not me,' Ilya squealed.

Sammy scowled. He gave a reluctant downwards nod.

'In my shirt pocket.'

'OK, I want you to lower one hand, your left hand, and take it out. Slowly.'

There was one buttoned-down pocket over his breast. He undid it, slowly as instructed, and fished out a small key. He held it out between finger and thumb.

'You want me to unlock them for you?'

'Very funny. Drop it on the floor.'

The key hit the wooden floor, bounced up and came to rest a couple of feet in front of them.

'Now step backwards, both of you. Slowly.'

The final instruction was unnecessary. Walking backwards

with their trousers round their ankles they had no choice but to go slowly. She followed them, step for step, until she was standing over the key.

'Stop there.'

There was a bare expanse of wall behind them, between a window and a wooden pillar. 'Turn round and put your hands flat against the wall. Above your heads. Higher.'

When she was satisfied with their positions she bent down and picked up the key. It wasn't difficult getting at the lock, but it was stiff. The loud click it gave when it sprang open was the sweetest sound she'd ever heard.

'Now move along the wall, to the left. Nice and slow.'

They shuffled along the wall until they were on either side of the wooden pillar. It was a hefty trunk of rough-finished wood fixed flush to the wall. But at the top, seven feet or so off the ground, it joined one of the beams that ran along the ceiling. At the point where it joined there was a curved section that left an arc-shaped gap between the wood and the walls. She bowled the handcuffs along the floor towards them. They landed at Sammy's feet. 'Bend down and pick them up with your right hand. Keep your left hand on the wall where I can see it. Now raise both hands above your head. No sudden movements. Put your right hand in the cuff and close it.'

She listened for the click as the handcuff closed.

'Now put your right hand up and push it through the gap between the wall and the beam. Good. Now you.'

She turned her attention to Ilya.

'You put your left hand through the other cuff and close it.'

Again she waited for the metallic click.

'Don't move. Either of you.'

She walked over to Sammy. She transferred the gun to her left hand and rammed it up between his buttocks against his testicles.

'I would advise you to keep very still.'

A muscle in his face twitched but apart from that he took her advice. She stretched out her right arm and checked the lock on the handcuffs. She backed away and stepped over to Ilya, going through the same routine. When she was satisfied that the handcuffs were securely locked she searched them both, one at a time, keeping the gun pressed hard against their private parts while patting them down and going through their pockets. She had never had more compliant subjects for a body-search.

She came away with Ilya's black-handled knife, a mobile phone, two bunches of keys and two wallets. She carried them over to the table. Between them the wallets contained about a thousand euros. She retrieved her handbag from the floor and added the money to the wad she had taken from Orhan. Now that she was calming down she was beginning to feel very cold again. She took off the bathrobe and put on Ilya's black leather jacket. She saw Sammy watching her every move.

'You want money?' he said. 'I can give you money.'

'I've got all I need, thanks.'

All she needed and more. Petrol, tolls, a ticket for a plane or ferry, more than enough to get home in style. She wanted desperately to be home. Only there were some loose ends needed tying up first.

She checked the front door and confirmed that it was bolted. It was also double locked. Lucky she hadn't tried to make a break for it. She found the key amongst the bunches on the table. She left it in the lock.

The men were muttering to each other. She couldn't hear what they were saying, but it didn't matter. Bound to each other through that solid block of wood they were every bit as helpless as she had been downstairs.

She climbed up the staircase next to the kitchen, the gun at the ready. She didn't think there were any more of them in the house, but she wasn't going to leave anything to chance. There were five bedrooms upstairs. They were all empty, but four of the beds had been slept in recently. Through the windows she saw white-capped mountains. She was less entranced by what she saw in the mirror. Her hair, her face and throat were smeared with dried blood. She stopped in the last en suite bathroom and rinsed it away with soap and warm water. She glanced covetously at the shower. She was desperate to wash this foul place out of her skin, but she wanted to be away from it even more. She hurried back downstairs.

'Where are the others?' she demanded.

'What do you mean?' Sammy answered.

'Four people were sleeping upstairs. Where are the other two?'

'They went into town.'

'Which town?'

'Grenoble.'

'How far are we from Grenoble?'

'Half an hour.'

'When will they be back?'

'Could be any time.'

'Then why is the door bolted?'

He didn't answer. She sat down on the arm of the sofa. There was a packet of cigarettes on a low table in front of her. She found a lighter in one of the jacket pockets. She lit up and tasted nicotine for the first time in over two years. She choked back a cough and filled her lungs with smoke. It felt disgustingly good.

'If they do turn up I shan't have time to worry about you,' she said. 'I shall just have to shoot you.'

'That wouldn't be smart. It makes a lot of noise, that gun, as you know.'

'Oh yeah?'

She reached back into the pocket where she had found

the lighter and drew out a long black silencer. It fitted snugly on to the barrel. Sammy attempted to look casual.

'If you were going to shoot us you would have done so already.'

'Fuck you!'

Her sudden explosion of rage surprised him almost as much as it did her. She had jumped to her feet and run towards him, the gun levelled at his head. Her finger was itching to pull the trigger and he must have known it. His face had drained of all colour even before she jammed the tip of the silencer into the soft flesh of his neck.

'You think I wouldn't enjoy blowing you away, you fucking bastard? Tell me, what exactly were you going to do with me when this creep here and that other dead fucking creep downstairs had finished with me? Put a gun to my head and throw me down a well some place? Or cut me up in pieces and bury me under the floorboards? Do you like to do the killing yourself? Is that how you get your kicks? You like looking into their eyes, you want them to plead for mercy? I'm so sorry I'm not looking my sexiest today, so sorry you didn't feel like having a ride on me first. If only I'd known I could have asked Dmitri not to knock me around so much. Maybe you'd like me to go away and slip into something comfortable? Would you? Go on, tell me exactly what you'd like, don't be shy. Or can you only get it up when you've got the gun and it's the woman who's chained to the wall? Do tell me, please, because I'd really like to know what makes a sick sad fucker like you tick.'

He yelped as she grabbed between his legs and squeezed him roughly.

'Is that the best you can do? About as hard as an ice cream in a heatwave.'

She released him and stepped back. She pointed the gun at Ilya.

'And as for this creep, look at him . . .'

She had become aware of an odd rattling noise but had been unable to place it. Now she twigged that it was caused by the handcuffs knocking against the wood. Ilya's hands, his arms, his legs, were trembling violently. She noticed that the thick hairs down the inside of one of his thighs were matted with moisture.

'Frankly, I think you need a torturer with a bit more guts. This one's peed his pants. Well, you know what they say about bullies. And I'm including you in that.'

She pointed the gun back suddenly at Sammy. He flinched.

'Come on, give me an excuse to pull the trigger. You want me to come the other side of you? Think you can make a grab for me with your free hand? That close enough? Go on, grab the gun. If you think you're tough enough.'

She had moved round to his left side and was only a few feet away from him. She thrust the gun into the space between them and left it there, inches from where his left hand was flat against the wall. He didn't move. She watched a bead of sweat break out on his forehead and trickle slowly down his face.

'I guess that answers that. I wonder, do you have any idea how ridiculous you look standing there with your trousers round your ankles like a mucky schoolboy? And you two are meant to frighten people for a living? If I didn't despise you quite so much I could have a bloody good laugh.'

She turned her back on him and walked to the sofa. The cigarette she had lit was in the ashtray, half smoked and barely smouldering. She lit another. She sat down on the arm of the sofa and tossed the gun on to the cushion.

'A couple more minutes and I'll be out of here. I'd like the answers to a few questions first, so perhaps you'd be kind enough to oblige. The girls in the cellar. Who are they?'

'One's a Latvian. One's Slovakian.'

'Have they got names?'

'Anna. Mira.'

'How long have they been here?'

'Couple of days.'

'They look like they've been there years. Ilya did that to them, right?'

'Yes. It was Ilya.'

'And you had nothing to do with it, naturally.'

'I –'

'Shut up. Next question. Your friend Martinez, or Gallagher, or whatever he's calling himself today. Name of his hotel, please?'

'Hotel Moulin Rouge.'

'How quaint. It's near Lyons, I understand. Exactly where, please?'

'To the north. Ten, fifteen kilometres.'

'Which? Ten or fifteen?'

'I'm not sure. It's signposted.'

'How reassuring. That's where babe shipments happen, is it, at a hotel outside Lyons? Don't look so astonished. He's got a big mouth, your friend, I know quite a lot about what's going on. Quite a lot. Now, suppose you fill me in about the rest.'

Once Sammy had started talking he became quite loquacious. He was anxious to convince her that he was only a small cog in the machine, and that the main operator was Mickey Martinez. The same went for the business he ran for the Rostovs.

'You mean you were only obeying orders?' said Grace, cutting him off in mid self-justification. 'Save that for the French police, will you? Have Anna and Mira got papers?'

'They're some place. Look, can we talk?'

'No. Either tell me where the papers are or I'll find them myself. After I've shot you both.'

'All their stuff is in the cupboard under the stairs.'

There were two battered suitcases sitting in the cupboard. On top of them was a large brown envelope containing keys, some cheap jewellery and the girls' passports. Grace retrieved the lot.

She went back down the steps into the cellar and stopped outside the first cell. She drew the bolt and gently eased open the door. The two girls were on the bed in almost exactly the same positions she had seen them in before. The blonde's eyes widened slightly as Grace came in, but there was no other reaction. Her face was a blank white mask. The brunette sat up at the sound of the door and turned towards her. She looked scared but at the same time there was a flicker of defiance. She said something in a language Grace didn't know.

'Don't be frightened, I'm here to help you,' Grace said in Russian.

Her words seemed to have no effect. She repeated them in English. The girl looked surprised.

'Who are you?' she answered, in English. She had a strong East European accent.

'My name's Grace. Are you Mira or Anna?'

'I am Mira. How do you know my name?'

'I made them tell me. Look, we haven't much time. Come with me and I'll explain everything in the car.'

'What car?'

'I'm taking you out of here.'

Mira didn't move. Her eyes were full of suspicion. Grace saw her staring at the gun.

'It's all right. Look –'

Grace checked that the safety catch was on and tucked the gun into her waistband. She showed her empty hands.

'Listen, they can't hurt you. Sammy and Ilya, they're my prisoners, upstairs.'

'Where are the others?'

442

'They're not here but they might return at any time. Come on, please, we've got to get out of here. I've got your passports. You can go home.'

The girl shrugged.

'There's nothing for me at home,' she said.

Grace walked over to the bed. She took the gun from her waistband and laid it on the blanket.

'Do you want it?'

The girl glanced up. She shook her head. Grace locked eyes with her.

'I know what they did to you,' she said softly.

'I'm OK,' said the girl, a little too swiftly.

'What about your friend?'

'She is not OK.'

'Then let's get her out of here.'

'Where are we going?'

'Does it matter? It has to be better than here, doesn't it?'

The girl nodded grimly.

Grace put the gun back in her jeans. She took one side of Anna, Mira took the other. Together they hoisted her up. She didn't help, but she didn't resist either. Once she was on her feet she stood unaided.

'Come on. Upstairs.'

They went up the cellar steps. Grace showed them their suitcases.

'You'd better put some clothes on, I think it's cold outside.'

Both girls were dressed in their underwear and T-shirts. Grace left Mira to sort the pair of them out while she went back downstairs.

She went into the cell where she had been kept. The pool of Orhan's blood had spread out in a great circle from his head. It had the colour and consistency of raspberry jam. She didn't look at his face. She picked up her suitcase and retrieved Tatyana's wig and fur coat.

Upstairs Mira had put on shoes, a plain black skirt and a pullover. She was trying to get Anna into a floral-patterned dress and not succeeding very well. Grace helped her. Together they managed to get Anna's feet into a pair of boots and her arms into a short woollen jacket. They steered her towards the door.

Anna let out a sudden petrified yelp. Grace let her go and yanked the gun out of her waistband, her heart in her mouth. She was convinced for one dreadful moment that the others had returned and had entered by a back door. Mira saw what she was thinking.

'It is them.'

The loathing in her voice was enough to make Grace understand. Both girls were staring into the corner, at the two men hanging from the beam by their wrists.

'You did this to them?' said Mira disbelievingly, peering around the room as if in search of hidden accomplices. 'Why didn't you kill them?'

Grace didn't answer. Half an hour ago she had killed a man, a thing she never would have considered herself capable of. A thing she would remember in vivid, horrific detail every day for the rest of her life, even though she would not, could not let herself regret it. These two would have killed her as casually as crushing an insect. And yet, even when Sammy had provoked her into an almost-blind fury, even when her finger had been straining to pull the trigger, something had held her back. She was glad of it too, glad to be spared one more set of loathsome memories. She could see that Mira would do it, now, if she gave her the gun, and she didn't blame her. But she knew that she could never, in cold blood, do such a thing again.

'Let's get her out of here,' said Grace, pulling Anna towards the door. She snatched her handbag from the table on the way out.

444

Outside was cool but bright. The sun glinted off the windows of a house about a mile away, halfway up a wooded slope. It was the nearest building. The only other buildings in view were in the distance, up the mountains. She could see the bare skeleton of a ski lift, looking incongruous without the background accompaniment of snow, but no sign of people. In front of them was a driveway that led into a narrow road that wound up a bare stretch of the slope. Anything coming up that road would be heard long before it was seen.

Orhan's key fitted into the only car on the drive, a red Audi. They got Anna into the back seat. Mira climbed in after her.

'I'm going to get our things,' said Grace. 'Is there anything you need?'

'Is there food? We are very hungry.'

'I'll see what there is. Stay here and look after her.'

Grace carried out all the suitcases and put them in the boot of the car. She went back into the house one last time and liberated what she could find from the kitchen fridge: some chicken pieces, cheese, chocolate biscuits, bottles of Coke and water. She piled everything into an empty beer box and went back out.

She ignored Sammy and Ilya. They had no means of escape and no way of calling for help. She had Sammy's mobile and the nearest telephone was on the wall by the kitchen. As far as they were concerned it might as well be on the moon.

As soon as she had got the girls safely stowed somewhere she would call the French police. She wasn't planning on identifying herself, but she knew enough to ensure that they wouldn't dismiss her as a crank caller. All she needed was a full address. She found it by the front door, on an electricity bill addressed to a Monsieur Martin.

She left the door off the latch for when the police arrived

445

and went out to the car. Anna was stretched out across the back seat, apparently asleep. Mira was now in the front. Grace handed her the box of food.

'You have cigarettes?'

Grace patted the pockets of Ilya's jacket.

'I think they're on the table inside.'

'I will get them.'

'I'll stop at the first garage.'

'No problem. One moment.'

Mira was out of the car before Grace could stop her. She ran up to the house. A minute passed. Grace turned on the car engine, ready and anxious to be going. Another minute passed. What was Mira up to?

Grace turned off the engine and got out of the car. She could guess what Mira might be up to. She imagined her taunting Sammy and Ilya, spitting at them, kicking them. What if she found Ilya's knife and attacked them? What if they got the knife off her?

Grace was halfway to the house when Mira emerged, a freshly lit cigarette in her mouth. She showed Grace the packet and lighter.

'I couldn't find them. Sorry.'

The two women got into the car. Grace restarted the engine. She indicated Anna.

'Does she need a doctor?'

Mira shook her head emphatically.

'No doctor, please. No official people. Where are you going?'

'England, eventually.'

'You take us to England?'

'That might be difficult. But don't worry, I won't abandon you. I'll get you to some place they won't come after you.'

Mira wound down the window and tossed out her half-smoked cigarette. She looked through the box of food as Grace steered the car down the drive.

446

'They won't come after us,' she said.

Something in her voice made Grace glance across. She sounded steely, yet at the same time indifferent. For a moment Grace sensed the same disquiet she had felt a minute ago while Mira was in the house. Deep inside this teenage girl, wherever it was that the spirit resided, was a cold empty place. Grace knew that place.

There was only one way to go at the end of the drive. She drove up the hill along a narrow unmetalled road.

Mira had started to demolish a chicken leg. She had slipped off her shoes and had one foot up on the dashboard, as if she were a kid out on a picnic.

Up ahead, near the top of the hill, was a road sign, bent and rusted with age. It announced that they were twelve kilometres from Grenoble.

'Look in the glove compartment, will you?' said Grace. 'See if there are any maps.'

The glove compartment contained a pair of aviator sunglasses, a bag of mints and a handful of maps. Mira sorted through them.

The road ahead widened. Grace could see it filtering into another road, one of those long straight French avenues bounded by trees that seemed to stretch for ever into the distance. She put her foot down on the pedal.

'Where now?' asked Mira, struggling to unfold a road map of France.

They had come to the junction with the main road. Another signpost told them that Grenoble was left, and added in brackets a list of other cities. It was 110 kilometres to Lyon.

'This'll do fine,' Grace murmured.

21

The only thing glamorous about the Hotel Moulin Rouge was the name. A squat, nondescript two-storey construction in redbrick and concrete, it was as thoroughly characterless an example of the modern roadside hotel as one could hope to find anywhere in the Western world. It was, in short, the perfect anonymous stopover for the anonymous traveller.

The brown Range Rover was one of only a dozen cars parked in the small front lot. There was space for another hundred vehicles at the back, but at this time of the day there were no takers. It was coming up to one o'clock. There was a restaurant at the side of the hotel and most of the cars seemed to belong to diners.

Grace had been sitting in the car on the other side of the road watching the comings and going for the last twenty minutes. She was alone. The two girls were in another hotel, a much smaller but infinitely more charming family pension halfway between Grenoble and Lyon. Grace had booked them in and given Mira half her cash, more than enough to settle the bill and get to Paris if anything should happen to her. Mira was adamant that neither of them wanted to go home. Nor did they want anything to do with the police. Grace decided to leave off trying to persuade them till later. Meanwhile she made some phone calls, using Sammy's mobile.

The first was to the gendarmerie in Grenoble. She said to the bored-sounding man who answered that she wanted to report a dead body. That got his attention. She ignored his questions and read off the address on the electricity bill. She told him exactly what to look for, and where, and finished the call.

Next she rang the Moulin Rouge. She found the number in the phone book in the lobby of Mira and Anna's hotel. She asked if Juan Antonio Cruz had arrived yet, identifying herself as his secretary. Monsieur Cruz had checked in half an hour ago, the receptionist told her, but he had asked not to be disturbed. Very well, she said, she would ring back later. She asked to confirm his room number. He was in room 204.

She had made just the two phone calls. She had debated with herself about making a third, but had decided against it. She didn't want to be given instructions by Bob or Dent or anyone. She had come this far on her own. She would finish it on her own.

She checked her face in the driving mirror. She hardly recognized herself. She had showered in Mira's room and changed into her blue suit. She was wearing a lot of make-up, enough to cover her bruises. She turned her head from side to side in the mirror, checking that none of her own hair was showing underneath Tatyana's wig. She put on the pair of opaque sunglasses Mira had found in the glove compartment. Now her own mother would have had difficulty recognizing her.

She started the engine and nosed into the road. At the next gap in the traffic she smoothly crossed over and drove into the hotel forecourt. She parked next to the Range Rover.

She picked up her handbag and walked boldly to the door. She had decided to go in by the front, in plain view, rather than try to find a side entrance. Boldness suited what she had in mind.

She swung open the double glass doors and stepped into a spacious but sparse lobby. The floor was covered in a thin blue-grey carpet and the colour matched the walls. The lighting was dim, and it took her a moment to register her bearings through the dark shades.

The receptionist was chatting to a big burly man she had seen park his truck and go into the restaurant about ten minutes ago. The receptionist was looking for something under the counter. He barely glanced at Grace.

'Une minute, s'il vous plaît, madame.'

He disappeared through a door into an adjoining office. She saw him open a filing cabinet and look inside.

The trucker leaned against the counter and stared covertly at her legs. She turned away and pretended to read the notices on a cork board on the wall. Bad timing, she reflected to herself. Her intention was to book a room, with the aim of attracting as little attention to herself as possible. If she'd asked for Monsieur Cruz then they would probably have insisted on calling him, and she didn't want that. But if she'd delayed her entrance by ten seconds she could have gone straight up, by the stairs or the lift down the narrow corridor beside the main door, without the receptionist even seeing her. Now that he had seen her she supposed that she had better stick to the original plan. Idly she read a tourist leaflet on the chateaux of the Rhone valley.

There was the sound of a car engine directly outside. Grace glanced across and saw a woman getting out of a taxi. She walked into the hotel.

The woman was about thirty, slim and stylishly dressed in a bottle-green suit of a cut that would have been conservative were it not for the shortness of the skirt. She had long blonde hair tied back with a velvet bow. Her eyes were invisible behind dark sunglasses.

The woman turned right at the door without hesitating. She didn't even glance towards the receptionist's desk, where the trucker had happily transferred his attentions to the new arrival. Grace heard a clunking mechanical sound.

She put back her leaflet on Rhone wines and walked up to the door. She was in time to see the woman getting into the lift. The lift door closed and the upwards arrow flashed.

The receptionist was still in his office. The trucker was opening a newspaper out on the desk.

Grace walked quickly to the stairs. A deafening alarm bell was ringing inside her head. She had never known her instincts to clamour so insistently.

She took the stairs two at a time and emerged breathless at the top. Thank God it was only two flights up. She went through the swing door and stepped into another blue-grey corridor. The blonde woman was walking away from her to the left.

Grace followed her, walking rapidly. The woman was slowing down. She was looking in her bag. She pulled out a piece of paper and read it. She stopped outside room 204.

'*Excusez moi, madame,*' said Grace softly.

The woman stopped in the act of raising her hand to knock.

Grace said, 'I'm sorry, madame, there's been a change of plan. Monsieur Cruz has had to cancel your appointment.'

The woman lifted her sunglasses to get a better look at Grace. She seemed nonplussed.

'I'm sorry, madame, but who are you?'

Grace put her hand into her bag and pulled out a clump of hundred-euro notes.

'This should cover your time and your expenses.'

The woman stared at Grace coldly.

'I'm sorry, madame, but this is impossible.'

Grace put her hand back into her bag.

'Nothing is impossible, madame,' she said coolly.

The woman did a double-take. She stared at the money in Grace's left hand and at the gun that had appeared in her right hand. She cleared her throat nervously.

'*Bien*, if you put it like that . . .'

Grace rather admired her sangfroid. She smiled sweetly as she folded the money and stuffed it into the vee of the woman's blouse.

'Best not to mention this to anyone, if I were you.'

The woman nodded. She started to back away towards the lift.

'One more thing please, madame. What is your name?'

'Isabel.'

'*Merci beaucoup, Isabel.*'

Isabel got into the lift. Grace waited for the doors to close.

She turned to face room 204. She knew exactly what was required, she was a veteran. She took a moment to compose herself, and then she knocked firmly.

There was a pause. She imagined him walking to the door. Did he stand to the side, wary in case it was an enemy? A man like him must have so many enemies. Perhaps he was armed. Well, so was she.

His voice came through the door.

'Hello?'

'*C'est Isabel.*'

'*Entrez, Isabel. C'est ouvert.*'

The door opened a fraction. She recognized the style. She waited a few moments, then she pushed it open the rest of the way.

He was walking away from her. Very casual, as ever, he didn't look back, though she saw him glance at her reflection in the window. He stopped in front of a sideboard on which sat a bottle of champagne and two glasses. He picked up the bottle.

He was wearing a white towelling robe and his hair was damp. Almost exactly as he had been at their first meeting. *Stripped and ready for action.*

'You don't mind if we speak English, do you?' he said, starting to pour. He still hadn't looked at her.

She kicked shut the door with her heel.

'I don't mind at all, Mike,' she said.

Champagne spilled over his fingers. He put down the glass and bottle and turned slowly to face her. She pointed the gun at his chest.

'Sit down in the armchair, please.'

He didn't speak. There was a half-smile frozen on his face. He walked, very slowly, to the armchair in the middle of the room. He didn't take his eyes off her for a moment. He had the glazed look of a sleepwalker.

He sat down. The armchair was facing the bed. She walked round to the foot of the bed and faced him.

'Put your hands on the arms of the chair.'

He did as he was told. She made a space for herself on the bed between his suitcase and his laptop and sat down. She removed her sunglasses.

'That's better, Grace. You look a whole lot better when I can see your eyes.'

There was a slight cracking in the voice, but she wouldn't have known otherwise that he was under duress. The expression in his eyes had faded back to his usual neutral. Idly he crossed his legs.

'Stay still,' she snapped.

He lifted his fingers off the arms of the chair in an apologetic gesture.

'It's OK, I'm not going to argue. You're the one with the gun. Where did you get it?'

'Does it matter?'

'I think someone must have been careless.'

'Maybe that someone was you.'

He gave her one of his thin smiles.

'So your people were tailing you all along, huh? I called it wrong, Grace. I guess you lied to me.'

'Guess again.'

'You want me to believe you're Harry Houdini?'

'I couldn't give a fuck what you believe. Keep your hands down.'

'I was scratching my knee.'

'Scratch it again I'll blow it off.'

'Whoa, now. You know how to use that thing?'

She didn't answer. He chuckled softly.

'Is it loaded?'

'Want to find out?'

'You put it like that, maybe not. Where's Orhan? Have the police got him?'

'You afraid of him talking?'

'He won't talk.'

'You know, you could be right. No need for him to talk, though, I think I know enough. Sorry to deny you the pleasure of the real Isabel's company. She looked rather gorgeous. Great legs. Blonde, of course. You only ever sleep with blondes?'

'Like the guy said about art: I know what I like.'

'You'd have liked her all right. Very cool when I pulled the gun on her, mature and sensible, perfect chauffeur material. You like someone with a bit of experience, don't you? No teenage ingénues for you. You told her to bring her passport and driving licence, I presume? Were you going to break her in gently, maybe even try her out in the casino for fun? Or were you going to go ahead with the shipment right away? The stuff's all ready. They were going to make the switch tonight. Such a neat idea, I guess it must have been yours. Come on, don't be modest, claim the credit where it's due. It has your stamp on it. You get the girl used to doing your driving for you, then at the last moment,

454

on the day you're due to go back to England, you say sorry, something's come up, would you mind going back on your own and I'll join you later? Natalie told me that's exactly what you did with her, only I didn't see anything sinister in it. Nor did she, nor did any of them. Only the car she drives through the Channel Tunnel isn't the one she's been used to. Meantime someone brings the genuine car over on the ferry and the next night, at your hotel in England, it's switched again. Then you wave your poor unsuspecting chauffeuse goodbye and off she goes, perfectly oblivious to the fact that she's just carried however many kilos of grade-A drugs through Customs. As I say, perfect in every way. The one thing that gives a courier away is nerves. But why should anyone be nervous when she doesn't even know she's carrying anything? If the worst happened and she was caught, then it's her lookout. Even the car's hired in her name. She gets pulled and you've plenty of time to escape. That's the worst. The best is that you get all the action you can handle and at the end the girl goes away thinking she's been very well paid, not realizing for an instant that it's a fraction of what a professional courier would cost you. No wonder you always look so smug.

'Orhan can sell the drugs through his contacts in the Turkish community in London, while Sammy is skimming off a small but lucrative fraction of the stuff Dmitri is sending him to sell through his club network in northern Europe. He must be a brave man. You all must be. You don't rip off a man like Dmitri lightly. Brave and cheeky, using his garage in Grenoble to stash the drugs. Perfect for Sammy. Whenever he has to send down some girls for disciplining, or whatever the charming Ilya calls it, he packs a shipment into the back of the van with them. No borders to worry about in Europe; you don't even have to bother to hide drugs these days once they're inside EU borders. Britain's another matter, which Sammy says is why Dmitri made the decision to get out and leave it to the Turks and Albanians. Hence an opportunity for you, knowing there's no danger of trampling over his patch. It's strictly a small-time operation, but since the drugs aren't paid for and the overheads are minimal, the profits must be vast. Too vast for the Albanians, I understand. They heard somebody was undercutting them and they assumed it was Dmitri. Dmitri protests his innocence, and for once he's right. It's an awkward situation for you, especially when Dmitri hears that Orhan is trying to move heroin in London. The Albanians think that Orhan is working for Dmitri and they don't like it. It must have taken all your fabled diplomatic charms to swing that one, Mike. You're the one who pours oil on troubled waters, first clearing the air between Dmitri and Orhan in England, then persuading the Albanians that they've got it wrong about Orhan and getting them to come to Dmitri's villa and kiss and make up. As an added bonus you even get Dmitri and the Albanians to agree on a peaceable division of the sex trade in London. You should have been Secretary General of the UN, Mike, you're wasted in organized crime.

'What you don't tell anyone is that Orhan has arranged with his Turkish friends to bypass London and sell your stuff in Glasgow, Manchester, anywhere the Albanians aren't too bothered. You're bound to step on someone else's toes eventually, but for the time being it's crisis averted. Babe shipments can continue. Or at least they could have done, if you hadn't got careless and hired girls from the same agency too often. The consequences for you are pretty serious, I'm afraid. No more leggy blondes where you're going. Not unless you acquire a taste for your own sex. There'll be plenty of opportunity. A good-looking boy like you should have no shortage of admirers.'

'Are you trying to frighten me?'

'Oh, rape isn't such a big deal, is it, Mike? I expect you'll get used to it, the same way as Ilya's victims. He had two girls in the next cell to me, did you know that? It was too late to spare them his attentions, unfortunately, but at least their testimony should save a few others from going through it. The French police should be there by now. What a fine old time they'll have. A body in the basement, a car bursting with heroin in the garage, and Sammy and Ilya to tell them a story. I'd rather you told your story, though, to my people. I'm taking you back to England. The French police might ask too many awkward questions if I hand you over to them. They can also be funny about extraditing people to the States, especially when they've got capital offences hanging over them. That's where you're going to end up, on trial for the murder of Ramirez and the Schultz girl. Don't worry, they won't put you in the electric chair, or whatever they do these days, at least not if you co-operate. Life without parole in return for a bit of help with people and places. Besides, prison will be the safest place for you, once Dmitri finds out what you've been up to. I think you're probably dry from the shower by now. Come on, time to get dressed.'

'And if I refuse?'

'I don't see how you can refuse. Unless you're really determined to find out if the gun is loaded. It is, by the way, and it works. I've already fired it twice today.'

'At Orhan?'

She didn't answer. She had no inclination to give him the gory details. All he had to know was that she was capable of using the gun, and she thought he'd got that message. Outwardly at least he seemed to have recovered his poise. She imagined that he was thinking that it was a long way to England, that he was bound to get some opportunity to take the gun off her. He wouldn't know she was alone, but he did know there weren't any gendarmes surrounding the building. Maybe she had already told him more than was necessary. She didn't have to tell him a damned thing; having the gun in her hand made explanations redundant. But she hadn't been able to resist it. She wanted him to know that she knew everything, she wanted him to know that no matter how clever he thought he was, she had outfoxed him, and that he was every bit as powerless and pathetic as she had been only a few hours earlier. She wanted to savour every moment of his humiliation.

She might have enjoyed it more if she hadn't felt so wrecked. Her body was rigid with tension. Every muscle was stiff, every nerve strained. She hadn't slept for a day and a half, by rights she should be on the point of collapse. Pure adrenaline sustained her, but her gauges would have to run down soon.

'Time to make a move,' she said.

With her spare hand she pulled his suitcase nearer and flipped open the catches. She shook the case open and emptied the contents over the bed. She fished out all his spare clothes and tossed them on to the floor.

'What are you looking for?'

She ignored him. In the side compartments she found half a dozen phone simm cards and as many computer disks. She also found the driving licences and passports of both Michael Gallagher and Juan Antonio Cruz.

'I don't have a gun, if that's what you're after.'

She opened a brown envelope and tipped out two thick wads of banknotes, one of euros, one of pounds. Some of it must have been the fee he had given her in London.

'How much do you make doing this detective stuff, Grace?'

'Enough.'

She zipped open his washbag and shook out the contents. She picked out a small plastic bottle half-filled with white powder.

'Is this what you gave me?' she demanded.

He nodded.

'How much did you give me?'

'A spoonful.'

She looked at the label.

'I've read about this stuff. The date-rape drug. You enjoy fucking comatose women, Mike?'

'I enjoyed fucking you.'

'Too bad you'll never have the chance again. Get dressed.'

'Would you mind looking the other way, please?'

'If you're trying to be funny I'm afraid that's pretty lame. Put your clothes on and don't make any sudden movements.'

He picked socks and underpants from the floor, a tan pair of trousers, white shirt, brown suede shoes. He affected nonchalance, but she could see that he was self-conscious about being naked. He zipped up his flies with an air of unmistakable relief.

'What now?' he asked.

'Sit down.'

He lowered himself back into the armchair. Grace picked up the bottle of Rohypnol and carried it to the sideboard, keeping him covered the whole time. She poured what she guessed to be a teaspoonful into one of the champagne glasses and topped it up from the bottle.

She carried the glass over to him and set it down on a small table within reach of the armchair, making sure she never took the gun off him for an instant. She returned to her place on the bed.

'Drink it.'

'You're kidding me.'

'No. Drink it.'

'Or what?'

'Or I'll shoot you.'

'You'd shoot a defenceless man?'

'You trying to be funny again?'

'I'm wondering what your story would be. What would you tell the French police? You say you don't want them asking awkward questions. Those are exactly the kind of questions they do like to ask when there's been a murder.'

'You think I wouldn't kill you? Your friend Orhan probably thought that too.'

'You say you're not a cop, but you're working with cops, and cops do things by the book. Your people want me, you already told me that. They won't be happy if you shoot me.'

'They don't even know I'm bringing you in.'

'You telling me you really are on your own?'

'I'm not telling you anything, except drink that glass down.'

'I've got a better idea.'

'Drink it.'

'No, hear me out. I already asked how much you make doing this detective shit. Not much, I guess. How would a million dollars sound to you?'

'You think you can buy me?'

'I already did, remember? Only this time it's for real. Instead of taking me to London, let's go to Zurich. One phone call and I can have the money in cash, no questions asked. I think you'd like the life of luxury, Grace. You're a natural.'

'I don't want your money. I want to see them put you in a cell, and throw away the key.'

'Yeah, I heard that line, in a movie. But you don't want that. Believe me, you don't. Because if you did, I'd come after you. You think being in a cell would stop me? If you don't want a million dollars I can think of plenty who do. A cool one million dollars to hit an English lady detective, real name Grace Cornish. That's way over the rate. You say you live in Guildford? Never been there, but I don't suppose it would be too difficult to find you. You in the phone book? Maybe you got an ad in Yellow Pages. You got a family, Grace? I don't suppose you're married, the way you put out, but you got brothers and sisters? A nice mommy, daddy? For one million dollars I know people will take out your entire family, including the cat. No matter where you try and hide. You think I'm kidding?'

'No.'

She knew he wasn't kidding. She might be the one holding the gun, but he was acting as if he were in control. He crossed his legs, idly swinging his foot from side to side. It was like in the casino. He had the count in his head; he knew how the cards would fall.

'What would you get for turning me in, Grace? Their grateful thanks? That enough for spending the rest of your life looking over your shoulder, wondering whether each stranger you see might be the one who's going to kill you? You want that, Grace?'

'No.'

She stood up. He was about eight feet away. She had measured the distance carefully in her head.

'I'm glad you're getting a grasp of the situation. As you so correctly point out, the only way I could save my neck would be to give them what I know about Dmitri and one or two others who might wind up feeling a little pissed with me. I don't want to be looking over my shoulder either. You think we got a deal here, Grace?'

'No.'

'I think . . .'

His voice trailed away. She saw his eyes widen slightly as she raised the gun and aimed it at his chest. For a split second their eyes locked and he knew what she was going to do. He tried to get out of the chair.

She pulled the trigger twice.

The first bullet struck him in the shoulder, spinning him half around and throwing him back into the chair. A puff

461

of smoke came out of the tip of the silencer, but almost no noise. She saw the look of disbelief in his face. He tried to rise again and she shot him in the middle of his chest.

He sat in the chair, staring at the bloodstains spreading over his white shirt. His mouth hung slack and open. He tried to speak. He coughed violently.

A trickle of blood spilled out of the corner of his mouth and ran down his chin. His head rolled to the side. His eyes continued to stare, but not at her. Not at anything.

She used a handkerchief from the pile of his clothes to wipe her fingerprints from the champagne glass and any other surface she might have touched. She did what she had to do. She adjusted the wig and replaced the sunglasses and went downstairs.

She saw no one except the concierge, who was back at his desk. He was reading something. He didn't look up as she walked past.

And she didn't look back.

22

Ryan missed the turning after Stamford and had to stop and take directions from a garage. Retracing his route he managed to spot the narrow high-hedged lane he'd been told about. After another half a mile he came to a row of old well-weathered almshouses. He parked and walked up the path to the house on the end. It didn't have a name or a number, but as soon as he had seen the face of the tall, slightly stooped man who answered the door he knew he had come to the right place.

His hair was grey, but it was apparent from the complexion that it had once been blond. He had her chin and nose, but most of all it was in the eyes: very blue, bright and inquisitive. He also had the same, slightly quizzical expression, and the same direct way of looking straight at you.

'I've come to see Grace,' said Ryan.

Her father looked taken aback. The round blue eyes narrowed with suspicion.

'I'm not sure she's in the mood for visitors.'

'I understand that. Please tell her Ryan would like to speak to her.'

'Ryan, eh?'

Her father smiled softly. It was an expression Ryan knew.

'She mentioned you, Ryan. Hang on, I'll have a word.'

He went inside the house. He left the door ajar, which Ryan interpreted as a good sign. He was gone for a minute. When he came back he opened the door all the way and stepped aside.

'Come in, she'll see you. I'm Leslie Cornish, by the way.'

'Pleased to meet you.'

Ryan was shown into a small neat kitchen. A door at the back led out into a long, narrow garden.

'Weather's been grim past few days,' said Leslie Cornish, inviting Ryan to follow him outside. 'I told her to enjoy the sun while she can.'

Grace was sitting in a deckchair at the end of the garden. It was a bright afternoon, but it could have been warmer. Grace was wearing a thick man's sweater and had a blanket over her legs. The opaque sunglasses that covered her eyes looked incongruous. So did her pale skin.

Her appearance was a shock. She'd had cut her hair very short, and whoever was responsible had not done a good job. She was wearing no make-up. The thinness of her cheeks, the colourlessness of her lips, made her look anorexic.

'Hello, Ryan.'

The wind, gusting suddenly through the trees at the foot of the garden, made it hard to hear her. Her father bent down and picked up a tray with an empty cup and saucer.

'You must be thirsty, Mr Ryan. I'll make some tea. You want another cup, love?'

'Thanks, Dad.'

'Make yourself at home, Mr Ryan. I'll be right back.'

A wrought-iron table and a set of matching chairs stood nearby in the shade of a pergola hung with climbing roses. Ryan helped himself to one of the chairs.

'Mister Ryan, eh?' Grace mused. 'Not many people call

you Mister Ryan. You can tell he spent too much time in uniform.'

'It's good to see you, Grace.'

'It is? Not too many people in your department, whatever it calls itself, seem to think it's good to see me.'

'Not my department, remember?'

'Oh yeah, you're one of the good guys, aren't you?'

'How are you feeling, Grace?'

'Fine.'

'You don't look fine.'

'I don't? Damn. You want the truth? I feel like shit.'

'I'm not surprised.'

'They send you down to spy on me?'

'No one sent me.'

'You mean this is a social visit? How did you find me, by the way?'

'Your office in Guildford.'

'Nikki? I told her not to give anyone the address.'

'She didn't, but she let slip you were at your parents. I tracked your father down through police records.'

'You should have been a detective, Ryan.'

'And end up like your friend Bob?'

'Touché. I'm sorry, Ryan.'

'Sorry for what?'

'Being in such a filthy mood. Lack of sleep, I'm afraid, always makes me grouchy.'

'You've not been sleeping?'

'With pills. Not the same. At least I don't dream.'

'I'm sorry you're in a bad way.'

'I'll get over it. I've only myself to blame.'

'Don't think that way.'

'I can't help it. I think of Natalie a lot. Seeing her die isn't something I'm ever going to forget. She left a kid, you know. A three-year-old girl. If it hadn't been for me she wouldn't have been out there.'

'Don't confuse cause and effect.'

'Don't try and blind me with science, Ryan. I blame myself because I seem to make a habit of getting myself into trouble. Someone else tried to kill me last year, a case I was working on. I said I'd keep myself out of danger after that. For their sake as much as my own.'

She nodded towards the kitchen. Her father was standing outside the door, a laden tray in his hand, listening to a small vigorous-looking woman with greying hair. She was talking animatedly and pointing at something on the tray.

'They've been wonderful to me,' Grace continued, a catch in her voice. 'They haven't asked any questions, they've just looked after me. Mum disapproves, of course, always has done. Thinks I should be raising kids and baking cakes. But she doesn't say anything. Nor does he. It would kill them if something happened to me. I'm sorry, I'm feeling a bit over-emotional at the moment.'

She wiped a tear from the corner of her eye and sniffed. Ryan gave her his handkerchief.

'Thanks. I've been crying a lot lately. Good to let it out, I think. Look light and cheery, will you? I don't want Dad to think you've been upsetting me.'

He laughed good-naturedly. Her father came and set down the tray on the wrought-iron table. He laid out cups and saucers and a big old earthenware teapot.

'I'd leave it to brew for a moment, if I were you.'

He cleared his throat. He indicated a plate piled high with scones and biscuits, all freshly baked from the smell of them.

'Try and eat something, love.'

'All right, Dad.'

He left them with the air of someone who had done his duty and been seen to have done his duty without any conviction that the effort had been in any way worthwhile.

'He seems a very sweet man,' Ryan observed.

'Deceptively sweet. He got two commendations for bravery, you know. Though he's not as tough as Mum.'

'Which of them do you take after?'

'I know I've inherited his obstinacy and I wish I'd inherited her common sense. The rest is my responsibility, I'm afraid.'

'Stop being so hard on yourself. Eat something.'

'I won't, thanks, but don't let me stop you.'

Ryan poured them both tea and helped himself to biscuits.

'Sure you won't try one? They're delicious.'

'You sound like Dad.'

'Suit yourself.'

'That sounds like him too. Only he adds, "you usually do".'

'Sorry?'

'Suit yourself. You usually do.'

'I see.'

'I wish I was as tough as he thinks I am.'

'I think you're tough enough.'

'I suppose that's a compliment, coming from a hard man like you.'

'I know what you've been through. I read Dent's debriefing notes. Even he was impressed.'

'He didn't sound impressed at the time.'

'That's because he wanted Martinez alive. There wasn't anything you could have done about that, though. He understood that you killed him in self-defence.'

'It says that in the notes?'

'Yes. I only had a chance to skim through them. They were marked strictly confidential, you understand. But I got the gist. He commended your exemplary fortitude.'

'That's what he called it?'

'It seemed like an understatement to me.'

'It seemed like recklessness to me. I shouldn't have been there, Ryan. I did a stupid thing, for all the wrong reasons.'

467

'You went after Jeanette.'

'And when she wasn't there I should have come straight back. But what did I do? We all know what I did.'

'You had a unique opportunity to get inside information on the Rostovs.'

'That's the official line, is it? It's not why I stayed. I didn't even know he was going to see the Rostovs, did I? You want to know the reason? The reason they didn't put in the report? I stayed because I was having a great time. I was living the high life in luxury hotels and casinos. I'd never been in a first-class airport lounge before, I didn't even know such places existed. I thought I was being treated like a queen and I knew I was behaving like a tart and I didn't care. It was like I was on some high-class Club Med holiday, if that isn't a contradiction in terms. Sun, sea, sex. I didn't even have to fake it. I loved every minute. You look shocked, Ryan. Don't worry, I'm pretty shocked myself.'

'I'm not shocked. Maybe a bit . . . no, I'm not shocked.'

'Maybe what?'

'Nothing. You didn't know Gallagher wasn't who he said he was.'

'No, but I knew who his friends were, and I got a buzz out of that too. I didn't know how bad he was, but I thought he must know more than he was letting on, and I think I liked it that he was bad. Maybe you were right, after all.'

'About what?'

'Remember that night when you drove me back to the mews? I snapped your head off when you started getting personal. Probably because you struck a nerve. Yup, I've always picked wrong 'uns. This was big time, though. I can't tell you how foolish I feel. He was the most evil, heartless bastard I've ever met. That's why I shot him. It didn't happen the way I told Dent. I lied to him. Martinez didn't reach for a gun in the hotel room. He couldn't have done, he didn't have a gun. He was as far away from me as you are now, and I shot him, in cold blood. I didn't think I could. But he told me he was going to . . . well, it doesn't matter what he said he was going to do. I killed him because I had to, the same as Orhan. Both of them deserved to die, I've never been more certain of anything. But I feel empty, and sick, and disgusted. That's what I feel, disgust. I should never have been there.'

'Of course you feel like that. Anyone who didn't would be a psychopath. I know that feeling.'

'I forget, you've been there. It's different, though, isn't it, when the other guy's taking a pop at you and it's your job to shoot back?'

'No, it's the same. I was eighteen the first time I killed a man, and I'm ashamed to say I felt elated when I saw him go down. But I didn't feel that when I saw his face later. I can see his face now. I felt disgust. I still do, even when it's people you know don't deserve to live, the Rostovs and the kind of people who hang around them. All killing is sick. It's butchery, whether you're putting a bullet into a guy's head or ripping his guts out with a knife. I don't want to have to do it ever again. I always say that, but I think this time I mean it. I wish you didn't have to know that feeling. But you do know it, and once you know it you can't unlearn it.'

'Oh my God,' said Grace, very quietly.

'What is it?' he said, alarmed at her expression.

Her face had gone ashen.

'I'm sorry, Ryan.'

'Don't be. It's my job, remember.'

'No, I don't mean that . . .'

She smiled faintly. It wasn't much, but it was the first time she'd smiled in weeks.

'I mean, Ryan, I'm sorry I didn't get it before. You were there, weren't you? You were on the yacht. No, don't deny it, I understand now. What you said about killing Rostovs makes sense of it at last. Dent was completely baffled. He didn't understand how there could have been this blood-bath on the yacht and yet I claimed not to know anything about it. How could I have known anything? I was uncon-scious and in the back of the car on the way to Grenoble when it happened. You did it, didn't you? You came after me. Christ, I'm so, so sorry.'

'There's nothing to be –'

'Yes, there is. You put yourself on the line for me. If it had gone wrong it would have been you in a body bag lying somewhere at the bottom of the Mediterranean, alongside Natalie. Dent doesn't even begin to suspect, does he? How did you get out there without anyone noticing?'

'I had some leave due.'

'And all the time I was behaving like a fool you were keeping an eye on me. Christ, I'm so ashamed.'

'You've nothing to be ashamed of. Quite the opposite. You didn't need anyone's help, did you?'

'I needed all the help going. What happened? Did the Rostovs put up a fight, or did you kill them because they wouldn't tell you where I was?'

'I killed Misha Rostov because he shot at me. I didn't kill Dmitri, that's the weirdest thing.'

Ryan explained what had happened. He described how he had left Dmitri tied up but alive, how he and his friend Johny had laid out Natalie's body on the beach and alerted the French police before driving hell-for-leather to Grenoble. How they had arrived in time to find the ski lodge in flames and police and firemen swarming all over it. How he had assumed that Grace was dead inside and only learnt the truth when he'd rung into the office and learnt from Jackie Harrington that Grace had just called in. He didn't tell her that he had been driving back down to the coast at the time, en route to kill Dmitri Rostov.

470

As it turned out, it would have been a redundant trip anyway.

'You weren't the only one who was surprised,' Grace told him. 'When I went back to the hotel to pick up the two girls there was no sign of them. I'd given them money, they could have gone anywhere. I should have realized Mira was up to something when she went back into the house. She said she wanted cigarettes, but it was the lighter she was after. Apparently she sprayed cooking oil over the curtains and set them alight. Dent showed me something from the French press. "Gangland massacre", that was the headline. By the time the firemen arrived the top part of the house was ablaze. They found the charred bodies of Sammy and his torturer still handcuffed together. Then, in the basement, they found the body of Orhan and a Range Rover packed with heroin. When they heard about the dead Rostovs they must have thought they were in the middle of World War Three. Who do you think killed Dmitri?'

'It had to be one of his own people. Found him trussed up and helpless and took advantage of the situation. They're all ruthless men.'

'And women. Tatyana, his mistress – was there any mention of her in Dent's report?'

'You think she could have done it?'

'She could certainly have done it.'

'She wasn't on the yacht.'

'She was there earlier and she's the only one not accounted for.'

'It was a pretty cold-blooded killing.'

'That's what makes her a suspect. You don't know her. Or do you still harbour illusions about ladylike behaviour? The French police said the safe had been cleared out. I'll bet you anything it was Tatyana, topping up her pension plan. Who else would have had the nerve to rob Dmitri Rostov?'

'Well, now you come to mention it . . .'

Ryan drew an envelope from his inside pocket. He opened the flap and showed her discreetly what was inside.

'I had a few incidental expenses and took the liberty of reimbursing myself from Mr Rostov's funds. This is left over, it comes to about three grand. I thought maybe you could use it, take all the time you need to convalesce, maybe take a holiday. I think you deserve it.'

'Taking money from criminals, Ryan? Whatever would Mr Dent say?'

'Oh, what the eye doesn't see . . .'

'My thoughts exactly. Sorry, but I beat you to it. Martinez had about twenty thousand pounds in cash on him. I filched the lot. I did wonder if stealing his money wasn't putting me on his level, but only for about one zillionth of a second. I took the money because I knew I was going to need it. As you say, I won't be going back to work in a hurry and I don't think that Mr Dent is going to be offering to tide me over. Thanks, Ryan, but you keep the money. You take the holiday. You're the one who deserves it.'

'No time, I'm afraid. I'm shipping out the day after tomorrow.'

'Where to?'

'Not allowed to say. Sorry.'

'Going back to your unit, are you?'

'Yup. It'll be a relief. Don't think Dent's brand of spook work is quite me somehow.'

'I've come to the same conclusion. How long will you be gone for?'

'Six months probably. Maybe longer. Then I think that'll be it for me. I'm getting too long in the tooth to be at the sharp end.'

'I know what you mean. What will you do?'

'When I retire? Dunno. I'm due a decent pension, the

472

kids are grown up, I can afford to take some time off and have a good look around.'

'I'm sure you'll find plenty.'

'I'd like to keep in touch.'

'Please do.'

'Can I write to you?'

'That would be nice.'

'Maybe we can meet when I get back?'

'Of course.'

'I'd like to see you again.'

'Sure.'

'Will you come and have dinner with me?'

'Oh. I see. Are you asking me for a date, Ryan?'

'Does that sound so bad?'

He covered his mouth and gave a little cough. He leant forward in his chair, his elbows on his knees, adjusting his weight awkwardly and staring down at the lawn. He picked a long blade of grass and looped it through his fingers. She smiled.

'No, it doesn't sound bad at all.'

She lifted her sunglasses from her eyes and took him in properly. She was remembering their first meeting, his intimidating bulk, his unfriendly silence. She remembered noticing his rough hands and tattoo, and putting him down for a Neanderthal squaddie. It was true, he did exude a kind of brute primordial power, but there was more to him than that. She watched the delicate way his fingers twisted the grass. A faint red flush had coloured his cheeks. She felt a sudden stab of tenderness in the pit of her stomach that was as queasily pleasurable as it was totally unexpected.

'I'm afraid I'm not much use for anything at the moment,' she said. 'Maybe in six months' time I'll have got my head straight.'

He nodded.

'I'd better be going. It's getting on. Long drive ahead.'

'To Poole? Yes, it is.'

They both smiled.

'Thanks for coming all this way, Ryan. I appreciate it. What you did coming after me, I'll never be able to repay you for that.'

'Don't mention it.'

The old gruffness was back in his voice. He got to his feet.

'I'll be making a move then.'

He stood awkwardly for a moment. Then he offered her his hand.

'Don't you think that's a bit formal?' she said.

He thought about it for a moment.

'You're right.'

He bent down and kissed her tenderly on the cheek.

'You take care now, do you hear?'

She touched the tips of her fingers to her forehead.

'Aye, aye, sir.'

She watched him walk, straight-backed, into the house. Her father appeared at the kitchen door to escort him out. A few minutes later he came back out on his own.

Her father sat down in the chair Ryan had vacated. He didn't say anything for a while. The pair of them sat, quite still, without any awkwardness, staring at the trees, and the sky, and the sun fitfully peeping out from between the thick white clouds.

'Seems like a nice bloke,' said her father at last.

'She on the phone to Moss Bros then?'

He laughed. It was a joke grown stale in the telling that every time she brought a man home her mother would be waiting by the door, tape measure in hand, to fit him for a hired morning suit. It had got to the point, Grace once complained, that she couldn't order a takeaway pizza without running the risk of getting hitched to the delivery boy.

'Oh well,' said her father, reaching for a biscuit. 'You could do worse.'

'Oh yes. I can think of a lot worse.'

Leslie Cornish chewed his biscuit thoughtfully. He had never had much idea of what went on in his daughter's head. It never used to bother him, but in the last year or so he had become concerned. Most of the time her job was mundane, even more so than regular police work, but he knew there was an element of danger that could not be erased. A year ago he had stood at the foot of her hospital bed, and watched her sleeping with the bandages wrapped thickly round her head and the plastic tubes sticking out of her veins, and the tears had flowed so uncontrollably that he had had to go and lock himself away in the men's room for half an hour. Despite his own long years on the front line of human degradation he knew there were darker places in his daughter's head than there had ever been in his own, and it scared him. Sometimes he caught a glimpse in her eyes. Or heard it in her voice. There had been bitterness in her tone, yet a kind of wistfulness too. Whatever thought had triggered it had left behind a residue of coldness in her eyes. When she saw him looking at her she glanced away. She put her sunglasses back on.

Her father finished his biscuit. He picked up the plate, and the empty tea mugs, and loaded them on to the tray.

'It's getting chilly, I think I'll go in. You coming?'

'I'll stay out a bit longer.'

'Suit yourself.'

He started to go. She cocked her ear, waiting for the next line. He didn't disappoint. She heard the mumbled words over his heavy footsteps as he loped away down the gravel path.

'You usually do.'

She smiled. He was right, it was chilly. She huddled down into the deckchair and pulled her blanket up to her chin.

She watched the wind rustling through the leaves of the trees. She listened to the buzzing of the bees in the flowerbeds. It was sweet to be alive.

Around her the shadows lengthened.

www.ingramcontent.com/pod-product-compliance
Ingram Content Group UK Ltd.
Pitfield, Milton Keynes, MK11 3LW, UK
UKHW022244180325
456436UK00001B/6